Has Anyone
Seen My
Sex Life?

KRISTEN BAILEY

Has Anyone Seen My Sex Life?

Bookouture

Published by Bookouture in 2020

An imprint of Storyfire Ltd.
Carmelite House
50 Victoria Embankment
London EC4Y 0DZ

www.bookouture.com

ISBN: 978-1-83888-236-5
eBook ISBN: 978-1-83888-235-8

Prologue

Back then I wouldn't have said I was a bitch exactly, but I was all the things that came from being a young professional Londoner: I was broadly cynical, deep into a free overdraft, my bloodstream was a mix of takeaways and watered-down cocktails, and I was prone to meltdowns over stolen teabags and my flatmates interrupting my sleep. I was a city girl working in magazine publishing, so naturally I was also a superficial douche. This was why when I first met Danny Morton, I was obsessed by his spectacularly ugly shoes. Footwear that hideous will brand itself into a girl's memory; that and the moment I barged past, half-cut, spilling my overpriced White Russian all over him.

'Oh bollocks…! Wow…' I said the wow as I glanced down at his shoes being showered in my cocktail. Maybe the drink would make them less ugly? I giggled to myself. We were in a Soho pub, full of London's finest cosmopolitan wankery, loafers and neon trainers and this gentleman had on clumpy walking boots, like he was setting off up a mountain or had come to fix my sink. 'Those look sturdy.'

He wasn't impressed or bothered. 'Where I come from, a lass would apologise.'

'Oooooh, "Where I come from"?' I mimicked his broad Northern accent. I couldn't pinpoint it. North for me was anywhere past Brent Cross. 'Manchester?' That's North.

He eyeballed me. Was he handsome? Frankly who knew, I was so boozed up. He held out a hand.

'Danny Morton, how do you do…'

I really was drunk. I curtseyed.

'Meg Callaghan, very well, thank you.' I said with a strange affected posh voice.

He smiled. 'I haven't had an apology yet.'

'Sorry?'

'You don't sound sure about that?'

'You're a bit bolshy.'

'You're a bit rude.' He turned his back to me. 'Fookin' South-erners.'

I'm not sure why but this struck a chord that I couldn't ignore. I was never precious about where I was from or who I was. I quite liked being a Londoner; it meant that I was trendy, metropolitan and globally aware by association. But he was surly and quite frankly, a bit of a tit. Have I mentioned I was also very drunk?

'Oh piss off, fucking Liam Gallagher.'

I'm not sure why I compared him to Liam Gallagher; it may have been the ape like persona and the fact I'd committed to him hailing from Manchester, but Britpop was all the rage back then. I was also fully aware that to support the fact that I was indeed a fully-fledged Londoner, I may have replaced my accent and gone all Cockney on him.

'Facking?' he said quizzically back at me.

'Fooking,' I replied.

He laughed. I wasn't sure why. He looked me in the eye and did this strange action where he seemed to be doffing an imaginary flat cap. I thought it was quite charming but I was still offended by his aversion to my Southerness and frankly confused by the shoes situation.

An arm reached over my shoulder at that point. 'Holy flaps, Meggers. We can't drink here anymore. Bloke at two o'clock, I think I may have shagged him and peed in his kitchen sink because I couldn't find the toilet in his house. I think his name is Ron.'

Bloody Beth. She stopped for a moment to check out my new Northern acquaintance. He, in return, stared intently at the sort of person feral enough to piss in a sink. Danny and I turned to see the man in question. 'Ron' had a strange centre parting and fringe curtains. I felt pangs of disappointment for my sister. Beth was still eyeing up Danny, but her expression read horror when she got to the shoes.

'I'm Beth. I'm the sister. She's Meg and she's single.'

Beth was newly graduated and excitable. Her main agenda seemed to be recreating her university experience in the real world but constantly moaning about how everything was far more expensive and that she didn't like it. She was training to be a teacher, with an agenda to save the kids from themselves. However, they swore at her and she was slowly realising poetry wasn't something that could be taught via the power of rap. It meant we usually ended our weeks with 'a drink to see in the weekend' that turned into us one hundred quid shy by the morning with handbags full of soggy spring rolls from hitting the all-you-can-eat Chinese buffet at 3 a.m. That night, Beth was off her face, varifocal drunk due to an uncontrollable set of Year 8s. It meant she shuffled on the spot, adjusting her vision like the sun had just hit her eyes.

'She's a journalist and that is all her own hair. She is a fricking *catch*,' she said, pointing to me.

Danny Morton started laughing. Beth had the awesome ability of letting people into snippets of conversations in which they'd had no previous participation. She was referring to when ten minutes previously, we'd been talking about a girl at the bar whose extensions looked like they'd been applied with a hot glue gun. Beth proceeded to stroke my hair like one would a spaniel.

'So, a journalist for what? Like the newspapers?' Danny asked.

'For *Red* magazine.'

'Don't read it.' It was an absolute answer. But strangely, I found it very compelling. Too often, you mention you're a journalist and people feign interest or come at you with their bullshittery. He seemed to have no concern about ingratiating himself to me.

'You're both sisters, eh? Got the same chin.' His tone didn't read as complimentary.

'Yeah… and what of it?' Beth replied. If anything, we were now starting to look like a couple of drunken townies out for a brawl. I was also very aware that Beth was losing rigidity in her legs. My main thought was how I was going to get her home. Fireman's lift to a cab or drag her about on the Tube?

'Were there dishes in sink?' he asked.

'What sink?' Beth replied.

'The one you urinated in after you shagged Ron over there.' He gestured toward Mr Fringe Curtains and Beth shimmied to the side of me to hide both herself and her shame.

'No?' Her indignant reply led us to believe she wasn't sure.

'How could you not find a toilet in someone's gaff?'

'I was drunk, it was one of those giant shared houses where every door I opened was another bedroom or storage. I was busting. It was either the sink or the floor.'

What Danny did next was brilliant.

'OI, RON!'

The group of men 'Ron' was stood with at the bar all turned around. Danny raised his beer at them. Beth went an even brighter shade of raspberry. The sheer audacity shocked me to silence; people around us went very quiet.

'YOUR NAME RON, FELLA?' He singled out the one in question.

'My name's Seb, mate.'

His friends were starting to puff out their chests in a territorial way. Man, this is how bar fights start, I thought. I was twenty-four and going to get glassed in a bar because my sister possibly took a whizz in this man's sink.

Beth clung on to Danny's arm. 'Please stop talking now—'

'NO BOTHER, BIRD HERE THOUGHT SHE KNEW YOU FROM BACK WHEN.'

Beth waved back. The men in the group shrugged and shook their heads. They also started to relax, wearing looks of pity now that perhaps Danny was just a bit of a social oddball. I was still trying to work out the Northern vernacular but as first impressions went was also surprised by the size of this man's balls. I may have laughed to that effect.

Beth punched him in the arm. 'I don't belieeeeeve you!'

'Just… there are a lot of people in London. Statistically, it can't have been likely to be him. Did you use his dishcloth after to dab yourself down?'

By this time I was in hysterics. I was protective of my sisters but there was also fun to be had in winding them up and this man seemed intent on being an accomplice. Beth wasn't getting the joke and hit him again. Another man appeared at this point, watching my drunken sister take him on.

'Making friends again I see, Danny? You got beef with them tossers at the bar? We could take 'em.'

Beth stopped play-hitting to give this gent the once over. I'll admit he was the better looking of the two; better taste in footwear and denim and a well-defined jaw.

'Ladies, I'm Stu… How do?' He waved a continental beer about his person. He was the more relaxed of the two lads, too cocky for my liking. Beth's demeanour changed and she re-jigged her boobs.

By the similarity of their accents, I had a punt. 'Brothers?' Danny said nothing but raised his ale bottle in the affirmative. 'Same chins,' I muttered. Danny smiled. Stu was giving Beth the eye while I tried to prop her up.

'These two are sisters,' said Danny. 'Meg and Beth. She's a journalist and this one likes to pee in sinks.'

I laughed. Stu did a thumbs up, the revelation clearly not deterring him from checking out my sister's arse.

'Excuse me,' intervened Beth. 'It could be worse, Megs here once shat outside someone's front door.' Oooh, deflection. Cow. She and Stu burst into laughter and I shook my head, slowly. Danny started sniggering but held a hand out for a high five. I placed my palm in the air and reluctantly engaged.

'It was a dirty protest. I was at university and he was a sexual predator who'd taken advantage of a mate.'

Danny's smile got broader. It was bizarre to think I was winning him over. He suddenly seemed more interested in me for being able to take a stand using the contents of my bowels.

'Meg, rhymes with smeg…' Stu joked. Beth thought this hilarious. It wasn't, but Danny and I both read their intention instantly and I allowed Beth to drape herself off the better-looking brother while I stood there in awkward conversation with the older one.

Was there a spark with Danny? There was something refreshing about his candour and he seemed a solid sort. However, there was something that told me he was the kind of straight man who was here simply to drink. After he finished his dark ale (heave), he'd go home via a curry house in time to catch a re-run of *Eurotrash*. In the morning, he'd wake without a hangover and do something sensible like go for a run or walk a dog, a sensible dog with a Northern name like Lad.

I'm not even sure I'd been on the pull that night. At that point, I was free, easy, just keeping an eye open. I'd sworn off relationships for a while after Dexter. Dexter was an artsy wannabe writer; we'd lived together and, at the time, I'd thought he was profound and deeply intelligent. I'd envisioned a future selling his poetry leaflets and living off love and creativity. Then one day I said I didn't get one of his poems. Next thing you know, he turned into a melodramatic shit who walked out and took my kettle. It was a bloody good kettle.

So you're probably wondering how this evening panned out. Stu and Beth probably got it on, right? Some drunken sex back in a three-bedroomed shared flat, some open-mouthed snogging, the night ending with their bodies sprawled across a mattress that came with the rental (and had been treated for bed bugs, several times) and the swapping of phone numbers that may or may not have led to the sparks of a potential relationship.

No.

After Beth laughed at Stu's rubbish smeg joke, we all got some shots in. The bar we were in played a rather lively mix of house music which Beth and Stu grinded away to quite inappropriately. Danny and I joined them like some sort of older sibling chaperones. There was gentle swaying on our part and a moment when the DJ played a dance remix of Britney Spears and Danny mouthed all the words to the chorus and seemed to know parts of the accompanying dance routine.

At about 11 p.m., Beth and Stu ended up outside the bar having a snog and a bit of inappropriate frottage against the doors of a closed artisan cake shop. They got a cab back to Beth's place in Hammersmith but when she got through the door, she threw up in the hallway. That girl never knew how to mix her liquor. She was lucky that Stu didn't take advantage of this. Instead, he waited outside the toilet for a while hearing her spewing, hoping it was just the one bout and he'd still be able to achieve congress that evening. However, after the toilet flushed for the third time, he popped his head around the door to wish her a good night. She didn't respond. She dropped her phone in the loo. Before Stu left, he threw a bit of newspaper and bleach over the carpet thinking it was the kindly thing to do, but this only discoloured it greatly meaning Beth never got all of her security deposit back.

We bring this story up a lot when Beth and Stu meet, even though they hate it. They've always held a grudge for each other which I feel is more due to the embarrassment that they half had sex in the street. Five months after this, Beth met Will who became her long-time boyfriend. Stu shagged his way around London and at one point had a very serious case of gonorrhoea, which I knew about as Stu showed up on our doorstep one day grumbling that his wang was falling off and asking Danny how he could fix it.

At the same time Beth and Stu had been dry humping in the street, Danny and I stood beside our siblings, staring into space about the wheres and hows of getting home and wondering if we were hungry. We watched Beth and Stu get into a cab.

'Come with us!' they roared.

Danny and I declined politely and watched them drive off, their faces attached to each other in the back seat. I thought about chips and jumping in a taxi. Or maybe a bus. It was summer. I thought about walking, about my aching feet. Should I go home and make oven chips? That was a bind. I worked out which was the closest chippy/kebab shop and which was the less stingy when it came to garlic mayonnaise. I thought about texting my roommate, to see how her date went. It was with a bloke she'd met through her new yoga regime. I thought about what if I got home and they were going at it all tantric in the front room? Maybe I shouldn't go home. I wasn't prepared for what I heard next.

'Fancy a fuck?'

I turned to look at Danny Morton. He said 'fuck' strangely – in deep guttural Northern tones. He was looking straight ahead so I wasn't sure if he was even talking to me. I didn't suppose he was so drunk that he was talking to the lamp post. He wasn't shy, or coy about it. He knew exactly what he wanted. I didn't know whether to laugh or cry. Chips were suddenly not a priority. Danny stuck his hand out into the street and a taxi stopped. He got in the back and left the door open. I followed.

'Victoria Park fella, Lauriston Road,' he said to the driver.

We didn't say anything to each other for the whole cab ride. I remember being sat on opposite sides of the seat and not even holding each other's gaze. I'm not sure what the taxi driver must have thought. To any outsider, it may have looked like we were mid-fight, a cloud of some sort of tension sat between us. When Danny stopped the cab, he paid for it and held the door open for me. He opened the front door – a plaque on it claiming it to be the 'Cumbrian Embassy' – to a flat that was above a bohemian clothes shop. When he got through the door, he stepped in and I followed. He turned, closing the door with one hand behind me. He was unfeasibly close.

What happened next? Oh my days. I remember him pulling his body into mine. The kiss was extraordinary, exceptional: the hand to the back of my head, fingers tracing my collar bone. He turned and pinned me to the stairs. He said nothing. He parted my legs with his hand and moved his head down to my waist, pulling my skirt up. I could feel his lips through my knickers. He used his fingers to move the fabric to one side and I felt his tongue lightly press against me. I put my hands down on the steps to steady myself, mostly from the shock that he had located my clitoris. He then moved himself up over me, unbuckling his belt, removing my knickers and well, we had that fuck he was after.

And I remembered feeling aroused but strangely excited thinking about the times when first-time sex had not gone like this at all: the sloppy misaimed jabbing against my perineum, the neck lickers, that lad who convulsed and I was worried the power of Christ had compelled him. The time I had nearly garrotted someone with my handbag, coats getting in the way, sex that's clumsy and you're constantly apologising to each other. I simply felt surprise, pleasant surprise. He was of reasonable size and girth and knew exactly how to move. I'd never felt that build-up of energy within me to reciprocate. I pushed my hips against his, hearing him moan slightly.

But there was something else, equally as unnerving: he was looking at me. Into my eyes. The number of times you'd be looking over someone's naked shoulder or have your face buried in a pillow. This couldn't be more different. He cupped a hand around my face and just kept staring. I'd never felt more appreciated, but I was starting to feel unnerved that perhaps I wasn't allowed to blink. I bulged my eyes slightly. His eyes creased and he laughed.

'Come…'

He said that word Northern too. But he kept moving over me. I wasn't sure it was a request, an order, or a competition but I could feel the energy, the warmth building up, my legs trembling. I remember coming. Hard, moaning loudly as his hands reached down to my naked thighs and he pushed harder, deeper into me. I remember having a momentary panic about STIs and pregnancy, set against the fact I'd just had amazing sex in a stairwell in East London and come like a fricking rocket.

He was still looking at me when the moment was interrupted by a key in the door. Stu stood there looking at his brother's naked buttocks set against my straddled legs.

'Oi!' Danny said. 'Close the door!'

I laughed.

'You cheeky bastard. Is that her sister from bar?'

I was very aware that Danny was still inside me.

'Would you close the door and give the lady her sodding dignity!'

I was hiding underneath Danny at this point.

'Whatever, I'm going down the shops.'

He closed the door. Danny withdrew. Truth be told, I was too shocked to move. He sat there and scratched his head.

'Y'alright?'

'Uh-huh.'

He sat there half-mast. What to say next? Tell him I came? Ask him if he came? Something wildly romantic and sincere?

'You fancy a cuppa?' he uttered as he pulled up his undergarments and buckled up his trousers.

It was everything I wanted and more. 'I quite fancy chips, too.' I added.

'I'll text Stu… there's a decent chippy down road.'

'And I'll take that tea if you're offering. Milk, three sugars.'

'Christ, how do you have any teeth left?' I found this wildly amusing. 'I'll put brews on then, Meg Callaghan.'

'Alright then, Danny Morton.'

He pulled me up and again our bodies folded into each other, his face next to mine, and he kissed me. The kiss was magnificent – and always has been since. The intensity, just the right amount of pressure, the way he pulls gently at my bottom lip, the perfect hand placement. But I also remember just feeling so incredibly safe. Danny Morton, I thought, with your ugly yet sensible shoes: go make me tea, bring me chips and fuck me like that for the rest of my life, please. I wish we'd written that into our wedding vows.

Chapter One

I always wake up the same way: a nest of hair, drool, fatigue aching through my bones, in one of his old T-shirts and a pair of multipack knickers that were once white but are now grey and sagging around the gusset. A hairy arm weaves itself around my midriff, weighted there like a log, and a bearded face rubs itself across my back. I'd like to say it's pleasurable or intended to arouse but it's become some sort of morning ritual whereby he's almost rubbing his face against me to generate heat and wake himself up. I imagine squirrels do the same of a morning.

He finds a safe spot in the small of my back and wedges his morning erection between my butt cheeks. He doesn't apologise for it anymore; it's a given that it'll be there, like his unnecessary need to grace the bedroom with a chorus of his flatulence. Most of the time it's there to simply wake me up, having the same function as an alarm clock. Sometimes I rouse to him playing with it, other times to him asking me for help with a cheeky 'hand shandy'. He's set his aims higher this Monday morning though.

'Fancy a fettle?'

I don't move. I consider his romantic proposal. He rubs his feet over mine and moves a hand over one of my breasts, giving it a squeeze like it might make a comedy duck noise. Unremarkably, I am still not aroused, but there is a possibility he's made me lactate. I turn to look at him.

'Do I have to take off my top?'

'Nah, just a flash… give me a visual.'

I nod, turn onto my back and lift my T-shirt to reveal unshaven armpits. I roll my knickers down, kicking them to the end of the bed. He clambers on top of me. I have vague flashbacks to a documentary about walruses. He rests an elbow either side of my head and looks me in the eye. I say *in* the eye – my eyes are closed and I drift in and out of sleep.

'I'll be quick. Just a speedy one before the girls get up. You ready?'

He kisses the underside of my chin so we can avoid offending each other with morning breath. His cock prods the inside of my flabby thigh. I push him back.

'Go get a condom on.'

'I won't come in you, promise…'

'Which means you'll come on the sodding sheets and I only changed them a couple of days ago.'

'You're killing this…' He sighs and reaches down to the bedside cabinet. 'Why is this drawer filled with Lego?' He finds a condom and then lies on his back, acting like sheathing himself up requires more concentration than is really needed. I won't lie, I put my legs down and use the moment to sleep for a few more seconds. 'Seeing as I'm here, hop on?' he says.

'Fat chance.'

He nestles his body on top of mine and kisses me on the nose. There is then a bit of wayward angling and poking until he finds his way inside me. By the way my body tenses, it's quite clear that my vagina's still asleep too. I will admit it is not unpleasant and I am grateful for the fact we can share some bodily warmth. Cosy's the word. He thrusts into me a few times. He buries his face into my neck then raises his torso so the covers fly off and his body is at a right angle to mine, trying to bend my legs back at the hip.

'Nah, that's not happening.'

'C'mon, I'll get better purchase that way.'

'It's too effing cold!'

He admits I may be right and pulls the covers over us again, chest against mine, flattening my breasts. He thrusts deep into me. I pretend to be into it and grab his arse. Danny's buttocks have evolved over the years but I've always overlooked the fact they've gone a little fuzzy given they've maintained their grabbability.

'Shit!' he says.

'What?' Please don't be a split condom.

'I forgot to take out the recycling bin…'

'Glass? It's fine. We'll have time before the school run.'

He thrusts more rhythmically as he pushes me deeper into the mattress, the effort seeing him release small, quiet gasps of air. Then a light comes on in the landing. Crap. He halts and collapses into me like we're frozen in a very close embrace. Small footsteps head down the stairs.

'You better hurry, they'll all be up soon.'

The rhythm picks up. You can see in his face that the thrusting may also be causing some over-exertion. Small beads of sweat form on his brow, his nostrils flare. A baby in the room next door whimpers.

'Danny, just come already…'

'I'm close… I can't do it on demand, woman…'

I grind my hips knowing it'll get him off. He freezes again at hearing a second set of footsteps, a toilet flushing. The baby is still whimpering.

'Yep, keep doing that. Just like that…'

'Keep your voice down—'

'IS SOMEONE COMING TO MAKE BREAKFAST?'

'YES! I'M COMING!' I shout over his shoulder. Not really, not even close.

The baby is starting to gather volume. I lift my knees a little higher, starting to feel a little unimpressed I've been made to indulge in such athleticism on a Monday morning. And then a noise, his body tenses, legs straighten and his eyes roll back in their sockets. He collapses onto me. I grip on to his shoulders.

'That's the ticket.' He kisses me on the ear then rolls off me.

'I'M HUNGRY! AND TESS WON'T GIVE ME THE REMOTE CONTROL!'

'WE'RE COMING! STOP SHOUTING!' I call back.

We lie next to each other for a moment and I watch him ping off his condom.

'Pass us a nappy sack.'

I grab one from my bedside table and watch him wrap up the offending item.

'You want me to finger you?'

I study the small cracks on our ceiling. I'm not sure if I have the time, need or concentration to summon up an orgasm amidst warring siblings and the fact my downstairs region is still on snooze.

'It'll keep—'

I retrieve my knickers and rise to tend to the baby next door. As I leave, I see Danny lying there, a semi slumped over his groin like an earthworm that's just broken through ground. His legs apart, his chest hair matted and glistening with sweat, seemingly unaffected by the fact the house is bloody Baltic. If he falls asleep, I will literally body slam him.

'I SAID, IS SOMEONE COMING TO MAKE MY BREAK-FAST?' thunders up the stairs. It's Eve, daughter number two who likes to be fed on time.

'Danny…'

'You've just taken me life force, give me a moment.'

'You want Cheerios and tantrums or croup and a full nappy?'

'Littl'un still have croup?'

'She does.' I know because I was up half the night with her. 'Now get up before I grab you by the bollocks – and there's leftover Vicks on these fingers.'

'Kinky.'

He thinks I joke. Next door, the baby is not happy. I open her bedroom door and she stares at me stroppily from the corner of her cot. Her hair whipped to a frizz atop her head, her cheeks scarlet. She barks at me like a seal. I pick up her warm, sleepy body and cradle it close to mine as I bring her back into our room. Danny pulls the covers over his naked body.

'Y'alright there Lemon Drop?'

Polly is Lemon Drop for no other reason than she has blonde hair and Danny is terrible with names. Yes, even with his own kids. I hand her over, slightly smug to know her bottom area is damp and fragrant. He sits up, putting a hand to her back and does that thing where he beats out a rhythm from a song in his head on her ribs. The dog pokes his head around the door to let us know he needs a whizz. The house awakens like a grizzly bear from hibernation except it's cold, it's always cold because I live in the North of England now and the version of cold up here is something my Southern bones have never quite got used to. Downstairs, I hear footsteps and the murmur of voices. The television? Eve is talking to someone. On the phone? To the cat?

'You see, Polly has croup,' she says. 'So it's probably why they've slept in and forgotten to feed me…'

'Oh dear, Princess Polly's not well?'

Bollocks. She's actually let someone in the house. I arch my head over the landing. It's Patrick.

'I'm sorry, Patrick. I'll be down in a minute,' I call out.

Danny is the one who's grinning now. I hope Polly pees on him. I tighten the sash of my dressing gown around my midriff and gallop down the stairs to find Patrick propped against the front door as Eve fills him in on the small injustices of her life. He smiles at me, as he always does. You see, our postman is a man called Patrick so essentially, we have a Postman Pat. I kid you not. When we moved up here, away from London and all that I'd ever known, it was the first thing that tickled me, making me think I'd like my new life in the Lake District. When my sisters would text me, cajoling at how I was miles away from the nearest revolving sushi bar, swapping the capital city for cowpats, sensible wellies and people who wore tweed without irony, I would throw Pat in their faces. Look at you with your toxic urban lives and your postmen who change every week and put junk menus through your door. I'm running around green hills like Maria frigging von Trapp. My postman is *actually* called Pat. He wears knee high socks and shorts, in mid-winter! And because the joke is also not lost on him, his wife has made him a stuffed black-and-white cat for his cherry red van window. I officially love Pat.

However, the unfortunate way in which our living room window is right next to the front door means that Pat often gets more than he bargained for when he delivers the mail to our house. The girls will answer the door when they see him trudging up the driveway so we never have any warning he's here, and he'll get to see me with a towelling dressing gown draped over my shoulders, Danny in his pants (the man feels no cold or shame) or a young daughter of ours screaming that we've given them the wrong colour bowl.

I've shared minimal conversation with Pat but in my head, he's lived in the Lakes all his life and comes from a family of ginger postmen. At Christmas, the girls always make him a card and we give him homemade shortbread. I like to think he eats them by the fire with tea served to him by a wife who likes a heavy wool skirt. I approach the front door trying to protect my modesty, knowing that Pat has seen me in worse states of undress, possibly at one time with a child still attached to my breast. It means there's always a lot of winking and mild innuendo with him – something I've tried to ignore so it won't spoil the image of him living his Lakeland shortbread idyll.

'Morning Mrs Morton. How do?' Wink.

Pat says this a lot and even after having quizzed Danny on what 'how do' means, I still never know how to respond to this.

'Oh, you know… this and that…'

The dog, Mr T (don't ask) comes over to observe. There was a time he used to launch himself at the postman but old age means he's far more chilled these days. I'm all too aware though that he could very well unload his old dog bladder on him if I'm not quick. Pat pets him on the head.

'Shouldn't you lassies be getting ready for school? Tick tock… how's little Princess Polly's croup? You manage to get some of that Olbas Oil?'

The trouble with a provincial postman is that they also know far more about your life than a normal one would. Pat has been witness to all our family dramas.

'She's not a real princess, you know,' pipes up Tess behind me.

'Are you sure?'

'Yes, because we're not royalty. We wouldn't be living in Kendal otherwise or be driving a Volvo.'

Tess is the eldest daughter, and there's a dryness to her sense of humour that feels more than a little familiar. Pat laughs, winks and hands me a pile of mail, including a plain cardboard box.

'And big day today,' he says. 'You wish ol' Bob a Happy Birthday from me, June and the kids.'

That's the other thing about Kendal, everyone knows everyone. Bob, my father-in-law, is part of the Kendal Golf Club mafia, which means if you drew some sort of Venn diagram, he was connected to literally everyone in this place. I once argued it was all a bit incestuous at which Danny kicked me under a dinner table.

'I will do,' I reply.

'IS THERE ANY BREAD THAT ISN'T 50/50?' Eve pipes up from the kitchen.

'And that is my cue to go! You don't happen to have any bread on you, do you?' I say to Pat.

'Only meat and two veg I'm afraid.' And there's your innuendo. I do believe my postie just offered up his member for breakfast. He guffaws and winks again. 'You have a good day now, Mrs Morton.' Oh dear, Pat.

'You too, Pat.' Are we talking chipolatas or a decent-sized Cumberland?

Tess is looking curiously at both of us. 'What sort of postman carries meat around?' she asks. She gives me her father's look; the one he gives me when I attempt to make popular culture references that he simply doesn't understand.

'It was a joke.'

'Who jokes about meat?'

'Postmen.' Mr T sidles up next to me doing his old dog sway. Poor Mr T. 'C'mon, dogface.'

I head to the back door to let him out. Outside, a fine Lakeland drizzle mists the air. Mr T looks as unimpressed as I do as he goes to water my rose bushes with his urine. I stand there, cradling the mail to my chest. Meanwhile, Eve stands in the middle of the kitchen, having opened every cupboard.

'There's nothing to eat,' she declares.

'There's bread for toast, white bread that you ate yesterday in a jam sandwich,' I reply.

'It's not white, it's that 50/50 stuff. You think I'm stupid.'

No, I think your father is stupid because he can't tell the difference. You're five and are one of those ridiculous children who seem to possess a discernible palate that knows when I've changed brands of baked beans or attempt to bring sugar-free fruit squash through the doors.

I refuse to fight over bread so take it out of the bag and pop it in the toaster. She has that stubborn face which makes me want to buy 50/50 for the rest of her life.

'There are Cheerios…'

'Don't like them.'

'Porridge?'

'I'm not a bear.'

'Eve Morton. Don't you dare be a sassy pants with me this morning…'

We exchange glances. Five-year-olds gunning for a fight so early in the morning can go do one. Upstairs, a baby barks in the distance. Mr T saunters into the kitchen, tail wagging, and I throw him a biscuit that bounces off his head because his youth and reflexes have abandoned him. He looks at me and the biscuit. I feel you, Mr T. I really do.

'What's in the box, Mummy?' Tess rifles through the mail. She shakes the box which makes a clunking sound.

I poke lamely at it with a butter knife. Part of me is half-excited we have a box in the house that I can turn into Tess' Viking ship homework due next week. The box is plain and mundane – it will no doubt be something for Dan's work. He's the boss at a paper mill which is as dull as it sounds but always means I'm sorted for A4.

Opening the box, I put it down for a moment so I can wrestle a biscuit-hunting Eve out of a cupboard. 'Biscuits are not breakfast!'

'Yes, they are. You can eat Belvita for breakfast – I've seen them on the tellybox.'

Tellybox is a Danny thing – a Northern affectation that means my daughters also don't know what meal dinner is and call cupcakes buns. Eve is hell-bent on a Hobnob breakfast.

'Belvita are special biscuits for people in a rush who have to eat their breakfasts on trains,' I say.

Upstairs I can hear Danny swearing as he's had to break open a new packet of wipes and can't handle the secret wizardry of the packaging. Things are falling to the floor. I'm having arguments over breakfast biscuits with a five-year-old.

'Mummy, what is a triple tickler?' Tess studies the contents of the box.

Tickling, what on earth? I shake my head; from biscuits to this inanity. I peer in at its contents. It's long and blue like a rolling pin. What newfangled kitchen nonsense is my mother sending me now?

'I don't know, Tessie. Is it important now? Really?'

'It says here that it has more features and better girth to help you come to organism.'

'You're talking gibberish now.' I grab the box and retrieve the item from the plastic moulding. Why is it blue? I hold it in my hands. It's huge. Why is it made of rubber? Then I realise it has bollocks. I shriek and drop it on the floor. It has impressive bounce. Tess and Eve's eyes seem to be glued to it. I have the urge to hurdle the table and carry them out of the kitchen to safety, like an earthquake has just hit. I scurry to the floor, hide it under my dressing gown and stuff it back into the box. What the actual mother of crap?

'GIRLS, we're done here. Let's get ready for school.' I clap my hands like a seal. 'Now! We can do breakfast after.'

Tess' eyes follow me suspiciously as I try to close the box back shut.

'Why are you angry?' Eve's eyes bulge, imitating my frazzled look.

'I'm not angry with you. I'm not… I'm just… Uniforms, please, please, please…'

Desperate pleas lead them to saunter out and up the stairs. I freeze for a moment. I open the box back up, slowly like the thing might escape. That is really there, isn't it? I get it out again and examine it, this blue dildo, with a curious eye. Mr T has gone back to his corner of the kitchen to fall asleep but the cat, Magnum (we went with an eighties pet name theme) gives it a curious look from his corner of the house. I feel the need to protect the cat. Shield your little feline eyes! I can't let this corrupt you. I shove it back in the box once more and force it shut.

Then there's the small issue over why it's here. In our house. Did I fill in some online survey and forget to tick a box? I do a lot of those surveys. Or maybe it was sent by someone to arouse me. Yikes, what if it was made in the image of someone as some sort of ruse to get me into bed? Like a 3D dick pic? I applaud the effort but am perturbed that someone would go to such lengths – extreme lengths from the looks of this thing.

On the flip side, maybe it was sent as hate mail. Maybe I was the dick? Not just any dick. I was an abnormally large dick. I thought of people I'd riled in the last weeks or so. There was that mum at the school gate, who's always held that grudge against me ever since Tess overtook her daughter on the infants' reading tree. Or maybe it was Trish from the gym who had finally worked out it was me who farted during yoga and blamed it on her. Then there's that ex-boyfriend from uni who I dumped because he wore boat shoes. It becomes quite the problem when you suddenly realise there is an impressive list of people in this world who might have cause to send you a dick.

But then I remove the invoice from the box. I notice the address on the front. It's for Danny. Danny's the dick? Or he bought a dildo for me? For himself? For… I freeze for a moment.

Danny enters with Polly under one arm in the way he's become accustomed to holding babies, like a farmer holding a newborn lamb. He's in his pants and an old T-shirt, completing the look with a pair of old man slippers. He takes a thumb and rubs at Polly's snot-crusted cheeks before sitting at our kitchen table. I clutch the box. Do I ask him why he's ordered a dildo while he bounces our youngest on his knee? I study his face, the way he takes a handful of Cheerios and uses his palm as a bowl.

I haven't used a dildo in years. Back when I was a single, independent woman, working as a journalist in the *Sex and the City* years, every woman owned one as a statement of owning their sexuality. When Danny and I first dated and had exciting, regular sex, it got brought out on occasion though my recollection was that Danny wasn't overly keen – especially as the one I had was glittery and he was convinced it wasn't wired up properly so was worried it'd overheat and meld to my bits. But then we had decent sex without it, we got married. Marriage didn't dry up the sex. The chaos of babies and family did. Where was that glittery dildo now? In a box in the garage, possibly. Or worse, in a box in my parents' loft.

It still begs the question why this blue one is here? Now? My throat goes a little dry as my mind runs through the possible reasons

why. He probably bought it as a joke for his brother. Maybe he
ordered it in complete error. Maybe he was looking for a rolling
pin and he wasn't wearing his glasses so clicked on the wrong item.
Easily done. I should ask him, make a little joke. Danny has always
driven that Northern straightforward sensibility through our marriage – a spade's a spade, a dildo's a dildo. I stare at the box for a
moment, returning to the worst-case scenario.

'So I told work I'd be in after lunch,' Danny says. 'We can
walk girls to school, grab Stu from station and then he can come
back here? He was going to stay with Mum and Dad but they're
putting up other guests for the party tonight. He can just bunk
on the sofa.'

The words are going in but I can't process them. I look back at
Danny smelling the top of Polly's head. Danny's younger brother,
Stu, has flown in from Sydney to be here for Bob Morton's seventy-
fifth birthday celebrations, starting tonight with some pasta and
sparkling wine at the famous Francesco's. Stu is our present. Then
again, maybe it's the dildo? Maybe it's from Stu? He is the sort. He's
stayed here before but once got so drunk he soiled himself on our
new rug which means our cat doesn't quite trust him.

'Yeah, that's fine,' I reply.

'Mum rang – table's booked at Don Francesco's for seven thirty.'

'Yup…'

'Dad'll love it. His golden boy's back where he belongs, not on
some surfboard halfway across the world. They're coming around
later to see their lad too.'

Danny talks everything through clearly, in the way that he does.
There is always a method. He'd have been good in the military,

or as a chef. Very little fazes him. I should just ask him, there is a reasonable explanation here.

'Daddy… Mummy called me a sassy pants and won't let me have biscuits for breakfast.'

Eve appears in a uniform covered in yesterday's squeezy yoghurt. Danny gives me that look where he sometimes dares to support the five-year-old before me. I see him pop Eve on his other knee to hear her woes and brush her hair.

'Thing is, Buttons, your mum is right. Only fools eat biscuits for breakfast. How you going to make your brain work on biscuits?'

I pause for a moment to see him balance both girls on his lap. Eve is Buttons for no other reason than she has big shining eyes like a cartoon kitten. She's the quintessential Daddy's girl mainly in the way she likes to curl into him and give me evils from across the room. I watch as she runs her fingers up and down his bearded chin.

'Can you go back upstairs and change that cardie, lovely?' I ask.

'You call me lovely when you want something,' she retorts.

'I want you to go upstairs and find a cardigan that doesn't smell like cat and doesn't have yoghurt down the front.' There's a tremble in my voice.

'Mummy's just mad because of that thing in the box.'

'What box?' he enquires.

'Junk.' I realise my turn of phrase is not entirely inappropriate. Eve saunters off and I hear her footsteps skip up the stairs. Now's good a time as any. I open up the box. I don't say a word, I just hold up the contents like I would a pair of skid-marked pants that he's left on the floor in the bedroom. *Care to explain?* I can't read his look. There is mild surprise but I can almost see his mind whirring like he's thinking of what to say next. It's not the reaction I was expecting.

'I don't think Polly should be looking at that. You'll blind her.' He shields the baby's eyes and she giggles.

Choked up, I manage to get an important word out: 'Why?'

He pauses for a moment. 'It were a gift.'

'For me?'

'For you.'

'Flowers are gifts.'

'But flowers die…'

'Well, the message you're sending here is that you want to kill me instead with a sex toy. This is bloody ridiculous…' To prove my point, I struggle to get my fingers around it.

'Geez, it's like a frigging marrow. Polly couldn't have been much smaller when you birthed her.'

It's very unlike Danny to not check the dimensions of something before purchase.

'What on earth would make you think I'd want to have a go on that?' Closer inspection alerts me to the fact that it comes with a suction cup attachment and has fake veins running through it. 'It'd be like making love to a tree stump.'

'I just thought, you know… go for something a bit bigger for the lady's pleasure…'

'So, it's for you? So you can watch me do myself?'

The baby seems a tad confused now. This has the potential to scar her for years, engrain itself into her consciousness. I try and hold it out of sight.

'But you know… if you were feeling that way inclined. It's been a bit slow recently. I know we had a jump this morning but I just thought it'd jazz things up.'

I let out a small laugh, almost in disbelief. It's what happens every time a baby comes along: the sex dries up for a bit. We find our mojo months down the line when my body recovers and we have the physical energy to partake in such endeavours again. But then we're constantly tired, I look like crap.

He comes over and stands next to me by the kitchen counter. Unsure of what to do, I hit him. With the dildo.

'That didn't hurt.'

'Shame.'

I think about his morning erections pressed up against me and how at times I've ignored it. I think about the sexual urges that haven't really been stirred for a while. I think about a husband who bought me a dildo to try and rouse those urges again. How ten years of marriage has turned into a couple standing in their kitchen, staring at a gigantic, if slightly forlorn-looking blue sex toy.

'If I wanted to have sex, I'd have it with you… surely?' I say.

'Yeah… but once you have babies, you go through a bit of a moment where you look like you could stab me most days, and when we do… do it… it's different? You don't always look that into it? I don't have full access…'

'Pardon me?'

'Well, your tits… you know, your tits are pissing milk every-where…'

We've gone from the ridiculous to the offensive in the space of a minute.

'So, you're saying… you're not keen on having sex with me at the moment so you've given me a dildo to tide me over until you're ready?'

'No.'

'So, you want me to use this on you?' I'm open-minded sexually – if that's what he wants. Though he's never really requested I go near that area before.

I hold the dildo up again. If anything, it's beginning to look like it could have a use as a weapon. Polly's eyes bulge as I hold it up – even the infant knows how absurd it is. He laughs.

'I'm OK for now,' I reply. 'If I need to get myself off, I've got a perfectly good hand. And anyway, an electric toothbrush has the same effects.'

'That's grim,' he replies.

'I don't use yours.'

'Thanks for that.'

'We could have had a conversation about this before you gave The Love Shack,' I study the invoice, '£36.99 on this contraption.'

'I'll bring it up over dinner next time, shall I?'

'Over mini kievs and potato waffles?'

'Why not? "Oi oi, once we get our chocolate mousses down, let's go upstairs and have a go on that big blue love cannon you hid in my sock drawer."'

Love cannon suddenly has me in fits of giggles. 'And you think this is what I want? I'm not sure what to say, Dan. It's far too early for this crap.'

He puts a hand to the back of his head, half-laughing. I still can't register the emotion – he doesn't even seem embarrassed.

'You could re-gift it,' he says.

'Ewww…'

'It's unused. Save it for school tombola…'

'They won't know what to do with it. I'd go round someone's house and see it being used as a dog toy,' I reply.

'Here Fido, be a good dog and go to your bed with your giant cock toy.'

We both laugh. Tess flies in and you've never seen me throw something in the cutlery drawer with such speed. She senses a moment between us and looks down at the empty box.

'Eve stole the biscuit jar you know? She ate three Hobnobs upstairs.' She loiters in the kitchen with book bags and school shoes.

Danny looks me in the eye. 'We should get changed up, don't want these girls to be late. Dimples, go get them hair tie thingies. We done here?' he asks me.

Tess is Dimples, simply as she has two of them carved into both cheeks – the first thing I saw when she was born. I watch them together as he smooths over the bumps in her hair.

'Are you just doing a ponytail?' she asks her father.

'It's ponytails or I do you a bowl cut with kitchen scissors, those are your options.'

Tess, as always, is tickled by his frankness and sits there open-mouthed. I study him intently. He doesn't even flinch at what we've just discussed: keep calm, carry on, nothing to see here. That was the thing with Danny. Fights were always easily resolved, there was never any grey area, always black and white. I bought you a dildo because we're going through a bit of a sexual dry patch. The idea was that it'd get your juices flowing. It hasn't? We'll send it back. Many more pressing issues to deal with today.

I, on the other hand, of course have a million and one questions. Like why blue? And somewhere, floating on top of the more vacuous concerns, is a little whisper. I look at his eyes darting about, wondering why he didn't address his concerns about our sex life before he clicked to buy. Why can't I read that unfamiliar, vacant emotion in his face? It whispers whether this was meant for someone else, for another reason. It tells me my husband just lied to me.

'Yeah, we're done.'

Chapter Two

We got Mr T when he was just a pup from a mill deep in remote Smardale, a small village to the east of the Lakes where the population of sheep outnumber the humans by about five hundred. Danny was adamant it was a rite of passage now we were living in the countryside. He had heard a friend of a friend knew a farmer whose border collie had got knocked up by the dog from the next farm over, and he now had puppies to give away. I had one condition: I got to name it.

The selection process took place in an old stone farmhouse, like one I'd seen in films about pigs that could talk and herd sheep. All I remembered was a caged-off area containing a mass of paws. It was completely unnerving that we were going to separate one of these babes from their mother so I left the decision-making to Danny, who finally opted for the chubbiest furball there. He had a scrunched-up little face and markings across his front, not unlike the shape of a medallion. The mohawk at the top of his head sealed the deal.

'We shall call him Mr T!' I exclaimed.

The farmer looked confused. 'What's that, love? Tea? Like Yorkshire Tea?

'No, like the eighties TV star. You know: "I ain't getting on no plane!"… "I pity the fool!"?' I mimicked aloud in my best baritone. I spied Danny shaking his head at me, half-begging me to stop but secretly pissing himself.

'What's her mother called?' I asked.

'Gyp.'

'As in pain?'

'Say what?'

'Like my ankle's giving me gyp.'

'Is it, love? Should have said. Did you fall?'

'What?'

I turned to Danny, who was in hysterics at this point. We'd been in the North for four months by that time. I may as well have moved to France for what I understood of people's take on the English language up here, but to Danny it was all a major amusement. I shook my head as he cradled his little bundle of fur.

I was not Northern, not yet, and in no way was I going to have a dog called Skip, Fly or Gyp. Welcome to the family, Mr T. This is the baby, Little Miss T. Three years later we got a cat that I was convinced had a moustache, so we called him Magnum, and we've had fish and other pets, gerbils called Cagney and Lacey and a giant rabbit called Hasselhoff.

This menagerie of animals was never my idea. That was part of some outdoorsy dream that Danny hadn't been able to fulfil in London where he could live in a field with his girls, scrambling up rock faces and befriending wild birds. I had grown up the eldest of five sisters with parents neither stupid nor brave enough to add pets to the equation, so animal husbandry was properly foreign to me. I was initially annoyed that Mr T lacked the communication skills to impart his wisdoms on to me (how did I know running in a circle and barking your balls off meant needing to go outside for a poo?). The breath that smelt of old ham coupled with the continuous moulting was not endearing either. Yet after a while, Mr T became a part of the furniture. Obviously, he likes Danny more than me; I still lack his dog-whispering alpha master ways, but I like to think that over time Mr T has come to respect the fact I am a mother of sorts – and will always give him some of my crisps. He's especially keen on Pringles.

Today, I use him as some sort of shield on the school run and he eyes me curiously; less enquiring about my emotional state but curious as to why I haven't brought biscuits. Danny walks ahead with all of the girls – one on each hand and the littlest strapped to his front swathed in fleece. It's a sight I'll never get sick of but it does mean Mr T and I follow behind carrying an assortment of book bags and rucksacks like sherpas. But having the dog means I can distance myself from Danny to ponder the events from this morning. It doesn't even seem real; normally drama at that time on a Monday morning is a car not starting or me having forgotten to launder a sports kit. Was he lying? Why would he lie about a sex toy? It conjures up images that dwell and invoke a tiny bit of bile. I look down at Mr T. If he was playing away from home, you'd know wouldn't you, Mr T? You're a member of the A-Team! Mr T looks at me. He sits waiting for that biscuit I haven't brought him. You stupid furry bastard.

We live in a townhouse in Kendal built from grey limestone, the same colour as the perpetually overcast sky. Danny had been less keen to live there. However, I was a city girl, not a rambler, and certainly not someone who understood the aesthetic appeal of waterproof trousers. I lack the ability to charge a car down a country lane, mount a hedge and overtake a tractor. I need to be within the safety net of an M&S Food Hall, and in the very least a Top Shop. I defiantly stood by this notion which led us closer to the town centre. However, to get his revenge on buying his central townhouse, Danny refused to buy me a car which meant that I usually walked everywhere, along the weaving ginnels of Kendal, usually pushing buggies and dragging a dog around. It was probably better than having to do this in London along streets littered with old kebabs, pollution and congestion charges but it would always make Danny laugh to see me take on anything with a gradient steeper than a road bump; his city lass out of her comfort zone, without a Tube or taxi in sight.

Given the school was just three roads down, it was also something we regularly walked, if only to escape the fight outside the gate with grown women fighting for parking spaces. As we approach the huge iron railings of the school wall, it's the usual scene of families milling around the windswept playground marked out with hopscotch and health and safety-friendly play equipment.

'We want Daddy to take us in!' Eve announces and I don't argue, pulling softly on Mr T's lead, glad that I can stand by the railings and escape the parents and teachers exchanging gossip and civilities. I distribute the girls' belongings and misplace kisses on cheeks. Danny looks pleased to be wanted, Polly cradled into his chest, and I leave him to escort them to their classrooms.

In the middle of the school playground, Mr McArthur is doing his headteacher spiel. He's also a Kendal native who went to school with the Morton brothers and if I remember rightly, Stu may have once dated his wife. Joanne McArthur is a nurse who works at the local hospital and together, they are one of those legendary all-star status couples. He even has the glossy American-medical-drama locks and teeth to match. They have three sons, run half-marathons together and live in a giant farmhouse on a hill somewhere that may or may not also be a hospital for dying kittens. OK, I made the last bit up. When I speak to the Mortons about him, they all say the same. He was one of those Scouting-Duke-of-Edinburgh-types who has an overbearing enthusiasm for life. I spy him squatting down to look at a child's rainforest project offering which looks like a sloth made out of a broom head attached to some loo rolls. Two mums stop conveniently behind him, most likely to check out his arse. Danny emerges from the school and when he sees McArthur, they stop to talk.

'Morning, why are you hiding back there?' A voice catches my forlorn-looking sad figure: Sarah, a mum acquaintance from school, married to Jez and mum to George and Maisy.

These mothers are sometimes the only people you speak to in a day and you end up knowing everything about their lives and more, whether it's through the class WhatsApp group, social media or the daily playground chatterings. You know who's married, who's split up, whose party you haven't been invited to and who's looking for a builder. Sarah is the classic Alpha Queen Bee – she's the one organising all the drinks, popping up on all the Facebook pages, the one who knows all the gossip because she's a childminder so has her ear in a lot of people's lives. It also means she comes with an entourage of little people who more often than not are running circles around her.

'Leon, put that stick down and your coat on! You OK, love?'

I don't suppose Sarah really cares much if I'm OK or not and I think for a moment before I divulge anything. Oh yes, all good. We had a dildo delivered in the post this morning that's the size of an Alsatian's hind leg and I'm not sure I believe why it's in my house, but apart from that I'm tickety-boo. That would get around this playground faster than the nits do.

'Nothing, just got Danny on dad duty today so I don't have to cross the threshold,' I say instead.

She gestures over to him as he stands there chatting with McArthur. 'I forget those two know each other from back in the day.'

Naturally, she also knows the social tapestry of Kendal and how the Morton brothers are woven into it. This means she always talks at me like she knows more than she's willing to let on.

'That is true,' I reply.

'I'm sure Danny has told you everything.' Her words ring with double meaning this morning, so much so that I can't reply. She doesn't seem to care but moves her attention to another mum who's more worthy of the conversation. All I know of this other mother is that she told us all off on a Facebook group once because someone had stolen her kid's Pokémon cards. I'd never seen such fury. They remain within eavesdropping distance so I can hear how they went drinking at the weekend and someone called Mandy left her shoes in the minicab. Danny and McArthur continue to chew the fat and I will my husband to hurry the hell up.

'I tell you, she were there and flirting with Marv all night,' drones Sarah.

'Speak of the devil.'

Their disapproving tones mean I can't resist but turn my head and try to work out who they're talking about. I scan through the railings and across the way. Oh dear. It had to be Briony Tipperton. I let out a resigned sigh. If Sarah was your Alpha, Briony was your classic caricature yummy mummy. The glass slipper in a sea of walking boots, a world away from sensible and hardy, she's the sort who tackles the school run dripping in fake tan, bottom-lifting animal print jeggings and towering heels. I spy her tottering over the tarmac in furry, diamanté-clad shoe-boots and what looks like a cashmere poncho. I'd have to go over and stroke her to make sure. I won't.

Briony and Sarah do not mix well – there's a competitive nature to their relationship that if anything, is fun to witness at boring school events. That said, I also have my own thing with Briony as when we first moved up here, I found out that she and Danny used to date in college and that she was the very person he'd lost his virginity to. I couldn't understand it, not least because they are chalk and cheese, and because she has that flashy, attention-seeking personality to match, a laugh that echoes around the school with the jarring dissonance of a small yapping dog.

Sarah and her mum companion glare over at her.

'Attention seeker, always has been. Her and Ian belong together, that's for sure.'

Ian, Briony's estate agent husband, likes a shiny suit, car and shoe, and when you walk past him, it's like he's been bathing in Lynx.

I watch as Briony's ample bosom bounces in time with her high-heeled shuffle. I look over at Danny, still in conversation with McArthur and his eyes shift towards her. There's a look between them.

'Back in day, when we were at school,' Sarah says, 'she'd be in the cafeteria doing her fifty layers of slap and combing through her extensions. Nowt's changed.'

I see Briony go over to Danny and McArthur and join in, a little three-way conversation. This is when I wish I could lip-read. McArthur says something and Briony laughs. Danny smiles and nods, not one to ever be too casual with his emotions.

'Oooh, she's such a flirty tart. "Oh, Mike… you're so funny! Look at my tits! Snatch is wide open for yer like a hippo's jaw."' Her friend's laughter goads Sarah's bitchery. 'I've heard she's had work done too. Her arse is filled with air. They attached a bike pump to her arsehole. If she landed on a hedgehog, she'd pop like a balloon.'

The ladies cackle with an assortment of children stood at their feet listening to every word, one of whom has lost a shoe and is making their way through their lunch.

I move away from Sarah and her friend to get a better view of this three-way. I'm not wearing cashmere, that's for sure. Just my Lakes mother uniform of sensible rain jacket that is not remotely stylish, although on a practical note the hood can be tightened around my rain-beaten face, peering out like a newly born babe from her mother's nether regions. I'm not in the same fashion postcode as Briony, nowhere near.

Why is she standing with her hip to one side? She and Danny start their walk back to the gate then engage in pleasantries. Or not? Is it more than that? She touches his arm, he nods.

This is what I hated most about relocating to the Lakes. It's full of history for the Morton brothers – three lads who'd dated around, got into trouble and had used this manor as a playground in their mid-teens. Every so often we'd bump into a woman in a supermarket or a pub. They'd recognise Danny and have a very brief conversation doused in Northern while I tried to join the dots. Then usually once they'd disappeared, Danny would say, 'Yup, shagged her back in day.' To which I'd normally spit out something through a nostril.

Briony and Danny were what I would define as childhood sweethearts. I never believed he divulged the full truth of their dalliance, but sources (his mum) told me they dated for two years through college. His mother was always disapproving of the length of Briony's skirts and the fact she dumped Danny to go out with Johnny Bagwell who was a wrong'un with slightly questionable political affiliations. But I always dug for more information, the details. Had we returned to the scene of the crime so they could rekindle old flames?

After the events of this morning, this encounter is loaded with suspicion for me. They continue to talk. *Remember that time we did it in photography room at school? From behind?* Why is he still there? Why do they have things to say to each other? Every time I ask Danny what happened on the school run, he tells me, 'Nowt, got my girls and left. Don't engage with the rabble.' Yet here he is, engaging. She knocks her head back and emits one of her cackles. What was so funny? Danny is many things but he is rarely funny. Why do they have their phones out? And then she goes in for the air kiss. Their cheeks meet. Because Briony thinks she's high-end (her kids are called Lexus and Chrysler) she goes in for the double which catches Danny off-guard, so she gets closer to his lips than anticipated. I stare on. I may have just retched in my mouth. Emotion swells deep in my chest.

Briony then moves on to another gaggle of mothers while Danny catches sight of Rufus and Rowan, two of his oldest friends. They are also part of that Kendal clique and this morning seem to be a stark reminder of how much I don't belong to it. My name is obviously mentioned and Rowan turns to wave animatedly at me and puts her hand to her ear to signal that she'll call me. I put my thumb up in reply. Their friendship dates back years and even though they have welcomed me warmly into their circle, I wonder if they know if there's something happening? Rufus similarly wears his youngest, River, on his front and they both stand there, this statement of modern fatherhood, and make their babies high five in the middle of the playground. It all looks so wholesome, so worthy.

Which is why you better not be shagging Briony effing Tipperton with a giant dildo, Danny. I would leave him. I would take his kids and take them far away from here, simply for the shame. I always had you pegged with better taste, Mr M. I cross my fingers for no other reason than to hope my husband hasn't let his standards drop and been playing away from home with someone so awful.

I thought we were fine, I really did. Images flicker through my head. This is just paranoia talking. You've still got a young baby, your body is recovering, your face is creased with a thousand lines that hint at age and lack of sleep. It was just a sex toy in the post. He explained why it was there. Perhaps it's wrong to doubt a husband who's never given you reason to before today. It was nothing.

I hear Briony's laugh again and my instinct is to set my aging dog on her. Not that he'd do much other than use her as a lamp post.

'Really? It's a school love... there are kids about. You better be picking that up...'

I turn to see a parent – one of the faceless sorts who is always manning a second-hand clothes stall and is most likely called Kate. Sure enough, in amongst my playground spying antics, I've failed to notice that Mr T has been squatting next to me taking a dump. He looks nonplussed. I can feel the embarrassment rise to my cheeks as I see his turds peppered with the remainder of the sweetcorn from last night's dinner. I pat my pockets down to find something I can use to pick up the offending pile, while a few other parents shake their heads at me in disapproval. *It's OK, I wasn't going to let your children eat it…*

'He chooses his moments, eh?' I say.

'When you're done, have you signed the petition?' Kate asks.

'The petition?' I enquire. She carries a blue clipboard that she holds closely to her chest.

'About the sex education classes?' Kate is not being too specific here.

'For the children?'

'Yes, the children in the infants are being taught about sex and homosexuality.'

Kate's eyes widen at the sound of that final word. I cringe. I know her kind, someone who was born and bred here, and never really left so hasn't had the chance to see the wonderful wide world beyond. None of them 'homosexual sorts' exist up here in the hills and spring water. We don't even have sex here. The children emerge out of the Lakes. It is an infuriating aspect of living out in the sticks and not one I take lightly, especially on a morning like this.

'Is that alongside their phonics because that's a big word to spell? Gay would be easier, or maybe queer?'

Kate can sense I'm enjoying mocking her and tuts in the same way when I occasionally walk into school concerts late.

'Well, I have twenty signatures on my petition.'

'You should have said, I could have picked up my dog crap with that.'

She glares at me with a smug look like she's some superior being. Don't even try, love. Her gaze shifts away from my scowling face, towards someone else more naive, on whom she can force her opinions. I swing the bag in my hand. *Don't throw the poo at her, Meg.* Maybe I can throw it at the person coming towards me though. Shame he has a baby strapped to him.

'Did dog pinch one off?'

'What do you think? Some bint was coming at me with stupid school petitions too. What did McArthur want?'

'This and that. Just shooting the breeze. He said he wanted to talk more about that article you wanted to write in The Wezzie about the school.'

I nod. However, I hate it when he does this. That was a five-minute conversation at most and I expect a play by play.

'I mean, I'll just stand here while Briony Tipperton rubs her tits in your face too.'

'Ooooh, someone's got their grumpy cat face on… wouldn't touch it with barge pole.'

Barge pole. Was he alluding to the dildo?

'Why were you trading numbers?' I ask. 'Or were you booking in a blow dry?'

My tone has gone full-on bitch now. Danny has been with me long enough to sense what's happening. He shakes his head, slowly, to let me know this is not the time or place to gun for a fight. I rarely do this, maybe once a month when the hormones are high and he's done something ludicrous like leaving the cheese uncovered in the fridge or throwing coloured socks into a white wash. But today every little thing is escalating my confusion.

'She thought it may be nice for us to go out for a drink,' he says.

'I'd rather poke my eyes out with kirby grips.'

'I'll tell her we're busy then.' He doesn't want to play.

Both Briony and Danny have encountered each other before, and usually we mark the occasion with nervous laughter, but today it's hit a nerve. We stare each other out. Danny turns to walk home and expects me to follow. I pull at the dog who looks like he'd rather be anywhere other than here.

'What did you say that was so funny?' I ask.

'Can't remember.'

'You literally spoke to her five minutes ago.'

'She's a daft lass, she'll laugh at anything.'

'Maybe it was the fact she used to shag you…'

At this point, Danny looks down at the baby, her eyes wide open, like I'm tainting her.

'Don't start…'

'Don't start what?'

If I had to list things that Danny hates about me, it's probably my propensity to start drama when all he reckons is needed is a bracing walk and a strong cup of tea. He doesn't like to have it out, blazing row style like I do. He doesn't want us to talk through the finer details. He likes to quietly simmer, silence me out and then make me feel like some overreacting harpy. What

I really want to announce to this cobbled street? *You ordered a dildo online and then gave me a shitty excuse of a reason which makes me think you're playing away from home! And then you went and engaged in conversation with a mumzilla who you used to shag in your teens! I want to throw dog crap at you!* But I don't. He won't let me. He wants to make me think I'm imagining things. He wants us to walk to the station to welcome his little brother back into the fold and then wait in anticipation for tonight when we'll sit and make nice over garlic bread and one of his mum's crumbly birthday cakes.

He walks a little ahead of me to prove his point. But whilst I'm dramatic and perhaps at times a little too fond of shrieking to prove a point, there is a nagging feeling in my gut that something has changed the landscape. Like a fly on the windscreen that refuses to budge. Fly away, you bastard. And though this may be nothing but intuition, my journalistic need to dig prevails, just so I can be proved wrong. I reach for my phone and pretend to react to something on the screen.

'Oh, that's strange?'

Danny stops in the middle of the street to heed my explanations.

'The Wezzie want me in... Something's happened on the Crook Road Estate and they're writing a feature and want my input. I can be back by 12 p.m.'

'They need you in now?'

'Yes.'

He doesn't answer, again very symptomatic of how Danny operates. He will not voice disdain but shows quiet disappointment in the style of a bearded Geography teacher.

'Well, do what you have to. Come on, T dog. Let's go for a shuffle.' He takes the lead from me, our hands brush past each other and he gives me a look. I'm still not sure what it means. It's telling me there's a story here that I don't know about. But it's almost pleading with me not to look any further down the rabbit hole. He turns, starting to walk up the hill towards our house and the light refracts off his body, breaking off into tiny shards, almost like little chinks in his armour.

Chapter Three

If there was anything I left behind in London of significance, it was my career. I wish I could have engraved a tombstone for it. *Here lies the career of Meg Callaghan, journalist and writer. Missed every month by the readers of* Red *and the sandwich shop where she spent her monthly wage on lattes and greasy bacon butties.* At the time, it wasn't something I mourned: I was leaving the superficial world of beauty journalism behind me. I had a baby girl. I was going to be living life in the country like a Brontë character decked in Barbour and Hunter. More importantly, I had found love and I was going to follow that love. It was wildly romantic, no?

I wasn't sure where my career had been going at that point. *Red* magazine was fantastic with all the fashion and beauty freebies, the discounts on haircuts and highlights, and it'd allowed me to meet the odd celebrity. At the time, I moaned about my commuter existence and the monotony of the nine-to-five but looking back now, I'll admit to missing the sophistication in how I dressed, the hot morning coffees I carried, the designer handbag that came as standard. When I relocated here, I did the odd freelance gig alongside the kids but then took on part-time work at the legendary local paper, *The Westmorland Gazette* aka The Wezzie Gezzie. And now? Now I write about flooding, planning applications, flower shows and tourism problems. There's not a free lip stain in sight.

I've had few regrets; I still get to write, investigate and balance that with family but in truth, it's a world away from what I did before. In fact, Jan opposite me knits covers for her stationery. Seriously, staplers can get cold. Perhaps the one thing I mourned most was that marriage gave me an awesome journalist name, Meg Morton, journalist at large with all the alliteration of Lois Lane but none of the skyscraper glamour, just me sat in a quaint parochial office, held together by regular tea-breaks and surrounded by a few watercolour prints of Windermere and Alan's A4 signs etched in Comic Sans telling us what printer isn't working.

'Meg, you weren't due in today were you? How's Molly doing?' asks Diana.

Diana Lovell is my boss, the grand dame of South Lakeland journalism. She is a sturdy force of nature, not one to shy away from a quilted gilet, her ruddy face mapped out with thread veins. In my previous job, my editors came with Yves St Laurent Touche Éclat and high-waisted pleated metallic skirts.

'Still croupy. And no, I had a tip on the Crook Road Estate that I thought I'd follow up on.'

'Excellent. Steam for the croup. Let me know if you want me to shout at Gavin on the council board again.'

I like Diana's confident earthiness; she's been known to chain herself to bulldozers and shout at local MPs as a front for being the voice for the community and the greater good. I watch as she goes around the desks in the office and plonks jars on each one.

'Pickled damsons everyone, handpicked. Excellent with gammon.' Her voice commands, travelling through the office.

Tim widens his eyes. He is my desk neighbour and new to this game, having come to us from Manchester with a journalism diploma and the idea that his words could change the world. Except that he ended up in a shared flat over the Sizzle Inn kebab shop and spends his days editing submissions about local football scores and how someone once stole a collection box from a chippy. He's the youngest in the office and attaches himself to me as for some reason he thinks I have journalistic kudos. I will admit to liking him even though he still wears what looks like an old school tie.

'Why would you pickle a damson?' he whispers.

'Jam, right?'

'I was thinking beer.'

I smile at him as he props his glasses on the bridge of his nose, and sips tea out of an Iron Man mug. In another universe, this kid is Jimmy Olsen, isn't he? I look around the office, trading smiles and nods and wait for everyone to return to their work before I boot up my computer. I know why I'm here. I just need to have a scratch at this to sate my own curiosities. I firstly go on Facebook, to stalk Briony Tipperton and seek out any clues. There's a lot of leopard print but otherwise, nothing.

Next. If this is as logical as Danny is making it out to be then there must be a chain that I can follow; there will be something in black and white. I reach into my pocket and find an invoice from the parcel that I squirreled away. I go to our banking website and bring up the joint account details, scanning transactions. Nothing. Surely if you were buying a sex toy for our joint pleasure then this is how he would have paid for it? We have no secrets (or so I thought) so I log into his current account. Nothing.

I can't access The Love Shack website here for obvious reasons, so I open it up with my phone. I look around with furtive eyes. Sign in? I click on the link and input his email address. Password. I go through the regular ones I know with dates of birth attached and without. I even put in Briony's name. My fingers move with expert speed. I just need to know. I put in our daughters' names, the dog's name, his mother's name. But then I think, would he do this through his personal email address? If I can't find the transaction, how did he pay for it? With a secret credit card? With an email address that I can't access? Work, I realise.

> *Login*
> d.morton@mortonpapermill.co.uk
> *Password*
> cumbrianembassy1

> *Welcome back to The Love Shack!*

Fuck.

'Tea?'

I throw two palms over my phone screen, my cheeks a deep cherry blush. Tim stands over me like the eager beaver that he is. Did he see the home page of the scantily clad couple on all fours and the special 2-4-1 on lubricants?

'Why not?' He scampers off and I return to the website. The bastard used his work address. My stomach grumbles to a low churn. He hid this from me.

A pop up appears on the screen:

You are a Platinum Customer! Click here to redeem your points!

Platinum? That's more than I've ever achieved on a credit card or loyalty points scheme. That says everything I need to know. I click on Purchase History.

'Margaret from accounts brought in some custard creams so I liberated a few for you.' Tim plonks a cup of tea down on my desk with a pile of biscuits.

'Thank you…' I have my phone covered again as he hovers, expecting a bit of small talk in repayment.

'No worries, Meg. I didn't know you were going to be in?'

'Oh, I just wanted to catch up on a few things.'

He hangs around awkwardly. 'I have to get on though… I also have a deadline for a match report against Workington. Let me know if you need my help,' he says.

I smile but can feel my heart sinking slowly into my chest, embedding itself in doubt. My fingers hover over the button. I need to know for sure.

No.

Please.

I hold on to the sides of my desk to steady myself, staring at the screen. I can't breathe. Why the hell are there three pages worth of purchases? It dates back a year. Christ alive, that's a lot of lubricant, enough to fill a bathtub. But there are all sorts on the list from dildos to cock rings, handcuffs to feather duster-style contraptions. Oh my good god, he's having an affair and a kinky one at that.

My face is so close to my desk I'm tempted to simply put a cheek down and just die right here, really quietly. The girls. Us. Our marriage. Our life. Who was this he's playing around with? How did it take me so long to find this out? Did I miss any signs? You can read, watch and hear about what it's like to be cheated on but the overriding emotion is feeling like a little crack has formed on the surface of your heart and it's carving its way into your cells like the ground fracturing in an earthquake. What I have with Danny isn't perfect but I love him, I loved him enough to be here with him, to mother his children, to have a life. With him. Is this an affair? Is it just sex? With more than one woman? I clench for a moment, thinking about his bits. My bits? Panic ensues.

What do I do with this? Do I confront him? Where will I live? The girls, my poor girls. How could he do this? Don't cry. Don't cry at work. I stuff two custard creams in my mouth. Geez, I hate custard creams. Chew. Just do something. Why is my mouth so dry? Where is all my saliva? Don't. Choke. I grip on to my desk again. It's stuck. Good god, I'm going to die here with a sex website open on my phone and an economy biscuit stuck in my gullet. A sharp hand beats against the back of my ribs. Tim. This can't be how it ends. He lifts me from my chair and pushes himself up against my back with surprising force. Jesus, Tim. I didn't know he had it in him. I cover my desk and laptop with regurgitated biscuit. The entire office turns in my direction. Len from marketing is holding a first aid kit.

'Meg? Are you OK?'

Tears fill my eyes, sweet clotted gunk spills out the corners of my lips. The tears roll freely down my cheeks. Tim looks me straight in the eye and for some reason, embraces me tightly. I may use him as a napkin.

'Do we need to fill in an incident form?' It's Len with the first aid kit again. I turn to the office with my hands in the air, in a mess of tears and snot.

'No, sorry everyone. I'll just learn to chew…'

Len hands me an old man handkerchief that I wish I could just shroud my face in. The shame. The utter shame. I turn and find Tim readjusting my desk and cleaning up. He hands over my phone that had fallen to the floor.

'Thank you.' His face is different, less eager now but a serious look in his eye. 'Are you OK?' he whispers. I want to hug him again and just nestle myself into him, sobbing uncontrollably. But he's young and I hardly know him; I probably have bras older than Tim. I plaster a smile over the last five minutes of my life.

'Thank you… seriously.' I give him a kiss on the cheek. 'I've found out what I need, I'll just call it a day. Tell Diana I went home. Maybe miss out the fact I nearly died.'

This doesn't raise a laugh. But he keeps a hand to my arm for longer than he probably should.

As I leave the office building, I can't tell if I want to throw myself in front of a bus or find my husband and push him in front of said bus. A one-off dildo, he can fob off with lame excuses but there was a shopping list that needs a better explanation – not that there's any way he's going to explain his way out of this. I think about what he said this morning, the way he made me think the dildo was for me, for my pleasure, there for the sake of a dried-up sex life, and I start to feel murderous. Bastard. You absolute fucker of a bastard.

He'll have picked up his brother from the station now and be at home. Do I storm in and embarrass him in front of kin? I could do it tonight in Francesco's. He's making a speech. I could heckle him and throw the dildo at the cake.

I can't seem to stop crying, or walking in a fierce marching style. But if he ordered all this other stuff, where is it? Where is the stockpile? Does he have a love cave where it's all stashed away? Is it at her house, her flat? And strangely, like a montage of old photos, my mind flickers to all the times I've had sex with Danny. Perfectly serviceable sex where we enjoyed ourselves and orgasmed and laughed and held each other and I thought it was fine. We'd been adventurous, from that first time on the stairs in his East London flat, to a beach in Cornwall, to my sister's wedding where we did it outside on a patio. And just times where it'd been comfortable sex with our socks on and he'd look at me, always, and cup my chin and say something silly so I'd giggle.

Sure, sex had become something of a rarity recently. The last time we did it before this morning, properly? Maybe a couple of months ago? Or maybe it was pre-Polly. She was now seven months old. That time may have also been a pity shag as I was a week overdue and I just wanted him to ejaculate in me as I thought it might dilate my cervix. The only way he could approach me was from behind. It wasn't romantic or in the least bit erotic. Even less so when he made a quip about a mate, Hobbsy, who once got cautioned for trying to mount a cow as a bet. Had it really been that long since we were last fully intimate? But I thought he was mature and loved me enough to get it. I thought it was an unspoken pact between us that there was love and friendship, that the sex was a glittering embellishment on an otherwise stable marriage. A marriage built on honesty: the way he would look at me, the way everything was so black and white. I thought he would never hurt me, ever. Not like this.

Lost in my thoughts, I have no idea where I am on the High Street but I suddenly look up and I'm in front of *Chic Boutique*. There's a mannequin in the window, the sort without a head or lower legs but she wears a red basque and suspenders in some very dodgy Christmas style promotion. I always used to laugh walking past this place; I thought it tacky. Who in their right mind had anything in their wardrobe that was feather-trimmed unless they were a drag queen or an ostrich? Maybe it was the fact I didn't have the body shape like that mannequin anymore. I mean, I had a head and legs but my tits were beyond redemption. Covered in stretch marks and hanging like flappy spaniel ears. Everything else was rounded and untoned, my stomach was creased like old leather. When your body and bits have just devolved with all the numerous pregnancies and births that it's endured, you are less inclined to stand at the end of a bed, prop your wobbly thighs up on the mattress and ask him to come and get it.

I had also worked in the industry so I knew how it worked when it came to bodies and perceptions of beauty. I was responsible for holding that ridiculous ideal up to women; I went to photo shoots and saw miserable girls who survived on Cup-a-Soup and air to retain their toothpick figures. I ordered more Photoshopping on images, I told women which slap would make them look younger and more attractive. I knew about the veneer so when it came to my own body, I knew it wasn't perfect but I also had enough savvy to not care or let it affect my confidence. I'd hoped Danny was attracted to far more than my body. Maybe I should have cared. All I have in my mind now is an image of Briony Tipperton wearing something fluffy, pink and crotchless, stood over my husband with her hands loaded up with 2-4-1 lubricant. I think I'm going to throw up. Here. On the cobbles.

'Meg? Y'alright lovely? Where's Polly?'

I've been stood outside the shop now for far too long. Where am I? Who's talking to me? Balls. Gillian. Morton. Mother-in-law. How?

'We were just headed to yours. Danny texted to say Stu's in so we thought we'd go round for a cuppa. I've bought a cake from the farm shop.'

She holds up a waxy shopper. Danny's mother. Of all the ruddy people.

'You don't look well lovely. You OK? You haven't caught Polly's bug have you?'

Your son might be cheating on me. Say it. Tell his mother.

'I just had to pop in the office for something. Polly's with Danny.'

Tell her. This is your chance to get the ultimate upper hand. Gillian takes off a glove and puts the back of her hand to my cheek.

'Bless your heart, you're freezing, your eyes are all teary. Best get you in the warm. Bob's just finishing up paying some bills in the Post Office. I tell you, he is so excited to see Stu again, after all this time.'

You could tell her. You could shit all over this big day, her perception of her son, her family. But I can't. She's the sweetest creature in the world, Gill Morton. She has a silver bob and Eve's bright blue eyes and loves a floral scarf over a mohair jumper. She solves world problems with cake and tea and has a cat called Blossom. She adores those boys, despite their quiet surliness and reluctance to partake in hugs or divulge details of their lives to her, she adorns her house with photos of them. And her grandchildren. She's taught my girls to make felt. Actual felt. I didn't even know that was a thing. I feel a tear roll down my cheek.

'Just a tough night really; sleep-deprived I think.'

She comes in for a hug and as her arms embrace me, I let out a sigh and a few more tears. Since my move up here, she has become a surrogate maternal figure. My mother came with fire: a by-product of raising five girls that she'd wanted to succeed and light up their corners of the world. With this came opinion and judgement when it was sometimes not needed. Gill was different though: she hugged me a lot, she loved the fact that the girls and I gave her female companions to fight her corner.

I can't tell her. Not here, not now.

I suddenly feel another pair of arms around us.

'Now that's my birthday made...'

It's Bob Morton.

'How's one of my favourite lassies doing? Lordy, you look a bit parky?'

Oh, Bob. He's like Father Christmas without the elves or the red coat. He's all beardy and cuddly and he's seventy-five today. You can't do this to him. I let him wrap his arms around me and inhale the familiar scent of jam and musty old coat.

'Birthday greetings, Bob. Are you having a good day?'

He breaks from the hug to give me a bristly kiss to the cheek.

'All the better for seeing you, love.'

God, these are two of the loveliest people I've met in my life. They've always welcomed me into their fold and they are part of the reason I've survived in the North. Every inch of my body is clenched, trying not to break down and cry.

'I saw Patrick this morning. He and his family send their best.'

He delivered a dildo to my house that was probably not meant for me.

'Lovely Patrick, will have to take him out for an ale soon,' Bob replies. Gill nods enthusiastically. 'Did you get the apple cake, you know it's Stu's favourite?' he asks.

'Yes, and those cheese twists he likes.'

'Lovely.' He hooks his arm around mine. 'Come on then, let's get you out of cold.'

I'm not sure how I make the walk home at all; it almost feels like I'm drunk. My legs have taken on a life of their own, Gill and Bob talk to me but I can't for the life of me process the conversation, responding in pleasantries and nods. There will be balloons tonight. But not those big number balloons because they're a rip-off so they've gone for your normal latex in green and white, which Bob was sceptical about because it'd look like some Irish theme party but actually matches the decor in Francesco's quite well. They speak for ten minutes about balloons. And they talk about a starter they had in there once which was pasta stuffed with fish but not ravioli and it didn't have a sauce but it was beautiful. *It's tortellini*, I whisper to myself. *My marriage may be over. My marriage to your son.* And yet I don't say a thing.

As we approach the front door, fear engulfs me. When I see him, maybe that is when this will all finally surface. I'll launch myself at him with superhuman force and grab him by his hair and bash his head against the cold hard floor. Or I'll just crumple to the floor and cry and sob and raise my hands to the air in despair. The door opens before I even have a chance to get my key out.

'Happy birthday, Dad.'

Well, I can't launch myself at him because he stands there with Polly nestled in his arms, all bonny and rosy cheeked. Gill crosses the threshold to get nana cuddles and Danny and Bob embrace with roars of greeting and emotion. My chest feels like someone is stamping on it, a hand is inside my chest, stretching my ribcage open and wringing out my heart.

'Well, where is he then?' asks Bob.

'In kitchen, having a brew.'

I'm the last to enter the house, knowing this moment isn't about me at all. Danny stops in the hallway as I take off my boots. He studies my face. I can't look at him. He comes over and takes my hand.

'Fook, your hands are freezing.' His touch feels almost painful. 'Brew?'

I nod. Let's fix this with tea.

'Get done what you needed?' I nod again. I give nothing away, not now. I follow the mass of people into the kitchen. I spy Polly's little face over Gill's shoulder, studying my expression. Gorgeous little Polly who looks like a cartoon chipmunk and who never sleeps through the night. What has your daddy done? I see shades of Danny in her eyes and I think about how as much as I hate her father right now, I will always love him for giving me these girls. I have to remember how to breathe. In the kitchen, everything sits as I left it. Uneaten toast on the counter courtesy of Eve, the butter knife next to it that I used to open Pandora's box. But in the middle of the room, a reunion of parents and their youngest son. Polly seems to be stuck in the centre of a silent hugging extravaganza. Gill is crying. Bob won't let Stu go. Danny stands there with his arms folded, looking on.

'My lad,' whispers Bob. It's been exactly eighteen months since they've last seen their son, when Stu decided he wanted to spread his wings again and explore the world. It's what Stu did. More often than not, he was usually doing a runner from a bad relationship. Actually, this sojourn to Australia was because his girlfriend had asked him to move in with him and he wasn't ready for that 'next level' commitment. But in running, he always fell on his feet, living off sofas and in communes, sending us pictures of him on beaches with his chest out and an on-trend procurement of facial hair. Danny would always call him a twat but I knew deep down there was a part of him missing.

'Smeg legs, looking lovely as always.' The smeg joke never wore thin, even after twelve years. Gill wipes away tears. Stu lifts me a little off the floor to hug me. 'It's like nothing's changed. I thought Mr T would have carked it by now?'

And for some reason this is the comment that leads my floodgates to open. And it's not even the comment about my ailing dog. It was the comment about change. *Nothing's changed.* The Mortons all stand there looking bemused. Polly's bottom lip pops out to see me looking so upset.

'Geez, didn't think you missed me that much.' He embraces me tightly which squeezes out more tears. He looks me in the eye. He's bronzed, with the same crooked incisors as his older brother and smells faintly of weed.

I am on an emotional roll and blub. 'It's just...' *I nearly died half an hour ago choking on a biscuit after seeing that Danny was a regular customer at a pervy sex website. I've held a foot-long blue dildo in my hands this morning and saw your brother flirt openly with Briony Tipperton. I also didn't sleep much last night.* '...It's so nice for Polly to meet her uncle, for you to be back...'

Stu looks surprised at my admission, Danny too for that matter.

'Bit of a shame she looks so much like her dad though, eh?'

Gill and Bob think this hilarious. Stu goes to take Polly off Gill.

'You and Danny don't half make cute babies though. C'mon littl'un, Uncle Stu had dollars to waste at the airport. Got a wombat for ya: it's like a hamster on steroids.'

Again, laughter.

We do make lovely babies and maybe that's the saddest thing about this all.

'Well, brew's on Dan. We've got a lot to catch up on...'

There's a clang of mugs and the kettle hissing into action. I grab at the kitchen towel to blow my nose. Gill is slightly alarmed by the noise.

'Danny, you're not looking after her. Bumped into her in the high street and she were looking like she were going to heave.'

Danny still looks curiously at me. I look back at him. We had a moment like this earlier this morning when we went our separate ways near the school. You can spend twelve years with someone, every day, every hour and it's still a shock to have that much unspoken between you, to feel like you don't know someone very well at all. How can just three hours have changed everything so drastically?

'You're going to be alright for the party, right? Why don't you go get some shut eye? I'll bring you up a cuppa and some cake in a bit, what do you think?' Gill's voice is warm and maternal.

Maybe I can sleep, forget, cry into my pillow and reassess. Maybe this is nothing. 'I think that's perfect. I'm sorry everyone.' I salute goodbye to the room.

'Don't be sorry, love.' She hugs me.

'Meg…' His voice used to be so familiar, so comforting. I turn to face Danny. He should see how legitimately upset I am, he should piece together what this it about and at least feel apologetic or enquire to look after me. 'Are you going to spew? You need the sick bucket?'

I look at him. I shake my head and leave.

Chapter Four

'So it's like pasta but it's stuffed with, like fish paste? Like a dump-
ling, almost like what we've had down the Chinese?'

'Tortellini?'

'That's the ticket… Go for it, Meg, bloody beautiful they were…'
booms Bob from the other end of the table.

Francesco, the actual Francesco the restaurant is named after,
looks down at me as I scan the menu. He is every stereotype you
can imagine, there's the waistcoat with buttons literally set to pop,
the dramatic hand gestures, the Super Mario moustache, but what
remains most intriguing is the hybrid Northern/Italian accent which
always makes him sound slightly drunk.

'I'll just have the mozzarella salad, please.'

'With the garrrrrlic dough sticks?'

'Why not?'

I am not sure how I made it out tonight. I didn't go upstairs
to sleep. I went to lie down and curl myself around a pillow, eyes
wide open as I went through all the alternative universes that
existed alongside mine; ones that involved Danny, ones that didn't.
I thought about what would have happened had I not met Danny
Morton. I'd still be in the sanctity of the South, in an office writing

about contouring and the perfect matte foundations. I'd still have my pre-baby body. I wouldn't have had my girls.

A strange confusion overwhelmed me, how had it come to this? In just a mere matter of hours, I was being forced to re-evaluate my whole life and I didn't really know the entire truth. It was a cocktail of emotions that made me feel heavy, ill. So much so that every time someone came in the room with tea and assorted snacks, I'd close my eyes and pretend to sleep. I heard Danny head off to work, I let Gill and Bob do the school run, the assorted squeals of excited girls echoing through the floor as Uncle Stu flung them around the living room and bestowed his airport purchases on them. My head was a mess, shrivelled with worry. I wasn't really sure what was happening. Was this an affair? Was it more? One day, would he just up and leave me? I was still thinking this at 4 p.m., lost and broken. So I picked up my phone.

'Megs? And to what do I owe the pleasure? You'll have to be quick, I'm sewing up a heart in a bit.'

Emma was sister number two. There were three others but Emma was the sensible, maternal one. She didn't just fix hearts for fun. She was qualified in such matters and doing very well from it too. She had the house in a leafy London suburb with multiple floors, the girls in private school, and was the sort of parent who pre-made dinners. If she weren't my sister, I would have hated her but I also knew that behind the veneer was normality. Because she had built this life with a fellow surgeon, Simon, who quite frankly, was a sex-crazed dickhead. None of us Callaghan sisters had liked him when she first brought him home and it was always a shock to us that someone so smart and assured could have fallen for such a smarmy pillock. When Ems told us about the first affair, none of us were surprised. By the seventh, we were really starting to wonder if some medical condition was affecting her judgement. It took him sexting at a family Christmas dinner for her to see the light and she has since divorced him, which is why today she felt like the one person who could give me something, anything.

'I just wanted to hear your voice.'

She went quiet on the other end of the phone. 'Is everything OK? Are you ill? Has—'

'No. It's just…'

'Spit it out.'

'I found out that Danny might be cheating on me.'

She went quiet again and I heard her sit down.

'Oh, Meg… Define "might". Did you catch him in flagrante?'

'No… but…'

'Did you hear it from someone else?'

'No. I hacked into an account he has on a sex toy website and it turns out he's been ordering shed loads off this place. Not stuff I've ever seen either…'

I could hear her almost giggle on the other side of the phone. 'And?'

I was annoyed at how calm she was over this revelation.

'I mean I know it's not someone sending you a pic of their minge over a mince pie but still…'

'Bitch.'

We've had to ban mince pies from our Christmas gatherings since that whole debacle.

'Cow,' I replied. 'This is serious, who on earth buys so many sex toys? I sure as hell haven't seen them in this house.'

'Have you spoken about this with him? Asked him to his face?'

'I can't.' I could hear her rolling her eyes at me.

'Well, I'm not sure why we're having this conversation then? It's Danny. Lovely Danny. He's like a *Countryfile* presenter, all honest and earthy. He's not a Simon. I know it. This is probably a misunderstanding. And if it isn't…'

'Yes…?'

'Well, when you have concrete evidence then that's when you call me so I can jump on the M6 and cut that man's bollocks off with a rusty scalpel.'

It was what I needed to hear: fire. Raw emotion had quelled that in me.

'Are you in bed? Get up, one foot in front of another and stop overthinking it.'

'You mean ignore it? I can't do what you did, Ems. If he's cheating on me then this is something I want to face head on.'

'True,' she said. 'I let too much pass but I also didn't sit crying to you lot about what a dickhead he was. I once caught Simon in our kitchen going down on a twenty-two-year-old Australian nanny. She had her legs akimbo on the counter where I make my toast. And you know what I did? I got on with life. I had daughters. I had a career and even though I knew the worst was happening, it was never going to destroy me. Has mum taught you nothing? You're a Callaghan woman, don't you know?'

The words were straight out of our mother's mouth. Fiona Callaghan didn't raise daughters who moped in their beds and cried about the state of their unions. She raised dragons.

'The Australian girl with the tattoos and the piercings?' I asked.

'Yup. Turns out she was pierced all over the place too. I'm a sodding surgeon and I swear I haven't seen a vagina in that much detail.'

'How does that work? A piercing right through the flaps?'

'That's not anatomically possible. She'd pee like an irrigation system.'

I laughed. The first time I'd done that today, properly.

'Good girl. Haven't you got that birthday thingy today?'

'Yep.'

'Go… Get drunk. You can have a slurry rant to me later if you want? I'll be back at about ten. Have to do this drinks date thing with an anaesthetist.'

'Is he fit?'

'I'm not quite sure. He drives a Kia.'

'Reliable.'

'Potentially a bit dull. I love you, sis. This is nothing and this isn't you.'

'Who am I then?'

'Ringleader of the Callaghan sorority. Grow a pair and have it out with him.'

'You make us sound like a prison gang.'

'Not far wrong. Just breathe. Kisses for my nieces. Chat later, got a registrar giving me evils.'

She hung up before I could respond. Love you too, sister. It was times like these when the distance was a killer. When I just needed the whole gaggle of the sisters, my protective herd. But she was right. We were Callaghan girls – we could stand on our own, without being propped up by men. So I slung my legs over the side of the bed and sat up. I sipped at a lukewarm cup of tea. I tried to find that fire. It led me to the bathroom where I located my shaver and dug out my nice pants from the bottom of my knicker drawer.

'This… this mozzarella, is it a cheese?'

I'm not sure who did the table plan this evening but I've ended up next to Aunty Mabel. Even though the family history has been explained to me on many an occasion, I've never quite remembered how she fits into the Morton jigsaw. All I know is that they've shipped her in today from Kirkby Lonsdale and she's gone heavy on the lavender. She was once married to Frank who is now deceased though I can't remember if he was the one who died falling off a cliff looking for his dog, or was the rampant alcoholic.

'Yes, but a soft cheese…' I reply.

'Like Philadelphia?'

'Hmmm, not quite. How about the minestrone? The soup?'

'Is it chunky? I've got me good teeth in today. Not sure they can deal with croutons.'

Francesco and I look at each other. Can you sieve the minestrone, Francesco?

'For you my love, we can do something special, yes?'

I am half-smiling, half-laughing – half-cut I think is the technical term. Francesco winks at me and I wink back.

'He's cheeky that one. Think he's got his eye on you, Mabel.' I place my hand on her arm. She shoos me away like a bird.

'Oooh, hush now. Not my type at all…'

We both guffaw, leading Danny at the other end of the table to give me dirty looks. I return the evil eye, but feel more like I've just done a bad pirate impression. Hell, if I'm going to be cornered here with Mabel I may as well have a laugh. I top up our glasses. How much have I drunk since I got here? Who effing knows? Let's just say I heeded my sister Ems' advice to the letter. She was a doctor, it would be like going against medical advice if I hadn't.

As I was informed this morning, the restaurant has been transformed into a sea of green balloons accented with holographic banners and table confetti. Since we moved to the Lakes, I've found the Mortons use Francesco's as their go-to celebration place, the height of fine dining for Gill and Bob. I've never been sure why they hold it in such high esteem: it could be the fresh linens on the tables, the soaring operatic music, though I've always hoped it may have something to do with the fake Statue of David sat in the corner adorned in coloured fairy lights which also doubles as a fountain.

I'm at the Mabel end of the table with some of Bob's friends from golf whose names I can't remember: Gina and John? Tina and Ron? I look at the other end of the table to see Bob surrounded by his wife and sons, all laughing and sharing jokes. Even their geeky cousin, Chris has got in on the action, and most noticeably has got that good centre seat where he can choose to dip into either table end's worth of breadsticks and wine. Why have I been relegated to the end zone?

Danny looks happy, relaxed in his best navy shirt. I love him in that shirt. I'm caught in the emotion for a moment. We haven't said much to each other since this morning. When I was in the bath, soaking the day out of me and shaving my legs, he came over, sat on the edge and kissed my knee. It was a tender, sweet moment. Until he exclaimed, 'Crikey, best not break that shaver… or block the drain…' before laughing to himself and tending to a crying child. Now he sits there trading jokes and insults with his family. I thought I knew him. I know exactly what he'll order today: Parma ham and melon to start, lasagne for main and to finish, the novelty sorbet that is served in a shelled-out orange with a cocktail umbrella. But I didn't know those kinky sexual vibes were his thing. I didn't think he'd ever cheat.

Don't cry at the table. Drink. I'm warm drunk at the moment, the sort of drunk where I'm comfortable without a jacket and if there were a dance floor, I'd throw a few shapes. Danny looks over at me and I attempt to catch his eye. I'm wearing the red dress he once complimented, my mousey brown hair in a makeshift bun. I may have even thrown on a bit more mascara this evening in some vague effort to capture his attention. He points downwards. Is he gesturing at my tits? The red? Head? Oh. He's gesturing at my breadsticks. I pass them down the chain of people to the left of me, one of whom has come in tweed.

'So tell me, how's the paper mill going?'

'I wouldn't know Jeron. Danny doesn't fill me in on much these days.'

I just called this man by a strange hybrid name, didn't I? He doesn't seem to have noticed but nods and proceeds to tell me about the architectural history of the paper mill, where Danny works. Riveting stuff. I know very little about the place except that it was the family empire and the reason we moved up here. When Bob had to step down because of health issues, the choice was either to sell or have a Morton brother take it on. Danny was always going to be the brother of choice: the stalwart, reliable one who'd carry on the family name. Jeron is still rambling. Drink. I roll the table red on the end of my tongue and swish it on my teeth. My teeth will be a lovely shade of blueberry now. I'm not sure there is anything else I can say to this man. He's in tweed, he's wearing dress shoes with jeans and his wife has the most symmetrical bob I think I've ever seen. But to make this evening bearable and to help things along, I will top up your wine glass for the evening. Drink, let's just have all the drink.

'Ladies and gents, if I can have your attention, please.'

We all turn to the top end of the table where my husband is stood.

'I was going to wait until the end of meal when the cake got wheeled out but I'll let the old man speak then. Just wanted to say a few words before your food arrived. I'm not normally one for speeches but it's a big day and things need to be said…'

There are laughs as Danny unfolds a piece of paper from his pocket. Gill, who sits beside him looks proud as punch. This is it, isn't it? This is when he's going to make a speech about love, family and pride and everyone is going to stand in a collective huddle whilst I lose my shit in between Mabel and Jeron. I can't listen to this, I need to leave. I stand up.

'There once was a man called Bob
Who had the most peculiar knob…'

Gill's head suddenly twitches. The Morton brothers giggle like they're at the back of a classroom.

'All the golfers would utter,

It was shaped like a putter.

How did Gill fit that in her…'

'DANIEL!' Gill hits her eldest son with a napkin. The old boy golfers around the table roar with laughter. Stu and Danny exchange high fives. That's it, that's his speech. I sit down.

'I didn't catch that, love… What did Danny say?' Mabel looks up at me, anxious that she's missed the best part of the evening. I'm not sure if repeating the limerick would see her dentures spat into her glass of red.

'He said Bob does a wonderful job… and that he loves his golf…'

Mabel nods. 'Oh, that he does. Loves a few cheeky holes.'

All this innuendo and nothing to do with it.

'But a wonderful job with those boys. Your Danny. If I were fifty years younger…'

I think it would be illegal given you're related by blood but she gestures over to him. The Brothers Morton are cackling with laughter as their mother tries to calm them down. And I look over at Danny as his face is creased with happiness, his blue eyes bright and shining with the radiance that only a dirty limerick and some cheap wine can bring. I've always thought he was attractive but I don't think he'd be picked on a dating show. He's far too surly for that, his receding hairline is speckled with silver, and his frame has slightly packed on the pounds now middle age is settling in. But he has a well-defined jaw, and when happy and relaxed, it reveals a softness to his face, a kind, sincere Danny that few got to see. *My Danny*. And for a moment, I feel that fire again: the fire to claim back what was mine.

*

The night flies by as the courses arrive. I watch Mabel pick out all the bits of her minestrone, and I nearly fall over myself in the toilet when I see that I did a shocking job trying to cover-up the dark circles under my eyes. I drink. I drink some more. Prosecco arrives over dessert. It helps wash down the golf-putter shape cake that Gill had made and means I can continue to blur the day's events a bit more. By the end of the evening, the bottle and I are best mates and I cradle one in my arms like one of my infant daughters.

'Dan's told me to come and escort you while he settles up. C'mon Mrs M…'

Stu. Hello, Stu. I look up. What was that, we're done? We must be as the taxis have come to collect us and the restaurant is emptying. I've hugged everyone a few times but I'm not sure I can move now so Stu's appearance at the end of my table is most welcome. Perhaps he can carry me home. I have on my decent knickers so it wouldn't be too unladylike.

'Where are we going?'

'I'm taking you home…'

'You're such a tart, Stu…' I pinch his cheeks. 'I know you've had your way with some of us Callaghan girls but I am not that sort of girl…'

He responds with a fake smile. Stu was likeable enough but my relationship with him was always a little laboured given I knew the many ways in which he'd seduced my sisters: not only had he half-shagged Beth but also slept with my youngest sister, Lucy, at my wedding, in the back of a Ford Fiesta in full view of half of the hotel's bedroom windows.

'Geez, you are wankered. How much have you had Mrs?'

'I am not your Mrs. I belong to your brother…'

He seems unbothered by the fact, relieved even to have not been lumbered with the burden. Back in the days when we were London dwellers, we all lived together for a while in the Cumbrian Embassy, a strange flat made up of three mezzanine levels and the world's most cavernous bathroom which housed a drum kit and Stu's equipment from his short-lived stint as a wedding DJ in one corner. He was a horrific housemate; he had an aversion to washing up, never covered the cheese, smoked in the bath, and many a time I'd caught him having sex with someone inappropriate: a work colleague, a best friend's fiancée, an ex. Sometimes it was on the communal sofa, other times it was loud whilst I was recovering from impacted wisdom tooth removal, but always his meetings with women were lustful, casual. He was the sort to tell a girl he'd ring and then delete her number immediately so I always felt that morally, we didn't have much in common.

'Where is my amazing husband?' I ask.

'He's paying the bill then getting the old folk in cabs…'

'You tell aunt Mabel to keep her mitts off, I know what she's like…'

Stu isn't amused. He puts my arms into my coat and places my handbag around my neck like he's hanging it on a hook. He then pats my cheeks with both hands.

'C'mon El Blotto, let's take a slow walk home… one foot in front of the other…'

We could be a while. In an attempt to seduce my husband, I went for some vintage stilettos tonight, only vintage given it's been at least eight years since I've worn them. I looked like Bambi walking in them to the restaurant. Lord knows how I'll be now I've got some alcohol in my veins. Outside, the cold air is like a hard slap. Stu and I huddle into each other.

'So, Stuart… why aren't you bladdered tonight?' True enough, Stu is usually the life and soul of such parties. I've heard legendary tales of his teenage drunkenness, including the time he boarded the wrong train home and ended up in Liverpool two hours and eighty miles later.

'I've had a few jars… just not out to get wasted tonight, that's all…'

'Am I really that wasted?'

'To be honest, I've never seen you like this, Smeggers. You had your tits all up in Jeff's face.'

'Who the monkeys is Jeff?'

'The bloke sat next to you.'

'That was Jeron.'

He laughs and guides me over a manhole cover. 'Mind yourself. Well, you made Jeff's night. Quite rare to see you letting your hair down though.'

'Are you calling me uptight?'

'No.'

There's a small period of awkwardness as I ponder what Stu implied. I like to go out and have a drink. I dance and stuff and know many people who'd say I'm good fun, people usually too drunk to know the difference but still. Stu is next-level fun which includes three-day benders, drugs and waking up in a field on the other side of the United Kingdom. But in the back of my mind, I wonder if it means motherhood and age have turned me into a shadow of my former self. I'd become a boring old hag who'd forgotten how to walk in heels. A tear forms in the corner of my eye.

'We had that house party at the Embassy once. I made cocktails and climbed on the roof. That's not uptight.'

'You were good value that night.'

'I'm still good value, right?'

I lose my footing. Stu puts me back in a vertical position but remains silent. I'm not deluded enough to know what I'm laying out in front of my brother-in-law here. Stu has just turned thirty, a slave to his wanderlust, bronzed and still vaguely handsome and interesting. I only have to catch my reflection in a shop window to see what I was putting out there: a woman in her late thirties, drowning in liquor, having squeezed her post-natal body into a dress a size too small, in black bobbly tights and her brown eyes racooned with mascara. This was not good value. This smacked of desperation, of very sad desperation. I pretend to smile knowing my value has slowly depreciated over the last ten years and it's only now, on today of all days, that I'm slowly being shamed for it. I stand there for a moment too long.

'Danny... you reckon Danny still thinks I'm good value?'

Stu looks confused now. I'm not sure if it's from the repetition or my gentle swaying. He puts his arms out as if he might have to catch me.

'I mean I know I've let myself go in some departments but I'm still a catch, right? You still think he fancies me?'

Stu doesn't read into it. He takes it as being lumbered with the drunk one at the end of the evening; the one who's delving into the emotionally lost and philosophical. Soon, she'll be crying to herself, hyperventilating and saying no one loves her and he'll have to feed her chips and water so she doesn't choke on her own vomit when she passes out. Instead he wraps his arms around me, something he's never really done before. I hug him back.

'Let's get you home, pisshead.'

We do make it home eventually, even though Stu has to piggyback me over some cobbles and there was a point where I thought I was going to throw up outside an Indian takeaway but instead let out the loudest drunken burp known to man. When we get to the house, the babysitter, Kayleigh, an eighteen-year-old from two doors down, opens the door.

'Oh, Kayleigh… such a sweet girl…' I hug her and hold her face in my hands. She is visibly scared and amused. 'You know, I shouldn't say these things but you are so pretty and just hold on tightly to that. Not that you'll get ugly. I'm just saying the time goes so quickly. I used to have a belly button ring like you and I could just snap into a size 10 and I thought I could get away with it but then things go wrong and… gluten. Gluten was part of the problem and lack of sleep and eye cream.' I take off my shoes and missile them towards the kitchen. 'When I worked in magazines, they always told me about eye cream and I should have listened because I didn't and now there's all this loose skin around my eyes like a sad little puppy.'

I pull at the skin for demonstration purposes. Kayleigh nods and looks at me with that youthful disbelief a teen exhibits when an older person gives them advice; standing there like it'll never happen to her. This doesn't deter me. 'And I know I shouldn't say this but go out there and get some. Like, look after your vagina but have fun. Real fun. Don't wait until you're twenty-one to have your first orgasm. Play around down there, let men know what they need to do.'

Kayleigh looks horrified. I feel a pair of arms around me.

'Right, Kayleigh. And that's Mrs M done for tonight,' interrupts Stu. I kiss Kayleigh's hand, hoping she's not one of them religious sorts who's saving herself. Stu is literally having to separate us.

'I'm not kidding, Stuart. She needs to know, she is of age.'

Stu de-coats me and takes my handbag, looking for my purse. 'I'll settle up here and you go upstairs and I'll put you on a brew. Go on now before you scare this poor girl off sex for life.'

Kayleigh looks at me humoured but with a distinct look of pity. No, don't do that Kayleigh. I'm just Mrs Morton, Meg from up the street! Don't look at me like an old mare on the pasture who's past her prime. Please. The eye cream thing is so important too.

I walk up the stairs like a sullen child, one step at a time as I hear Stu usher her into the kitchen and the click of the kettle as it hums into action. Bloody tea. They all think the world's problems will be solved by tea. I get to the top of the landing and poke my head around the girls' bedrooms, watching their bodies lain over pretty patchwork duvet covers, clutching at blankies. Eve, as normal, her mouth fully agape and hair in starburst patterns over the pillow, Magnum the cat nestled into her; Tess sleeps straight like she's a princess waiting for a prince to come and awaken her; Polly crawls to the corner of her cot and nests there like a kitten. I stand over

Tess for a while in her top bunk, watching her chest rise and fall. We found out we were pregnant with her when we were living in London. We'd been married for about a year and were no longer in the flat share but a rented maisonette in West London which we thought was a step up in the world but in reality it had a shower that was placed directly over the toilet. Danny sat with me in the loo when we did the test. It was neither planned nor a shock but the natural progression of things. When the second line appeared on the stick, he cried. He lifted me up off the floor; a rare moment of exuberance for Mr Morton, someone who was normally the straight man, not dour and unlikeable, but who never really broke through the emotional barrier unless really necessary. I liked how straightforward that made him, how it was easy to work him out. When he hugged me in that bathroom, the happiness felt purely sincere, it felt so very real. You were real, Tess. You are real. How could he have done this? To us, to you.

I stand in the middle of the girls' room for a while, drenched in the glare of the street light outside and look about at all the other very real stuff in there: the little clothes, the creased books, the drawings, the McDonalds Happy Meal toys of which we own far too many, the shoebox full of mismatched hair ties. I then stumble out, stepping on a toy which makes it talk, scaring the crap out of me and I shush it with my finger. I go to the bathroom and turn on the light and shush that too. I then take a look at myself in the bathroom mirror. Wow. Who the hell is that jagged up wench? I take off my dress and peel off my tights. They are the decent stomach flattening ones but as I roll them down, I feel my gut expand out of them and regain a capability to breathe fully that had been lacking before. I look in the mirror.

Nothing is more sobering than looking at yourself in your underwear under a fluorescent bathroom glow. My stomach looks like a collapsed cake. My thighs look like rolled pork joints. I poke at them to see if I can carve out a thigh gap. What is more worrying is that my pubes do not seem to be contained within my knickers. I remember when Tess was little and she called them my 'spider legs'. Well, tonight the spiders look like they're escaping en masse.

I can jump in the shower now and neaten up. I take off my knickers, grab my Venus, straddling the side of the bath. Baby shampoo, that'll do. I lather up and shave and rinse off. Is that straight? Meh. Look at this Danny, I've done pits, legs and now lady garden. Does your new lady friend go to this much effort? I attempt to lever myself out, slip and fall on my arse. Ouch. But funny. I laugh. I hear footsteps on the stairs.

'Are you alright in there?' Oh, go away, Stu. I remember a time when he was so drunk in our shared flat that he fell down two flights of stairs and slept on the landing. I laugh and tell the heated towel rail to shush.

'I am fine.' I go to the sink, brush my teeth and wipe some of the collected gunk and make-up from under my eyes. She's in there somewhere, that girl Danny Morton lifted off the floor in a radiant delirium. She's not going out without a fight. I put my knickers back on. They're some of my sexier ones given the lace to cotton ratio. I catch myself in the mirror, a tattoo on my lower back (a mistake from my twenties), a C-section scar from when Eve was born breech. My bra leaves interesting dents in my flesh from where the wire sat. It'll have to do. I hear a key in the door and slowly tiptoe to my bedroom.

How do I do this? Shall I just strip and get under the covers? Maybe I can adopt a sexy pose on the bed? On all fours? Like a cat? Or on my knees, holding something? Where'd that dildo go? I can hear Danny milling about downstairs with the others. I lie on the bed, opting for my side and my head supported by my arm, the other on my hip. Shall I bend my leg or is that too obvious? I look down. Jesus, where are my boobs and stomach going? It's like they're trying to flee from me in different directions – gravity is not my friend. I look down. Crap, I put my knickers on inside out. I lie on my back and lift my legs in the air to rearrange them. The bedroom door opens.

'Now that's a sight…'

I rearrange my undergarments and watch as he comes in and starts de-robing: watch, shirt, belt. I lie on my front and prop myself up with my hands, pouting.

'What doing tipsy-tits?'

'Nuffink. Just watching.'

He sits next to me on the edge of the bed to take his shoes and socks off and pats me on the head. I kneel up and drape myself over him. I may lick his ear. He flinches. I'll make him remember how good I could be in bed. He won't even think about his other bird once I'm done with him. She'll become but a ghost. I burp quietly under my breath.

'Tickles.'

I then kiss the side of his neck and work my hands over the top of his chest.

'Oi, oi. Something's got you randy.'

He turns to kiss me on the lips. I try to engage the kiss further and swivel my body around to straddle him. It's slightly ungainly but he's responsive and kisses me back. This is what's been missing. We hardly kiss anymore. I put my tongue in his mouth and go for the full-on teenage pash. He laughs and grabs on to my buttocks.

'Should take you to Francesco's more often…'

But I don't want him to laugh. I want him to remember who I am, why we're here and that most importantly, he is mine. I look him deeply in the eye, still slightly inebriated so lacking in focus and whisper into his ear.

'Fuck me.'

He looks back, slightly confused. 'Twice in one day? Not sure I've got the juice?'

'Now.'

'You're really shitfaced.'

I grab him by the cheeks. 'Now. Hard, any way you want.'

He's looking less confused, more surprised. I stand up at the edge of the bed and pull down my knickers.

'What in the hula has happened to your fanny?' I look down. I'm not exactly sure but there's not much left there except a line of pubic hair the breadth of a small hamster's tail that I obviously missed. I move his eyes to my face and place his hands on my boobs.

'What's got into you?'

'You, hopefully, in the next thirty seconds.'

He laughs.

'This isn't funny.'

'Well, give me a moment. That lasagne's landed in my gut like a brick. Let me get my undercrackers off.'

I stand there whilst he takes off his vest and rolls down his trousers in the slowest, least impassioned way ever. He sits there in his underpants where I can obviously see that me standing here naked and talking as sexually as I can has had absolutely no effect on his genitalia. I take one of his hands and lead it to my vagina. His fingers stroke me gently and he stands up, pressing his body into mine. I roll his pants down to his ankles.

'Do me against the wall. Like we used to.'

'Back when we were twenty-eight…'

'Like you did in the kitchen that time.'

He stops for a moment and smiles. We were newly married and it was a warm summer's day where we'd spent the whole day at the pub drinking and came home, not able to even make it upstairs. All I remember is wearing a short summer dress, Danny rolling my knickers down and pinning me to the wall next to the fridge. My legs wrapped around his body, one hand grabbed both my wrists above my head.

It's enough for Danny to push me into the space between the door and the dresser. I flinch as my back hits the cold wall but I immediately feel the intensity in his kiss, the urgency in his touch. I part my legs and lift one on to the dresser, one of my hands reaching down to grab at his cock and guide it towards me. He enters me and we both sigh. I try to lever myself upwards so my other leg wraps around him.

'Woah there…'

Danny may have had a point. Back then, he was stronger and I was lighter. He grunts slightly to have to support my weight and I don't know whether to be offended or ashamed that I've lost all my sexual athleticism.

'Just keep going… I want you so much…'

He keeps going. It's sex on a mission. It's always pleasurable enough with Danny but I want him to come hard and quickly so he can remember that time I was my sexual self and not just the mother of his children, the maker of tea, the washer of clothes. I was also the lover. 'You feel so amazing… do it. C'mon…'

I need to make him remember. I move my hips up and down in a more laboured way than I'd care to mention. I headbutt him in all the movement.

'Ouch. Don't do that…'

'Yes.'

'No…'

I bounce harder. A vein on his forehead looks like it's going to pop.

'Yes, Danny…' I moan, pleasured but in feigned ecstasy. He puts a hand over my mouth. Why are my tits wet? Is that sweat?

A light comes on in the landing and Danny panics. 'I can't… Fuuuuck…'

And no, that's not him coming. That's him realising he's not twenty-eight, collapsing to the floor and dropping his wife. His wife who has her leg propped against a dresser. I'm not sure what happens next but my body contorts as he vacates me and my leg kicks the dresser out of the way so a drawer comes flying out. I hear my ankle click and lie there spread-eagled on the cold wooden floor. The bedroom door flies open and Stu stands there, seeing me naked. Not for the first time, but covered in shards of wood – and what appears to be quite a lot of my own blood.

Chapter Five

'It's fine. I'm fine. I'm really quite fine. Seriously, I am fine.'

Despite the fact that my husband couldn't pin me against a wall and give me the seeing to that I thought might repair our marriage, I am shocked that he and his brother now possess the superhuman strength to carry me over the threshold of the A&E department at Westmorland General Hospital. I have enough alcohol in my veins to numb a donkey so the pain I am feeling is nothing compared to the shame; the shame that my left shin is covered in blood, my ankle has ballooned to the size of a small grapefruit and I have nothing on bar a man's dressing gown and a pair of Ugg boots. I couldn't even get my knickers on. I have a Morton brother either side of me: my brother-in-law to my left, to my right my husband, who keeps adjusting the tartan gown to protect my modesty. I hook my arms around their necks, feeling the homemade bandage Danny made with our best bath towels unravelling as we walk. They lift me over to a row of plastic chairs where a sea of people part to make room for me.

'Stay here with her and I'll get us checked in. When's your birthday again? Fifteenth June, right?'

I am not too drunk to have a go. 'Bloody hell, Danny. July... July!'

A lady next to me, who appears to just have a heavy cold, widens her eyes wondering if this is the reason we're in A&E. I can't focus. My leg pulses to its own disco beat. I hate hospitals. I hate all the arrows and sliding doors and nurses who always look prim, proper but slightly judgemental that you haven't looked after yourself better. Danny hovers at a desk and I see him trying to book me in. He has his hoodie pulled up over his head and looks bewildered that less than an hour ago, we were having slightly energetic sex that has led us here. He keeps looking over at me but I refuse to look him in the eye. You dropped me, you tool. Do you drop your other bird when you're shagging her? Poor Stu tries to sit me upright.

'Careful there, Meggers. Don't need the whole world seeing your growler…'

I laugh hysterically at the mention of the word and do a lion impression. Stu giggles. The lady with the bad cold watches us curiously, trying to fathom our relationship. Maybe we were having a threesome and something went horribly awry. Maybe we're a family circus act and we landed on a tent peg. Another man who looks like he's just tripped over and knocked a finger out of joint doesn't look too impressed. Maybe he's had a look at my half-shaven growler. I laugh and purr to myself again.

'Judith on 111 just said to put a compress on it and elevate it.'

I kick my leg up. That man opposite definitely just saw my lady bits.

I was adamant there was very little wrong, I had a good supply of plasters in the house, but Stu and Danny thought otherwise. Google didn't give specific instructions of what to do when you have a large split in your shin after landing on a dresser drawer after failed sex so the assistance of 111 it was. Judith had many questions and at one point, I had both Morton brothers staring at my leg trying to work out if it was going blue. It was just cold. But Judith's evaluation was that I may have fractured something and it was important to get me into a hospital for further evaluation. So, in essence, this is all Judith's fault.

'I bought the bumper box of plasters, cotton wool, bit of Savlon. I would have been fine.'

'Stop kicking your leg up, you're scaring people.'

Danny comes back to us with a wheelchair.

'Stu's right. Come shift over to this so we don't have to lug you around anymore.'

The brothers support me over, Danny nestling his face in my forehead to give me a kiss. I'm in the sort of mood where I want to headbutt him in return. He can sense I'm less than amused. The three of us sit there in silence.

'Stu... lad, you got any shrapnel? Could you get us some chocolate for peg leg here?'

'Shame that dresser didn't land on your todger really...'

Our small section of the waiting room freezes. A pregnant woman gets up and moves to get closer. The lady with the cold is still putting the jigsaw together. He was shagging the dresser? Danny hates the attention. Stu, meanwhile, is patting down his pockets for coins so he can escape. I was once happy and powerfully drunk but now I'm bleeding and a pulsing feeling stings with every beat. Bitter drunk is rising to the surface and she's got a bit of a gob on her.

'You didn't even try and catch the dresser when it fell on me. It's like you wanted me to die, out of the way...'

'Lucky it's that cheap IKEA crap you bought. Solid wood dresser and you'd have been a goner.'

Stu has no change. He sits there wondering whether to referee or magic some Maltesers from somewhere else.

'Was Kayleigh alright to come back and stay a bit longer with the girls?' I ask.

'I'll have to pay her double rate though, it's past midnight,' Danny replies.

'Then geez, go back then. Stu's here. Stu can stay with me.'

'Quiet now…'

'Idiot.'

Our section of the waiting room is loving the unfolding drama. The pregnant woman who was possibly in labour before is no longer that bothered about impending childbirth.

'Meg Morton?'

I don't see who's called my name but I put my hand up in the air like that kid in class who knows all the answers. The nurse approaches me from behind.

'Stewie Morton… Christ, haven't seen you in an age!'

Stu looks up with wide eyes. 'Joanne McArthur?'

Danny looks to the floor. Great. We have a nurse but it's a) our kids' headteacher's wife b) someone who used to date Stu briefly at school. I look on at her perfect nurse's hair.

'And Danny too… it's a Morton brothers two-for-one tonight. How are you, love? How's your mam and dad?'

I haven't seen Jo McArthur that much, only at school fairs when she appears with her family entourage to support her husband. She's the chatty sort, forever smiling, the kind who wouldn't shout and let life get her down but glosses over everything with a Pinterest meme of a rainbow and an inspirational quote.

'Good to see you again, Jo. You know the missus…' Danny says, gesturing at me.

'Only by face… Meg, I'm Jo. I'll do triage, I just need to take a look…'

She peels back the towel from my leg. The lady with the cold jumps back in her seat.

'Flipping Nora, what on earth did you do?' Jo asks.

I glare at Danny.

'She fell…'

'Does it hurt?' she asks.

I look down. Mother of bollocks. Is that leg even mine? There's a large split to the middle about four inches long and little splinters encircle it leaving rivulets of blood trickling down my skin. It's like an acupuncture session gone wrong.

'There were quite a lot of blood.'

'He's lying.' The room is starting to swirl a little. 'He's lying.'

'Meg, are you feeling woozy?'

Danny tries to hold my head upright. 'She's been drinking like a fish all night…'

I pull a fish face. 'Well, maybe you're the reason I drink…'

Danny stares at me. Not now, not like this. You know who this is; she'll just go home and tell her husband over a brew about our marital woes, the man who is supposed to be educating our kids. Don't be a daft drunken mare.

'I just need a strong cup of Yorkshire Tea and I'll be right as fooking rain…' I say in my best Northern accent, oblivious to the fact I'm probably insulting most of the occupants of the waiting room. Jo shines a torch in my eyes and places her hands up and down my leg. I flinch when she gets to my engorged ankle.

'How did you fall? Like on to the dresser, or through it? Did it fall on you?'

'All of the above, really.'

Her eyes shift between myself and Danny. Her gloved hand goes to my ankle and she tries to circle it around the joint.

'OoooooOOOOOOOwwwwww!'

Danny rolls his eyes at me as I make the noise.

'I'm sorry, lovely. Have you tried walking on it?'

'She tried but collapsed on bed. Then again, could be because she's half-cut.'

Her glance turns to Danny and his complete lack of sympathy.

'It's OK. I'm an idiot, I know…' I say.

Tears start to flow, rolling down my nose without ebb. Stu looks on in the way someone might do in a horror film. Jo realises the entire waiting area is now eavesdropping and starts to push me towards the cubicles. Danny and Stu follow, keeping a suitable distance so they don't have to associate themselves with me. My head knocks back in the wheelchair and I follow the strip lights to a corner of the emergency ward. I stand up next to a bed then sit down again almost immediately. Danny tries to put an arm around me and I shrug it off.

'Slowly now… hop on. Now lads, I'm just going to examine her with the curtain closed. If you could step aside…'

They vacate the cubicle and she draws the curtain. I'm still crying. Mostly because my leg hurts like it might fall off but everything is coming to the surface: the emotion, the alcohol, the knowledge that to the occupants of the waiting area, I will be a story they recount to their friends and family. Embarrassment has a new name and she's at Westmorland General in her husband's dressing gown.

'Now, tell me lovely. That's quite a fall from height. Did you hit any other part of you? Your head?'

'No.' I look down and try to arrange myself on the hospital bed.

'There's some bruising on your buttocks…'

There are two of her in front of me. I try and re-focus.

'I got that by falling off the bath while I was trying to shave my muff…'

'OK.'

We wait for a moment to let that revelation sink in.

'There was some tension there before though. You two in the waiting room. I mean, I don't want to assume but this is a safe space. Did Danny hurt you?'

The tears flow and she comes over to hold me in half an embrace. I don't even know this woman. All I know is that her husband has great teeth.

'No, no, no, no… not like that…'

The pulse in my leg is now in my head, travelling through my whole body and flicking at my heart.

'We were having sex. He couldn't support my weight and the dresser fell on me. I think. It was a bit of a blur of flesh and bits and the floor.'

'Oh… but you're…'

'Crying… because I thought if we had sex like we did when we were younger then he'd remember…'

'Remember?'

'That I was his wife, that I can still do things… because I love him. I love him so much and I don't want him to leave me for someone else. I don't want to lose him to sex toys. I love him. It was just such a big dildo and it caught me by surprise…'

Jo McArthur can see I'm going off piste here in quite dramatic directions. If I was a dog, this is when the muzzle would go on. She pretends to adjust the sides of the bed.

'And I can't lose him to someone else, to another woman. It would kill me. It would…'

And with that, the curtain is pulled back and Danny stands there with his brother. Oh, that curtain wasn't soundproof, was it? Stu looks confused. Danny. I can't quite read it. But his head shakes, a look of infinite sadness in those cloudy blue eyes. I can't bear to see it. So I grab on to my bed railings, lean over and throw up over the side of the bed.

I lost my virginity when I was eighteen. I'd snogged and done all the other stuff in college but by the time I got to university, I knew I was late to the game and doing 'it' felt like something I needed to cross off the list with some urgency. So who did I do the deed with, who was the taker of my flower? Why it was one Alex Gamble.

I'm not exactly sure why but for some reason, as I am in this hospital bed, flitting in and out of consciousness in a state of pure delirium and pain, I can see his face. His blonde curly hair like a bath loofah, the potent taste of tequila on his breath, a room adorned with a clothes horse drying sports socks and a Breville sandwich maker in racing green with matching kettle. And not just his face, his contorted sex face is etched into memory; flared nostrils and biting on his bottom lip. I recall after some preliminary poking, Alex asked me to navigate him towards where he needed to be. This hadn't been the first penis I'd touched but I remember his felt like how I'd imagine a very soft snake might feel. He poked around for a while until he entered me. I have no memory of the sensation but will always remember Alex Gamble's face, framed by a very random poster of Damon Hill on the wall, a polyester orange curtain and some cork tiles.

Needless to say, the experience was not arousing, for me at least. I felt friction, the sort of nagging irritation that comes from wearing a badly fitted shoe. Alex came in about three minutes which he announced via his legs straightening and him saying to the room, 'I'm gonna go! You ready?!' I wasn't sure what he meant so I nodded. But I felt a strange feeling of relief; this wasn't special, I didn't love him, but it was now done. I got it out of the way; from that moment on, I was a non-virgin.

But why can I see his face? Why is he telling me to wake up? That there'll be a wait for an X-ray?

The light suddenly goes bright white and I open my eyes. Joanne McArthur's face is there. It's not a face I expect so I appear shocked and move my eyes from side to side. I'm no longer in Alex Gamble's bedroom. I am in a cubicle, on a hospital bed on crispy sheets and the side guards up for my own safety. I burp quietly. There is no Danny.

'You need anything? Water?'

'What happened?'

'You were just having a little nap,' she tells me. The large circle of drool on my pillow tells me differently. I look down. I'm in a gown that allows for a peculiar draft to my downstairs region. My leg is bandaged around the shin and another tighter bandage encases my ankle. She finishes writing on her charts and comes over to adjust my pillows. She's close enough for me to notice that her hair smells like summer berries. She's the sort of woman who looks perpetually beautiful. She's probably spent most of this evening dealing with drunks in various states of incapacity like me, but still her skin radiates health, she has emerald eyes and a soft curve to her cheeks. She would never have been dropped during sex.

She senses me staring deep into her soul and smiles awkwardly. She vacates the cubicle with a smile conveying pity, all the pity. Have Danny and Stu just left me here? I feel my lip wobble and I picture how it must have gone down. My allegations of infidelity would have enraged Danny. After me spewing on the floor and then passing out, he'd have cast me looks of scathing embarrassment before disowning me. She's no wife of mine! You can keep her with her shredded leg and accusations! A tear rolls down my face. I feel Danny's abandonment in every part of me, even more so than this morning when I found evidence of all those sex toys, when I saw him flirting with Briony Tipperton. What did Emma say? I'm a Callaghan woman, I don't break. At least not here in this soulless clinical room that has curtains for doors and a bed with a rubber mattress. In the cubicle opposite me is the pregnant woman from before, strapped to monitors as she glugs from a two-litre bottle of Diet Pepsi. She notices me and says something to her companion in conspiratorial whispers. I bow my head from the shame.

A voice. 'Chuffing hell, Meg. Just shut your legs. You're not wearing panties.'

Danny? 'I thought you'd gone?'

'Yeah? To drop Stu back home. And get you some clothes from home. It's nearly two in morning.'

More tears well in my eyes. You're still here. His face reads confusion but also sadness. In his hand is a Dora the Explorer rucksack filled to the brim. He's still wearing his hoodie that has remnants of baby porridge smeared down the front. He stands by the end of the bed for a moment too long, then draws the cubicle curtains and comes up to sit next to me, tentative, nervous. He looks down for a moment to compose himself. Just spit it out, man.

'They'll amputate tomorrow when they've got a theatre free then they're going to fit you with a bionic leg.'

He laughs, nervously. I have no words or tears left. He looks me in the eye and I bring him in to nestle my head into his chest. He's here, he's not gone; that's everything at the moment. He still looks worried, delving in the rucksack to find some M&Ms, hoping that may break the impasse. He kisses the top of my head gently then looks at my leg.

'You might have a scar,' he pauses. 'And you've got a bruise the shape of Australia on your arse.'

'That may have been when I fell off the bath.'

'I guessed. You told McArthur's wife that much. You also told the doctor who was gluing you back together.'

'There was a doctor?'

'Yup, you told him about the dildo from this morning too. You asked him if it was possible for an appendage to be too big, and he told you about a woman who came in once with a deodorant stuck up her parts.'

'I don't remember that.'

'You asked if it was a roll-on or spray. He explained to you that your vagina contracts when it's aroused so can feasibly house quite a large penis if it wanted to. It was a comfortable conversation all round.'

He sits next to me like someone making nice with an elderly relative. He puts a hand in mine. He seems fraught, the way he's trying to endear himself to me so completely different to his usual surly self. Is his hand shaking? I grip it tightly.

'Did you explain to them about the dildo this morning then?' I ask.

'I didn't.'

I am silent. 'Maybe you need to explain to me then. Maybe give me the truth this time.' I stare him out, fear consuming me about what the truth might be.

'I'm sorry. There's no one else. I promise you. I wouldn't do that. I thought you would know me well enough to know that.' His voice is wobbly and emotional. The revelation makes my breath stick in my throat.

I pause. 'I hacked into your Love Shack account.'

'Oh.' He takes his hand off mine.

'You should also know me well enough to know that I wouldn't let the appearance of a monster dildo lie.' That may have come out a bit wrong but instinctively I knew he had lied to me, which was probably the worst feeling of all. He looks into space. Is he trying to come up with more excuses? 'Danny, something's going on and you just need to tell me what this is. I don't care at this point what you're up to but just be honest.'

Do I need his confession to be made here? Maybe not. But if the past day has taught me anything it's that I don't do well with not knowing. If there are things to be said, secrets to be revealed, then I need full disclosure. Right here, right now. He's using the sex toys on himself? He has his own shop? He's moonlighting as some sort of customer reviewer? He's a bigamist? All those business trips overseas sourcing paper and he has a whole different family over in Hong Kong? My inquisitive mind is not helpful here.

He sits there for a moment, gearing himself up. He reaches down to the rucksack and pulls out two hardback notebooks. He places them on my lap. 'Open these. I also went home to get these, to explain.'

I don't say a word. This is it? What's in these notebooks? Letters from a lover? Names and addresses of all he has lain with? Notes on a scandal?

'Just open them already,' he pleads.

I do as I'm told. Nothing can quite prepare me for what I find. It's a vagina. Or not. It's the outer bit, the vulva, I guess. A lady's parts, hand-drawn on sketchbook quality paper. In quite good detail, truth be told. It's in ink with some realistic hatch shading and a commitment to including some pubic hair. The picture is signed by someone called CM and dated eighteen months ago. I exhale loudly. I don't understand. I shut the book hoping no one's seen anything.

'So, who is it?'

He gives me a quizzical look.

'Well, it's you, innit?'

'I don't remember posing for this? Was I asleep?'

He laughs. 'It were from memory. An artist's impression?'

'Back when my vagina looked like this?'

'You seem to have this impression that your vagina looks like a windsock since childbirth. I'll have you know, it looks and feels pretty much the same as it did when we first met.'

I think that was a compliment.

'Bar all the undergrowth, of course,' he adds.

Negated in mere seconds.

I re-open the book and turn the page. Wow, that's a penis. This one is in charcoal. It's quite large and veiny. I thumb through the pictures with more speed. A fine display of skill and detail but mostly consisting of genitalia.

'I don't get the signature. CM?'

'It's my username initials.'

'Username? So, *you* drew all of these?'

'Yes.'

'They are very good.'

It's like a bad improvisational comedy as we try and eke reactions and dialogue from each other. I don't know what to say. He doesn't look as flattered as I thought he might but I think he's trying to gauge if I think he's a complete pervert.

'I draw sex things, nudes… which is why I order sex toys in. To draw from life. It's hard to draw from images sometimes and I wanted to draw more than just my own appendage.'

This makes me laugh more than it should, to think of Danny curled up downstairs, legs akimbo and trying to find the right angles to draw his own cock. He laughs back nervously, our voices still in hushed tones so no one else can hear. Danny had always been an artist. When we first met, he was involved in graphic design and he had a real eye for art. He'd studied fine art in college and was always a sketcher, a doodler. His career fell by the wayside once he moved up North and went into the glamorous world of paper production but every year, he'd hand draw a card for his girls on their birthdays, and he was the one in charge of the art-based homework projects. I flick through the pictures, the doodles, the penises that have been practised and crossed out, the girl-on-girl action, the accurate conceiving of every sexual position that I know of, and one where I have to angle my head slightly to understand how the gentleman is actually achieving penetration. There are many questions. How he had the time is one of them.

'I guess the overriding question is… Why?'

'I don't really know. It just happened.'

'You lied to me about all of this, you kept it from me.' He's silent at the accusation. 'You could draw fruit. People draw fruit.'

'Well, bananas and penises are kind of the same thing.'

'Or not… You said username?'

'I put these pictures online. I have an Instagram page and a website and I copyright the images so they can be used for tattoos and bespoke art.'

I imagine someone's walls adorned in vag, a natural pairing for a couple of corduroy cushions, no? I am trying to rationalise whether this is wrong. If it doesn't hurt anyone and the pictures are not exploitative then surely it's an artistic expression of the human form. I saw nothing there degrading women or men. They are for the eyes of the more discerning adult, but it sounds like he's selling these pictures. This isn't bad. This isn't the worst-case scenario I had imagined. But there's also something here that doesn't make me feel good. He sits there gauging my reaction. He looks like he was expecting angry, and for me to launch the book directly at him. Instead I hold it close, almost cradling it in my arms. My thoughts are scattered. When did he do this? What is going on here?

'So it all eventually ends up online? For people to see?'

He nods. He goes to his phone and starts scrolling through some pages. There is a lot to process here. This was all on his mobile. Our kids use that phone to watch YouTube clips of baby pandas. Why did I not know this? He shows me an Instagram page of all his pictures. I scroll through the comments. It seems that people are fans. He slides to another page. I take the phone from him. He has a webpage. He has followers. He has fifty thousand followers. It's linked to Twitter and Instagram and there's even a PayPal link. People pay for this stuff. By the bollock? And it's only then do I see the username heading it all up.

Captain Mintcake

'Say what now?' I mutter. 'Captain Mintcake?'

He nods.

'You're Captain Mintcake?'

'Yes.'

Mint cake is their thing up here in Kendal, their regional foodstuff. It's an overly sweet mint confection that people take up mountains for energy. I never really understood the appeal myself. It has the consistency of firelighter and tastes like you've downed a tube of Colgate.

'That's the unsexiest username I've ever heard. You've also spelt it wrong. It's two separate words.'

That doesn't seem to be a concern to him. 'People like it. It sounds reassuring. Not in your face, or overtly sexual like…'

'RockHard4U? VatofPussy1?' We are both surprised that these roll off my tongue so easily. 'Because the giant pictures of the knobs aren't too in your face, you know?'

I'm veering into sarcasm now and I can tell Danny doesn't know if this means I'm bordering on bitchy too. It's all a bit hard to process in my fatigue and delirium and a leg half-cocked up in the air. I open the book again. There's a woman there with her mouth open like a basking shark. That's a pretty large tallywhacker. She's going to take that in her mouth? No, she's letting it rain down on her. Like a sprinkler.

'I don't know what to say, Meg. This is it, this is what the dildo was about. I didn't tell you. I didn't know what you'd think of all of it. It was just fun to start off with, just something silly to bide my time. I didn't think anything would come of it.'

'Well, who knows? Does Stu know?'

'No, and I want to keep it a secret.'

I am silently processing everything. The date on that first picture was eighteen months ago. Polly wouldn't even have been born. Was this because I was pregnant and he didn't want to scare me by saying, 'Oi, look what I've drawn here!' in case it'd send me into premature labour? I feel more confused by the fact this was a secret, that it was hidden and that he didn't think I was open-minded enough to accept it. Besides that, there is this feeling in the pit of my stomach because there are pictures of many many women here, women who aren't me. I stop at a picture of one of these women on all fours in the middle of a bed. That was me, once, maybe. When my stomach was flatter and I had time to wear matching underwear and condition my hair but now I'm more inclined to sit in the middle of a bed and eat a packet of prawn cocktail crisps while playing Candy Crush.

'These people on your website… do you converse with them? Have you met any of them?' I ask.

'Only online. I did research. It's not cheating or anything.'

He says that last sentence defensively. I'm not sure now is the moment to discuss the moral aspect of what he's done. To be honest, I'm still taking it in. I'll admit to baulking slightly that a mere five hours ago we were attempting to indulge in the sort of sexual act he draws about. Damn it, we even did it this morning. Twice in one day which is a record for our sex life. I bet in Danny's scenarios no one's leg falls through a dresser. A sadness still prevails that I can't seem to shake.

'I'm sorry.' I don't know why the words fall out like they do but I feel apologetic, I feel guilt. I feel ashamed because I don't know why he's done this. Is it a hobby? A career change? Why did he hide it from me?

'You're sorry?'

'Just because…'

He shakes his head. I put the books down, lower myself down the bed and prop my head up on a pillow. I curl into the foetal position away from him. He sits on the side of the bed space next to me, a hand to my back.

'Are you alright? Do you need anything? Do you want to talk about it some more? Are you in pain?'

'I'm kinda tired.' I can't look at him. Not for feeling prudish or shocked but just an immense feeling of confusion. What has just happened today? From thinking that my husband was having an affair to finding out he's someone called Captain Mintcake. And now, I'm in a hospital bed and I've just looked at pictures of curves and body parts that are definitely not mine anymore, of sexual thoughts and scenarios all drawn by Danny. And deep down, this nagging feeling like these pictures are some sort of artefact of who we used to be, that he's almost had to document these moments so he can verify they actually happened once. It makes me feel like a bad wife, a failed lover. They're not bad but they don't make me feel good. Danny takes his arm off my back. The curtain opens. Joanne McArthur stands there with a wheelchair.

'OK, love. X-ray is ready for you. Let's check if you're still in one piece.'

Chapter Six

I'm not sure what cocktail of drugs they give me at the hospital but that night, I dream about a person having sex in a picture. In truth, it looks very much like an a-ha video from the eighties except there are no mullets. And all the people having the sex are myself and Danny, except that we have sketched out bodies and our heads are ripped out of old wedding photos. I can't feel the sex, but I am looking down at my new sketched body in complete awe. I have these pert, rounded boobs and a sculpted, almost concave stomach. It is picture sex so naturally I am amazingly bendy too – my legs are being flung about to the wonderment of my sketched out husband who engages in intercourse with me in a range of unrealistic positions, and at one point I can do a bridge which I haven't attempted since junior school gymnastics. The dream appears to me like a cartoon flick book, in stills. Morten Harket, the lead singer of the band even runs in at one point. I pause to wave to him. 'Your name is Morten! Like us!' He runs off again. My eyes open.

I awake to an empty bed back home. I have vague recollections of getting here, mainly involving Danny and Stu angling me up the stairs with the same noise and exertion one would move a piano. I remember my husband dressing me in his favourite Stussy T-shirt, a mug of lukewarm tea, a stilted kiss goodnight. Where's Danny now? It's 7.30 a.m. A pillow that once elevated my ankle is now on the floor. The dresser that I wrecked is now pieced back together awkwardly. Undergarments that were tossed aside in the heat of drunken passion are folded in piles. Maybe this time he's actually left me. I shuffle over to the wardrobe with my dodgy ankle. Well, if he has left then he's gone without clothes. Maybe where he was going he didn't need clothes. The room door flies open.

'And what are you doing out of bed?'

Of all the people who should be standing there, this one is welcome. I smile and exhale loudly to see her carrying Polly close, followed by Tess and Eve, all dressed and ready for school.

'What the hell are you doing here?' I ask.

'Well, when you hear your sister's fallen down the stairs and there was blood everywhere then you make the effort to ensure she hasn't done herself any serious injuries… You numpty.'

Emma. Relief and emotion pour out of me and Tess immediately comes over to embrace me. Eve is more tentative.

'What did you do, Mummy? Daddy said you fell because you drank too much wine.'

This will no doubt be what she reports in her writing diary at school.

'Daddy's here?'

'He was,' Emma informs me. 'He rushed off to work, said he had an early conference call with Asia? All OK?'

Emma knows she can't say too much but comes to offer me a hand while I shuffle over. Tess fluffs my pillows up for me. When I sit down on the edge of the bed, Eve comes over and hugs me tightly.

'I was scared,' she mumbles. I push her back to cup her face and kiss her forehead.

'Honey, it's just my ankle. I'm fine.'

She passes me a get well note on a Post-It that she sticks to my leg then runs off. Tess examines my leg and stares at my toes.

'How did you fall? Like did you tumble down the stairs or belly flop?' she asks.

'I can't quite remember.'

'That'll be the wine.' I told you she was dry. Tess smiles at me, looking all at once like her father. 'Granny Gilly is making our packed lunches by the way and she's giving us granary bread. Eve is gonna flip out when she sees that.' She giggles, cupping two hands to her mouth.

'I'm sorry. Mummy should have been more careful.' I rake my fingers through her hair, soft curls springing back in my fingers.

She hugs my midriff for a moment too long. 'Uncle Stu is downstairs just sitting there in his pants. Nothing else. He still thinks he's in Australia. There's also a man called Jag who has Maoams in his pockets. He came with Aunty Ems. Can I go now?'

I nod. No doubt she's gone to mug this man for his sweets. She skips away while I pull faces at Emma who sits pretending she hasn't heard a thing, Polly purring like a contented kitten in her arms.

'So… all OK?' she asks.

'Jag?' I reply.

'You go first, let me check out the patient.'

She leaves Polly to crawl on the bedroom rug and pulls back the duvet to examine the damage, unpeeling tape to assess the handiwork and moving my foot around on the joint. I wince a little.

'Danny said they did an X-ray, not broken but a heavy sprain? Nice glue work though. You'll have to shower with your leg in a bin bag. Any pain, warmth? And Tess has a point… How did you fall?'

'None of the above and I didn't fall, Danny dropped me.'

'Because… you accused him of cheating on you?'

'Because we were having sex and it turns out he can't stand up and support the weight of big old heifer me.'

'Right, which is why he had all the sex toys?'

'No.'

We are interrupted. The door opens and an Asian gentleman walks in carrying a tray of tea. I try to work out whether I am on the good drugs, whether he's a very kindly intruder, or this is Jag with all the Maoams. I give him the once over and am immediately taken with the trendy Vans trainers and Oxford shirt with the sleeves rolled up.

'Oh, this is Jag,' Emma casually drops in.

'A pleasure to meet you.'

I suddenly remember I am wearing very little so creep the duvet up my legs.

'Hello? My daughter mentioned you…'

He smiles. He has the most amazing skin and smile; the sort of wide smile that's toothy and joyous and leads you to imbue trust very quickly. He also delivers tea which helps.

'Jag and I were having a drink when we got a call saying you'd fallen and yes, we are both here now.'

I smile broadly. It explains why she's in a dress. She never wears dresses.

'You drive a Kia.'

'I do?' he replies confused. I feign an expression like I just guessed that out of thin air. He glances over at my leg. 'Your leg is still attached then?'

'Just about… are you staying? You should stay. The Lakes are lovely. Go for a walk or grab some lunch on Windermere Lake or something?'

'It's a lovely offer but I have a scheduled surgery at 7 a.m. tomorrow so I was going to take a slow drive back via Wolverhampton, my sister lives there.'

There is a moment between him and Emma where if I was able, I'd leave the room. He smiles broadly and my liking for him increases again.

'At least stay here for a nap before you set off?'

'I'm filled to the brim with services coffee. I'll be fine but it was lovely to meet you and I'm glad it's nothing serious.' He does a thumbs up and glances over at Emma before leaving the room. I glare at my sister.

'Follow him,' I whisper, angered by her hesitancy.

'But I was going to stay, I have some days off…'

'I mean, to the door. He just drove six hours through the night to get you here. Go to him…' I shoo her away like a pigeon.

'Ungrateful cow,' she says.

'You love me really.'

I'm interrupted by my phone ringing and I take a deep breath. 'Mum.' Emma widens her eyes at me and tries to contain her laughter. I have to take this, don't I?

'Meg. Is Emma there? Did she make it up safely?'

I smile to myself. Emma is my mother's chosen one: the doctor, the one who veered down the golden path. I veered up North, away from her, so she's always held some resentment over that – especially as I took her grandbabies away from her. I'm fine, Mum. Thanks for asking.

'Emma is here. She is safe. She got a lift up here from a friend…' Emma shakes her head at me. Don't you dare tell our mother. 'A male friend, someone she works with?'

Emma snarls. All at once, we're fifteen again and she's telling on me for having been hanging outside the chicken shop with the boys from school.

'Who? Is he handsome?' Mum enquires.

'I only met him briefly. He drives a Kia. Would you like to hear about my leg now?'

Emma shakes her head. Revenge is coming. She leaves the room sticking her middle finger up at me. The revenge begins by leaving me to take this phone call on my own.

'Oh yes, what happened? Gill was in such a state when she called,' she says, matter of fact. 'Your father is here on speaker too. Say hello, David.'

'Hello, Meg,' pipes in Dad.

'Hi, Dad.' A dad hug would be good around now. The mum lecture that will follow less so.

'How on earth does a woman of your age fall down the stairs? You really should be more careful.'

'Indeed. I think that's why they're called accidents, Mum.' Do I tell both my parents via speakerphone that my husband dropped me during sex? Probably not. Still dizzy with sleeplessness, I hear her lecture melt into nothing. Make sure you elevate. You were always my clumsy one. I'd be able to help you if you lived down

South. What a bind for Danny to have to look after you. Thanks, Mum. Yes, poor Danny to be lumbered with old me.

'Is there anything we can do to help?' My father's voice.

It's a jolt to hear him get a word in.

'It's silly really, Dad. A few days will put me right.'

'Your Aunt Sylvia fell down the stairs tripping over her cat, and they had to bolt her hips together with titanium. She sets off scanners in airports now,' Mum informs me helpfully.

'Ems being here is good,' I say.

'Yes, it's a wonder she can find time out of her schedule. She's been so busy these days,' replies Mum.

'Being a doctor and all,' I add, mockingly. I hear Dad giggling.

I want to say it all. My husband draws willies. And fannies. Emma's husband was a horrible cheating tit. I know I'm not your favourite daughter. I hope I'm at least third in the rankings though. My leg looks like it's been attacked by a large cat. But no. I am too tired. I don't want to worry them to the point where they might jump on a train and actually come here too.

'I'm tired, folks. But really, I'm fine. Thanks for checking in. Give everyone my love.'

'Can we talk about Christmas soon?'

It's October. Don't start a fight now, I tell myself. Not today.

'Yes, Mum. Of course.'

I fall asleep after that and awake to find a bunch of yellow tulips and a packet of Minstrels on my bedside table. From Danny? Downstairs, I hear people milling about and miss being in that hive of action and conversation. I look around the room helplessly, my eyes feeling like bees have stung them several times, my mouth furry like a cat's slept inside it. I am irritated by that horrible ick from not having showered or removed my make-up properly so I am basically a giant blob of mascara gloop. I think about texting Danny but refuse to, almost as punishment. I had to ferment in all of that suspicion yesterday, feeling broken and hurt. I almost feel he deserves the same. His sideline hobby in erotic art still confuses me. My ankle feels achy and alien. I am in a strange sort of limbo where fatigue and uncertainty are not playing nice in my head. Strangely, I am also craving Jaffa Cakes.

A firm knock on the door gets my attention. 'Come in?' I say.

'Are you dressed?' It's Stu. Obviously approaching with caution even though it's very probable he's seen all of me that there is to see. I pull up the duvet to my neck to make doubly sure.

'Yes.'

He opens the door and appears with a mug of tea. 'What doing?'

'Not much, really.'

'You still take like forty sugars in your tea, right?'

I nod and smile, glad that he's remembered, thinking back to a time when we used to sit in our shared kitchen, fixing each other's morning brews before work.

'You need anything?'

Quite frankly, I do need a wee but am not sure if Stu needs to witness or assist in that after last night.

'I'm good.'

'Who's Tim then?'

'Kid from work. Why do you ask?'

'I've been like the doorman all day. Chocs and flowers are from him.'

I feel pangs of disappointment that they're not from Danny but I panic at how Tim would have known I was poorly. Did Danny tell them? It's always worrying when your gossip reaches the local news outlets. Am I to become a headline outside a newsagent? *Woman twists ankle in sex gone wrong!*

'Rowan also popped around with some New Age medicine rubbish but I told her you weren't taking visitors.'

My expression reads confused. I never said that. Or is he trying to hide me away? Rowan's warmth and all-embracing hugs would be just the ticket right now.

Stu collects used mugs from about the room and glances over at the drawer hanging out of my dresser, looking slightly puzzled but reticent to ask how it all went down. He glares at me, his brain obviously loaded with questions that he can't quite bring himself to say out loud. I take a sip of my tea. He wasn't joking – this is laden, even for me, but I am polite and get it down me. He looks out the window then turns to glare at me, a sterner expression than I'm used to.

'I need to tell you something,' he says.

'Yeah?'

'Dan is many things. He's a miserable bastard. He is stubborn and he don't look after himself. And I don't know what's happened but he left house in a flat cap this morning…'

His dreaded flat cap. I'd been hiding it under the stairs.

'But he loves you. That much I know. I don't know what's happening with you two but you've got kids and this house and a life and he wouldn't cheat. He wouldn't. I know my brother.'

'I didn't accuse him. I was just confused…'

'I've lived with both of you. I've seen this thing from the beginning.'

'And we've not seen you in eighteen months.'

How has this suddenly become my fault? How qualified is he to come and lay these grand assumptions at my feet?

'I know he loves you. I know he held your hand in the hospital when they were gluing you together, and didn't say a word when you were all drunk and ranting and being a fool.'

'He dropped me.'

'It wasn't on purpose? You did nothing to defend your husband's reputation in that hospital… and that's piss-poor behaviour. That man would do anything for you.'

I feel bile rising to the surface. Do I add here that his beloved brother likes to draw sex stuff?

'So you come in here on your moral high ground, giving me relationship advice? That's rich.'

I'm not half wrong. I'd seen the flocks of women he'd got through, the utter contempt he'd held for commitment and the long-term.

'Look, this ain't about me. If you're having some sort of mid-life hormonal crisis then don't drag him into your drama. Don't be a bitch and accuse him of things he wouldn't do.'

Bile turns to anger. Mid-life crisis? I take the things closest to me on my bedside table – a bunch of yellow flowers, and sling them at his head. He puts his hands up to shield himself but not before yellow petals spray across the room. He glares at me. I hear someone hurdle up the stairs. Gill enters as the petals float through the air and on to the floor.

'What on earth is going on here?' she whispers, shocked. She gestures that there's a sleeping baby in the room next door.

'Stuart? Stuart!' Gill pleads.

Stu doesn't even dare to look at me but turns to leave, his footsteps heavy on the stairs. I can't read Gill's expression but before she leaves, she turns to glare at me in a way she's never done before. The look makes me heavy with sadness. I also realise now is not the time to ask her for biscuits.

'Yo hop-a-long, I'm back.'

I awake from a nap to Emma standing at the end of my bed, prodding my leg. On my bedside table is a giant iced bun, a cup of tea and what looks like codeine. She looks over and smiles. If I could, I'd launch off this bed and hug the crap out of her.

'Get that down you before Gill comes up here with her lumpy-looking soup. Make sure you hydrate and up your fibre with the codeine or you'll get backed up… I don't fancy giving you an enema. I also sorted the little one's croup.'

The joys of a doctor sister who recognises the need for the stronger drugs.

'I'm sorry I abandoned you. I had to tend to Jag.'

'Tend to?'

'Don't go there.'

'Mum can't wait to meet him.'

'I hate you.'

I smile. 'What about your girls, work?'

'Lucy has the girls, you've got me for two days.'

'Did you do the school run?' I ask.

'Yes, and some woman accosted me as well, asking about your leg. Blonde, lots of kids?'

Sarah. How this had got to her already was beyond me. 'What did you say?'

'You fell on some cobbles? I didn't know how we were playing this… And there's something going on with Gill. She and Stu… They're not happy?'

'I had it out with Stu earlier.'

'Oh, that's why he's packing a bag then.'

'He's gone?'

'Loitering. Staying for soup.'

'And the anaesthetist?'

'Went at lunch.'

There is a pause. We both need to divulge but neither of us want to go first.

'What happened with the sex toys then? Did Gill find them?' Emma asks.

'You go first.'

'You.'

I gesture down to my leg that I am the invalid here who has suffered pain and deserves the honour of going second in this exchange. Emma rolls her eyes back at me.

'Jag is lovely. He's so nice. We drove six hours here overnight. We had a lovely day yesterday. We had a stroll. He brought me flowers. Like flowers from a florist, not even supermarket flowers. They were wrapped with twine and he opens doors and we had Greek food.'

'And you love hummus.'

'I do love hummus.'

We sit here silently. Emma has been divorced from sex-pest Simon for nearly a year now. She keeps her walls high and lets few in. Ninety per cent of how she handles herself is done with grace and poise but I have the privilege of being her sister. I'm allowed to see the fractures, the irreparable damage that prevents her from participating in a relationship with her whole heart. Jag was doing everything right: trying to cement her back together with some Mediterranean dip and accompanying her six hours up the motorway to see a sister who'd fallen arse over tit. But Emma's recovery will take time and lots of digging deep into her soul to be able to trust and love another again. I pat the bed as only a big sister can and she puts her head down next to my hip.

'Your turn.' She sits up, knowing my story is going to be a hell of a lot more interesting.

I pause, unsure at what to tell her. Lying here on my own has given me the time to look through Danny's art. It still brewed a strange feeling of resentment in me, all these hours that he spent on it and I had no idea. I feel like I've been taken for a fool for not having even noticed that his time had been divided between me and this new hobby. I reach for my phone on the bedside table. Emma peers over for more information. I find Instagram. The news feed is an assortment of friends' pictures of food, holiday sunsets and celebrity portraits. I go to the 'Search' box and take a deep breath.

Captain Mintcake

And there he is. I notice he has a blue tick. He is verified. Because there are imposters? I happen upon a version of a sketched picture with a man sat on an armchair, schlong on full view. He looks very comfortable in such a position. It has 52,014 likes. I show it to Emma.

'Holy granola, girl, it's not even past the watershed.' She looks away like I've shone a laser in her eyes.

'That's what Danny was doing with the sex toys.'

Emma looks confused. 'Like masturbating with them and looking at porn?'

'No, that's Danny…'

'He's life modelling? No offence but your Danny's a bit more… rounded?' She gestures as she says it, almost as if he's pregnant.

'He drew it. He draws about sex and stuff. Like a pastime. I think?'

She takes my phone and scrolls through the content. Everything I need to know is communicated via her eyebrows and one picture that makes her quickly draw breath and turn the phone a full one hundred and eighty degrees.

'I see.'

Strangely, she doesn't recoil in horror at the images displayed before her. She may not be the prude that I thought she might be.

'Anatomically, these are all very accurate. I'm impressed by the detail and the fact he's been quite honest.'

'Huh?'

She shows me a full-on vulva. 'Like take this, I'd expect when most men fantasise about the perfect lady parts, they're wanting tight, shaved – that sort of early twenties porn look. This is a proper labia with full on bush.'

'Proper?'

'Overgrown, flappy.' Her eyes widen as she realises it might be mine. I feel a twinge of shame. 'But then you look on here and it's another one, not quite perfect like in a textbook. These are natural images, the labial lips are more pronounced.' It's suddenly all gone a bit *Gray's Anatomy*. 'Lady parts are strange-looking entities, most men don't know their vulvas from their vaginas but this is someone who knows them, who understands them. Look at the shading on that clitoral hood, he knows exactly where the underlying glans are too. I mean he knows where it is… that's a start…'

I forget that Emma's looking at this with a detached medical mind. As long as Danny's remembered to dot in a urethra then she'll be happy. She studies the page intently.

'Look at this one where the lightning is shooting out of this woman's vagina.'

I have a look. It owes a lot to Thor and I hope that anyone else involved is wearing something with rubber soles.

'Saucy,' she says.

'Absurd. The last time I felt a sensation like electricity down there was when Polly's head was emerging.' I reply.

She laughs scrolling through more images.

'Having fun?' I ask.

'This is almost as fun as Tinder,' she replies.

'Say what now?' I say, surprised.

'Tinder, it's a dating app,' she explains.

'Yes, I know what Tinder is. What the hell are you doing on it?' This was Emma, newly divorced but also a woman who's only ever worn white knickers since she was a teenager.

'It was our darling Lucy, wasn't it? Signed me up to get me back on the horse.' I can't quite decide if this is an act of pure genius or idiocy which defines the littlest sister perfectly.

'And have you ridden any horses?' I ask her.

'No, I have not,' she replies, shocked at the comment. I look at her and she knows what I want. She reluctantly gets out her phone and shows me her profile.

'And this is for finding a new bloke? How you found Jag?'

She shakes her head. I'd heard the rumours about Tinder but had always thought it was mostly for random sexual encounters. You don't want to imagine your sensible siblings having sex but I always supposed what she liked was wholly vanilla and missionary, not random punters.

'It's been a curious exercise. Quite amusing really. When you haven't dated since the nineties, it's interesting to see what men want these days.'

'And what would that be?'

'Well, most of them want to ejaculate on my actual face.'

I laugh in horror to hear Emma talk about things so plainly, sat there sipping her tea in her well-fitting jeans and pinstripe shirt.

'Have you had any hook-ups from it?'

'I met one man for a drink – we were both embittered divorcees. All going well until he opened up his wallet and still had a photo of his wife in there.'

'Oh.'

'Then he cried and I sat there for an hour like his counsellor hearing about how she cheated on him with a dad from the school run who was a Zumba instructor.'

'Did you do the deed?'

'Hell, no. But Lucy bought me new lacy pants in case it went that far. Never let Lucy buy you pants. Completely see through and no gusset.'

I shift her a look to see if she may be lying but it's Ems. It's so matter-of-fact that it hurts. I imagine her inviting a random punter into her house and the first thing she'd do is tell him to take off his shoes then make him a cup of Earl Grey. Ems continues to scan through my phone, licking the icing off her iced bun in the same way she's done since she was little.

'They do much better buns up North, I tell you. There's a lot of knobs here too. The big shiny one – is that him?'

I shrug. I mean how closely does anyone ever examine their partner's penis? It's of size and I reckon I'd recognise it in a line up but possibly by feel as opposed to pictures. That's awful. Something that has come near me so intimately, that has made babies with me and I don't think I could recognise it. Emma seems surprised.

'You don't know what your husband's penis looks like?'

'You'd have known Si's?'

'It was very straight, like a fleshy baguette. It got to the stage where I had to etch it into memory so I could catch him out.'

I retch a little. Emma chuckles to herself.

'So, is this a problem? What's the deal here? Man's found himself a hobby. It's just drawing. Could be worse.'

Emma seems a little narked that I seemed to be overthinking this. She gives me a look that tells me that *she* was the sister who has suffered with first-hand experiences of infidelity and lies. When it came to matters of the heart, she has truly bled, her heart's contents spilled out in the worst possible way. A few pencil sketches do not spell the end of a marriage.

'But he lied.'

Did she have some sliding scale of what a lie in a marriage really was?

'I think we all lie in our marriages to some extent. We hold back, we're not immediately open with our spouses. I can see why he kept this to himself...'

I'm less convinced.

'Bottom line, I don't think this is drastic. And not the end, most definitely not divorce. Divorce is good for some people, it was the best thing I ever did and I'd tell you if you needed to go down that route, I would take your hand and lead you up that path with me.'

There's a creak on the stairs, Emma sits up. I shrug it off.

'It's the dog, he can smell the buns.'

'So, you would look after me?' I ask.

'Always. We could live down South together and I'd buy us a big house like some sitcom family.'

She squeezes me tight. I needed this more than anything.

'Speaking of which, we've got to clean that wound in a bit. And give you a shower. You're starting to smell like a tramp.'

'Takes one to know one.'

'Can I tell the sisters?' she asks.

'No, you bloody can't.'

As I say it, Gill suddenly arrives at the door with a tray of the aforementioned soup. It does look exceedingly lumpy and she's given me a side of granary bread that I know will hurt my teeth. I smile knowing where Eve must have inherited her proclivity for baked goods. My mother in law is strangely quiet with us, most likely still confused from the flower-slinging incident. Emma picks up on the tension.

'I'm going out in a bit, Gill, to pick up some supplies. Do we need anything?'

She shakes her head. I notice her looking down at my phone on the bed, wide open at a picture of a naked man spread-eagled in a chair. I'm quietly relieved that he's flaccid. I don't think Gill sees it that way.

By the evening, boredom settles in and certain things are already starting to grate and catch my eye: the socks tangled and trying to worm their way out of the drawer, a thin film of dust over the windows and the pile of clothes in the corner of the room that are neither dirty nor clean but sit there hiding a very lovely armchair that no one ever gets to actually sit on.

Ems gave me my bin bag shower a while back. It involved me standing like a flamingo in a shower cubicle while she pointed at me through the glass, falling into absolute hysterics as she saw the mess I'd made of my bush. I fell out of said shower cubicle and my hair is now lanky from not having washed out my conditioner properly.

The bedroom door opens.

'Seeing as you can't move, would you like to read with us?' asks Tess.

Two freshly bathed children with partings combed dead centre stand in the doorway wearing pyjamas that look suspiciously like they've been ironed.

'Where's Polly?' I ask.

'Downstairs, having milk with Granny Gilly and being forced to watch *Coronation Street*.'

'And Stu and Aunty Ems went out,' adds Eve.

I smile and gesture for them to come over. Naturally, they launch themselves onto the mattress and I have to shield the dodgy leg. Any parent will tell you a little break from your sproglets is sometimes needed but I've missed them today. I was slightly jealous to hear them doing homework with my sister downstairs, to hear the chaos around the dinner table and the little snippets of inane conversation that normally fill my day.

'Did you lot have soup for dinner?'

Eve pulls a face at me. 'It had chunks. I prefer your soup.'

I smile thinking about Eve, my cream of tomato fan who likes to lap hers up with cheesy toast fingers and dredge the bowl so it leaves red rings around her mouth like a lion cub. I kiss the top of her head.

'What's happening at school then?' I enquire.

'Noah farted today in the classroom and I thought I was going to be sick,' says Tess.

'Did he apologise?'

'Did he ever? Have you met Noah?'

Tess talks to me like this small adult me sometimes. She turns her nose up at boys and has done ever since nursery when she decided they were the inferior species who dealt in willy and poo jokes. It was all very beneath her which made me wonder how she got on with her father at all. Eve is in hysterics.

'OK, what are we reading?'

'We've picked *The Twits.*'

I sigh deeply, thinking about when Danny first grew a beard and hadn't got used to the fact it was like a giant crumb catcher. A picture pops to mind of a little Eve picking croissant flakes out of it; some halcyon, sun-drenched image I'm completely in love with.

'Any time this evening would be good.' This was when Tess was her father's child, impatient to a fault.

I flick through the pages.

'Arabella said I'm not allowed to use the word *fart,*' Eve pipes in. This was me. I liked to come back to conversations at opportune moments. Tess rolls her eyes. 'What's wrong with the word, fart?' Eve asks. 'Arabella says it's rude. You should say words like poot or parp.'

I laugh to myself.

'It's not funny. Apparently, you can't say ballsacks either…'

I choke a little on my own breath.

'Where on earth did you…'

It's Tess' turn to have a little chuckle. 'Don't you know Daddy then?'

I pause as she says it. That's the thing little chica, I thought I did. I mean, how well do we know anyone really? You can't open up their brains and spoon their thoughts out to have a look but you assume that marriage gives you licence to access at least eighty-five per cent of everything. I have a moment and kiss the top of Eve's head.

'Daddy always says he's scratching his ballsacks.'

'And you know what ballsacks are?'

'They're the bits behind the willy where Daddy keeps the baby seeds.'

'He told you this?' I ask this a little too calmly given they seem to know the ins and outs of baby-making at such a tender age.

'He sure did.'

And in the most well-timed manoeuvre ever, Danny's figure appears at the door. Eve bounces off the bed and throws herself at him. He stares over with the glimmer of a smile. I'm not sure what he expects; I've nothing left to throw at him bar the paperback in my hands which would hardly leave a scratch and I feel a little bereft to lob good children's literature at him. His face is ruddy, his eyes sunken. He's here. This is far from over but he's here and that's a start.

'Come read with us, Daddy,' gestures Eve.

I nod. He glances at the book in my hands.

'Am I Mr Twit?'

'Naturally. I'll be Mrs Twit.' I ache to hug him but the dodgy ankle and the girls prevent me. Instead, he throws something in my direction.

'Peace offering.'

It's a packet of Jaffa Cakes. I clasp my hand around them. He knew.

Chapter Seven

Climax. This picture is just called 'Climax'. It involves a woman who seems to be climaxing so strongly that her body is vibrating in the fashion you might see a washing machine go in for a final spin. I suspect it would make for quite a good flick book. Rowan stares at the paper intently, nodding thoughtfully. I knew she wouldn't be the sort to shy away from the content and so far, nothing has shocked her. Not the vaguely seizure-like orgasm or the numerous sketches of penises stood to attention page after page.

'Bloody hell, Daniel Morton. Who knew the boy had it in him?'

My thoughts exactly. It's been a week since my discovery of Captain Mintcake. Emma has gone back to London, my ankle is still dodgy and Danny and I carry on with life, marriage and such. In between readjusting to kids, work and learning to walk again, I've been digesting Danny's new canon of work, usually at night, before I go to bed. How am I dealing with it? With looks of disbelief over cornflakes, or staring at the ceiling in bed thinking about why he never told me and wondering what it all means deep down in his psyche. It's left conversation affected, the atmosphere barbed and awkward. I haven't probed (not like that) but am just glad that this isn't a death knell to our marriage. I think it's maybe why I'm here today.

When Rowan called seeing if I wanted to come over to her house for some tea and chat, I thought the escape might do me good. Rowan's heart has always been in the right place – on a slightly different cosmic space to mine, yes, but when we first moved to Kendal she was the one who took me under her wing and made sure I felt welcome. She and Rufus were true childhood sweethearts who'd traversed the awkward years of school and college together before travelling the world and ending up exactly where they started. Rufus now ran a small farm making cheese and interesting concoctions with nettles, whereas Rowan was a sculptor and artist. It was all earthy and New Age, from the kids – Sage, Zenith and River – to the ethereal home on the hill which was built by Ru himself and was at least sixty per cent hemp and alpaca products. Despite their differences, Ru and Danny remained the best of friends growing up, that shared heritage of joyriding down country lanes and learning how to roll joints at the beating heart of their friendship. That said, Rowan had promised tea today and intriguingly, also new information. Whatever that may be, I feel safe here. Her friendship and some fresh Lakeland air will cleanse my soul and clear those clouds hovering over me.

'So, tell me what you know,' I say.

I sit here knowing little will shock me now. Rowan looks on calmly and smiles.

'Danny was here – the morning after you found out,' she tells me.

Is this the new information? He hadn't told me where he'd been but I'd just assumed he was at work. Again, more lies. Ro reads my confused expression and puts the book down.

'He showed up at 7 a.m. He was crying, Meg. The only time I've seen Danny cry was in Year 9 PE when someone hit him in the nads with a cricket ball. He thought he'd really messed up… that you were really angry with him.'

'I'm not angry, I think,' I reply.

'But we calmed him down. I did some meditative breathing exercises with him. Ru took him for a walk, they talked. They then dug a trench and got all that emotion out. It was very cathartic. We made sure he went back to you.'

I smile. And that he did. 'He probably would have skulked back anyway but thank you for pushing him in the right direction.' Ro returns the smile and gets up to pour me more nettle tea and offer vegan biscuits (both tasting a little leafy) as she adjusts my ballooned ankle on a Peruvian woven footstool. I wince slightly. She then grabs a couple of sketchbooks and sits down next to me.

'I need to show you something too.'

She starts opening them and leafing through the pages.

'A couple of summers ago, remember when you went down to London to spend time with your sisters? Danny enrolled in one of my drawing classes at The Brewery.'

She opens the sketchbooks. It's all charcoal, blurry and smudged, but there's a theme: naked people. I feel my eyes have seen far too much in the past week, like I need to cleanse them with holy water. That said the sketches aren't as graphic as the ones he's shown me but definitely reveal talent, a real eye for the human form. I flick through the book and suddenly realise something.

'So you guys knew about Captain Mintcake?'

She makes a face and nods. I feel strangely embarrassed.

'From an artist's perspective, of course. Not like some weird perverse orgy angle. He'd show me the drawings and ask me for advice. I told him to put them online. I was stoked he kept at it. I just saw it as erotic art. I thought you knew though. I really did.'

I blush because the revelation was not the fact he drew other people's bits and bobs but the fact he didn't share this with me at all. He opened up to his mates and they'd studied the quality by which he'd shade in someone's foreskin but, from me, it was a guilty secret.

'I didn't know. And I'll be honest Ro, it's making me feel a little crappy.'

'Why?'

'I think it's the secrecy. It's just a jolt to reality; what it says about our sex life, our marriage, my body.'

She embraces me and then holds my shoulders, head cocked to one side.

'My love, don't read too much in it. You know Danny, he keeps to himself.'

'But I'm his wife.'

She doesn't have to say anything. Her look says enough. He should have told you.

'But try not to internalise this, sweets,' she says in return. 'I think this is just a journey of expression for Danny. These pictures just feel like him. At school, he was never out of the art room. He was always sketching. It broke my heart he went to that sodding paper mill.'

I pause for a moment. It's not escaped my attention that this hobby is a manifestation of repressed professional desires too. I'd been there when Danny had been asked to give up his cool London graphic design job to take over the mill. His dad was wired up to machines, an unsavoury grey pallor about him. Think about all those people we've known for years who would lose their jobs, he was told. It was emotional blackmail at its worst. But I always knew he'd take over the business, not because he had a thing for stationery but because he had heart, he was driven by his unwavering love for others over himself and that made me love him all the more.

'You don't think it's too much though? All the sexual pictures?'

Ro shakes her head very slowly.

'It's the human form, lovely. It's all very placid imagery too. Trust me I'm an artist, I've seen the whole spectrum of where this can go…' She stands up and picks a book called *Erotica Masters* from the bookshelf, turning to the page of a woman giving herself head. I'm pretty sure such contortionism would require the removal of a few ribs and her tongue would need to have the ability of corkscrew, but I study the picture with new eyes. Sure enough, Danny's work doesn't veer into surrealism or the sexually violent or kinky.

'Honey, there's a difference too between erotic art and pornography. To me, a lot of Danny's images are not meant to arouse. They are born of appreciation, observation. They're actually quite tame. I knew someone once who was into vomit.'

Ro sits there very calmly as she says this, almost as if she's telling me an item on her shopping list. She reads my lax jaw.

'His name was Gustav. He was Latvian and a fetishist. There were all sorts of rubber and adornments involved.' I realise Ro has just burst a bubble.

'But I thought you and Ru…' For the longest time I'd always assumed they were childhood sweethearts skipping through cornfields, who'd bestowed each other's hearts to one another from year dot.

Ro smiles broadly. 'We went to university, we went on breaks. It was necessary when you're young and full of sexual curiosity. I spent that year in Berlin where I got all my piercings and almost lost all my hair from the number of times I bleached it. We both experimented sexually. Ru was very into men at one point. I thought I lost him to the other side. Went out with a gorgeous Liverpudlian called Greg.'

I love how matter of fact she is about everything. Ro sips her tea looking out the window as Ru entertains the children in one of the large fields outside. Despite all those distractions, they got their curiosities sated, they had their fun, and there was a point where they gravitated back together and carried on having that conversation, building that intimacy into marriage and beyond. It's a modern-day love story. That includes a vomiting Latvian. 'But now, do you go there… do you still experiment?' I ask.

Ro seems surprised. 'Lovely, sex is a constant experiment, no? Finding those positions and things that someone likes. It's a work in progress. Sometimes I feel intensely connected to Ru on so many levels. Other times, I'm lying there wondering how we've spent twenty years together and he's still working out where my clitoris is.'

I choke on my tea. It could actually be a bit of nettle.

'We tried tantric for a while, sex outdoors. Ru had a thing for feet at one point. It comes and goes in waves, the foot thing actually.'

My expression says everything. I am brought back to the very beginning of this business when the thought of having a monster dildo in my foof scared the bejesus out of me. I can't imagine a size nine stuck up my lady parts. Not least Danny's with his fungal toenail issue.

'But you guys still have sex, right? I am sure you have your things,' she says. She gives me a look that tells me *You are free to do as you wish, I won't judge, my husband sticks his feet up my fanny.*

I nod. We used to have a go with sex toys though I wasn't always keen on the element of surprise and the fact they often induced thrush. Maybe that was part of the problem, maybe Danny and I didn't have a *thing* anymore.

'How often do you have sex?' I ask.

'Depends, doesn't it? Once a week if we're lucky.'

Oh. My face says it all. I think about all the things I do once a week: do a white wash, take out the bin, shave my armpits, sign a homework diary. All things that take priority over sex.

'You seem a little worried, hun. You're internalising again. This has nothing to do with your sex life.'

'But… maybe this is him expressing some sort of sexual frustration?' I open up a notebook to a picture of a group situation.

Ro laughs, a little too hysterically. 'Trust me, the last person I'd imagine in this sort of situation is our Danny.' We both cock our heads to one side to study the many limbs.

'Lilac. Remember her? She was into all sorts, mostly the group thing.'

I'd met Lilac once back in the summer of Ro and Ru's house raising. Danny had been trying to convince me to move here so brought me to the Lakes to show that we could have a life building houses and gambolling across the sun-drenched dales like Heathcliff and Kate frigging Bush. Lilac's hair matched her name and she wasn't keen on bras so caused quite the commotion when asked to mallet in some tent pegs.

'She lives in Staveley with a fifty-year-old man called Colin but last I heard they were also experimenting with thruppling.' I don't know how to react to this given thruppling sounds like something to do with birdsong. She tilts her head to one side. 'They go to sex clubs. The way she describes it, it just sounds like a gaggle of dicks flying about. You wouldn't know who's sticking what where.'

I giggle to hear this smidgeon of disapproval from someone normally so free-spirited and non-judgemental.

'People think we're a bunch of weird hippies, well Colin plays the chuffing didgeridoo.'

I smile. I hope that's not a euphemism.

'Are you worried about what people will think?' she asks. I shake my head. I've never been one to bother with people's opinion.

'This is nothing. Behind closed doors, people get up to all sorts and far worse than what Danny's doing. Just look at our school gate. I know at least one mum up there having an affair, one experimenting with lesbianism and a dad whose Prince Albert gave him gangrene.'

I sit there, slack jawed. One of the dads has his bellend pierced? 'But you don't even talk to anyone at the school gate.'

'You're right. Half of them are toxic but I talk to you, lovely. And my ears work perfectly well,' she says, smiling. I think which dad it might be. My bet's on the one with the funny running style from sports day.

'Oh, and Sarah the childminder. Her Jez is a complete manwhore. Though I knew that from when we were at school together.'

'Really?' I reply disappointedly.

She nods. 'It's always shocked me that she's stayed with a man like that, void of any sort of worth. Makes you wonder what's going on behind that awful facade she puts on.'

I feel immediate twangs of sympathy for Sarah but also confusion that any woman would want to go near Jez. He looks like a potato with legs.

'But it proves my point. Who knows what secrets lie behind any four walls, what sex people are having? It's the last taboo really and it's essentially the most natural thing in the world.'

I take in her wisdoms and stare out the window watching children emerge from the trees and head back towards the house.

'At least we know that behind Captain Mintcake isn't some cheating pervy twat,' says Ro to prove a final point. 'It's our Danny. Boring old Danny.'

I'll allow her to call him boring. We both smile. Maybe she's right. The door to the living room swings open and Zenith stands there covered in mud to the tops of his knees and holding something feathered and bloody.

'Mama, we killed a pigeon! Daddy said we can pluck out the feathers and try and cook it!'

This may be my cue to leave but soon Rufus enters with the other kids, followed by the other reason that I'm here. Stu. He comes in cradling Polly whose cheeks are flushed from the cold. When I first arrived, he spirited her away outside in some vain attempt to try and avoid me but now he's back. I hop to a standing position and hobble over to Ru as he comes over to embrace me as Ru always does, sandwiching little River in his sling between us.

Don't look at Ru's feet. Don't look at his feet.

'Beautiful day! Next time, get Danny and your girls up here and we can all go out together,' Ru says.

Ro watches Stu and me and senses the friction immediately. 'For Pete's sake, just hug this out already.'

I laugh. Stu does not look impressed. I've not seen him since he stormed out of my house in a huff and called me a bitch in the midst of a mid-life crisis.

'Where have you been sleeping?' I ask.

'Ru and Ro let me doss in the caravan.'

'It's nearly winter.'

'It's fine.'

Polly looks up at him and strokes his chin. He pretends to bite one of her fingers and she giggles.

I'm supposed to be here to clear the air. Of course, this would be easier were I allowed to talk about the circumstances of what happened: your brother is an erotic artist under the pseudonym of Captain Mintcake but I've been told to keep this a secret and breaking Danny's confidence would only make things worse. I need to apologise but like all good people, will not budge until he does it first. Maybe I can reach a compromise.

'You should come back and stay with us. The girls would love to have you there. Danny would too.'

He seems surprised. I won't say anything more than that. Even if he doesn't want to apologise then I've done the decent thing by extending an invitation back into my house. He seems sheepish and too darned right. I, however, said a few misplaced things myself in my anger. I also threw some flowers at him. Maybe I'll start there.

'I am also sorry I threw those flowers at you.'

Ru and Ro are nodding their heads at my openly contrite ways. Stu still stands using the baby as some sort of human shield.

'I thought you wouldn't want me back,' he says.

It's my turn to be surprised. I'm not that much of a bitch. He misread the situation, I couldn't be truthful and we both said regretful, hurtful things. I wasn't the sort of person who'd turn it into some sort of family feud. Life was too short.

'Stu, you're family. You're Danny's brother. Come back and be with the girls.'

'So, you're fine with everything that happened with Emma? I mean, it was just really sudden and we were drunk...'

I turn my head to one side. Ro closes her eyes at the treaty negotiations breaking down somewhat. What was that now? He was drunk? My sister? The expression on my face says it all. I will for Polly's little baby hand to give him a slapping.

'Tell me.'

'That fella she were with had gone back. We went out for bevy before I came here.'

There's a brief pause as I see him clutch Polly that bit closer.

'One turned too many and we got chatting – about her divorce and stuff… And then we just did it.'

'Just did it?'

He nods.

'Where?'

Gill would have been at our house and my girls would have been there too.

'Round the back of the squash club.'

Now that better not be a euphemism. Ru is doing his best to hold in schoolboy giggles. Stu's doing it again, isn't he? Making my sister look like some common backstreet slapper. For one, she's only just out of a messy divorce but also my serious, strait-laced sister. I've seen Stu in action. I've seen him use that Morton charm to prey on the emotionally vulnerable and do his cool wink thing so they jump into his bed. He would have instigated this. I am beyond furious. Why didn't Emma tell me? The shame, no doubt. Poor Emma.

'She were well up for it. It's not like I took advantage.' And there he goes again. 'She's an attractive single lady, it's not like we did anything wrong.'

'She's my sister. Beth was my sister. Lucy was my sister. Shall I give Grace a call? Perhaps then you can accomplish the Callaghan Grand Slam?'

I realise that this is the wrong phrase to have emerged from my lips. Ru ushers his little ones into the kitchen whilst Ro attempts to umpire the fracas.

'I never shagged Beth. We just had a snog and a fondle. And if memory serves, I've never given you one either.'

'You are carrying your niece. Your brother's daughter. Shut your face!'

Polly's glance shuttles between this verbal game of tennis. She's wondering what side to pick. The lady who breastfed her for eight months but is looking slightly purple with rage or the man carrying her with the strokeable facial hair. I glare at Stu. Maybe it's the disrespect to me that hurts the most. Did he do this to get back at me for apparently showing contempt towards his brother? Some sort of sibling payback?

'Ro, seriously… who does this?'

She puts her hands up so as to leave her out of the argument.

'Oh, give over. I wouldn't touch you with a shitty stick.'

'Stu, please. Don't be a tosser…' pleads Ro.

'No, she can't come at me with all her sanctimony. You know what she accused Danny of doing? My brother! Spreading lies about him!'

'I said nothing. You assumed—'

'Do you know how much Danny loves you? Do you? I don't think you do.'

'Who are you to be talking about my marriage?'

'It's Danny, he's a good'un. You know that.'

'Good'un? Well, you know what your darling brother gets up to? He draws cocks! Lifelike cocks and vaginas and sex stuff. And he buys dildos online. Dildos that are in my actual house.'

Stu looks at me like I've officially lost the plot. A small person stands at the kitchen door.

'Mummy, what's a dildo?' asks Zenith. We all freeze.

'It's a fake penis, darling,' replies Ro very calmly. Zenith stands there taking it all in.

'Why does Danny need a new one? Has his fallen off?'

Chapter Eight

Since the whole Mintcake reveal, all my dreams involve sex. Except they're not *those* sorts of dreams. Tonight, I am Anastasia Steele in *Fifty Shades of Grey*. I'm the reporter come to Christian Grey's penthouse office in search of a searing, honest interview and I'm wearing the sort of sharp tailoring I used to don when I was a Londoner, hair and make-up on point, as the youngsters would say. I strut about as I come out of the lift and sit cross-legged in his waiting room sipping on an espresso. Christian and I make eye contact as he leaves his office and I bite my lip which gives him an instant erection to the titters of his reception staff. He follows me in.

'Why, this is quite an office you have, Mr Grey. Thank you for seeing me today.'

'I'd like to see far more of you, Miss Callaghan. It is Miss, isn't it?'

I put my expensive Italian leather handbag down on the floor and start to undress. His eyes widen. With horror. I look down. Holy nuggets. I look down to see that I'm wearing the worst pair of knickers in my arsenal. They are reserved for when I'm on my period or need to hold in my gut with a nice dress: flesh-coloured granny pants. Pubes sprout out the top and down my thighs. I'm also wearing a nursing bra; not even the nice one – the greying one that has a yellow patch of stained milk.

'I think we're done here, Miss Callaghan. If you don't mind, I'd prefer to do this interview by phone.'

I run out of the office in shame and get to the lift realising I've forgotten to put my clothes back on.

I wake up, slightly clammy. Grabbing my phone, I seek out the time. 4.35 a.m. Next to me the bed is empty. Where's Danny? He's not particularly happy with me given I brought Stu home earlier. Stu who now knew about Captain Mintcake. This resulted in merciless ridicule, dead arms, headlocks and Danny threatening to tell everyone about how Stu once shagged the fifty-year-old landlady of a local pub just so he'd get a free carvery dinner. To be fair, telling Stu did mean we got to clear the air and he now understood why there were tears and accusations. However, in return, he also told me what happened with Emma. I got a glimpse of an apology. I berated Emma, telling her to check her bits.

Normally, I wouldn't overact at Danny's absence – when Polly wakes up in the night he often ends up passing out on the floor next door, propped by a giant George Pig pillow. But maybe he's downstairs drawing sex things. Maybe this is when he does this stuff, when I'm asleep. I'm not sure how he'd manage it now though with his brother on the sofa bed in the living room.

I suddenly hear the door creak open and pretend to close my eyes. It's Danny in his pants, dressing gown casually draped over his shoulders, holding Polly close to his chest. He goes to stand by the bedroom window and does that little baby jig he does. He also sings. It's the only time he'll sing, to his girls; some nonsensical lyric to a made-up tune. In the twilight, I catch Polly's little hand reach up to his cheek and he kisses it. I sigh and he turns to try and catch me out.

'What doing Meg the Peg?'

He's on baby patrol. I need to show some sense of alliance. 'Is that my new name?'

'Came up with it myself.'

'What's Polly doing?'

'Woke herself from a coughing fit. She's drifting back.'

He tiptoes out of the room, the sash of his gown dragging on the floor. I hear him settle Polly back in her cot and then the light switch goes as he traipses to the toilet, the sound of him relieving himself. Flush. Tap. Maybe I should pretend to go back to sleep. He returns to the room, sitting on my side of the bed, rearranging covers and the pillow that elevates my leg.

'You in pain? Need some meds?'

I nod. He turns on the bedside light. After popping out some meds he props me up, holding a glass of water to my lips. I have a flash forward to when we're sixty-four.

'I think our ballcock needs replacing, that toilet cistern isn't refilling like it should.'

I don't know how to respond to that. His boxers have a wet patch where he hasn't shaken off completely. He taps my ankle like one would the base of a loaf of bread. There's a look between us. It's nearly 5 a.m. but at some point, we're going to have to talk. We need to dig out a layer of conversation that goes beyond broken toilets and ankles. So far we've just allowed real life to gloss over the issue. We need to fix something else. I go first.

'I'm sorry I told Stu.'

'Done now. I'm sorry he's such a twat sometimes.'

An apology. It's a start.

'Now Stu knows, can we tell your mum too? So she'll stop hating me.'

Danny's eyes read horror. Gill hadn't been quite right with me since she witnessed my fight with Stu. I always knew she'd side with her son but I hated that she thought the worst of me.

'Hate is a strong word. Mum doesn't hate anyone. Even that cat that poos on her begonias. I'll make something up.'

I sit there, confused. Captain Mintcake is out now, right? Or is he going to wear this like a secret identity? Does he think he's Batman? Actually, the thought of a costume is a tad arousing and I think he'd especially go for the idea of a utility belt. However, the problem I have with this whole thing is that it's remaining a secret. I don't want my mother-in-law asking me what we got up to last night and me having to make up some lie when really Danny was putting the finishing touches to a threesome in acrylic.

'I told Emma,' I inform him, in an attempt to wring out some honesty.

He sits up in bed. 'What'd you do that for?'

'Because she's my sister and I was confused, hurt and I wanted her opinion.'

'I thought she were being funny with me when she were here. What she think?'

'She thinks you have a very good anatomical sense of what's going on down there.'

Danny shrugs off the compliment and pauses. He turns to face me in the bed, a fuzzy leg visible and wrapped around the duvet. This was his signature duvet thief move. He's leaving me to make all the moves in this conversation, which builds my resentment. I can feel Danny looking up at me.

Not knowing what to say next, I grab my phone from my bedside table.

'I looked at your Instagram today.'

'Oh?'

'I found a picture that lacks realism.'

'How so?'

I open his Instagram and scroll through for the offending piece.

'This woman making love to her iPhone. That level of moisture would kill a device. She'd have to put it in rice.'

He looks at me strangely.

'It was allegorical, commenting on her love affair with social media.'

I say nothing. Silence.

'What did you talk about with Ro?' he asks.

'What do you think?'

He squirms on the bed.

'I'm just sad you didn't think you could tell me about the Captain. You didn't even tell me you did those art classes with her. We tell each other everything.'

Up to that point, our relationship was underpinned by friendship and we never had problems as such – we always managed to laugh them off. I thought I'd seen everything when it came to Danny. When you're married, you do. You hope that having lived with someone, having been intimate with them and seen them at their lowest ebb – tummy bug saga of 2001, I had to steam clean the mattress – means you know everything. I saw him cry when these daughters of ours were born. He'd seen them emerge from me. I'd cradled him in my arms when he thought his father was dying. When he did the Three Peaks challenge, I helped apply Vaseline to his gooch so he wouldn't chafe.

'I was just embarrassed. I just… didn't know what to think of it myself.'

'Why did you go to the classes?'

'To support Rowan. She invited me along as she only had five people sign up. You and the girls were away. It got me out the house.'

It's comforting to hear that he went to support a friend at least.

'It snowballed from there. I enjoyed having an actual hobby that's not childcare, paper or walking the dog.'

'So it wasn't because we're not having enough sex?' I blurt out a little emotionally. I think back to all that sex talk at Ro's and how it's made me preoccupied with the sort and frequency of sex we've been having. Danny's taken aback by my admission and sits up to look at me. That's the problem with my husband, he always makes great eye contact. He holds your gaze and is never the first person to look away. If they ran a World Cup in it, he'd excel in blinking competitions. It's a look that made me first fall in love with him because it was so reassuring and safe.

'Don't be a silly mare. Not that at all. Just liked drawing it, imagining it. It sparked something. It's not like I was drawing pussies and wanking over them.'

I can't tell if he's lying again. He kisses me on the forehead. We're never normally up at this time of night unless it's with a teething child but it feels like these words need to be said – or at least until my painkillers kick in.

'So how did you know what to draw? I'm assuming you did other sorts of research?'

'I went online, some sites and apps and stuff.'

'Like?'

'There are swinger groups, dating apps, quite a lot going down on Twitter…' I get a little twitchy at the thought of him actively engaging with people.

'Oh. I found out Ems is on Tinder.' I inform him.

Knowing my sister as well as I do, he laughs a little. 'Geez, times have changed. First, she's bonking my brother and now picking up men online. Tinder was one of the apps I used, actually.'

My husband went on Tinder? He senses my unease.

'I set up fake profiles to see how these things worked. I used fake pics, names.'

'What name did you choose?'

'Matthew. I was twenty-seven and a personal trainer.'

I may laugh. 'OK. Did you make jokes about your plank?'

'Naturally.'

I pause for a moment. 'Did women engage with you?'

'A few.'

'Did they send you pictures of their tits? Did you send them pics of your dick? Did you wank over them?' I blurt out nervously, shocked that he's actually engaged with other people.

'No and no… because that would have been wrong. I usually wank in the shower in the morning if I feel the urge.'

We've blurred the lines of right and wrong I feel. I am also now thinking about those times I've found trails of what I've thought were mis-squeezed shampoo in the shower.

Danny continues, 'Research on things like Tinder helped but you forget, I take a walk on the factory floor most days and have banter and a cuppa with some of them lads and it is pure filth. Half of what they tell me is in them pics. And that's how it is these days. They make friends online and hook up for sex.'

'Like prostitution.'

'Like how we used to hook up with people in bars and pubs and clubs except now you don't have to leave your house and waste cash, you just pick someone you like and invite them round for a bit of Netflix and chill.'

I feel strangely prudish.

'So, show me what you did. What your research entailed…'

I'm not sure what I'm suggesting here. Some of it is fuelled by curiosity to educate myself further but a part of me wonders after today's conversation with Ro about whether I need to up my game. It's an experiment in pushing the envelope, in trying to convince him and myself that I am on board with this, that I want to understand this more so it doesn't become an issue in our marriage. I grab my phone and download Tinder. Danny watches me curiously. I can sense he wants to sleep but also understands there's a bit of urgency in me needing some answers to things he's hidden from me for so long. He grabs my phone and creates a profile for me.

'Let me. I'm calling you Olivia, you're thirty and looking for fun. I'll use some stock photo.'

Olivia sounds like the classy sort. He writes some fake bio scattered with emojis. Her Spotify anthem is 'Yellow' by Coldplay.

Done. I press a button and suddenly the Tinderverse starts looking for suitable men to show me. Danny and I sit there in anticipation. Who will they give us? Shite. A picture pops up. They've given me Kevin. I don't believe he's forty-five I'm afraid. Kevin sits there in his front room in a football shirt with a look that says he might want to kill me, eat me and hide the rest of my remains under his patio. Danny gives me a nudge.

'He might be hung like a stallion.'

I flick through his photos.

'There's a lot of pictures of him with his cat.'

'Maybe he's subliminally trying to tell you he's good with pussy.'

We're both laughing.

'So aside from browsing through Tinder, where else did you go?'

'Well, there are all sorts of sites where I could see what people are into: the swingers, the ones into kink, hot wives, cross-dressers. It was insightful. No meet ups, just conversations to see what the landscape is like in sex these days.'

'Hot wives?'

'Ladies whose husbands allow them to hook up with other men.'

'OK then.' I am still dubious as to whether this was alright or whether I've been a prize mug. I distract myself with the men provided before me. Brett is the sort of man I would typically call attractive; that unshaven, lumberjack look. His profile picture is him with a guitar and an eyebrow raised.

'Skinny jeans… not a good look.'

'Hmmm, he's a little bit fit. But I'm thrown that he's twenty-four.'

'He's from Carlisle which should be a warning sign. Are you going to swipe?'

'And engage with these people? Hell no. I'm just window shopping.'

Hello, George, 29 from Cockermouth. The place name alone is promising. I open his profile.

Likes wine, travelling, good food, dogs, health and sleeping. Looking to meet the one.

I laugh. I like that he values his health (don't we all?) and has made it clear he doesn't like bad food. I like the optimism too. I hope you find the one, George. I swipe through a few more pictures.

'Tinder is just the tip of the iceberg though. Look here…' Danny takes my phone off me and logs on to a swingers group. He's in a swingers group? That said, he is not wrong. Whereas Tinder consisted of mostly selfies and middle-aged men in Lycra telling me how tall they were, this is pictures of people in their actual pants. I scroll through some of the profiles.

Looking for GS/BDSM/BBW only. Love queening. Huh?

'What's with all the letters? Is that a medical qualification?'

'Golden showers, bondage, big beautiful women.' The words roll off his tongue. I look at him, curiously. 'I've taught myself some of this terminology given my new line of pastime.'

'Queening?'

'He wants you to sit on his face. He is the throne.'

'Would I have to wear a crown?'

'That would be optional. Or we could pick you up one from Burger King.'

I giggle.

Single looking for couples fun luv going down on a dirty bird filming role play

'Where's the punctuation in that sentence?'

Danny looks over at me confused. Apparently, that's all I got out of that sentence.

'No beating around the bush with this lot. It's all about the sex,' says Danny. 'It's certainly an education.'

I don't know what to think. It seems like Danny wasn't using these sites to get himself aroused and I certainly don't feel anything seeing all these overtly sexual images but it makes me wonder how much my sexual spark has diminished. Given that half of these people want to communicate via Snapchat also makes me feel incredibly old.

I open one of the profiles. Oh my giddy aunt, that's a real life penis. It's of reasonable size. I'm not sure where his pubes are though. This gentleman is not just content with the one though; he displays a half-dozen pictures at different stages of erectness.

'Jesus, you put all these pictures together, it's like he's showing us the different phases of the moon.'

Danny is creased up with laughter. 'Total eclipse.'

In fact all the pictures here may be explicit but also speak of extreme confidence. I'm almost jealous that these people know exactly what they want sexually. I don't even know what I want for dinner most days.

'I don't think I could ever do this…' I mutter.

'Do what?'

'Take pictures of my bits? Stand there in our bathroom mirror and take a picture of my arse?'

'Why not?' Danny asks, confused.

'Well, my angles would be all out and you're going to need some epic filters to make my bits look picture-worthy?'

Danny looks a bit sad for me.

'Nonsense. I'll show you. Get your tits out.'

I give Danny a look that registers both horror and *never*. He smiles.

'You have a great rack.'

I like the compliment but even I know that motherhood has ravaged my boobs a little. There are hints of stretch marks and flappiness and they most certainly need a bra during the day to give them a bit of a boost. Danny doesn't seem to get the message. He leans over and puts his hands to my sides and takes off my T-shirt, tracing a finger down my side. I wasn't wearing a bra in bed anyway but now I sit there topless, and frankly, a little cold. My nipples say that much. Danny flicks one playfully.

'Oi!'

'Lie down for me.'

I giggle nervously.

He's smiling and puts my arms down by my sides so it props my boobs up from the side, meaning they don't spill into my armpits. He stands over me in the bed and takes a picture.

'What are you doing?'

'Having fun?'

He comes back to lie back next to me, has a cheeky crop, adds a filter and then shows me the picture.

'See, beautiful.'

Danny puts an arm around me and kisses me on the shoulder. I can't quite tell if he's being facetious or actually paying me a compliment but he looks at the picture for a moment too long. Don't you dare make that your wallpaper.

'We'll start slow. Tomorrow I want your legs wide apart and we'll stick that dildo up you. That'd be a pic.'

'It'd look like I've got an arm hanging out of it.' We are both in hysterics now. You idiot. Danny snuggles into me. The last time we shared phone and bed space like this was to watch *Line of Duty* on a tablet with a packet of chocolate Bourbons and a bottle of wine. Across his face is an expression I've come to know and adore: there are lines around his eyes, crinkled with laughter, a broad and warm smile away from the usual scowl.

I have to give him the benefit of the doubt now, don't I? That he didn't do all his research looking for kicks and affairs and quiet wanks in the living room over pictures of people's private parts. To be honest, I still don't know what to think about it all. Have we sorted anything? Have we touched on the fact this was kept secret from me for so long? I want to ask him so many questions. I want to drown the twilight in them and talk until the sun comes up. Who do all those vaginas belong to in your sketches? But maybe these answers will trickle in at a later time. Maybe I want too much, too soon. Because he's here. He's next to me exuding warmth, rubbing a stubbly chin over my bare shoulder. There is a desire to still be by my side, and talk and laugh and connect in all those tiny ways.

I pull him towards me and look him in the eye, trying to draw out that same level of intensity he gives me. Has anything tonight turned me on? No. But I need you, Danny. I need you here, next to me. I want to feel like some pictures are not going to get in the way and for whatever it all means, I'm not going anywhere. I just want him; I want to be held, to feel him.

He studies my face, looking a little sad. It'll be light soon and those little people and real life will get in the way of us ever finishing this conversation. 'I am sorry. I am sorry if this has made you feel bad. You're my wife, my magnificent wife. It all means nothing.'

And this is what's arousing, this is what I need to hear. He kisses me gently, moving his lips to the side of my chin, down my neck, our feet touching at the end of the bed, with caution obviously given my fragile leg. But it's not broken. He does that strange manoeuvre where he tries to kick off his own underpants by lunging his crotch up into the air. I laugh, let him kick them to the end of the bed and nestle himself close to me. Let's take this slowly but it really isn't broken.

Chapter Nine

'Tea?'

If I had a pound for the number of times anyone up North has asked me if I wanted a cup of tea, I could buy that island off Richard Branson and possibly another one on top of it. No one ever refuses a cup of tea either so it always feels bad form to say no. This usually leaves your thirst quenched but is often followed by being out in the cold with a very full bladder.

'Why not? Cheers, Tim.'

I'm at work today for the first time in a fortnight since ankle-sex-gate (Danny's name for that little episode). I'm back at my desk putting my husband's hobby to one side, trying to write an article about a local school raising money for some new football goals because their last ones were stolen by thieving gits, leaving the poor kids kicking balls in between a couple of bins. I've been given photos of the year six boys looking forlornly towards a barren school playing field. Life could be worse. For them, and me. I could have been given the football to report on, which is Tim's allocated task. Kendal Town FC's nickname is the Mintcakes which could have made things a little awkward. Bloody mint cake. It's just like eating a giant chewable Polo. It's the least sexual thing in the world and now every time it's mentioned all I can think about are phalluses. Thanks, Danny.

Speak of the devil, a text pops up on my phone:

What doing?

The furore that all Danny's sketches caused has simmered down. I guess the difference now is that he doesn't hide away to draw them anymore. I'll be doing the dishes and he'll be behind me rendering a bellend in charcoal. Once he accosted me at the kitchen table and turned me around. It was quite a moment and I thought that we might be engaging in something quite erotic despite the fact I was wearing Disney print Primark pyjamas. Alas, no. He was just drawing something and had to figure out the configuration of limbs. Turns out what he had in mind would've meant my kneecaps being able to rotate at 360 degree angles.

Important journalistic shit. You?

Paper

Are you really doing paper or drawing porn at your desk?

Yes. Drawing a series about a wife who sexts her husband from her office.

Does she put bulldog clips on her nipples and pleasure herself with a hole punch?

No one puts a hole punch up their fanny unless they have a bucket minge

I do it all the time

No comment. I got pizzas in for tea

Yum. Laters xx

I stare down at my phone. The dialogue has always been like this, with a casual affectionate cajoling, but now it has an added dimension. I don't mind. But I wonder how much there is to say about this. I've just accepted it for now. I've wanted to avoid any more conflict so have just tried to see it as an added part of our fabric, almost relieved that it wasn't the worst-case scenario. He's still here, with us. We're still married. People go through much worse; true sorrow through circumstances they can or can't control. This is just pictures. For now, to seal over the cracks, I can make out that everything is fine.

'Meg! Wonderful to have you back! How's the leg?'

Diana's face booms through the office like a comedy foghorn and a few colleagues jump up in their seats. I pretend I wasn't looking at my phone on company time and hold a thumbs up. Diana claps in the same manner of an enthusiastic gym teacher.

'I need everyone on editorial in the meeting room in twenty minutes please.'

I look over at Kirsty, who is compiling obituaries and catches my eye over her computer. I lied. Maybe things could be worse and

I could be prioritising whose death is more worthy of the column inches. 'Rumour is Di's got a huge article on the go,' she tells me. 'She was approached by a national.'

'Is it about the Crook Road development and all the council payoffs?'

Kirsty shrugs. It's not the most sensational story, but Di has uncovered evidence of councillors taking backhanders and so I can understand how in the current political climate, it may be of interest. Certainly beats stolen goal posts.

My phone bleeps again:

> *I don't get these bags lined up at the door. Do I have to get in the water at the swimming class? I don't have trunks.*

Stu is still with us and as payment and penance for having slept with my sister, he's paying his dues and helping us with the school runs and extracurricular activities. I'm not sure if this is a good thing. It seems he's very good at giving our girls biscuits but has yet to master how to put on a nappy or put the toilet seat down.

> *Blue bag with butterflies is ballet, 4–4.30 p.m. at the Town Hall. Purple drawstring bag is swimming, 6–6.30 p.m. at the Leisure Centre. Other bag is a change bag for P. You can get in the water if u want but you may be asked to leave.*

> *Who's P?*

> *Polly*

Just pulling your chain

Don't do that

He replies with a thumbs up. They'll be doing ballet in their swimming costumes, won't they?

A cup of tea appears on my desk.

'Three sugars and there were Nice biscuits today. Did you know that you say it "niece" not "nice"? Apparently, they're named after the French town.'

'That's proper pub quiz trivia knowledge right there, Tim.'

He smiles and props himself next to my desk. I've seen Tim with new eyes since he came round to the house with gifts when I was incapacitated. Before, Danny and I would joke that he kept me close because he was crushing over me, but the gesture he made was real and honest. I don't think he fancies me and it'd be weird if he did, but I quite like his sincerity and the fact he brought me Minstrels when I was broken. I've liked people for far less. We also have that common bond where we both relocated to this part of the country. I was lucky in that when we moved here, I inherited friends and family and could start friendships at school gates but he's been dropped into a local newspaper in a small town knowing no one. I feel for him, recalling the memory of what it's like to ache with loneliness in a new place. It's made me promise to try harder with him.

'Good weekend?'

He freezes hearing me initiate some idle chit-chat.

'I... ummm, I've joined this walking club. It was cool. You?'

'You know… the kids and family and stuff. You should come around and meet the girls sometime actually? We have Danny's brother, Stu staying with us too. You'd like him, he's younger and cooler than me and arguably more fun.'

He shifts his eyes awkwardly.

'OK?'

That was easier than I thought. There's a moment of silence as we sip our tea. I study his face. There is a lot between us that is unsaid. You possibly saw a sex shopping site on my phone that morning at work. But you did save my life when I choked on a biscuit. Then you visited me with flowers and chocolates. I still don't know if your liking of me is professional or personal. But then again you're completely non-threatening. And you make me tea.

'You're cool.'

I'm not sure if he's means that or whether it's just him being sweet but I'll take it. I am cool. Wassup.

'I was, back in the day, maybe less so now… so… how are you finding Kendal? Have you sorted the dodgy pubs from the good ones?'

He laughs. 'There's not much of a scene, eh?'

'Unfortunately not. And are you dating anyone?'

Again, he looks surprised by my line of questioning.

'I'm seeing people… nothing serious.'

'Just asking… as a curious friend.' I emphasise that last word to let him know the boundaries but also that I'm someone he can talk to. He relaxes slightly.

'I'm out there having fun. Just don't want anything serious. When I was at uni, I was going out with someone for a while but we're not together any more so… yeah…'

He talks about the ex with a touch of mist in his eyes. I don't pry further. But a lad this young and reasonably handsome surely shouldn't be so preoccupied with lost love and broken hearts. The benefit of fifteen years on this kid is that you want to pass on that knowledge. Not like the sort of drunken advice one would give a teen babysitter, but you want to tell him to have fun. Life will soon be serious and filled with children and mortgages and your life not being your own so go out there and do it all. Go out and drink and dance till you're drenched through with sweat, take cheap flights to Europe, experiment with your hair, pick up a stranger on the night bus home and shag them in the kitchen of your shared flat. Have that sort of carefree sex all about pleasure and gratification, when it isn't about love. Be able to look back on it fondly while you're sitting at your office desk and remember that person you once were. Don't sit here with an old hag like me eating office supply mega pack biscuits and drinking tea from a mug marked with Margaret's name from accounts. I don't tell him all this of course.

'Well, you're young. Jen from advertising is single.' I try to think up some alternatives.

He stops for a moment. Jen is lovely. She's partial to coloured knitwear and I think she makes her own earrings but I've been out with her on a work do and she likes a bit of karaoke and can hold her drink. It's a good start.

'Is Jen the one who has the handbag in the shape of a cat face?'

I nod. His silence tells me that may not be happening. We smile at each other. He's still studying my face when Neal comes over to our desks.

'So, what's this about then? This big article?' If I'm Lois Lane then Neal is a wannabe Perry White. He has none of the power mind but he has a ruddy face, rolled up sleeves and drinks an abnormal amount of coffee which always makes him seem slightly on edge.

'I have no idea. Crook Road?'

'That old chestnut. Nope, this is bigger than that. C'mon troops.'

He gestures to the few people heading for the meeting room.

'Kirsty said it was a big story…' I tell Tim as Neal plods through the office.

'Kirsty thought the new Costa opening on the High Street was a big story.'

I laugh. He made a joke. He grabs our mugs and in return, I pick up some pens and paper for him, pocketing the last of the biscuits. Tim covered for me in my fortnight away too so I've a newfound respect for him. He finished and edited some of my articles and demonstrated an articulate command of language and facts. We could be an awesome double act. And look at him carrying my tea. That's the sign of a good upbringing. That doesn't make me sound old at all.

We head over to the meeting room where Diana has set up piles of printouts. Our editorial team is a select few, of which I'm privileged to be a part. Next to myself and Tim, there's Neal who doesn't like a chair but prefers to prop himself up on a windowsill and manspread himself. He prefers a cultural interest story set on a hill whereas Lisa and her statement beaded necklaces like to hang around Carlisle Crown Court finding wrong'uns who sell drugs out of prams. I'm the token Southerner, also known as the one who has all the babies, the advocate for arts and education. Tim's on sport. Di dips in and out but likes big debate and opinion pieces.

'So, what's this all about then, Di… there've been whispers, you know?' Neal enquires. The boss closes the door. She's gone for a comfortable slack today with a striped shirt and pearls. She always looks serious. I know she's married and has children but she's the sort whose spice rack is in alphabetical order. Go on Di, live a little. Get your ground ginger mixed up with your chilli flakes.

'This isn't about the job cuts at the paper, is it?' Neal continues.

I look at Tim for a moment. There were cuts? Was this something I missed from being away? As much as I joked about the small-town trappings of my job, it was also a source of earnings for me, a newspaper that fit around my life and for which I had great affection. Was this some sort of group cull? Neal has three sons to get through university so is more on edge than usual, his eyeballs literally vibrating in their sockets.

'Oh god, Neal, no. Our jobs are safe. Just the rumour mill going into overdrive after Prestwich ordered that stupid redesign.'

She starts passing around the handouts. Neal's question about job security still in the air, I take a cursory glance at them before nibbling on a biscuit.

'So I've been approached by two sources now: one a tabloid newspaper and the other, one of those gossip mags, both raising a potentially interesting Kendal-based story and they were hoping we could get involved, maybe do some investigative work.'

Lisa looks at the printout, goes a bit blush and covers her face. Is this Crook Road? What have those councillors been up to now?

'What the hell is this, Di?' huffs Neal.

'Well, apparently, this stuff is everywhere at the moment. It's generated a huge following. Publicists, promoters, even art buyers are desperate to find out who it is behind this.'

Tim is giggling under his breath. Neal throws the handout down on the table and walks out of the room. 'Not for me, Di.'

I pick up his discarded page. It's a collection of pictures. It's cocks. It's all cocks. Shit. Shit, shit, shit. I know this cock. Why are they here? Lisa has taken a pen to hers. She's literally highlighting the willies. Tim is still laughing under his breath. It can't be, can it?

'So, I've studied a fair bit. Suffice to say, it's all a little racy but the publishers think that the artist is local to these parts. He goes under the pseudonym of – and you'll love this – Captain Mintcake.'

There are sniggers around the table. I laugh, probably louder than I should. Di gives me a look. 'Right, ridiculous?'

Bloody effing mother of crap. I can feel sweat pockets start to form in my bra. I know him. I'm married to him. I need to do the best acting I've ever done in my life, even better than when I was a shepherd in my school nativity thirty years ago. Crap bags.

'Do you really know he's local? How many tourists come through here, it could be someone passing through? A fan of the area?' I say.

Di nods. 'True, but sources have also linked this up to a local PO box. Definitely someone who's at least lived here for quite a while. I'm thinking a genuine local. Some of the pics are drawn in local settings. That plus the username is a giveaway.'

I feel a little sick. If I threw up now, it'd just be a mess of coconut-flavoured Nice biscuits. What the hell is this? Need to put her off the scent.

'We're also assuming man, perhaps Captain Mintcake is a woman?'

Di looks impressed by my thorough line of questioning.

'True, and these are all things that I want you to look at. Maybe the Captain is part of a local artists' group? It'll be a bit grubby but check out these local dogging sites too – perhaps this is where it all started?'

I want to stand up. NO! This is just a man with a good imagination. He doesn't convene in car parks looking for hook-ups and sucking random strangers off by the conifers.

Tim interjects, 'You want us to go dogging?' Lisa laughs under her breath.

'No. Just investigate – do what you do? Who is it? Is this person a primary school teacher, do they stack shelves in Asda or is it the parish vicar?'

'So an exposé?'

My heart aches now, panic darting through me. Di has just assumed he is a pervert and more would do the same if this were ever to come out. It could ruin the family business. We have really young daughters. I know how newspapers work. We'd plaster his name across the pages with family pictures and question this man's integrity and everything he's about. I tear up slightly at the thought.

'Realistically, this is more of a way to help people make contact. Mr Mintcake is ignoring all private messages and letters…'

'Captain Mintcake…' I correct her. I shouldn't have done that.

'He has a quarter of a million followers across different websites and social media platforms. He draws, he paints and he's built a fan base.'

Say how many? How did I not know this? I was so busy looking at the penises, I didn't register this information. That's like the population of Sunderland. That's a shed load of people. They're all liking his stuff, they're all fans. Danny has fans. I sit silently as Tim makes notes next to me.

'So, I don't know enough about these things. It may not always be the most pleasant of research – let's look at the underground scene here in and around the Lakes. I'm sure there's all sorts of sordid shenanigans going on. Of course, be safe and don't do things you don't want to do but people just want to know who this Mintcake person is…'

Captain Mintcake, I mumble under my breath. Crapping hell, Danny – you even chose a moniker that was completely Lakes inspired. Why couldn't you draw porn on the Tube or in a Geordie accent and throw people off? I can't think. My only urge is protective, to guard the man I love.

'And there are rewards, finders' fees in this for us.'

Tim looks up from his paper. 'So we're like bounty hunters?'

Di gives him admonishing looks. She's still getting to grips with his youth and at times fails to get the sense of humour.

'No, Tim. The money on the table for the big reveal on this is massive. He's played this so well – everyone is speculating about who he is. Like that secret artist who draws on the walls. This man has the potential to be the next big thing in social media, art, he could go into publishing – the extent of the online following speaks volumes. We're talking big money – one million pounds on the table to start.'

I can't quite read my own reaction but I think it veers between catatonic and someone sitting on my chest. Lisa and Tim are scribbling down notes. I nod and pretend that went in.

'So someone who's lived here for all of their lives?' Lisa asks.

This is good. Danny did live in London for a while.

'Or maybe someone who was born here…'

Damn you, Tim. Di's words still echo in my ears. A quarter of a million followers, one million pounds. It's all an alien currency to me. This isn't a hobby anymore. This is the prospect of paid work, something that Danny could do that would satisfy his heart – and sort us for life. It makes me beam with pride and excitement for him though obviously I don't show it. I try to sit here cool and aloof but in my head I'm thinking about booking a Disneyworld holiday. We could have breakfast with Mickey.

'I've got it!' exclaims Lisa. My blood runs cold for a second. Lisa is a decent journalist but I hope my face didn't give it away.

'Must be Neal!' There are peals of laughter throughout the room. I join in reluctantly. Thank balls for that.

'So, someone born in the Lakes, possibly a man who could be involved in some sort of sexual kinkiness/artists' groups… narrows it down…' Lisa says.

'Well, do what you can. It'll make for an amusing piece in any case. Meg—'

I snap out of my trance. I can't breathe, let alone speak.

'Yes?' I squeak.

'I understand that this might be difficult for you to take on…'

'Why's that then?' My muscles freeze up.

'It's all a bit distasteful and you have young children. It may be the wrong thing for you but that's your call.'

I look down at the pictures in front of me. There's one where a man is exploding like a jet wash. I feel nervous, a little sick. But the only way to protect Danny is to take this on and try and deflect Lisa and Tim.

'It's fine, Di… really…'

She nods and marches out of the room like she does. Lisa follows, leaving Tim sitting next to me. I pretend to scribble notes.

'Well, this is a bit different to football scores.'

'Yes, it is.' I can feel a ring of sweat forming on my forehead. Soon, it will leave a tide of foundation creeping down my face and shame the truth out of me.

What do you call a Captain's wife? I've seen all the pictures, all of them. Evidently, Danny's talents mean we're sat on a goldmine but it's not about that right now, is it? This is about protecting our family. Tim is staring right at me. Does he know? How would he know? He may have seen me looking at sex sites.

'Are you doing anything now?' Like, you said I should come over – maybe we can chat about this over dinner. Sorry, that sounds like I'm inviting myself around. I know you have kids.'

I look at his spritely face; this is huge to him. It's a story not talking about penalties, free kicks and lower league football teams, something where he doesn't have to sit in a cagoule in a wet and windy pitch-side press box on a Saturday morning. I think about the young lad who brought me flowers to my bedside. But I also think about a chance to take the lead on this, to keep him close and have his prying eyes cast in the wrong direction.

'Do you like pizza?' *You should come and meet the man in person.*

Chapter Ten

There are many things I dislike about my husband. Marriage throws up all those minor flaws and foibles and magnifies them completely so they become things you slightly obsess about; things that would see you murder him in his sleep if you could. He snores on a scale that could shift tectonic plates and he eats ice lollies strangely, inhaling a lot of air on sucking, making this horrendous vacuum-like noise. Never have I wanted to murder him more than in the summer when he has his chops around a rocket lolly.

Today, he's doing that stupid thing where he's not answering any of my calls or texts. The Lakes is notoriously bad for phone reception, but once he checks his device, he'll see I've left thirteen missed calls and twenty-three texts, one of which I had to write in the work bathroom and is completely nonsensical due to autocorrect, my nerves and Margaret from accounts who was hovering outside my cubicle. *It's not hard Danny, just pick up the bloody phone.*

I sometimes envisage moments where I could be in real peril, hanging off the edge of a cliff face with Mr T and I'd call Danny and nothing, and then I'd fall to my death screaming out, 'Just bloody answer iiiitttt…' Pick up, pick up, pick up. Let me tell you everything I've just learned and prepare yourself for the fact a young man who knows about Captain Mintcake is coming over tonight. And the fact we could be millionaires. This could be everything. We could have fitted wardrobes and do things that millionaires do like pick up the weekly shop in Harrods. But no, he ignores me. If he's left his phone at home then I'll fricking sucker punch him in the throat.

With an hour to kill before I head home, I attempt to do some research by way of Google. Diana wasn't wrong. Danny was a member of a few sites that I was unaware of and all that connectivity meant that everything was being shared and liked and followed across quite a broad range of social media sites too. In a market that was saturated with artists, he'd captured the imagination of a loyal fan base and amassed a following that most could only dream about. All by accident of course, too. I don't think Danny wanted this when he set out to explore this creative endeavour. The pseudonym wasn't some clever marketing ruse but just a way for him to avoid the attention. I have a few websites out on my computer when Tim comes over, coat on and ready for pizza. Maybe this is the point where I come up with an excuse: migraine, puking kid, home emergency.

'Are you OK with dogs? I have a dog. And a cat.'

Please be allergic.

'Totally. I didn't know you had a dog? What's his name?'

'Mr T.'

'Like T-Bone?'

'No, like the eighties dude with the Mohawk.' He goes blank. I feel bloody old.

'Are you browsing the websites then? Found anything interesting?'

'Some of his spelling is a bit off,' I say.

Tim nods. 'He seems to have an aversion to apostrophes. Though I reckon he's not young, definitely older. Trying to work out if he's single or married?'

'Single, I'd say. And I'm going to explore the female angle too.'

I may as well be walking my dog and throwing balls in different directions so he won't go and roll in piles of fox poo. I get rid of all my browser windows. I glare at my phone. Effing nothing. Stu is also not responding. It's a Morton brother thing, must be.

'Why single? You think these are manifestations of fantasies then? Could be repressed married sexual frustration,' he says.

I pause. Mainly because I've just stood up and have to do that manoeuvre where I have to adjust the gusset on my tights but deep down, that thought still lingers. Even though Danny denies it's anything to do with us, it could be a subconscious thing. Maybe all these feelings and desires lay beneath the surface.

'Maybe.'

'Am I OK just rocking up to yours? Do I need to bring anything?' he asks.

'Wine.' I respond, a little too quickly. He smiles. We're going to need it.

I spend a deliberately long time selecting and purchasing wine this evening, hoping it might give Danny a few more minutes to call me. Of course, he doesn't make any contact but it does lead me to appear like a wine snob to young Tim as I make him read every label on the shelves looking for something aromatic and woody. As we stand in front of our house cradling the precious bottles, I take a deep breath. You can tell Stu's been in charge of the household as every conceivable light is on and I can hear the excitable screams of girls running up and down the hallway.

'It's a bit of a madhouse, you know?'

He laughs. 'Youngest of four. It'll be fine.'

I smile and open the door. As soon as I step in the house, I'm accosted by Eve whose hair is washed but not dried or combed so it makes her look vaguely like a little feral beast child we acquired in the woods. She wears a vest and knickers and a superhero cape. I lift her on my hip.

'Mummy! You have returned! Who are you?'

Tim smiles at the regal if slightly forward greeting.

'Eve, this is Tim from the office. He's come round for pizza. Pyjamas? Hair dryer?'

'Uncle Stu didn't know how to work it so he said I could air dry. Are you staying the night, Tim?'

Tim laughs. 'No, just here for dinner.'

'Get upstairs, comb your hair and put on some clothes.'

'Yes sir, Mummy sir.'

'How was swimming?' I shout up as she scrambles up the stairs.

'Wet.'

Tim grins broadly. I lead him into the kitchen where it looks like there's been some sort of riot involving pepperoni and child-sized cutlery. Mr T saunters up next to Tim to have a perfunctory smell. I remember a time when the dog would launch himself at anyone who'd come through the door. Now he just checks if they're packing bacon and treats. Tim gives him a pat on the head. I assess the damage and decide the best course of action is to reach for wine glasses. Tim is very proactive and fumbles through the drawers looking for a corkscrew. One drawer opens and some cling film jumps up to attack him. I notice a huge box on the kitchen table, the size of a standard laundry basket, unmarked bar an address label. I stare at it for a while. Ever since the dildo, I am cautious of the goods that come into the house. I don't know what the hell would fit in that though. If it's a sex toy then I don't want to know. Tim hands me a glass of wine. I hold it to my lips and take four or five large sips, draining half the glass. To hell if this is aromatic or woody, it's alcohol and it's good. I lift the box. It's lighter than expected.

'You don't mind if I just leave you here, Tim? I'll just check on the little people.'

'No, go ahead.'

'Don't eat that pizza on the table. You don't know what the kids have done there and Magnum the cat's probably had a go. I will be back.'

He is seemingly unfazed and sips at his wine. I shuffle along the hall and gallop up the stairs. Where the hell is Danny? Why does it sound like there's another swimming lesson happening in the bathtub? Why are all the effing lights on? I go around flicking switches and picking up wet towels off the floor. Stu is many things but he's no Mary Poppins. He's not even Mrs Doubtfire. When I open the bathroom door, Polly is sitting up in the bath with her baby hair formed into soapy devil horns whilst Stu is topless and using his T-shirt to mop up pools of water on the floor. Polly beams to see me but is also having far too much fun flooding the bathroom. Eve's hair is still a wet tangled mess but she's traded the superhero cape for fairy wings.

'Why was your phone going to voicemail?' I ask.

'It were dead. What's in the box?'

'Don't know, it's addressed to Danny. Where is he? I need to chat to him. We've got company downstairs. Friend from work. Put on a shirt?'

'What, like your boss?'

'No… but… have you tried calling Danny today?'

He shrugs and starts rinsing out Polly's hair with the tumbler we use to hold our toothbrushes. I say nothing.

'Eve, please put some clothes on and find a comb? Where's Tess?'

I throw the box on to our bed next door and enter the bedroom where little piles of school uniform sit like molehills. I pick up cardigans and tangled tights and discover Tess in a corner, reading quietly, Magnum the cat in her lap. They both don't look overly excited to see me but both seem to nod in unison to acknowledge my presence.

'How was everything today, Tessie? Did Uncle Stu pull it off?'

She closes her book thoughtfully. Her hair is combed and parted and she's wearing matching pyjamas. Eve still skips around the house singing to herself. It sounds suspiciously like Rihanna.

'He's very flirty at the school gate. He seems to know everyone and he was chatting to Liam's mum and kept touching her arm.'

I applaud the judgement in her tone but then it is Stu so I am hardly surprised. She's on a roll as she continues to report the day to me.

'And Polly was very noisy at swimming and I think Uncle Stu may have given her half a pack of Rich Tea biscuits to make her quiet but then the lifeguard told him off for having food poolside and then I'm not sure but I think Uncle Stu called him a bad word.'

I close my eyes. I'm sure the Little Fins classes have never seen such action.

'Does that mean we might not be able to swim there anymore?' she asks.

'I'm sure it will be fine. Thank you for getting yourself sorted honey. We can read later if you want?'

She nods. 'Oh, and Uncle Stu had a fight with George and Maisy's mum at the gate.'

'Sarah? How on earth?' I enquire.

'Zach was throwing mud at Eve and so Stu told him to F-word off.'

'Really?' I say, aggrieved at the further drama but relieved that she knows how to self-censor.

'She told him to mind his language and he told her to do her job and mind her kids.'

Oh, Stuart. I applaud the bravery though.

'He also gave Eve Haribo after swimming. I told him not to.'

I freeze for a moment. I am not averse to sweets but there's something in the magic formula of Haribo that turns Eve into a strange sort of growling creature. I'd imagine crack would have the same effect. I look over at her as she sways on the spot and I see that bewitched glazed look in her eyes.

'Eve, for the love of my sanity. Put a nightie on or something.' I grab a comb and start trying to neaten her hair. Her body fizzes with energy. I wonder whether I should just let her loose in the garden with a ball.

'Who is Tim in the kitchen? Did he bring anything for us?' asks Eve.

'No… and you need to stop doing that. Every time someone walks through our door, you expect them to be clutching presents for you. It's very presumptuous.'

'I don't know what that means…' she replies.

'It means you're an idiot,' adds Tess.

Eve launches herself at her. I hold her off like a cub on the attack.

'What's going on here then?' Danny says.

He stands there nibbling on a slice of pizza that I told Tim not to eat. I glare at him, a little murderous.

'What are you eating?'

'Waste not, want not.'

'A little help here? Stu gave her Haribo.'

He rolls his eyes back, stuffing what's left of the pizza in his mouth. 'C'mon hyper Buttons, let's go brush them teeth.' He carries her away kicking and screaming while I hurriedly kiss Tess and scowl at her simultaneously. I go to follow them. In the bathroom, Stu fishes Polly out of the bath.

'Stu, do Eve's teeth… I just need to chat to Danny…'

I drag him into our bedroom and close the door softly before slapping him slightly across the arm.

'Where the hell have you been? I called like a million times!'

He reaches into his pocket. 'Oh yeah, you did. Sorry, it's been on silent as I had meetings. What's up?' That look, that nonchalance, makes me want to murder him with the comb in my hand. He looks at the package on the bed. 'Did my stuff arrive? Is it because of that?'

I hit him again. I can hardly catch my breath for wanting to tell him. 'Tim, in the kitchen. Did you say hello?'

'Well, yeah. I wasn't going to ignore him.'

'He knows.'

'He opened the package?'

'What's in the bloody package?'

Danny strolls casually over to the bed and uses his car key to slice open the tape on the box. I don't want to know but I must suffer this anguish as part of this ruse. He pulls out a harness. A climbing harness. Wait, no… it has a penis attached. It's a strap-on. He bought a strap-on from the internet and it's on my bed. The bedroom door opens. Danny drops the strap-on to the floor. Stu holds a wet baby under one arm wrapped in a towel, flailing her limbs about as she can't see anything.

'What do I dress this one in? Does she wear a nappy to sleep?'

We both stare at him, in wonderment at the question but also fretting whether he saw anything. He looks at both of us curiously. Eve appears at the door dressed as Wonder Woman. I should have brought my wine upstairs.

'Nappy, vest and sleepsuit in the second drawer down. Eve, get in your bedroom.' I point at Danny. 'You need to give Daddy and me two minutes together.'

The bedroom door closes. Danny turns to me with a look. I am close to wrestling him to the bed with anger.

'Captain Mintcake.'

'Yes?'

'Tim knows.'

The look drops from his face. 'Well, what'd you tell him for?'

'I didn't. He doesn't know it's you… but we got the lead on a story today about some wannabe erotic arty person living in the Lakes and our job is to reveal his identity.'

'Oh. So why's Tim here? Surely that's not a grand idea.'

'Never mind that, you didn't tell me people offered you money from this. A million quid. What the hell?'

Danny shrugs like it was none of my business. For all the times we've sat at our dining room table chatting about bills and how we'd finance the mortgage, I can't understand how he'd not lap up the opportunity to have the financial freedom that amount of money could bring. I am angered by his casual rejection of something that might be so important to us as a unit.

'Because I don't want people to know,' he replies. 'I'm not doing this to be famous. This is my thing. You want me to do this full time? For my kids to say that their dad draws minge for a living?'

'Then why do it?'

He doesn't quite understand which way I'm riding in with all of this. He assumes I'm OK with a strap-on lying on my bedroom floor? I still have all the questions. I'm shocked that he thinks I wouldn't have residual feelings about it all. There is a knock on the door and it opens slightly. Stu stands there with a shirt on this time and a baby with a sleepsuit wrapped around her.

'I'm sorry. I have two degrees and a masters but even I can't figure this out.' He stands there and senses the tension between us. Danny gestures him to enter the room. I'm not sure what Stu used to wash Polly's hair but she smells a lot like Lynx Africa.

'Meg's work fella downstairs knows about the Mintcake situation.'

'Why'd you tell him?'

Why has this been the assumption, twice already?

'I didn't… It's out there. There's word at the paper about some mysterious sex artist and we've been asked to try and find out who he is.'

'Aye Danny, you're like Banksy. Better than that, Wanksy.'

Neither of us laugh. I look over at my husband. It takes him thirty seconds to dress Polly, bundle her into his arms and kiss her on the forehead. She giggles. Stu looks on in amazement.

'Look, people want to know who he is. And if Danny doesn't want people to know then it's our job to protect him. So, Danny… you stay upstairs and get the girls to bed and Stu and I will go downstairs and entertain Tim.'

They don't question it. I can hear the girls squabbling next door and feel I have drawn the better straw given the wine is downstairs.

'And you…' I point at Stu. 'Next time, I'll give Eve Haribo for breakfast and you can deal with that?' Danny casts him a look in agreement.

'Guys, is that a strap-on lying on the floor?' He raises an eyebrow. 'Didn't know you were into all that nonsense?' Danny kicks it under the bed and glares at his younger brother.

'I'll bloody 'ave you. Behave!'

'Bunch of pervs.'

I hold my head in my hands. Too many different threads to pull together tonight. I've got a guest in my kitchen, sex toys on the floor, a kid high on gummy sweets and wine to drink. In another life, that would be a perfect chain of rap lyrics. I clap my hands and literally push Stu out of the room. 'Get the oven on for pizzas. And

I want alcohol.' Danny and I retreat to the girls' room where Eve is going through the hallucinatory part of her sugar high. Soon, she will come down and lie there crashed out with her tongue hanging from the corner of her mouth like a sleeping puppy. I kiss Tess on the head.

'Daddy's doing bedtime tonight.'

'Don't get too drunk.'

Oh, geez. She assumes I abandon her because I'm out to drink all the wine. I don't feel like a failed parent at all. Danny laughs under his breath.

'Anyway, Daddy does the voices better when he reads the stories. You always say my Scottish pig sounds Jamaican.'

I go to the bookshelf and pick something substantially thick with multiple characters that Tess will demand have an array of accents for reasons of authenticity. I smile to myself.

'I'll send Stu up with some milk. Night.'

I look at Danny as I exit the room. How many things are left unsaid between us? It worries me that one day, Polly will finally fly the coop and we'll be left with four walls and the time and space to finally resume a conversation we started eighteen years previously.

Danny needs to stay upstairs because I know what will happen. We'll start talking about it. There will be comments where I'll be unable to hold my tongue and I'll unmask him. Tim will have the glory. Danny would be a front page story on the Wezzie. We'd be social pariahs and he'd never be able to sell paper in this town again. I tiptoe down the stairs. I can do this. I won't drink all the wine. I'll be the calm and professional journalist that he's come to know and respect and have the poise and steeliness of Anna Wintour about my person.

'So I hope you like a meat feast?' asks Stu as I enter the kitchen.

'I could handle a meat feast?' replies Tim looking a little confused.

'I'm so sorry, Tim. Kids, bedlam. Have you had more wine?' Maybe the key here is to get him so drunk that he will have no recollection of this evening and forget even if the information is leaked. 'Has Stu been entertaining you?'

'Naturally,' interjects Stu dryly. Tim laughs awkwardly. I find my wine glass and refill it. Tim picks up a letter on the kitchen counter and hands it to me.

'Have you read this?'

It's on the school trademark mint green letter paper and I scan over it quickly. There's a meeting in the school hall in a few weeks about the sex education debacle. I hadn't really heard anything about it since that woman at the gate wanted me to sign her petition. Tim's face doesn't look wholly impressed with the content.

'What's that?' asks Stu.

I wave the letter in his face. 'Some letter. Are there others?'

He looks at me, blankly. 'There was something about them all having to wear red for a charity thing, I think on Friday.'

'Head to toe red?'

'I weren't really listening. And they want us to collect milk bottle tops to save the hedgehogs, or maybe it were badgers. I think.'

Breathe, drink. Tim is giggling. Must distract the company.

'So, Tim… how do you like living in the Lakes?' It is the most unnatural lead into a conversation ever. I take a huge swig of wine and let it sit in my mouth before swallowing it.

'It's wet. There's a fair few hills too. But what we were talking about before? There's not much of a scene, eh?'

'Well, that's where someone like Stu can help. You know where the action is, don't you Stu?' My brother-in-law is sliding pizzas off their foam bases onto oven racks with all the diligence of an untrained ape. 'Stu's been away. He was in Sydney for a while but he's from here. He knows the Lakes well enough.'

'So, where is the action? I haven't found it yet.'

'The Brewery. Back in the day,' replies Stu.

'I didn't get that vibe.'

'Maybe it's died down a bit since I was last here but always guaranteed action there.'

Tim nods, a bit suspicious. I mill about clearing up the detritus from the girls' dinners and try to distract myself so I won't say or do anything untoward. I look over as Stu is trying to rearrange shelves in my oven. There's a hint of his pants poking up from his jeans and a flash of crack.

'I mean if you want the more hardcore party stuff then I'd head down to Blackpool,' mentions Stu. 'Me and some of my mates were thinking of heading down next weekend – welcome to join us?'

Tim seems surprised that the invitation is so forthcoming but it's very Stu to be inclusive and matey. Unlike Danny, who verges on hermit status with his unwillingness to socialise, Stu is one of those people who throws parties and sends out Facebook invites to all, just telling them to bring tinnies and a bag of sharing crisps. I study all the litter left out on the kitchen table.

'Did you give Polly pizza too?'

'I gave her the crusts to gnaw on, she quite liked them, then she had some yoghurts for pud.'

Nutritional requirements fulfilled for the day then. Tim looks impressed that Stu's been involved in some house husbandry. From the contents of the bin though, it would seem that pudding was a whole six-pack of Petits Filous. I don't critique him knowing that even though he is serving his penance, he also does this without payment or complaint.

'So, what do you do Stu?' Tim asks.

'This and that…'

'He's in-between jobs.' Stu gives me a look. It's a classic line that Gill would dole out to protect her son's integrity even though I know her son isn't hugely bothered at all. We can class it however we like. He's a free spirit, biding his time, finding the best fit, but there was always a sense that he had no affinity to anything in particular. His time and space was his own and he wasn't bound by the chains of what was socially required of him. I know Danny was vaguely jealous of the freedom that came with that, whereas to me, I wondered if it wasn't all a bit selfish, where he was only out for himself.

'Back in Kendal for my pa's birthday celebrations but thinking ahead, might head down to Chamonix for ski season – plenty of money to be made out there chalet-hosting.'

I think the problem is that all this flitting about also makes Stu sound a bit thick. He lives for the adventure but he is admittedly the smartest person I knew bar my doctor sister. He has degrees in philosophy and law and can speak at least four languages fluently. In another world, he was a high-flying litigator with holiday homes on each continent. That said, he's still trying to figure out the controls on my oven. That's the grill, Stu.

'So, not back to Sydney then?' I ask him, realising we've not really had the conversation about his next move.

'Been there, done that. Need a change. My pal can get me a decent gig. And as Danny will tell you, it's a hotbed of action down there.'

I cringe a little. One, he's brought Danny into the conversation but he's also referring to what I call my husband's underground years. Back when he was young, a bit more reckless and had the freedom to get in a car with Rufus and Rowan, head for the slopes, snowboard on their own crudely made boards, eat raclette, and get wasted out of their faces. The first I heard about these good old days was at my wedding, as part of Rufus' best man speech.

'Sounds cool,' adds Tim.

Or not. If the stories are anything to go by, when the younger brother Morton was of age, he got dragged into the debauchery. To me, it'd be like going back to the scene of a crime. I am all too aware that talk has also gone over to matters of a sexual nature and I need to swing things back to something more neutral. I get some plates out. Plates are very neutral. And napkins.

'So, Tim… I'm under no illusion that you're up here for the work experience but any idea what your next step is?'

I sound like an old aunt. Tim takes a sip from his glass and smiles.

'No idea. You know what it's like… journalism work is thin on the ground but maybe a bigger city next, editorial on a magazine. Problem is so much is digital these days. London would be good… which is why this Mintcake story is quite appealing, you know? It's different. If I get an angle on it then it's good for the resumé.'

Darn it, my deflection attempts did not work at all. Balls. Stu's ears have pricked up at the mention of Mintcake. I stare at the back of his head. How good will he be at playing along here?

'What's this then? A story about mint cake? Sounds a bit dull, sorry...'

'Nope... Basically, there's a man/woman we think lives in the Lakes who is making a living out of drawing erotic art under the pseudonym Captain Mintcake. We're trying to uncover who it is.'

Stu turns his nose up. 'Sounds like a bit of a wrong'un. Plenty of them live around these parts I'd say.'

Well played Stu. You called your own brother a wrong'un, but I think he'd forgive you that.

Interesting to hear that Tim thinks Danny makes a living out of this though. I can wish.

'So, what happens when you find out who it is?' asks Stu.

'Oh, it's part of a bigger story. The reveal alone could make him quite the celebrity. A million on the table to start, apparently.'

Stu stops to give me a look. And this is why you buggers should check your phones more. He's slightly lost for words and I worry he's going to give the game away so I click my fingers.

'Garçon, oi! My pizza's burning.'

Still stunned, he turns to the oven. I see him steady himself over the counter. I try to distract Tim by pouring him more wine, hoping his journalistic instincts aren't honed enough yet to read Stu's reactions.

'The one way to catch him out is maybe via Instagram? Apparently, he sells the images so we could purchase one and make contact that way? Offer him cash for his story?'

Oh, Tim. That's a great way to approach him – well thought through but you can't go there, you really can't.

'You still think it's a man? I think we should reserve judgement. People write or draw under all sorts of noms de plume. Let's think outside the box. I also think it's someone single. I mean I don't know any married person who'd have the time to do all of this?' The last part stings a bit. I say everything calmly. I have had some wine.

'Maybe their partner knows about it.'

Maybe they *don't*. Maybe all those times she thought he was downstairs, watching *The Wire* box set and asleep on the sofa, he was drawing schlongs.

'Nope, lots here to assume he's married. There's real fantasy stuff here: threesomes, dogging with a partner, work affairs.'

Stu realises any initial shock he had is now mine. He swoops in to be my wingman.

'But isn't it just that: fantasy, a fiction of that person's imagination?'

'Or maybe some married man who isn't getting enough and just writing everything down out of frustration?'

There's not enough wine in the world to mask my inner turmoil. Stu looks at me. I guess he hadn't thought about the situation in that much detail. To him, his older brother had a new hobby which was amusing and meant he could torment him. He hadn't thought about the motivation. I wrinkle my nose to try hide the fact that I'm holding back emotion. Stu springs into action to try and divert Tim's attention.

'I'll put the pizzas in the middle of the table, just dig in mate.'

Stu doesn't break my gaze. I can't quite read him but he seems concerned, protective. It's the first time I've ever felt that from him.

'Bit of a harsh assumption?' Stu suddenly pipes in. Stu, please don't. He continues. 'Maybe he is an artist. Maybe he's not frustrated but the sex he's getting is so good that he's drawing some of that shit down.'

He looks at me when he says this. Bless you, Stu. Not the truth at all but thank you.

Tim laughs. 'Well, you've obviously heard better things than me about married sex. Isn't it the popular conception that you get married and you just don't do it anymore? One of my big sisters is trying for a baby; she has sex on a schedule. It's on the fridge.'

Stu laughs but takes a quick glance at my fridge door.

'I mean that's half of Captain Mintcake's following, no doubt,' Tim carries on. 'Bored housewives whose best sex lives are behind them…' I have a feeling Tim may have had more wine than me when I was upstairs so the barriers are down and the lips are looser.

Am I in that bracket? Is my best sex behind me? We don't do it to schedule but I know what it's like to put other things before sex. Like sleep. I can't believe I've become a cliché that younger folk like Tim look at and jest about.

'Or maybe it's more than that?' Stu whispers quietly. He takes a bite out of his pizza. 'Like take Meg and Danny here.' My eyes widen. Tim listens on intently. 'I was there when they got together, we all lived together in London.'

'Good times,' I add. Stu attempts to high five me. I am reluctant but join in.

'They used to do it a lot. Flat had thin walls. Then they got married, moved here, had the babies. I don't know what sort of sex they're having…'

They both look at me. I say nothing to hint that it's a private matter but dudes, we did it twice in one day about four weeks ago.

'But man, they're like best mates. It's like what my parents have. No doubt the old codgers aren't at it every day, dad's heart wouldn't take it for a start, but it's more than that. It's life. It's finding someone you want to spend your life with. I'd kill for what Meg and Danny have.'

I pause for a moment to look at Stu. Is this an act or a moment of sincerity? Is this why he was so angry before? Not to protect his brother but to safeguard a relationship he'd seen grow from the roots? He looked up to both of us, our marriage, our family.

'It's more than sex that's for sure,' admits Stu.

Both Tim and I smile at the admission, for different reasons, of course. I raise a wine glass to him hoping he wasn't bullshitting. He smiles back. The kitchen door opens. Danny. He shouldn't be down here. In his hands is a wide-eyed Polly.

'You said you were bringing up milk?'

Arse. 'Yes, I did.'

I jump to attention, glad for the excuse to leave the table and gather my emotions. Danny gives Tim a curious eye, never one to be able to mask how he feels. He goes to sit down next to him. Shit, no. Go in the front room.

'So, this is Polly, eh?' Tim introduces himself by shaking her hand. She giggles. Stu and I study the scene on tenterhooks. How much did Danny hear? Please don't make a scene, he's young and kind and just trying to do his job.

'So, Meg's told me you had work things to discuss? Something about porn in the Lakes?'

I stand by the counter filling up a bottle for Polly and like some sort of really bad spy trying to gauge the conversation by looking at the reflections in a really dirty stainless steel toaster.

'Yep, an amateur erotic artist – trying to track him down. We've just been talking about it.'

'Well, something a bit spicier for the paper than Spot the Dog.' That was Danny trying to make a joke. Danny doesn't really joke which Stu and I know about so we both fake laugh.

'Hopefully, Meg will show you some of his stuff. It's a bit raunchy… probably not to be looked at around the little ones. Some of it's really funny too.'

Oh dear, Tim. You need to stop now. Is there any garlic bread that we can stuff his mouth with?

'Funny?' asks Danny. Oh, Mother of Ballbags, he didn't.

Stu sits there glaring at his older brother. We find it funny because we know the artist but I am sure there is humour there that is not intentional. I turn with a lukewarm bottle of milk and approach Danny and Polly. Polly's doing the little bird mouth thing looking for a teat but Danny is distracted. I shove the bottle in her mouth and squeeze his shoulder to try and calm him down.

Tim reaches down to his bag and retrieves the printouts that Di gave us earlier in the day. Danny peers over to have a look at them, a grave look on his face. He points to a picture of a vagina rendered in ink in a pop art style. There's a little speech bubble above it. 'You get me so moist.' Stu comes and stands behind us, blushing, then looking up to the ceiling, assuming the passage to be about my nether regions.

'What's wrong with that?' Danny asks.

'Moist is a really bad word. According to polls, it's one of the most hated words in the English language. It sounds like the perfect conditions for growing mould…'

I bite my lip as I've already told Danny this but he refused to listen. Stu is pretending to stuff his face with pizza.

'So, what would you say then?' Danny enquires.

'I'm gushing like a tsunami…' hints Stu.

Tim and I laugh. Danny is not convinced. I study Danny's face. I can't quite tell if he looks hurt or annoyed. Polly finishes her milk and like the pro that Danny is, he hoists her on his shoulder to wind her. He holds her a little tighter than usual.

'They look like proper paintings…' asks Danny, innocently looking through his handouts.

Tim nods, 'Oh yeah, they're actually very good. They're really well done. Lots of different medium. He's good in watercolour.' He spreads out the images he has on the table. Stu can hardly contain his giggles and behind Tim's back he points at Danny, instantly recognising his brother's manhood laid out before him. Danny gives him evils. 'It's decent.' suggests Tim.

I sit down next to Danny and squeeze his hand under the table. He can't be angry anymore because his art has just been complimented, surely? I've always liked it. He's always had talents.

Tim is still scanning the papers before him. 'Just hard to know where to start, really? Maybe married, maybe single, maybe male, maybe female?'

Stu's face takes a funny turn and I squeeze Danny's hand again. A squeeze that says if you're so desperate to keep this a secret then you need to stop making faces that look like you're passing a kidney stone.

Tim explains. 'It's hard to tell; the stories tell me man but the drawings are male and female genitalia.'

'Maybe he's just a fan of the human form in general,' murmurs Danny. He puts a hand to my knee. My form? Or any form? 'Maybe he just found something he was good at drawing and it snowballed from there?'

I think about what I know already. He went to one of Ro's still life drawing classes and thought he was decent and it sparked something, something that was lacking before.

'The contracts are pretty mega though. Is there a reason he wants to stay out of the spotlight? Maybe he's an MP or someone vaguely famous?' Tim pipes in.

'Maybe he's already loaded…' Stu suggests.

'Or maybe he just doesn't want the attention?' Danny hints. 'Most creatives don't do it for the attention; it's self-expression. Not all of us want to be Kardashians.'

It's a jolt to hear this. To think that Danny needed this in his life, or that there was an anxiety that I didn't pick up on. Stu studies his brother's face as he speaks but realises the tone of the conversation has turned and become a little weighty.

'Or maybe he's some weirdo and doesn't want people to know,' Stu adds.

Danny's face lightens and he sticks his middle finger up at his younger brother as Tim turns to retrieve his phone going off in his coat. He scrolls through but then pauses to laugh. I know that face; that face where you receive a cheeky text that makes you glow happy.

'Is that from a new friend then?'

He smiles at me. 'Maybe?'

Danny and Stu don't seem to be particularly bothered but it would be both rude and uncharacteristic of me not to pry. As said, he's bordering on drunk and seems excited that he has someone to partake in gossip with.

'I've hooked up with them a few times. Cute. Adventurous. Older but I don't think they want anything more… Which is fine by me. I thought it'd be a single hook up but…' He shrugs and blushes. I feel a little awkward as it's obvious he's never crushed on me at all so I feel like I've slipped into old aunty territory again.

'Friend with benefits then?'

Stu rolls his eyes. 'Fuck buddy. You're so square, Meggsy.'

I cast him a look.

'What's her name then?' I enquire.

There's a pause as Tim gives me a look of disbelief. Have I crossed a line? I've always been a teensy bit nosy but maybe it's someone we know? Someone in the office? Did he get it together with Jen from advertising?

I see Stu giving me the same look. 'I thought you were supposed to be a journalist? How have you not worked out he's gay?'

Meat feasts, the 'scene,' the way he complimented Captain Mintcake's penis. I smile. It all makes sense, even if I do feel like a prize idiot to have not realised. What finely tuned journalistic instincts I have. Then again, it took me a year to work out my own husband was a willy scribbler.

Tim turns to Stu. 'You're not though, eh?'

Stu doesn't flinch. 'No mate, but still, come to Blackpool. I'll show you where to find the decent wanger.'

Tim gestures down at the watercolour cock on the table.

'Something like that would be fine, mate.'

We don't say a word.

Chapter Eleven

'So, what happened?'

'I went to the wedding with him and it was kind of fun. I learned how to bhangra.'

It's Sunday morning and I'm on a Facetime call with Emma after she went on a date with Jag; he who accompanied her six hours up the motorway after I fell tit over arse over ankle. Last night, she was his plus one at a family wedding which she was hesitant about, but she got to wear a sari at The Dorchester which pales in comparison to my usual date nights eating takeaway in my front room.

'Kind of fun?'

'His ex-girlfriend was there… I just… I don't know if I need that drama.'

There is something she's not telling me but I don't want to drag it out whilst a screen separates us.

'And did you sleep with him?'

'No,' she says hesitantly. 'But he introduced me to all his aunties who were very impressed that I'm a doctor. Turns out the man can dance too. Si never danced.'

I smile at her. She's doing a classic Emma-swerve so I won't dig for information but she also needs to stop the comparisons and throwing Simon into every conversation.

'Why am I still hearing that berk's name?'

'Because he was my husband for ten years.'

We look at each other through our relative electronic devices. She still smarts from it all, he's still part of the fabric, which is why it's important to give her that sisterly dose of home truth and unravel her from his clutches. She needs to leave him behind, to go to weddings, to dance, to live again.

'Anyway, you told me not to sleep with anyone until I got myself tested after Stu…'

I retch a little. 'YES! Do! I don't even let him use our bath towels and I let the dog use them.'

She laughs. 'Is he about? Can I say hello?'

I stick my middle finger up at her. 'No, you can't. He's taken the girls out with the grandparents to some farm fair thing.'

'That's nice. Tell him I said hello.'

'I will not.'

'He did me a favour, you know? I think I needed to have some sex and feel wanted like that. He wasn't terrible.'

I put my hands over my ears like earmuffs. She laughs and changes the subject.

'And that whole Mintcake thing, is that sorted?'

'He's a Captain I'll have you know.'

I pause for a moment. There is extra information to tell Emma – she doesn't know about this wild witch hunt that has been started by the Wezzie. But now doesn't feel like the right time especially when Danny and I are still processing the information ourselves. I am still urging him to consider the money, to go forth and take advantage of things. He wants anonymity. He didn't do this for fame and fortune. It's a bone of contention and I don't want to start dragging other people's opinions into it.

'He's doing his thing. He's upstairs drawing as we speak while I pair socks. It's all glamour here.'

She pauses. She knows I'm lying but doesn't pry.

'Mum will be here soon with the girls. You should wait and then you can talk to her too.'

'I'm fine, thanks. How is the Mother?'

'Wonderful. Telling us all how to run our lives. She often says I'm her cleverest one but I think that might be you for getting away when you did.'

'It comes with its cons though.' I go a little misty-eyed to say that out loud. 'And Beth, Luce? All good? Anyone heard from Grace?'

'Make sure you check in on Beth. I'm herding them as best I can. Grace is AWOL but alive from what Instagram tells me.'

'Hugs for all,' I say.

'I'll bring a gang up for half term maybe?'

'Is that all I'm good for? I'm the holiday destination sister, aren't I?'

'Yep. Love you, sis.'

'Laters, ho.'

She hangs up and my phone reverts to home screen with a photo of all the Callaghan sisters. Bitches the lot of them, but *my* bitches. I need to catch up with the others. Beth now has her own baby, Joe; Grace was globetrotting after the year from hell and Lucy was currently earning money playing Elsa at kids' birthday parties. Sometimes when my girls can't sleep, we ring Aunty Luce and she sings to them down the phone. Life had spun us all into its intricate web and left very little time to be in each other's lives but I missed their faces, I missed the chat, the camaraderie. A voice snaps me out of my ponderous mood.

'MEGS! Can you come here for a minute? MEG!'

Why does he insist on doing this? He feels the need to screech and booms his voice across the house.

'WHAT IS IT?'

There is no response. If this is him asking me to get a new loo roll then he can do one. I put down the piles of socks I was hoping to sort and climb the stairs to our bedroom.

'For the love of crap, Danny. What are you doing?'

It's hard to explain what my eyes see before me. I thought I'd seen and heard it all in the last month: the sex toys, my brother-in-law with my sister, our good family friends who are into sex with feet. However, currently my husband is sat on our bed with a large sketch book. At the foot of the bed is Honey Bear. Honey Bear is one of those stupid four-foot bears gifted to us one Christmas, whom I haven't had the stealth nor energy to hide or donate to a charity shop yet. I always thought Honey Bear didn't have a use. I was wrong. Today he sits there with the strap-on that Danny bought a few weeks previously. His sewn-on smile takes on a whole new meaning as he sits there in a harness with an impressively lifelike protruding cock.

'Poor Mr Honey Bear, you're corrupting the little bugger...'

'Well, he's a shit model. Furry git won't sit up properly.'

I grab him by the shoulders and try to pull him back.

'The dildo's too heavy, it's weighing him down. He's filled with cotton wool, he can't support it.'

I look over at the edge of the bed where several pieces of paper are scrunched up on the floor. He wasn't wrong; Honey Bear needs to find a different vocation in life.

'Come here, I'll put it on?'

He looks at me. I'm not sure what I've offered up here but it seems a better option than defiling a child's toy.

'Really?'

'You don't want me to use it on you, do you?'

'No,' he mutters sarcastically. 'I just need to see how the straps sit around the leg and groin area.'

'What are you drawing?'

'Stuff.'

I'm hoping it's not a couple of bears having sex. Isn't there a whole group of fetishists who have sex with furry toys? I don't question it. I just take the harness off the bear and start to fasten the straps around me.

'Do I need to take off my pants?' I ask, slightly horrified.

'Nah, just put it over your leggings.'

I do as I'm told. It is very much like wearing a climbing harness. I tighten the straps around my thighs and stand there looking down. Is this what it's like to have an erect penis? I expect a real one is not as malleable nor has such bounce. I stand there and jump up and down, rolling my hips to make it circle in the air like a wand.

'Whenever you're ready…'

I put a leg on the bed and lunge forward.

'Where do you want me?'

He flares his nostrils, trying not to laugh. 'Just stand there, legs slightly apart... maybe your hips slightly forward?'

I try a variety of positions. 'There... just like that.'

He starts making rudimentary sketches. I put my hands on my hips. I'm reminded of someone I went out with at university called Ben who was always very proud of his erections and used to adopt this exact pose. Truth be told, he had very little to be proud of, though I never told him that.

'Well, we've never done this on a Sunday before...'

'Beats going to church.'

'Draw me like one of your French girls, Jack...'

He laughs before falling into a deep concentration as he moves the pencil across the paper. I watch him as he does it. I've never studied the process before but it's quite intense and dare I say it, a little sexy. By the look of his trouser regions, it's not arousing for him but there's definitely a strong focus there, a look in his eyes which is engaged and absorbed.

'So, is this for your Instagram then?' He doesn't respond. 'Maybe I could get a hashtag out of all this? #mywifewearsitwell #pegginginleggings?'

He smiles. His hand curves down the paper and I wonder what he's just drawn; a thigh or an arse cheek?

'So, how's the Insta page doing these days? How are the pictures selling?'

There were no rules against talking and making chit-chat.

'OK.'

'Is there a market for strap-on art then?'

'You'd be surprised. Someone asked for one of my pics the other day so he could turn it into a tattoo.'

'Was it one of my vajayjay?'

'Yep, wanted it right across his back.'

'That'd go down well at the swimming baths.'

We both don't flinch.

'How much did you sell it for?'

'Well, I gave it him for a hundred quid in the end, grateful that he didn't just take it to a tattoo parlour and ask them to copy it. That's what most would do.'

I pout and shake my head from side to side. That'd keep a kid in shoes for a year and a half. He sees where I'm going with all of this though.

'It's not a million pounds but it's OK.'

The money thing has been a sore point recently. To me, it's like sitting on a winning lottery ticket but being told I can't cash it. Danny's argument is that he doesn't want the associated hassles the money would bring. He likes being in control of his material and doesn't want people to know who he is or nosing into his life. It's a perfectly respectable take on things, I get it. But it doesn't mean that I still don't push my agenda which is to be able to go on holiday past Europe, have a second car and extend the house so I can have a separate utility room with a shower for Mr T.

'You're not letting that go yet, are you?'

'Call me materialistic but it'd be kind of awesome. You could still go incognito, like Stu said, you could be a sexual version of Banksy.'

'That Wanksy thing weren't funny.'

'It wasn't. Maybe Prickasso?'

He doesn't respond. Of course, this is his thing. I'll keep trying to wear him down but at least we've got to this place where I can enquire about his work in a calm and supportive manner. It's progress and secretly, something for which I can congratulate myself.

'Have you tried drawing anything else?' I ask.

'I tried landscapes but it was dull as dishwater. Tried animals too but it turns out I can't do feathers. I tried to draw Mr T once but the fur I drew made him look like he'd been through the dryer.'

I giggle. Why didn't the dog tell me? And how does one make the jump from realising they can't draw animals to thinking they'll sketch a good knob instead?

'You seem to enjoy it? You said the other night that it was to escape everyday life. Like… To escape me?'

'If I wanted to escape you, I'd just leave, no?'

I nod. Blunt but true. The fact he's still here is something.

'Maybe it's just to escape being the Kendal King Of Paper Manufacturing. It's a dull enterprise really, not much call for creative know-how.'

I don't know how to respond to this. Somewhere in that labyrinthine mind of his there is something that craves more than paper. For that I feel guilt, and some anger that he feels trapped in what he does.

'Then you could do this full-time, as a career.'

Except I know what he'll say. He's doing this for his dad, the family, for a lot of people who work at the mill and have lives and families and mortgages to pay. His pencil slows down on the page. I change the subject.

'I think this strap-on goes particularly well with my hoodie.'
He smiles. 'It's a strange old beast though, eh? If I were a lesbian,
I don't think I'd bother. You'd have to break the passion to fiddle
with the straps and cue it up.'

Danny chuckles, returning to his sketch.

'So, if you were a lesbian… Wish list?'

'Kylie, obviously.'

'Naturally.'

I pause for a moment. I never really think about my girl list
because I'm never quite sure what I'd do when faced with some
lady bits that aren't my own.

'Is J Lo too obvious?'

'Nah, she's still got it.'

'And someone a bit off-kilter I reckon… Grace Jones?'

Danny's pencil moves off his page and he cracks up.

'What the actual… Meg?'

I laugh with him. 'Who doesn't bloody love Grace Jones? She's
a formidable woman. She'd bring her hula hoop. It'd be amazing.'

'That's proper dominatrix shit.'

'You're just not as hardcore as me, Morton.' I do a little move
in my strap-on.

'She'd eat me alive,' admits Danny.

'What a way to go though? Here lieth Daniel Morton, husband
and father who died peacefully while Grace Jones sucked his testicles
through his actual cock.'

Danny who usually tries to pretend I'm not hilarious can't quite
take it and creases up with laughter. There are actual tears while I
stand at the end of the bed wearing my dildo contraption. 'I have

beds to strip, get back to it.' He picks up his sketch book, wiping the tears from his eyes as the giggles subside.

'Well, can I ask you the same question? Celebrity male fantasy shag list… Go!'

'Seriously, no one… not my bag.'

I look at him. Is he lying to save my blushes?

'C'mon, Keanu Reeves in *Speed*?'

'No.'

'Harry Styles?'

'I'm pretty sure I'm about three times his age.'

'I'd totally support it if you wanted to experiment.'

He smiles. 'I'm good. I am.'

'Really?'

He puts the sketch book aside and comes to my side of the bed. There is a dildo between us turned up like a happy elephant's trunk but he comes and puts a hand to my face and gives me a kiss on the forehead.

'You know I was there when Stu and Tim were talking about married sex and all that bull. I heard. Polly and I had a little nose by the kitchen door.'

I don't know what to say. There is so much to vocalise here. Is this some manifestation of suppressed sexual desire that he thinks is more socially acceptable than an affair? I wait with bated breath to hear his take on everything. 'Stu is an idiot most of the time but he has a point. What we have, our girls, this life… that's what I'm here for. I wouldn't be without you.'

It's a strange and frank admission of love.

'This. The drawing stuff is not about us and the sex we have. You need to start believing that.'

Whilst I appreciate the sentiment, it might be easier to believe if I wasn't stood at the edge of our marital bed wearing this thing.

'Is there anything you want to try?' I ask.

Danny pauses for a moment. 'There's something new we could do?' I hold my breath. Please don't let it be nipple clamps. I've breastfed, my nipples have been through enough. 'Can you send me photos?'

'Of what?'

'I dunno… it was fun taking pictures of your tits the other night.'

I nod, my eyes scanning the room. I think I can do that.

'Do you want to try anything new?' he asks back.

I pause for a moment. I look down at my fake penis and the body holding it up. I have no bloody idea what I want. All my bodily parts that I once associated with sexual pleasure were loaned out to babies and now I have a complex relationship with said bits. They don't look like they once did, they've succumbed to age. It's a natural part of the process, but at times I just don't see the attraction. It's a sobering admission to make to myself let alone to someone I love.

'I just want to feel like me again. Like us. Like back when we first met…'

'When we had sex on stairs…'

'Right?' I smile. 'Sex is a feeling as well, an energy, being confident in yourself. I don't really feel like that about me, my body…'

I purse my lips as I realise talk has made me a little emotional. I sit here, the world's saddest wearer of a strap-on ever.

'Why are you getting sad, you silly bint? Come here.'

He unstraps me from the harness and brings me in for a hug. For the first time, I think he may finally realise how all these pictures have made me feel about myself.

'It's not like I'm some frigging model of thirtysomething fitness. Have you seen my six pack recently?'

'Family pack…' He pokes me in jest. I rest my head on his shoulder. 'My babies grew in that body. That's everything.'

That's the thing about Danny Morton; he doesn't do full disclosure emotional outpourings too often so when he does, they're the sort of moments that you know mean something. I look him in the eye, grab his cheeks and kiss him.

'I love you,' I mutter near his mouth. He kisses me back. And maybe this is what I've missed the most: the chance to have a long lingering kiss with my husband. Because I forgot that he is a great kisser, forgot the way he runs a tongue over my bottom lip, and places a hand to the back of my head. I get lost in it for a moment as he pulls away from me and studies my face, from my constellation of freckles all the way down to the wrinkles on my chin.

'You're a terrible model, you're very distracting.'

'It's because I'm not paid.'

'I can think of ways to pay you…?'

We both laugh. He continues to kiss me but this time takes off my top, and unclasps my bra with one hand. He lays me on the bed and kisses down my neck, my cleavage and my breasts, slowly circling my nipples. I giggle and he smiles knowing it's a well-rehearsed move that is guaranteed to do what's needed. He trails down to my stomach where his tongue moves all along my skin, rippled and stretch-marked but he takes no heed. He then pulls down my knickers and leggings together and stands there at the edge of the bed getting undressed. And before he comes to join me again, he looks at my body up and down with a raised eyebrow. There's no hiding my doughy, creepy flesh in this Sunday morning light, but he smiles, grabs at my ankles and pushes my knees up to my chest. It catches me by such surprise that I put my hands over my head and I wait for him to enter me, catching my breath as he does and his face comes to meet mine. For the first time, in a long time, I feel it. Electricity. He looks me in the eye and smiles, all those finely engraved lines by his eyes creasing up.

'Hi,' he says. 'I'm Danny. Nice to meet you.'

'Meg. Nice to meet you too. You come here often?'

'Once in a while if my wife allows for it.'

'You're married! I'm shocked.'

'So are you by the looks of that ring. Your husband mind you're here?'

'He's fine with it. He's a Captain.'

Danny laughs.

'Sounds like a right posh twat.'

Chapter Twelve

I definitely pulled the short straw here.

LOL, tough titties. I did the last unicorn disco. I had to throw glitter in the air and make unicorn wishes with a woman in a rainbow tutu.

Can you defrost the chicken for dinner?

One step ahead of you. Have they started serving alcohol in that place yet?

No and they're missing a trick. This place would be better with wine.

And a tranquiliser gun. Laters

It's the following week and even though we asked Stu really *really* nicely if he'd fill in for one of us today, I am doing the parental chaperone duty for the birthday party at Cheeky Monkeys Play Pit.

Today it's a joint endeavour celebrating Jimmy, Poppy and Emillia's collective sixth birthdays and what better way to do that than gather thirty odd classmates and family members in an enclosed space, throw some sugar at them and blast some Disney tripe over the speakers for an hour and a half.

I have a love/hate relationship with soft play. At times, I like the fact it gets us out of the house and the girls can run off some steam and make a mess of somewhere that isn't our home. However, I always leave with a blinding migraine and more often than not, an injured child who was usually flattened by an unsupervised kid who went the wrong way up the bloody slide.

'Meg, lovely to see you. Thank you so much for coming!'

Jimmy's mum, Vicky, is the lovely benign sort of mum who you know signs her child's reading record every evening and always has healthy snacks in her bag. She also had to chase up my RSVP for this party, for which she may or may not now hate me.

'No, thank you for the invite. I'm sorry about the present.'

Turns out I didn't read the back of the invite either which stated that we just had to donate a fiver each and the birthday trio were going to use it to 'have a special friends' day out. I'm not quite sure about a six-year-old's social life but I am pretty sure that the money gathered could buy you dinner at The Ivy with decent wine. In any case, instead of a fiver, I've shown up with some shoddily wrapped parcels that contain some cheapo arts and craft sets. No doubt, the presents will be stored and recycled for parties and school tombolas later in the year. I see Jimmy roar with the feral excitement that only a birthday gathering can bring and watch him tackle a young child into the ball pool. The child disappears, sinking rapidly into the germ-ridden plastic cesspit possibly never to be seen again. Vicky runs off to the rescue, clapping her hands and trying to maintain some order in this place. I've never seen that happen before but bravo on her for trying.

'Mummy! Mummy! Watch me!'

Eve waves at me from a rope bridge and hurls herself across. I flinch slightly to see her land but she gets up and follows a small gaggle of friends she's with. Eve has always been quite hardy, which I attribute to her being born in the Lakes. It's like the wilderness is part of her. Tess is different. Born a Londoner, she has a cautious side; she would usually arrive at one of these parties scowling, physically attaching herself to me. Eve comes to the edge of the play area and talks to me through the rope netting. Her face a shade of rhubarb, she takes off her cardigan and passes it through.

'I'm so thirsty. Can I have a drink?' she says, already scooting off.

It's what they do here too. They crank up the heat so you're forced to buy them drinks. I nod and look to the party table. Nada. I approach Rosie, mother to Emillia. Did we add the extra 'l' in the birthday card? Who knows? All I know is that if we didn't, I will be judged.

'Umm, is there anything to drink?' I ask.

Rosie is one of those mums I never can quite read. She's obviously a little posh, was probably part of the school hockey team and is very deadpan so I can never quite tell if it's sarcasm or she's being deadly serious.

'Well, we're providing drink with the meals.'

I don't know what she means. Does this mean we're expecting them to run around like loons for an hour and a half without hydration? I don't want to question it or appear ungrateful for her hospitality.

'That's totally cool. I'll get something for Eve.'

I head over to the food and drinks kiosk counting the coinage in my pockets. Kiosk girl has those sorts of eyebrows which make her look like she's drawn them on in Sharpie. Even after all my years having worked in fashion and seeing fads come and go, from berry liner around a pale lip to two tone highlights, I fail to understand the appeal. Why on earth would anyone want to look like a demonic kabuki performer?

'Hi, do you do squash?' I ask.

'We do squash jugs for £2.00.' As I anticipated, the customer service is lacking. She looks like she wants to stab everyone in this room with a wooden coffee stirrer. I would too if I had to spend forty-two hours a week in this hell hole.

'I don't want a whole jug, just a cup.'

'We don't sell by the cup.'

'Then can I just have some tap water?'

'There's Buxton over there.'

I need to make a point. They should provide water free of charge. I think it may be the law but I can sense someone standing behind me and I don't want to be the mum who makes a scene, spoils a party and made small children cry.

'I'll take a jug then. Do you do blackcurrant?'

'Yeah.'

She hands me a ready-made jug with five cups. I'm going to have to drink half of this to prove a point, aren't I? Down it like shots. A better mother would have brought gin in an unmarked bottle and used this as a fruity mixer. I put my jug down and take a seat. Three boys are next to me, and there's no other way of saying it, they're beating the shit out of each other. My money's on the one in the Minion T-shirt who looks like he's about to bite. Is it terrible I don't know any of their names?

My phone goes off in my pocket. For the love of Christ, Danny. It's a sketch of someone wearing a strap-on, the one he started the other day when I was his model.

Finished it.

FFS, I'm in soft play. This goes against the rules of conduct.

Should be OK as long as you're wearing socks

It's very good. Put it away you dirty bugger. Just paid £2 for a jug of squash.

Daylight robbery. Go take a piss in the ball pool.

Charming. And tempting.

I still have yet to figure out where we are with all of this. Last week, we had some pretty extraordinary sex – the sort where I forgot that we look like giant marshmallows and where we just enjoyed each other without distraction or hang-ups. Since then, the spark re-ignited, he sent me his first dick pic. He even put a filter through it to look vaguely arty. It's a development, one that I'm not averse too. I still have yet to send him any snaps of my lady parts as I'm not sure I see the attraction but one day I may be brave enough to do so.

I pour myself a cup of watered-down squash and glare at Eyebrows in the kiosk who's taking selfies. I could have urinated something stronger. I also look up to locate Eve who's forgotten she's thirsty. Darn her.

'I think she's up the mirrored tunnel thingy,' gestures a mum next to me. I say 'a mum' as I can never remember this one's name – she looks exactly like one of the other mothers in our class down to the blonde bob and the Converse… Jen, Jane? It could be anything. I was quite happy to dawdle at the end of this table and faff about on my phone but she's drawn me into her small circle of mum gossip and if I ignore them again, I'll be judged.

'Thank you. I swear they need electronic trackers in these places.'

That raises a guffaw from Tash with the big laugh; the one who's particularly good value at school events because she always gets drunk and heckles the headteacher. Next to her is Sally who I actively avoid as I may have not returned an Avon catalogue to her after Danny used it to scoop up cat poo in the kitchen.

'How's your ankle? Sarah said you broke it?'

There are sympathetic looks from all around the table. I don't know these women well enough to tell them the truth. You know, going for it hammer and tongs and my tosser of a husband couldn't handle my weight and dropped me.

'An over-exaggeration really – I twisted it, good as new.'

They all nod and smile. Tash studies my face for longer than needs be though. I smile back. I'm fine, Tash. She puts her hand in mine and pats it. I've never really spoken to her that much so I'm not sure why she's choosing to break the boundaries of personal space now. I reach over to my squash and down a cup to handle the awkwardness.

'Remember that time I twisted my ankle trying to ride Henry's scooter back from school?' Sally utters to break the mood. 'Oh Jen, thank god you were there to drive me home. Talk about looking like a complete tit.' I laugh simply from having witnessed the incident. She went over the handlebars in her bootcut jeans and I remember how the qualified first aider ran out of the school playground, placed traffic cones around her and put her in the recovery position. There is a small scream from the climbing frame. We all turn simultaneously. Not our child.

'So, Meg… we were all chatting before. Tash was talking about something her book group discovered online. Have you heard of this Captain Mintcake fella?'

As soon as the words come out of Jen's mouth, I feel my shoulders shudder. Not here Jen, not in front of the children. How the hell do you know? Did she just see that sketch that Danny sent and she's now trying to get me to fess up?

I laugh awkwardly. 'Who on earth is Captain Mintcake?' My mouth dry, I sip on my over-diluted squash. 'Sounds like a cartoon character?' That strange laugh comes out again. The ladies all around the table giggle in response. Tash leans in.

'Well, I go to a book group every last Wednesday of the month and one of our readers showed us these online pictures written under the pseudonym Captain Mintcake. It's amazing – all a bit raunchy, *The Joy of Sex* style. It's brilliant stuff.'

Tash looks genuinely excited and for a moment, I feel I need to capture this moment for Danny. Look here, I have found a real-life fan of yours. Captain Mintcake is out in the open. How am I expected to handle this level of secrecy when actual people know and are discussing it in soft play centres? On the other hand, I can't resist having a little dig.

'So, how raunchy?'

'It's real people, having sex. And the sex is pretty off the scale. I wouldn't mind being Mrs Mintcake, if you know what I mean?'

The table erupts into hysterics while it dawns on me that I *am* that woman. I am Mrs Mintcake. There's the Captain out in the world making a name for himself like a Kendallian sexual superhero while Mrs Mintcake waits indoors for him to come home. In my mind, she's wearing stockings and suspenders but making a pie of some description. Maybe a pork pie.

'Like there's this picture that's set in a forest and he's got this girl up against a tree and he doesn't even get his dick out.'

I crease my brow for a moment as I realise this may be one I haven't even seen. Our heads are all lent forward in conspiratorial whispers.

'Like it's just pictures of her orgasming with him using two fingers.'

'And a tongue, surely?' adds Sally.

'Nah. Just his hand… and in both holes.' She does a strange gesture with her hands which makes her look like she's at a rock concert and we all gasp. I definitely haven't seen that one. Our corner of the table cackles briefly.

For a moment I do wonder about an alternative scenario, where I hadn't found out that the Captain was my own husband. I'd be sitting around this table with these women and I would probably find it all a bit absurd. I'd probably have turned my nose up at it and said it was some sort of desperate housewife's endeavour. I'd have gone home, had a glance and got very angry at some of the cliché. I'd have watched his rise to popularity with bemusement and maybe bought a coffee table book of the art for a sister for Christmas as a joke present. But that's not how this panned out. The Captain is my husband. It's artistic talent, expression, freedom and I sit here feeling a very strange mixture of emotion but knowing that I am in no way ashamed of him.

A small baby crawls up to me and starts to climb my leg. I look down at her. You're not one of mine. The baby looks up expectantly. Sorry, I don't quite lactate on the level I think you need. I look around. One's escaped. Anyone? I reach down to pick her up.

'Stealing babies now, are we? It's Sarah. The other mums smile politely as I stand to hand her back. Sarah takes her from me but puts her right back on the floor to crawl in the opposite direction and start going through someone's handbag. Sarah is always the grand dame at these parties. She's a given at these events so will know the staff, the parents, the regulars and has her own spot.

'Haven't seen you in an age? How's the ankle?' she asks me.

'All good. It's just been a mare. Work and that.'

'I see Stu's been at the gate. He your manny now?'

I remember he may at some point have had words with Sarah about her childminding skills. I won't bring it up.

'He's helping us with the kids.'

'Thought he was kipping over with Rowan in her mud hut.'

I pause for a moment. At the slur on Rowan for a start but also to figure out where she would have learnt such information. I think of the gossip that Rowan imparted about Sarah's husband. If she knows about Jez's philandering ways, she doesn't let on. She just carries on, business as usual. It's reminiscent of Emma's marriage but it makes me think about that sliding scale of lies we all have in our relationships; the lie I got told, how Danny and I are repairing it.

'No, Stu's at ours. He's off soon, back on his travels but he's making himself useful.'

'I bet he is.'

'What does that mean?'

The atmosphere between us is barbed and awkward for reasons I'm not entirely sure.

'He's such a flirt at the gate, that's all. Lots of mums were hoping he was going to be here today if you know what I mean.'

I smile through gritted teeth. Thank God he's not because knowing him, we'd have received some sort of lifetime family ban from Cheeky Monkeys.

'But you and Danny are OK now?'

It's that sort of leading comment where she's asking me to divulge details but I'm not biting. It's soft play and a party so I don't let my discomfort rise to the surface but pour myself another cup of overpriced squash and hold the IKEA plastic tumbler to my mouth to down it.

'Mummy! That's for me!' Eve stands behind me with her class friends who all stand there expectantly.

'C'mon then, squash all round?' I look around for suspiciously missing parents who are sat at tables drinking cappuccinos while I'm hydrating their sweaty kids. The little ones all down their drinks and venture into the pit again. Sarah still stands there waiting for information.

'It's just I know your babysitter's mum and she said your ankle was fine when you got home but you told people you twisted it on the cobbles.' Sarah stands there smug, like she's worked this out for herself. 'Was it something to do with Danny? It's just… did he hurt your ankle?'

I freeze for a moment. So that was why Tash held my hand. People think Danny hit me? I am horrified that anyone would think Danny was capable of it.

'Well… Why lie and change your story? People do that when they have something to hide.'

All this hearsay and assumption angers me.

'No one's hitting anyone. It's really dangerous to say those things out loud too.'

She's affronted by my judgement.

'Danny and I are fine. Thanks for your concern but don't put two and two together and get five. It's nothing, really.'

I feel the need to unleash a few home truths now. Look closer to home, focus on your relationship, don't judge others? Now I know why Rowan rarely comes to these parties. She has issues with all the plastic anyway but it's the way people talk about other people's private lives like they're some sort of conversational currency. I imagine what would happen if Sarah actually found out about Mintcake.

'Are you Eve's mother?' a voice pipes up behind me just in the nick of time before I unleash some home truths on Sarah.

I turn around to see Ros, a meek mouse of a mum who toes the sensible line in woolly hats and wellies. I smile. 'Yes, I am.'

'Did you give my Lola squash?'

'I did…' I say hesitantly.

'It's just she reacts badly to the sweeteners in squash. We always give her water. Next time, you should really ask.'

Little Lola curls herself around her mother's legs, smiling. I'm confused. She looks fine. It's obviously not an anaphylaxis situation and it was as good as water anyway with the minimal amounts of squash inside. I just smile and nod as she goes off to reprimand her daughter and tell the other mothers present. This is starting to rate as one of my worst party experiences ever – and I've been to one where there was a twenty-year-old kid dressed up as a poor man's Obi-Wan Kenobi who called a kid a prick when he stabbed him in the balls with a toy lightsaber and a dad lamped him. My phone pings in my pocket. I don't look at it fearing it may be Danny being inappropriate again. A voice booms over a loudspeaker.

'Calling all Cheeky Monkeys! If you are here for Timmy, Poppy and Emily's birthday party then please can you come to the Jungle Party Room located by the toilets!'

There's a brief pause and crackle.

'Oh sorry, Jimmy and Emillia's party. Please don't forget your shoes!'

I look over at the entrance area where there seem to be five hundred pairs of children's shoes that are supposed to be in pigeon-holes but are lain there like some TK Maxx jumble sale nightmare. I scramble to retrieve what look like Eve's hand-me-downs and watch as thirty odd children cram themselves around tables and really tiny plastic chairs. One child circles the party crying because she can't sit next to her friend, one picks his nose, two others scream at each other like harpies, one squeezes ketchup straight into his mouth from the bottle. Children are given platefuls of beige food and you'd think that's where it'd all go quiet but no. They throw chips around. They spill juice. There is one child who I swear should not be given the privilege of cutlery. This is the image they should use on contraception packaging.

'Meg? Hi!' I turn next to me. Tits. What was that about the worst party experience ever?

'Briony? How are you?'

'Just checking in to see if you're alright. Heard you were in hospital?'

'Oh, it was nothing. Just fell on my ankle, but it's good as new…'

'Thought as much. Saw you up and about on it… but saw Stuart as well at the school gate. He's looking well.'

She scans me up and down like she always does. I think about how tight you can make jeans before they're an actual part of your skin. She really has gone for bringing the glamour to the jungle. Who wears heels to soft play?

'You free to talk?'

I wouldn't say free, more trapped in this corner as there's a small group of grandparents with cameras blocking the entrance. I nod.

'I just wanted to give you some advice.'

I pause for a moment. 'Danny will always be important to me because of who he was. I know you know, no point hiding it.'

Crap, is she going to tell me she's in love with my husband in the jungle party room of Cheeky Monkeys Play Pit? I'm not doing this here with two kids sat below us shovelling crappy cheese and tomato pizzas down their gullets.

'So when I hear tattle at the gate about him, it does me nut in. He's one of the good 'uns and I like you. I know we don't know each other well but it's nice to see Danny settled and with a family.'

I pause to hear her talk so fondly of him.

'So my advice… is when certain people are spreading rumours about you, ignore them. It's what I've been doing for years.' She glares over at Sarah, taking selfies with some of the mums in the corner of the room with the painted murals of zebras in party hats.

'What has she been saying?'

'That you and Danny had a fight and you fell down the stairs. The implication being that he pushed you. He'd never do that. I were fricking furious when I heard.'

My eyes widen and my heart prickles with sadness.

'It wasn't that at all. It really was an accident.'

'I know. We all know she makes up this shite to divert attention from her husband being a complete slag. I just won't hear Danny being talked about like that.'

'I'm glad I know. Thank you.'

'No problem.'

We glance over at Sarah. I feel many things but mostly sadness. I've always been civil to her. I can't believe the others just follow her like sheep. They'll believe anything she says.

'I tell you, if I see another of her passive-aggressive memes or hear her go for Danny again then I'll have her.'

I don't want to think about what that entails but I hope I can be there when it does happen.

'You lucked out there with Danny, you know.' I know. 'I mean I wouldn't trade my Ian for the world but I always thought Danny was set for bigger things, that he'd go exploring and trade up.' I *think* that might be a compliment. 'He still decent?'

My eyes widen in horror. Did she just say that?

She smirks. 'Lad had moves.' She's doing this at soft play, isn't she? 'When we heard he were coming back to Kendal, we were all wondering about the lucky bird who ensnared him.'

She makes me sound like a bird of prey. I scrunch my face up almost territorially. She reads my expression and laughs.

'But that's long gone. He were a quiet moody bastard too.' I nod; we can agree on that much.

'Who does your hair?'

Ah, there it is. She's going to attack my split ends now. 'Ummm, no one really.'

'Well, when you're ready, you come and see me.'

I smile. It's like we've both walked up to the line drawn in the sand and shook hands. That was a sweet thing to do, to defend someone you used to have feelings for. It's really grown up, probably more grown up than me.

'She told people I had implants put in me arse. Who the heck wants their bum to look bigger?'

I look sheepish as I believed that rumour. She laughs at my reaction.

'Squats, love. Kids made me arse cheeks droop down me thighs. Had to lift it back up somehow. Ian's an estate agent, he's not a millionaire.'

I giggle. Behind me, Vicky emerges, looking a bit cross that I'm ruining her entrance and carrying what looks like a three-tiered ombre cake with sparklers, candles and all three birthday children's names made out of iridescent fondant. Someone starts singing. In the wrong key so we're all stretching for the high notes in the end. One child is sobbing in the corner because he can't see the cake. There's an odour in the room that makes me think someone may have wet themselves. We reach chaos mode yet again as kids wait for cake and start throwing sachets of salt at each other. Sarah watches us both closely. 'Ignore her,' says Briony. But there's too much noise. And I'm not sure if I know how to mute the volume.

There's something about the first inhalation of air after you step out of a soft play. The air feels clean and quiet again, it's a chance to restore your sanity and feel less murderous. Eve, a whistle in her mouth, skips down the pavement clutching a bit of cake in a napkin, having stuck a line of emoji stickers down my coat. I wasn't quick enough – she got to the Haribo in the party bag before I could. This would be the opportune moment to take her to a rave and have her bounce off the walls so she can come down. She runs on the spot in a six-year old *Flashdance* style.

'Mummy, can I have a dance party for my birthday?'

I hate these conversations. We have six months to prepare for it and every party she will attend between then and now will become a comparative exercise whereby she'll change her mind and get swayed by whatever the craze happens to be, whether it be cupcakes, ceramic painting or slime.

'Will I have to dance?'

'No, because that would be awful.'

I laugh trying not to act offended. If it means I just fire up a playlist to our Bluetooth speaker in a church hall then I might be in. My phone suddenly rings, an unknown number.

I pick up. 'Hello?'

'Hello Mrs Morton, Meg? It's Mike McArthur here from Ferney Green Primary School.' I stop in my tracks and pull my shoulders upright. 'I know it's the weekend but I was wondering if you were at all free? Now maybe?'

Now? There's a strange urgency in his voice that rouses panic in me. Is this about the girls? If this is school related, why is he calling me at the weekend? Has he heard from his wife or the grapevine that Danny is a stair pusher? Is this an intervention?

'I can be… Is everything OK? Is it the girls?'

'Oh, no no no no.' There is an echo in his call which I attribute to my rubbish reception. I'm not sure where he would have got my number otherwise but I like my tone here. I am official and parently. I'm sure that it is down to something as simple as the girls' uniform not being labelled. I write it in biro. I know it washes off.

'I mean it would be really helpful if you were free… to come around…'

'Oh, to your house?'

'Yes.'

For what, a cup of tea and a chat? This must be serious. I can't let them see Eve all hyper and manic like this though. I don't know what to say. He's the headteacher so I need to reply. Balls.

'Well, I have Eve with me so I'll need to drop her home. Is everything alright, Mr McArthur? Should I be concerned?'

'Oh, everything is fine! Please call me, Mike. I'll text you my address.'

That suddenly went very casual. What on earth is going on? 'Alright… See you soon, Mike.'

He hangs up.

That wasn't weird.

'Then we could have a cake in the shape of a giant shiny ball?'

'Say what?'

'Those shiny balls that people dance around?'

'I need to ring your father…'

'Big shiny disco balls… shiny big balls…'

She stands there, high on sugar, singing a self-penned tune about shiny, disco balls. Giant ones at that. A parent walks past and tuts. Something is most definitely up. Danny, answer your sodding phone.

Chapter Thirteen

The McArthurs have shutters. I don't really do interior design or covet many things but I like shutters. I like that kids can spill things on them and you can wipe them down with a damp cloth. There are clipped bay trees outside the front of the house making it look both stately and modern.

'What's that tree that people plant outside their houses to show they're swingers?'

Danny laughs at me. 'It's not bay trees, it's pampas grass, you nutter.'

I scan the garden. 'Is that it?'

Danny gives me that look, the one where he questions the extent to which I've been appropriately educated. 'It's a bush. And not that sort of bush either.'

I wasn't going to come alone so I'd rushed back to ours, deposited a hyper Eve with Stu and told Danny to put on a decent shirt to make him look like a proper dad. We'd been summoned and I wasn't quite sure why.

'Didn't Stu shag McArthur's wife? Maybe this is about that? Maybe he's being banned from the school run… can they do that?'

'Doubt it. They went out for like a month at school,' Danny informs me, staring up their drive.

'Then maybe it's just for a chat, a cuppa? He sounded weird though.'

Danny doesn't look impressed. He's not a social butterfly. Chances are I'll natter on and he'll just sit there grinning like a ventriloquist's dummy. But at least there might be tea and I don't doubt they'll be the sort of people to have decent biscuits too.

'So, Mike and Joanne – is it a Ru and Ro scenario? Childhood sweethearts?'

'Well, she had a thing with Stu but I think McArthur were sixth form and they've been together ever since. They stayed local, don't think either of them went more south than the M60 for university. At least Ru and Ro spread their wings a bit.'

'Did you know Ro once shagged a Latvian bloke who was into vomiting?'

Danny closes his eyes, like he's wondering how on earth that would have come up in everyday conversation.

'C'mon,' he gestures. 'We'll look like a proper pair of idiots stood here on their drive.'

Danny grabs my hand. It's a strange gesture, one we rarely have the opportunity to do given our hands are usually hijacked by little people. I forget he's the firm grasp and handshake sort. This speaks volumes about people, I feel. No one likes a weak hold. Our feet shuffle over gravel and we get up to the front door. Danny rings the bell. The lights are on in the hallway and front room, but nothing.

'Can you hear music?' asks Danny.

I nod. I can. It sounds like Lionel Richie. Danny curls his hands around his eyes, looks through the front window and knocks again at the front door.

'Are you sure he said today? Weren't someone taking the mick? Could have been a prank?' Danny bends down and opens the letterbox. 'EY UP, ANYONE HOME?' I cringe at his lack of reserve. It's then that we hear it.

'MRS MORTON! IS THAT YOU?' shouts a voice, hesitantly, from somewhere in the house.

I push Danny out of the way of the letterbox. 'YES!'

Danny looks at me, confused. Why aren't they coming to the door?

'IF YOU JUMP THE GATE, THE BACK DOOR IS OPEN. LET YOURSELF IN!'

Danny and I look at each other. What the hell is going on here? This is a trap. I'll have my arse halfway up that gate, a dog will come at me and I'll lose a foot.

'What do we do? Do we go in?'

Danny shrugs. 'Well, we're here? May as well.'

He walks to the side of the house and puts a foot on a stone wall to lever himself over in the same way you'd imagine a late thirtysomething man might indulge in parkour. I help get his feet over the threshold and hear him land like a bag of potatoes on the other side.

'I'll go in and open front door,' he whispers through the fence.

I wait, wondering what this is all about. The front door opens.

'Now then. Fancy meeting you here,' he mumbles dryly. 'Just walked through kitchen, they're not in there.'

I cross the threshold. I can still hear Lionel. I notice lines of shoes all lined up by the door, the exact opposite of what I witnessed earlier at soft play. The school shoes are all unscuffed and pristine, the trainers all have their laces undone and ready to be worn. There are no double knot situations here where people are screaming at each other because they're going to be late.

'Take off your shoes,' I whisper to Danny.

'Why are we whispering?'

'I don't know but looks like they're the sort who have a thing for shoes.'

'Oi oi.'

I push Danny playfully and we fumble with our laces, adding our shoes to the mix. There is almost something too calm about this place. I can't quite put my finger on it. We walk past a corridor lined with studio photos of their whole family in denim and white. Darn it, they are a photogenic bunch. The sons are older but have inherited the swishy hair genes and some crazy good dental chops too. All five of them are looking at the camera too, something which we've failed to achieve yet as a family. No one is gurning, smiling with flared nostrils or having a meltdown. As we walk into the kitchen, Danny puts a cheeky hand to my arse. For the love of balls this is not the place Morton.

We walk through to his kitchen which is as I expected given the decor and layout of the house thus far. It's all white and light wood with shiny appliances that don't have handprints, and countertops not adorned with half-torn cereal boxes. Behind the kitchen is a sofa area that leads out to the garden and views over Kendal. They have monogrammed oven gloves. I now know what is missing from our lives. Danny looks at me. Are we reading each other's minds correctly right now? This has the glow of Stepford about it though, right? There's the smell of something coming from the oven. Danny goes over to open it and then turns it off.

'They're burning their lasagne.'

What the hell are we doing here? Danny points up to the ceiling. That voice from before came from upstairs, didn't it? They're upstairs.

'Danny, I'm not comfortable with this. What on earth is happening? Why have they called us?' Danny is just as shocked as me. He leaves the oven door ajar to let the lasagne breathe a little. We hear footsteps above us.

'This is a posh house. Maybe they've been held to ransom and we're the messengers and they're going to kill us,' I mention.

'Maybe you watch too much *Luther*.'

'We don't even know them that well.' I clasp my hand to my mouth. 'You think this was an invite… to something a bit saucy?'

McArthur's words echo about how I could be helpful. In what way? To hold a sex toy in place? Danny's face creases in confusion but he remains very grounded and rational in his reaction. He shrugs his shoulders.

'I doubt it. Let's just go upstairs and take a gander. You walk behind me just in case. It might be nothing.'

We head for the staircase. Their carpet is obviously from a luxury range that melts in between my toes. I've seen this in a film. We'll get up there and there will be a room full of beautiful naked people in masks shagging. I'm in jeggings. I haven't even got on nice pants and I'm wearing over a week's worth of leg stubble. I'm not sure Danny has showered since yesterday. Maybe the McArthurs know about the Captain. Maybe he's worried for our children. Shit. Halfway up, I hear voices in amongst Lionel's dulcet tones. I feel the urge to respond.

'HI! IT'S MEG MORTON. UMMM, I HAVE DANNY HERE WITH ME, IS THAT OK?'

My husband stops in case it may be a problem. The voices upstairs discuss what I've just shouted.

'Yes, it's fine.' I recognise McArthur's tones.

We get to the top of the stairs and I scan the doors that are open. I count all the bedrooms and realise the door the voices are coming from must be a bathroom. I knock on it lightly.

'Hi!' I say in an almost sing-song tone. 'It's me and Danny, is everything OK? We switched off your lasagne. It was burning?'

Maybe that's why I'm here. Maybe the kids' headteacher was too lazy to get out of the bath and needed me to switch off his appliances. Not the reason I am here at all and I know it.

'Hi, Meg… and Danny. So, if you go to the sage dresser in the hall…'

Danny looks at me blankly. I mouth 'green' at him.

'The one with the orchid and the photos?'

'The very one. There is a drawer to the left with a key. Can you locate it? We're locked in here.'

We. Danny looks at me. He rifles through the drawer and finds the key. He puts it in the door, twists it, and we wait for it to open. Do we turn around? Would they like us to run down the stairs? Naturally, we don't. And when it does open, Danny and I stand there in silence to see three people stood before us.

Righto.

Hello.

For some reason, I raise my hand to the air like I'm waving. Mike McArthur stands there with a towel tied around his waist, hair slicked back, face bright red. I can't quite tell whether it's from the embarrassment or the steam. He looks like he's just stepped out of a deodorant commercial. Must not stare at his garden path. He holds a hand out. Danny is not one to refuse a handshake so grabs it firmly.

'Danny, mate. Meg, I am so sorry. It's a dodgy door that sometimes locks itself. We just panicked and we didn't know who to call… we couldn't call family or the police because of—'

'Tim?'

Tim from work. I point at him. He stands there, also wrapped in a towel, looking a little sheepish.

'Guys, hi.'

I realise he told us about McArthur: the older, cute, adventurous hook up? Words fail me so I wave to him. Next to him is Joanne McArthur, also in a towel, looking fresh and dewy like she's just come out of the sauna. They had a meeting of minds in their bathroom and locked themselves in. As you do. Danny and I stand there slack jawed as we take in the scene before us. Three people can just about stand in my bathroom, let alone engage in sexual activity. I'm not sure where to look so I gaze over McArthur's shoulder. They have one of those large corner tubs that no doubt has jet functions and a lovely standalone shower. Nice tiles. *Oh.* I think that may be a tripod.

'And you guys know Tim and he said he knew you… and…'

Well, this is a side of McArthur I've not seen before. He's normally so self-assured and confident and not having to talk himself out of a corner. I get why we've been summoned. We know Tim. How else would they have explained to anyone else about the naked man in their bathroom? He'd come to fix the taps? I don't know whether to feel flattered or scared. At least I feel a bit more secure that I'm not here to be murdered. McArthur scurries to a bedroom next door to put some clothes on. I feel grateful for the towels and that we didn't see more.

'Joanne.' Danny gestures to her.

'Danny, bloody lifesaver. Thank you for rescuing the lasagne too.'

This is how we are helpful, saving people trapped in a bathroom and a baked Italian pasta dish. It takes forty-five minutes for a lasagne to cook. Is that how long they usually have sex for? Were they all going to eat the lasagne together after working up an appetite? Or do kinky stuff with the béchamel?

'We have some explaining to do, eh?' she tells Danny.

Danny puts his hands up. 'Love, we're glad we could help but your business is your own. We can leave now. It's no bother.'

I nod. This is their thing.

'Meg. I am so glad that ankle's better. Any problems with it?' she asks.

'Oh god, it's good as new. Obviously just fell on it strangely…'

'That were a funny night, eh?'

Not as funny as what's happening right now. I look at Danny, slightly confused. We're doing chit-chat, aren't we? There is an awkward silence as Jo and Tim take their leave to the master bedroom to get changed. Do we leave now? Danny and I loiter in the corridor. *Don't look in the bedroom*. All I find myself thinking is that I hope they're looking after their bits. But then she's a nurse, I'm sure she has this in hand. Danny waves over at me to look through the cracks in the bedroom door. I don't want to watch them get changed you dirty sod. But then I see it. It's a bloody swing.

'How old are your lads now?' Danny politely enquires as we make our way downstairs, led by McArthur. He's much better at acting normal in these circumstances while I'm quiet and shell-shocked. We've left Joanne and Tim upstairs and said our goodbyes. Do I remind them to be safe and look after each other? Don't forget that lasagne too – it'll dry out and be inedible otherwise.

'Max is the same age as your Tess, then Riley is eight and Evan is four.'

They have a son called Max McArthur. He sounds like he'd be a property magnate when he's older, with a sideline in evil empires. I can't say these things out loud. I have all the words and the puns and the sarcasm but they must be kept deep within me. Until I get to the car at least. I smile.

'Your youngest bairn is—'

'Polly's coming up to nine months.'

'Fantastic. Who'd have thought Danny Morton would one day spend his life surrounded by a bevy of lovely girls?'

Danny laughs. I don't. I just smile maniacally as he's passed a very strange compliment my way that could be construed as a little bit creepy.

'I'm not sure what to say, Danny,' he mutters awkwardly.

'You don't have to mate. You really don't.'

'Er, can I offer you a cuppa?'

I stare at my husband. I know you love tea but really, don't. Not now. A shot of tequila would actually be the answer. Danny shakes his head.

'We tried to force the door open. We ran through all the options and then Tim said your name, Meg, and how he trusted you so it felt safe to ask you to help us… I have to be careful because of who I am and what I do but it's a lifestyle choice and one that's private and not for the consumption of others.'

'Well mate, you have our discretion,' replies Danny.

This is unlike any parent/teacher conference I've ever had.

'And besides Tim vouching for you, Jo also mentioned something when you were at hospital with your ankle. Something about dildos and some adventurous sex and another woman and we just thought you'd understand…'

Wow. So they also have us here because they think we're like them? Danny covers his face like it might hide his reaction. I've just about rekindled sexual relations with my own husband. I giggle a little under my breath. Danny knows I can't actually speak.

'We're adventurous, Mike, but not with other people.'

I am tempted to applaud my husband's diplomacy. That was a perfect answer. Adventurous is overstating it a little – we just managed it over the duvet in the middle of the day about a week ago. But I guess we *are* a little more open-minded and understanding than most. I'll take that. McArthur gives him a thumbs up and I take that as our cue to leave so he can continue his evening's activities. McArthur goes to embrace Danny who baulks at the physical contact.

'Well, you lot have a nice evening. Mum's the word and all that,' says Danny.

'Again, we are so sorry we dragged you into this.'

'Mate, I've known you for years. This is new but no more awkward than you knowing I was doing my wife up wall when I dropped her on her backside.' He said that out loud, didn't he? 'You're both decent folk. Is what it is. We know Tim, good lad and all. Nice to see the gaff too. I remember when this place belonged to Martin Longdale.'

'Yup, him with the tractors. Bought it a shell and have just done it up slowly.'

'Doing a nice job with it. I heard Longdale moved to Amsterdam and opened up a titty bar.'

They both laugh. Compared to the open marriage here, cock-sketcher and Martin with the tractors, I suddenly feel like the most boring person in the room. I'm not quite sure what has happened but tomorrow I'm going to have to say hello to McArthur at the school gate without smirking. While we talk, we tread over to the front door. Escape feels necessary now. Keep up with the small talk, Danny. Ask them if that's magnolia on the walls and how they keep it so clean. We slip our shoes back on at the front door.

'I guess I'll see you tomorrow then Meg? Music concert in the hall from 2 p.m.?'

I nod. Christ, will you be there shaking a maraca? I may not be able to keep a straight face. He leans in to give me a peck on the cheek.

'Well, take care…'

We head down the gravel and Danny faces away from the house, trying not to make a noise. Hold it in, Morton. I turn and wave again.

'Don't you dare, you bugger,' I murmur under my breath. Our pace picks up and McArthur waves to us as we reverse out of the drive. 'Wave, wave, wave,' I say urging Danny to retain some form of normality. He does so limply, making out that concentrating on reversing is taking up more energy than is actually needed. The car finally out of view, we sit there grinning at each other. We can't speak for exactly thirty seconds as the information washes over us.

'And you thought it were about an unnamed school coat...' Danny mutters.

'What just happened there?'

'I'm not quite sure.'

We both stare into space. Danny continues along Serpentine Road winding down from their house.

'I think I may have broken their fence as I tried to get over it too. Do I tell them?'

'I'll get billed for it with the school dinners.'

'I didn't know where to look, feel a bit boss-eyed now. And was it me but that house was very white, eh?'

'And clean. All wipe down surfaces too.' Danny starts tearing up with the laughter. He pulls into a passing space on the lane to steady himself.

'Did that seriously just happen?' I ask him.

'I went bivouacking with him once... did I tell you about that?'

I pause for a moment and raise an eyebrow. 'You did the *what*?'

Danny forgets that London is in my bones. Scrambling is something I do to eggs, fell is the past tense of fall. I have most never certainly whacked a beaver.

'It's wild camping. Anyway, one night we're all out, it's a cold night. And there's McArthur, getting up close as we all passed out beside the fire. Told me it was all an exercise in body heat exchange but now, hindsight and today tells me it may have been something else.' He looks out the window looking a little perturbed.

'Did you...?' I am a little disturbed that Danny is choosing to tell me about this key sexual moment right here, right now.

'Fook no, it was awkward but I haven't had relations with the kids' headteacher.'

I am relieved, and surprised that he hadn't thought that was a clear sign that maybe he swung both ways.

'I don't know what to do with today's information...' I tell Danny.

'We keep it to ourselves. They entrusted us with it. It's like their Mintcake really.'

I let the realisation sink in that they must have really trusted us, and that feels good. We did something good. But I'm still struggling to process my day having gone in extremes from soft play to orgies.

Danny looks pensive. 'I'm so glad I moved out of this town for a while.' He's stopped the car in a perfect place on the road where the glowing lights of Kendal shine up from the valley. 'Can you imagine if I'd stayed?'

'You'd be running a paper mill with Briony Tipperton as your wife.'

'Swinging with the McArthurs every other fortnight...'

'I saw Tipperton at that party earlier.'

'Did you scrap?'

'No, it was surprisingly civil. She also divulged that you were decent. You had moves apparently.'

Danny laughs, shocked. 'It were known. You scored yourself the town hottie, you did. All the lasses wanted a slice of Morton.'

We both go a bit quiet. It's past five so the sky has darkened and out beyond the thickets and bushes, sky and landscape roll out for miles. The one thing you have to love about this place is the clarity of the night sky, the stars shine that bit brighter. Danny puts his hand out to grasp mine. We interlock fingers.

'You seriously don't want to get up to things like that then?'

Danny shakes his head. 'We don't have enough bath towels for a start. We'd have to put the swing in the hallway.'

I laugh. If we were inviting someone else in, I'd have to change the sheets too. And shave. It seems like too much hard work.

'I feel a bit dull in comparison.'

'You're not dull. I am though.'

'But you're Captain Mintcake.'

'On paper. In real life, I like my sex with the one person. Less complicated that way.'

'I hope that person's me.'

'Yeah. Always been you.'

And then something quite untoward happens. I'll admit, I'm a bit of a sucker for Danny's aloof wordsmithery but tonight, coupled with the dark car, the stars in the sky and maybe in an attempt to prove myself a little sexually adventurous, I reach over and kiss him, grabbing him by the collar and pulling him in close to me. As I bite gently on his bottom lip, he smiles and opens his eyes.

I undo my seatbelt, take off my coat and then roll my jeggings down my legs with my knickers, fumbling and giggling at the awkward movement. Danny doesn't have to say a word. He pushes the seat back and pulls his trousers down from his waist. I try and climb over to straddle him.

'Don't fall on gearstick now. Unless you want to…'

I laugh and lower myself over his lap.

'Mrs Morton. We're having sex in a car. Around the corner from the headteacher's house.'

'I know.' What the actual hell are we doing? I smile and run my tongue along the inside of his neck, feeling him harden under me.

'The suspension won't take it. It's a Volvo,' he whispers.

'You need to have more faith in the Swedes, they're a reliable breed.'

'I love it when you talk about Sweden.'

'Ikea.'

'Fuck.'

'Meatballs.'

'Billy Bookcase.'

I laugh, my head knocked back. He takes this as an opportunity to run a tongue along my collar bone. I feel the effect immediately and gasp. His hands reach down, cupping my buttocks, lifting them and slowly lowering them over his cock. We both sigh as he enters me, a long exhalation with our lips barely touching.

'Viggo Mortensen.'

'He's Danish.'

'Same thing.'

He smiles broadly and pushes his hips up, telling me I don't need to talk about Swedish people anymore. I grab on to the car seat and lever myself up and down, hearing the effect in his moans, building a rhythm and a movement that sees the car sway from side to side. He looks me in the eye, that goofy smile still plastered to his face. But then he squints. Light. Where's that light coming from? Crap, that's bright. Shit. I see the flash of a hi-vis jacket, a knock at the window and someone shaking their head. Oh fuckety fuck fuck fuuuu—

Chapter Fourteen

You have kids, you own a house, you get married and are in charge of your own laundry. It puts you on a different plane of maturity, you are grown up and answerable to no one but yourself. You can eat chocolate for breakfast, crisps in bed and occasionally walk around the house in outdoor shoes (unless you're the McArthurs). It's the best thing about being an adult, except it turns out you are answerable to certain people in society: the taxman, bus drivers and… the police. Namely, Constable Walsh sat in front of us at a desk peering over his glasses and making both Danny and I feel about two feet tall. The problem is we wouldn't be sat here if it wasn't for Danny. Danny who assumed the policeman who caught us having sex in a very public passing place was just a snooping passer-by and had an array of irate and colourful words to say to him. It was made worse when I screamed in his ear, 'It's the rozzers!' I hopped off him a tad too hastily, possibly bending his penis at an unsavoury angle and he responded by opening the car door forcefully. Into Constable Walsh's face. There was blood (not Danny's). There was swearing. There was a point Constable Walsh reached down to what looked like a taser and I started crying in fear thinking he was reaching for a gun and my children were about to become orphans which is stupid as police in this country don't carry guns, let alone Lakeland police who usually have to deal with little else but lost sheep and speeding cars. But that's not what shoots through your mind when you've collapsed out of a car into a country lane without any knickers on, trying your hardest to pull your T-shirt over your bare arse and convincing a policeman that you're not a violent criminal.

Constable Walsh looks at me now with a look of judgement, like the secretary sat outside the headteacher's office and what suspiciously looks like a tampon stuck up his nose. I shield my face with my hands to hide my shame and mortification. Danny is the opposite, he feels he has nothing to hide or at least be apologetic for – he adopts a rebel's slouch in his seat and is close to churning out some sort of rant about how they should be spending our tax money hunting down real criminals, politicians and tax dodgers. In short, the ground needs to swallow us up pretty quickly. Please.

'Can you at least try to look a little repentant?' I say.

'Not my fault he was stood so close to the car.'

'Danny! You made his nose bleed. Even if it's an accident, you at least should say sorry…'

I feel like I'm talking to a small child.

'He should be apologising to us. That light was like a frigging laser in our eyes. He could have blinded us.'

By the way he's still cupping his nether regions then I assume he's less concerned about his eyesight but more worried about damage to down below. That and his ego.

'There's a better way to dismount a man, you know.'

'Then next time, I'll gently hop off when the police are knocking at our car window…'

'You can break a penis, you know. You could have broken my penis.'

'What a load of bollocks, you can't break a penis… it hasn't got bones in it.'

'Do you have a penis?'

Constable Walsh is picking up on the drama unfolding in front of him, never mind an apology. He gets to witness a comedy domestic as compensation. This could be far better. I am glaring at my husband.

'No, I don't have a penis. I can't believe it's taken you eleven years of marriage to realise this.'

I'm going to go dry and sarcastic with him now and that's dangerous territory. Grow a pair, you absolute tool.

'There are tubes, a urethra in a penis that you could have damaged.'

'You're worried about not pissing right? I've had three sodding children. I haven't pissed right since 2008.'

Constable Walsh hides his face now; never mind he's seen my bottom half naked, he knows more about it than he really needs. Danny is still sulky, cradling his nether regions. I'll break it now if you want. He doesn't dare look at me. Oh, how the tide can turn so quickly. Ninety minutes ago, we were rescuing a threesome stuck in a bathroom. Forty-three minutes ago, we were having some of the hottest post-baby sex we've ever had, in the family Volvo, littered with old breadsticks and juice cartons. I felt that spark shiver through me, I felt like my sexual self of old, wanting to be fucked and touched and held. Now we sit here and I could seriously nut him and draw blood, giving each other serious concussions and I wouldn't bat an eyelid.

'What are they doing? Are we going to be charged?'

Danny gives me that look wondering what happened to my education.

'And charge us for what? Like you said, it wasn't intentional?'

I whisper out the side of my mouth. 'I believe the sex in the public place thing is pretty much frowned upon.'

'It's not like we were strangers doing it on a park bench? Or that there were people about? Two consenting adults, married adults.'

'Having sex in a car.'

This makes Danny smirk a little. I don't smirk back. I elbow him before Constable Walsh catches sight of him and thinks he's totally incapable of repentance.

'Then why are we here? Maybe you just need to apologise and draw a line under all of this. We need to get back to Stu, the girls.'

He looks at me. I know mention of the girls will strike at Danny's better conscience. It wasn't our finest moment being dragged here in the back of a cop car. We were forced to re-dress in the middle of the road as a man rode past on his bike. A bike with a basket no less, carrying loaves of bread. It was like we'd tainted this small Hovis ad village lane with our sordidness. Constable Walsh was still wary given Danny's profuse swearing so handcuffed him (this didn't help) and we were both shoved in a car and brought here without any explanation. I am just glad I wasn't drunk; this is around the time I'd try and use some sort of journalistic swagger to complain about my civil liberties and rights to legal advice.

Danny goes to stand and Constable Walsh puts a hand up.

'Can you take a seat please? We took the cuffs off on the condition that you behaved yourself.'

I pull him down immediately. He's baiting Danny for a reaction so he can take this further. It's cruel but I see the tampon-like thing protruding from his nose: fair play, sir.

'What about our car?'

To be honest, our rusting Volvo is the last thing on my mind but well done to my husband for thinking practically.

'That will be towed away, Mr Morton.'

Danny throws his hands up to the air. It feels like unnecessary punishment for the crime and a fine that we'll have to cough up but I don't question it. It's the law, we did something wrong. Danny is gearing up for a fight though, his jaw is rigid, his nostrils flared. Please Danny, for all the times I've wished and hoped for you to show grander parades of emotion, this isn't one of those times.

'Maybe I should request they put those cuffs back on…' I say under my breath.

'You'd like that, wouldn't you? Kinky lass,' he whispers back.

'You can talk, sex sketcher.'

We talk in whispering insults so much so that Walshy – he's seen it all, he may as well have a nickname – leans forward trying to get an ear in. This is how Danny and I fight, it's a battle of insults. We could go on like this for hours until someone admits that they have no words left and waves the white flag. As we wage our war, the station doors open and a police officer pushes in a gentleman who's obviously had a bit too much to drink.

'This is called police brutality. This is what happens in America and people die. You two got camera phones? I want evidence of this to give my kids at the tribunal asking why I died in police custody.'

Danny and I sit there in stunned silence. The gentleman walks like he has no ankles and his body is anchored into the ground at forty-five degrees. We don't reach for our phones but Danny alerts me to the fact that maybe we should try and text Stu to tell him we might be later than anticipated or at least try and hitch a ride off someone who could come here and transport us without question or judgement.

'Lee was caught pissing off the roof of the pub again. He stood there with his privates exposed in front of a crowd of pubgoers gathered for a wake singing that *Monty Python* song.' Constable Walsh and colleague are completely deadpan while Danny and I muster everything inside us to stifle the laughter. Unfortunately, this goads Lee on knowing he has an audience.

'They were too touchy. It's not like I was pissing on his corpse. And that woman who said I was wanking, I was just shaking off the snake.' Lee looks on as Walshy takes notes. 'Who took a swipe at you then?'

'None of your business.'

'Was it Rocky over here? Nice one pal!'

The other policeman looks over, not too impressed.

'Let's just say you're not the only case of indecent exposure we've had in today.'

Danny and I feign shock.

'Oi, oi! You and your lady friend doing a bit of al fresco. No shame in that.' He comes over to high five Danny but is hoisted back by his police escort.

'It wasn't indecent. We're married.'

I elbow Danny sharply in the ribs.

'Spicing it up so it don't go stale. Good on yer. You wouldn't be the first to have a bit of Lakeland outdoor fun.'

I lied before, *this* is when the ground needs to swallow me up. The police officers stand there and don't give anything away. They just glance over at us like we're reprobates, lowlifes, scum. You judgemental pricks. Walshy, you might like to do it blindfolded and dressed like a clown. Whatever floats your boat. We just found out the headteacher and his wife are in an open marriage, and that they're shagging my colleague.

'We were in a car,' Danny says, completely deadpan.

'Dogging?'

And at this precise moment, the police station door swings open and there stands the last person we need to be stood there.

'Mum?' exclaims Danny.

Balls. Gill glares over at Danny and myself. She looks no different to usual with the quilted jacket, floral scarf and sensible flat loafer but there's a look in her eye that I recognise from my house after ankle-gate; a look of mistrust and disappointment. After my fallout with Stu, we'd seen her but there was a bit of awkwardness still there. This is a new face to me given she's normally so sweet and upbeat. It's Lee's turn to be in hysterics now.

'Crikey, they called your ma. Hello, Mother of Doggers.' He does something which resembles a curtsey. 'Someone's been a naughty boy. No pocket money for him this week.'

The officers present have to compose themselves now. Lee gets dragged off as Gill approaches the desk.

'Gary, how are you, love?'

I look over at Danny. His mother knows Walshy? What screwed up version of weird is this? How on earth did he think calling your mother was a good idea? My mother-in-law who now thinks we abandon our kids to go dogging down country lanes. Danny looks completely vacant. Gill senses this and rolls her eyes back.

'Gary Walsh. He was Stu's mate for years,' Gill informs us.

'What? That nerdy one, with the big teeth? The one who used to wear a cape thinking he were in Pink Floyd?' Danny is not helping our cause here.

'The very one,' replies Gary, still remarkably unimpressed. 'The one who used to give you all those free pints down The Wine Bar.'

'Yeah, you did.' The memories seem to flood back in an instant.

'And remember the night of that New Year's do, when you kissed my girlfriend in full view of me.'

I turn to Danny. He needs to say sorry, all the apologies, right now. Get on your knees, man.

'Well, mate,' Danny replies, 'she were a bit of a village bike back then, you know.'

'That's now his wife,' Gill interjects.

Oh, my days. Who is this man sat next to me? Don't know him at all. Danny's eyes widen. Well done. Walshy's face is a strange shade of strawberry.

Gill intervenes. 'You'll have to forgive my idiot of a son here. Gary's wife, Natalie, is a teacher down at the comp. She attends my quilt-making classes on Wednesday evenings. They have five bloody kids together.'

Oh. You can half tell that Danny still has trouble placing this man at all. Such is the problem with someone who has no interest in building his social circle.

'You still mates with Stu?' Danny asks.

'Yup, I messaged him on Facebook. He thought this was hysterical. Told me to call your ma.'

'You pair of buggers.'

'You're free to go. We'll send you details about how to get your car back. As an officer of the law, I am giving you an official caution, in front of your mother, that sex in public places can be seen to be in violation of the Public Order Act and if caught again then we'd be inclined to press charges.'

He salutes us, sneering but touché my man. He's probably been coming up with ways to get his revenge for years and now he's finally done it. He can sleep well tonight but I'm thinking he may have possible questions for the missus over their roast dinner this evening. Gill stands there, arms crossed, shaking her head. Danny has been muted, shamed and has a sore crotch. I don't know where to look, not least because Gill thinks we've been dogging. We rise to leave.

'Thank you, Gary. I apologise these two have wasted valuable police time. Give my regards to Nat, I'll see her next week.' She looks closely at his nose. 'Best get some ice to that before it bruises.'

She turns and literally pushes us out of the door. She mumbles under her breath and we head over to her red Fiat Punto like sullen teenagers. This is a side to Gill that I've not seen before. She has always been bright and embracing; I thought very little could faze her but now I'm seeing a volcano bubble up to the surface. It's a side I'm sure she often had to unleash as a mother of teenage sons, one which she hasn't had to tap into for a long time. Until now. I'm a bit scared at how this might pan out. I've grown up with a mother who was a force of nature but that was who she was; she was unapologetic about her fire, every day, all day. This has all gone a bit Jekyll and Hyde. But Danny seems to know the score and guides us into the back seats. He holds my hand. Gill gets in.

'Seat belts, please.'

She eyes us both up in the rear-view mirror. We do as we're told.

'Wind down your window and see how close I am to that bollard, Daniel.'

She's using the full Daniel. I rarely hear her do this.

'Bags of room, mum.'

I sit there in silence as he helps her negotiate out of the space. She exits the car park, edging out onto the main road, slowly picking up speed to a steady thirty miles per hour. I nudge Danny's knee with mine.

'I'm sorry you had to hear all of that Mum, really I am.'

She says nothing but keeps us both in her sight.

'For the record, we weren't dogging. It was a misunderstanding,' he adds.

'I'm not sure how being caught having intercourse in your car is a misunderstanding, Daniel. You know I thought I was done with this sort of bullshit now you're a grown man. And to be honest, it's the sort of tomfoolery I expected with Stu. Not you.'

'You've been arrested before?' I enquire. Gill still doesn't look too impressed with me.

'Teenage sons, Meg. I wouldn't wish that misery and shame on anyone. If they weren't nicking my cigarettes, they were pissing about in school and shagging someone's sister and I'd have the coppers, angry fathers, exasperated teachers, the lot of them telling me about it, making me out to be the one who should have done better.'

She is a little glassy-eyed now and I feel all the empathy as a parent for her. What have we done? I didn't want to make lovely Gill feel shitty about herself. I lean forward in my seat.

'Gill, we really are sorry. It was a moment of madness.'

She steadies herself as she drives. 'You're just lucky I answered the phone and not Bob.'

'Dad would have found this hysterical.'

Gill and I both shift Danny a look. I go as far as to slap him across the arm.

'What is the deal with both of you? I'm not getting the whole picture. That whole thing with the ankle. My mind was racing at a million miles per hour. I thought that Danny had hurt you. Then, when I was stood on the stairs in your house I heard your sister talk about divorce and seriously, I thought I were going to fall down them stairs. It broke me.'

Danny and I look at each other. We realise that we haven't fixed this. We had let Stu into the secret but Gill had quietly thought the worst of us. I know Danny didn't want her to know anything about Captain Mintcake but it's important we put her mind to rest. Deep down, she just cares and we've given her two months of anguish thinking something was wrong with our marriage. I feel awful.

'I don't know how to put this, Gill.' Danny glares at me. 'With the ankle thing, it was as simple as Danny and I were having sex and I fell.'

I should probably not be telling her this while she is driving and negotiating a one-way system. She doesn't flinch.

'Then why was Stuart so upset?'

Danny intervenes. 'Megs made a bit of a scene in the hospital when we got there and the nurse had assumed that I'd hurt her which is untrue but it was all cleared up.'

Gill doesn't respond. She's having problems switching to third – that clutch needs a look at – but I can see her processing the information. I also feel like she has something to add to the conversation.

'Then explain to me the toys.'

Please be talking about cuddly toys. It's endemic in our house, we have far too many. Please, please, please.

'What toys would they be, Mum?'

She adjusts herself in her seat. 'Well, to be frank, they seem to be everywhere.'

I take a cursory glance at Danny. Yes, Danny… where are these toys?

'I've been helping Stu with things like laundry. I found a dildo in the linens.'

I turn to face my husband as I see him trying to concoct excuses to both of us within the confines of this metal box. Better be good, Morton.

'And the other day, there is no other way of saying this but I found a strap-on under the bed while I was hoovering. Stu tried to make out to me that it was his and some sort of climbing apparatus but I wasn't born yesterday. I watched that lesbian drama on BBC One.'

My eyes have glazed over. What does she think of me if she thinks my vagina can take that dildo?

'And…'

There's more? That's all the toys that I know about.

'…I went into the mill recently. Your dad sometimes likes to have a look over the books and I bring in cake for the lads and have a catch up.'

My husband's face turns a funny colour and he squirms in his seat. For crap's sake, Danny, we talked about full disclosure, about no more secrets. What on earth is at the mill?

'I found a filing cabinet full of the stuff. I'm an open-minded lady but I didn't even know what half of it was. I had to come back and google it. I'm not even talking about a few things, I'm talking a three drawer filing cabinet filled to the brim.'

You can tell Gill is riled as she's crept up to thirty-five miles per hour. I look over at Danny, not even angry anymore. His Love Shack stash. I'd just assumed he'd thrown everything away or returned it. He kept it? It feels like I may be drip fed this type of information forever more; a new fact per day until I've run out of reasons to be shocked.

'I do not know what you two are up to but anyone could have gone in that cabinet. Someone from work: a cleaner, Olive on reception, one of the work experience lads. We have a reputation to uphold at the mill. You have a responsibility.'

Danny looks suitably put in his place but is equally quizzical. 'Mum, that cabinet is locked with two combination padlocks and a key.'

'1981. You've not changed your combo since you were a lad with a BMX. The key was in the top drawer of the desk in the Star Wars mug.'

I give up trying to not act disappointed in my husband's complete lack of discretion.

'The padlocks are so people can't get in there. You went in on the hunt.'

Gill gives him an evil from her rear-view mirror. 'The mill is still owned by the Mortons and I have a right to know what's in them drawers. We're not a storage facility for your sex trinkets.'

I like how she refers to them as sex trinkets. My eyes are still glued open at the thought of what she found. Jesus, Danny. He could have hidden them anywhere. The spare tyre compartment of his car, the loft, the shed, the wood store. But, no. It pains me to think that he probably had that shit delivered to work too. I feel even more stupid. Danny shifts awkwardly.

There is a very easy way to explain this whole ruse. It's a new hobby I've got, Mum. I draw those toys and penises and vaginas. Come back and I'll show you my latest piece that features butt plugs. But he can't. Part of it is because she'll crash the car, no doubt, but I can see a doleful look in Danny's eyes; words still ringing in his ears about responsibility, the mill, the reputation. It's a look which makes me want to burst because I know what he wants to say deep down. The mill isn't me. I'm there because it was the right thing to do and I cared. I took on that responsibility. I changed my whole life, I transported my whole family up here so it could still exist. And I see him stare out the window, sat in the back of his mother's car, being told off and told that he's not doing the right thing by a company he's sacrificed his soul for – and that cuts him deep. He won't fight with his mum, that much I know. He won't tell her about Captain Mintcake either, partly due to embarrassment but also because it'll make her worry. If you're in the erotica game now, who will run the mill? How will I break it to your father with his dodgy heart? And what pains me, is that I can read all of this from just a single look and prolonged silence. But I know.

'Gill, they're mine. I am so very sorry.'

Danny breaks away from his silence to give me a curious look. I study the perforated ceiling of her Fiat Punto, trying to look for a cover story. Time to think on your feet, Meg.

'It was for the paper. They were running a feature on erotica, sex toys and the like. I had to try them out and write some reviews for a Valentine's Day special. The article never got to print, bit too risqué for the Lakes but these companies were sending me lots of the things. We were overrun and we obviously didn't want them in the house near the girls so I told Danny to keep them in the office. Danny, I thought I told you to throw them away?'

For this to work, Danny needs to play along but I forget he's not very good at this game.

'I thought we could keep them?'

I'm literally trying to put the words in his mouth. Work with me here, hubs. I was busy, I didn't have time to dispose of them, I forgot they were there. Don't make us out to look like we had some sex paraphernalia library hidden in the office.

'You tried out all those sex toys?' asks Gill.

I have to play along, don't I?

'For journalistic integrity. But I'm appalled that Danny kept them.'

Gill nods in agreement. I nod at Danny in jest. He raises a wry smile.

'I'm not sure this explains today though?'

It doesn't, does it? I have to break with tradition here and talk about my sex life with my mother-in-law.

'Well, the toys obviously spiced things up for us a fair bit so Danny and I have been trying new things…'

Danny is very close to sticking his fingers in his ears and blocking out the noise. He slowly sinks into his seat, shaking his head ever so slowly.

'And today was one of those new things.'

Gill is thoughtful as she drives. I have a feeling she can sense that I am lying through my teeth and beads of sweat form around my collar and inside my bra. There are things which should remain unspoken between you and the mother of your husband but I am saying them aloud out of love, to protect said husband, to save his pride. I grab his knee hoping he knows that this horrific awkwardness is for a reason. He puts his hand on mine. Please Gill, please say something.

'Back in the day, when you wanted to try something new, you just bought a fancy pair of pants and a suspender belt. Maybe a silk stocking and some saucy lingerie.'

And there is the image that Danny really needs at the forefront of his mind. I smile without showing any of my teeth. Look out the window, focus on the tarmac and the passing trees.

'Or when you had sex outside, definitely not a main thoroughfare where you'd likely be caught by the passing traffic.'

Danny and I pause for a moment. There was an inference about Gill's sex life there which we don't want to question any further. They liked a walk in the fells, dear Gill and Bob. I did wonder why they were always so keen to take a rug. I try to contain my laughter whereas Danny is grey. This is the torture that I am sure Gary Walsh was hoping he could witness.

'So really, you are a bunch of fecking idiots.'

I emit a small noise at hearing Gill swear.

'I'm sorry, Mum,' groans Danny, in a seventeen-year-old teenage grunting tone.

'I mean, think about the girls. Or what if that story had got to the paper? And god forbid, what if it'd got to the mill.'

'Can't be worse than what half the lads on the factory floor get up to.'

'That's not the point, Daniel. You head up the mill, you set the example.'

She's going to that place again and I see that look return to Danny's eyes. I want to get back to ours and invite Gill in to see her son's talent. Look how well he can render all those naughty bits in acrylic, all that artistic talent squandered. He hides it away from the world and refuses to pursue it as a career because of the bloody mill. Still, such bitter words would do nothing at this point. I just squeeze Danny's hand a little harder. The car pulls into our road and Gill looks for a place to park. The car squeaks to a halt and we sit there in silence. I'm not sure what she wants. We've done the apologies and the explanations. And I'm not sure how much longer Danny and I can keep this charade going.

'You think Bob and I are old farts but we've done stuff and it was always behind closed doors. Of course, we don't do those things since his heart but I get it. Just be smarter about it.'

'Yes, Mum,' Danny and I say in unison. We look up at the house where Stu stands at the doorway with Tess and a highly strung out Eve.

'I won't come in. It's well past dinner and I left a gammon on to boil before heading out of the house. Lord knows Bob won't know what to do with it.'

'Thank you, Gill.'

She turns and looks me in the eye one last time before I get out of the car, almost studying my face to gauge if I'm telling the truth.

'One last thing though. It's a bloody relief. I seriously thought one of you was having an affair or something. All those whispers of divorce. And the thought of you two splitting up and the girls, I won't lie… I cried…'

'Gill…' I stop in my tracks to hear such an admission.

'I know relationships can be strange things but you two are fine, right?'

'Mum, we were just caught having sex in a car…'

'Danny!' I squeal.

Gill smiles, almost out of relief. 'Go now.'

I awkwardly hug her from the back seat, Danny and I take the long walk of shame to the house and the group of us assembled outside wave Gill away. Stu watches us stumble in, Danny looking emotionally drained from the last ten minutes in his mother's car.

'What's Mum doing dropping you back?' enquires Stu, smiling broadly.

'I'm going to kill you when you're asleep brother.'

Stu's heard that five thousand times before. I smile faintly. Yet again, my sex life and misadventures are the butt of the jokes. I am the laughing stock.

'Why didn't Granny come in? Granny always comes in?' asks Eve.

Because she has already ritually humiliated us in the car and unwittingly hurt her son's feelings and we've also partaken in details of each other's sex lives which means that we won't be able to look each other in the eye for at least a fortnight. 'She was boiling a gammon.'

The girls are confused and tired. Hugs are forthcoming. Danny picks up his Buttons, who still has party and sugar fizzing through her veins.

'I gave littl'un a bottle and put her down.'

I nod at Stu's surprising efficiency.

'Head down pub, lad. It's been an evening,' instructs Danny.

'What happened at McArthurs?' Stu asks.

'You saw Mr McArthur?' asks a curious Tess.

I can't even recall that part of the evening, it feels like it happened to someone else.

Danny nods. 'I'll tell you tomorrow.' He literally shoves Stu out of the house. I put an arm around Tess and we take the long trek up the stairs to the girls' room.

'Did you brush your teeth?'

They both nod. They might be lying but I'm not sure I care too much at this precise moment. The girls are escorted to their beds and we wish them goodnight, turning the lights low so the stars on their ceiling illuminate the gloom. Danny goes around picking up used T-shirts, books and pens without their lids on. I kneel next to Tess' bunk and arrange her hair on the pillow, resting my head on the duvet.

'Is it school tomorrow?' asks Tess.

'Yes, it is,' I reply.

'Did I ever tell you the story about what Clara Lowry did the other day in lunch?'

'No.'

'Clara has started wearing starter bras and Marcus made fun of her and he got slices of cucumber and told everyone they were his new boobies.'

'So what did Clara do?'

'She slapped him and told him he was a sexist pig.'

'And who do you think is in the wrong here?'

'Marcus?'

If anything else, I've done something right. I kiss her on the forehead and she rolls over. Eve has passed out like a giddy puppy. Danny takes my hand and we go to Polly's room to find her spread-eagled in her cot like she may have landed badly after a sky dive. I'm not sure what she's wearing but it's clothes and I'm just thankful that she's asleep. I pat her to check Stu remembered a nappy. Danny bends down between the railings in her cot and reaches for her tiny hand. He then curls up on the floor space next to her cot and lies there in a foetal position. I lay down next to him, spooning him, placing my cheek on the curve of his back.

'Are you OK?' I whisper. He doesn't reply. I put my arms around him and squeeze him tightly. And that's when I feel it. The shudder in his chest, a tear drip on to my hand. I make him turn to face me.

'Was the sex that bad?'

He laughs through his tears. I know why they're there. I felt the mood turn in that car; I knew she made him question who he was and why he does it. I grab his hands and kiss them.

'Thank you for covering for me.'

A little person shifts in their cot and we lower our voices again.

'What is it you think your mum and dad get up to behind closed doors?'

'Please don't.'

'It's tarmacking, isn't it?'

He grabs a cuddly toy from near his head and hits me with it. 'Shush now or I'll have to gag you.'

'Or a dirty…' He puts his hand over my mouth, trying hard not to laugh cry. I bulge my eyes.

'And a whole filing cabinet full of sex toys? Now I know. Did you try them on yourself?' I joke.

'I tried them on you when you were sleeping.'

'Didn't feel a thing.'

'That's because of your giant vajingo…'

There's a moment of silence.

'Are you really OK?'

'We just lied to my mum.'

'I lie to my mum all the time.'

'Like how?'

'I tell her that I'm feeding the girls organic; that I tried to call her but I had a problem with my phone.'

'You know what I mean…'

'You shouldn't listen to her. You do what makes you happy.'

'I know.'

And maybe that's what's at the crux of this. Happiness. Is Danny happy? Because here he lies on our youngest's bedroom floor and I'm conscious that up till recently, I didn't really know him all too well. There's this whole side of his life that he kept from me, a brain lined with curious artistic leanings. I haven't been scared off. But I'm lying here with this brain and it's very confused. It doesn't know where it's supposed to be. I cross everything that I at least make him a little bit happy. Because there's no other place this brain should be but right here, next to me. Look at those sad glassy eyes. Don't look at me with those sad eyes. I run a finger down his cheek and trace the outline of his chin. You muppet.

'It's been a day,' I say.

'That it has. You couldn't make it up.'

'I'm really sorry I nearly broke your cock.' I touch it through his trousers to ensure it's OK.

'Stop pestering me for sex. It's getting boring.'

I laugh and rest my nose against the stubble on his cheek, my legs entwined around his.

'Are you really OK?'

He doesn't answer.

Chapter Fifteen

The one thing I like about the Lakes is that it has a very artisan side to it exemplified by the number of places where you can get a hand-stitched throw, a hand-raised pie, any number of pastel sketches and paintings (usually of a lake). There are little villages scattered around filled with galleries with these curiosities, next to shops selling overpriced cream teas and outdoorsy clothing joints where one can obtain a sturdy cane and a hardcore hooded jacket that has more pockets than any person really needs. These places are also usually filled with artsy people who love a Peruvian poncho, corduroy and are gnawing on some damsons; people like Rufus and Rowan.

Today, we are at The Brewery where Ro is exhibiting some of her drawings and sculptures. I'll admit, some of it is very Rothko and beyond my understanding, but there are a few phallic pieces that catch me off guard and make me glad we've left the kids with Gill, who has extended her forgiveness to us for all recent sexual misdemeanours. It's a very civil affair, by which I mean the home-made alcohol has been limited to one glass and there are bowls of nuts and seeds about the place that I believe Ru grew and smoked himself. Ro looks her usual radiant self in a green velvet dress, her hair long and tousled whilst Ru has gone full tweed with a pair of very battered old Doc Martens. They welcome everyone in the room with warm hugs and celebrations. It's contagious and makes me want to hug the gentleman next to me as we examine a large metallic structure that I am pretty sure is supposed to be a penis. I take back everything I said about that dildo in the post. This is *big*.

'Visceral,' claims the gentleman who is wearing a T-shirt that has either been attacked by moths or may be a fashion statement. 'There's a real command of the material and the subject matter: sexual dominance I think?' I don't know what to say. This penis doesn't have bollocks.

I feel a hand in mine. Danny. He pipes in. 'I disagree. I think the metal points to one's relationship with their manhood being a reflective experience; you are always looking inwardly during sex.'

We both nod. I'm slightly in awe at my husband's artistic insight. We both cock our heads to the side. Moth T-shirt man moves on.

'Have you tried the nuts?' I ask.

'It's like he dragged them across the floor. Told you we should have eaten first.' Danny curls his body into mine. 'I love these guys but how long can we stay before we skedaddle?'

'You look at everything once and then congratulate the artist, feign interest in buying and then on to the pub.'

'I think the giant metallic penis would work well in the bathroom.'

'To hold the towels.'

'Exactly.'

I dressed down today in an attempt to appear casually chic. I'm in a three-quarter skirt and pointed flats that Tess said made me look like a witch but I also made an effort with a coral lip and a touch of eyeshadow. I know the Wezzie was thinking of dropping in and I know there's nothing worse than being in the local paper looking like a surprised tramp in one of their shots. We head in different directions across the room in an attempt to cover more ground. I move on to another mixed media piece drenched in every shade of red but splattered in white. It's like a bukkake session gone terribly awry. A fellow art appreciator nods at me.

'This is so powerful. How one's femininity does not equate to a loss of energy.'

I nod in agreement. Let's go with that.

'How do you know the artist?' I ask.

'We went to college together, here in Kendal before she went overseas for a while.'

Alas, it's another Kendallian. I want to ask if she has any intimate knowledge of the Morton brothers but one of them beats me to it.

'Steph! You are having a ruddy laugh? Seriously?'

It would seem she knows Stu then, who's also here to give him a break from the kids. The two embrace as I stand there and they laugh trying to work out how long it's been since they've seen each other.

'Steph, this is Danny's wife, Meggsy. Steph used to live next door to us with her brothers. Jesus, it's been an age.'

It's actually Meg but I don't correct them and smile politely. Steph is a vision in many different clashing prints, her hair swept up into a messy bun held together with a tie-dye headscarf. I bet she's very into the nuts.

'Last thing I heard your mum said you were in Australia training to be a lawyer.'

'Trying to get on *Bondi Rescue*, more like,' I joke. Steph gives me a strange look.

'Stu was like the cleverest kid I knew. You and Bradley were in the same class and they got them professors in from university to give you harder maths.'

I glance at Stu who, as usual, has no interest in gloating. He nods and looks away sheepishly. 'What are you up to these days then Steph?'

'Own a vintage clothes stall and we travel to markets and fairs and stuff.'

'How old's Betsy now?'

'Get this, she's eighteen this year.'

I nod politely assuming Betsy to be a car or a very elderly dog. Steph gets her phone out to show Stu a picture. Betsy is a girl, a proper person and it dawns on me that it's her daughter. She smiles at me.

'I know, don't look old enough – I had her back end of college. Do you remember? Your ma used to help me babysit her so I could finish my art foundation course.'

'She were dead cute. Remember Danny used to take her on drives in his Citroën? It were a village affair raising that one.'

'And now she's off to Manchester to study French and Philosophy so we obviously did something right.'

I smile. The fact that Danny used to take Betsy out in his Citroën also makes me slightly wary about Betsy's parentage. Danny enters the scene and reaches over to embrace her.

'Now then, blast from past. How do?'

It's turned into a strange Northern vernacular where I will take a few seconds at the end of each sentence to digest and translate.

'Just telling Stu, Betsy turns eighteen this year,' she says.

'You're having a laugh. Bonny little baby she were… You here examining the art then?'

'How could I not? Powerful stuff – girl done good as usual.' She gestures to a man at the other side of the room. 'We'll catch up later boys, eh? Just going to check on the old man.'

We smile as she heads over to an elderly gentleman in a tank top holding a couple of pints. 'Not sure her dad will appreciate the art?' I say with a giggle.

Danny and Stu snigger. 'That'll be Steph's husband.'

'Que?' I seem to utter in a snort-like way.

'That's Mr Glendale. He were head of art. When she left school, they hooked up.' Stu informs me.

'How old is he?'

'Forty-four when they got together.'

They both glance over with shades of judgement.

'But… he…'

'Looks like he should be drinking the last of the summer wine?'

I try my hardest not to stare. He's not a sprightly gentleman and not in the silver fox territory either.

'It were all Kendal could talk about. He was married with two kids and left her for Steph. Steph's mum used to be in our house most nights crying into a cuppa. It were mental.'

Old Man Glendale looks over and waves and we all gesture back hoping the giggles didn't give us away.

'I tell you, if it were any of my daughters he'd be at bottom of Windermere.'

The couple chat further, laughing and deep in conversation.

'You can't say that, Danny… they're still together, proved people wrong?' They support my point by going into a full on snog. I see tongue. I retch a little just because I know they're not drunk and I'm pretty sure the last time I kissed someone like that was when I was fifteen and didn't know any better.

'It weren't right, Meggsy. I'm with Danny here. They're my nieces too – I'd help you throw that body in a lake and weigh it down with bricks.' They shake hands and I feel like I've become accomplice to something I shouldn't know about. 'And the sex now… geez, bet it's all Viagra and low impact so they don't bust his hips.'

'But you helped her, with the baby.'

'It's what you do, innit? She were young and lost and we helped them out. Her own dad weren't around. Wasn't Betsy's little fault she were born into a messed up situation.'

I watch on as Danny and Stu stare into some point in the past where they were more than just your typical lads but honourable youngsters helping single mothers find their way. Relief that Danny is not Betsy's father is replaced by shock that Father Time is. I wonder what happened to his wife and other kids? I also make a mental note to recount this story to Emma who's always looking for divorce stories to outdo her own. Could have been far worse and your daughters could have a schoolgirl as a stepmother. I feel a pair of arms extend around my midriff.

'Meggy, I'm so glad you're here! Thank you, thank you!'

I turn around to a slightly squiffy Ro, giggling with nerves but full of warmth and wild abandon as usual.

'Is it OK? Is everything OK? What do you think? How's the music?'

I hadn't really put my ear to it but there's some low-grade French mumbling happening over a drum and bass beat. I want to say it's not too offensive but then I'm not too sure what the rapper is actually saying.

'It's all amazing. Calm yourself.'

'I can't believe how many people showed up. My old art teacher from school's here.' I nod: Glendale, I know the scoop. 'And there are some people from Paris too who are doing a whole installation thing and they want my input. It's… it's…'

'You're amazing. Go, don't babysit us.' I say 'us' but the boys Morton have disappeared. Ro is not done with me though. She takes my hand and pulls me over to a piece hidden in the corner. It's not as ostentatious as some of the other pieces but it's a well-crafted series of drawings that look like the stages of a flower opening. Wait, that'll be a vagina. Yes, it's someone's labia.

'It's Danny.' She attempts to whisper but says a bit too loudly given her state of inebriation. We interlock arms and giggle.

'Last time I looked, Danny doesn't have those parts.'

'No, silly. It's Danny's drawing.'

I twist my head around to try and find Danny who's seemingly disappeared from the room.

'I had to include it, the detail, the idea was so beautiful. Dewy female anatomy blossoming to life.'

Also known as *Study of a Vagin*.

'Does he know?'

'Kinda. He just didn't want his name attached to it, not even the Mintcake one, but someone has already asked how much it is.'

I glance at it again. It has the hallmarks of one of Danny's pieces: the attention to detail, the sense that what's being drawn is neither done for perverse reasons or for titillation. There's an underlying appreciation there, a story. I can understand Danny's caution though in exhibiting anonymously. His Mintcake alias has made him a bit nervy recently. The soft play mums were not wrong. We were hearing utterances of the Captain's name in strange places and ever since that moment where it was obvious to me at least, that pursuing the Captain as a full-time job clashed with his own personality and his loyalties to the Mill, we've not really spoken about it.

'So, are you the person from the Wezzie sent to interview me?' she asks.

'Oh no, I am simply here as an art fan. I'm not sure who they've sent actually…'

I glance around the room as Ro is waylaid by one of her guests: a lady in linen dungarees who's already uttered the words, 'matrixial trans-subjectivity'. I know when I'm out of my depth. The room is a bizarre mixture of art fans and locals. I am compelled to stand here and protect Danny's work, or at least watch people's reactions to it. I think that may be born from pride. Where is Danny? Or Stu?

'Oi, oi…'

The voice struts up behind me. I am not wholly prepared for who I expect to see when I turn around. Quite bizarrely, it's school gate Sarah's Jez: the husband of the rumours and the affairs. He is over familiar and reaches out to kiss me on the cheek. We've met a few times through school events and such. I've never really understood the attraction myself; he's about five foot four, bald as a coot and is a massive purveyor of bullshit. This is the problem when you open these events up to the public.

'Rowan did all of this?' he asks.

'I believe she did. That's why her name's on the door.'

'Yeah, yeah… looks a bit random to me.' He looks over at Danny's sketch and tries to stifle his giggles.

'I didn't consider you much of an art fan…'

I know I sound slightly snobbish here but the truth is I'm also feeling protective of Ro. Jez is a heckler; the sort of man who likes an anecdote, to raise laughs and be the centre of attention. He'd try and dry hump a sculpture knowing him.

'Oh, just popped in… I've been at cinema watching the new *Fast & Furious*. Saw your Danny in gents and he told me you were in here. Free drinks, I'm there.'

One free drink. Bloody hell, Danny. Jez fingers a price tag on a sculpture. This one is a papier mâché sculpture in the shape of a missile condemning violence.

'£250 for what looks like a knob piñata. More money than sense some of these artsy fartsy crew. Proper load of benders in here…'

'I'm not sure you're allowed to call us that anymore?'

Tim's figure appears beside Jez and I suddenly realise who they've sent over from the Wezzie. Jez seems to hold no shame or understanding that what he's said is hugely offensive. I air-kiss Tim to show where my allegiances are.

'Tim, this is Jez, a dad from school. Tim works at the Wezzie.'

'How do?' Tim doesn't reply. 'I'll be seeing ya then, Meg.' A woman by the door of the gallery gestures at him. This woman is not Sarah but she seems to like her lace and a badly-fitting bra. My look gives him all the judgement he needs and he saunters off, slinging his arm around her and taking her to the corner of the room to poke further fun of the art.

'A friend?'

'Far from it. Welcome to The Brewery.'

'Is this what you meant about the "scene"?'

'Naturally.'

Tim smiles. I've seen Tim since I rescued him from the McArthurs' bathroom. He was honest with me, which removed any hints of awkwardness. He'd hooked up with McArthur before but this had been his first threesome with them. They were well-rehearsed, as he described it. He panicked a bit when the bathroom wouldn't open, thinking it was a ruse for them to keep him as a gimp in the linen cupboard. But he wasn't sure he'd do it again, not with them at least. It appeared to him that they were simply introducing new things to the bedroom to keep it exciting. I like how our friendship is evolving, that he could trust me with information so personal. He looks around the room now making notes on his phone. Oh young person, you will never understand the joy of having to extract shorthand notes on a spiral notebook made with a chewed-up Bic. He sips at a glass of the free wine.

'Interesting.'

'Elderflower.'

He smiles back at me.

'So, this is very different to a football match. Have they given you a promotion?'

'Oh, I volunteered. Di was interested to see if this linked into the Mintcake angle.'

I freeze for a second as the words come out of his mouth. I hadn't thought of that at all and feel a bit stupid that I hadn't. Tim looks around, studying everyone in the room. He gives special attention to Ru and Ro who are still merry off the wine and adrenaline and command the room and all their guests. Do I deviate his attention from them? From Danny? Look, there's Mr Glendale. He was an art teacher and ran off with an eighteen-year-old. There's Jez who likes a bit of playing away from home. There's a cross-dresser and a woman in actual art overalls. How the hell do I play this?

Danny and Stu suddenly return into the frame, having obviously raided the bar with more drinks and snacks to their liking.

'Tim, mate. If I'd known I would have got you a bevy in. How do? Interesting one this one, innit?' says Stu.

I try and catch Danny's eye but he has a pint in hand and is stood next to me so it's nigh on impossible. He's not here for the art, he's here to potentially unmask you, I want to say. I spy Danny's piece in the corner of the room and wonder whether it's too obvious to make a beeline for it and manoeuvre the big silver phallus to go right in front of it. Is this on the Captain's Insta?

'Do you, as locals and art fans, have any comments?'

Stu nods, attempting to look knowledgeable. 'A strong statement about male dominance in society.'

'Powerful,' adds Danny.

I'm a bit stuck for words here. I need to throw him off the scent – this is Ro who wants her art and her message to be seen and heard. There is process, a complete lack of mystery and subtlety. It's very unlike Captain Mintcake. However, the words don't come out as such.

'It's all very in-your-face.'

Danny pulls a face. Where are your big words, journalist lady? He looks at me and suddenly comprehends my stunned mullet face.

Something is awry. Come on Morton, you know what this is about. He offers me a crisp which I refuse through sheer disappointment that he can't mind read and the fact it's cheese and onion. Tim seems to be glaring over at Ru and Ro. I have to intervene.

'Danny, Stu… Tim thought today was a good way to investigate the Mintcake thing.' I let out a nervous laugh at the end of the sentence. Danny is quiet.

Stu tries to act along. 'Good shout, Timster. What were you thinking?' He offers up a pork scratching as some way of distracting him.

'Well, the artist Rowan O'Shea… seems like she could be connected to it some way?'

Danny looks over open-mouthed at Ro like a confused child. Get with the programme, Morton.

'You know that Danny, Rufus and Ro are old mates? He was best man at their wedding,' adds Stu.

'Oh… I didn't… I mean, they're very unlike you.'

Danny finally steps in; he's heard it before but he always feels the need to defend their friendship. 'Salt of the earth, Ru. Top fella. Ro's class act as well…'

'Is he an artist too?'

'Farmer…'

'So they're both from Kendal, interesting…'

I have to act here. I let out that nervous laugh again. 'To be honest, I'd be surprised if it was either of them. They literally live in a field in a house they built themselves. I think Ru has a Nokia 5310. Techno-phobes, not that way inclined,' I suggest awkwardly.

'When I want to meet Ru for a drink, I literally have to send a pigeon out with a little note tied to his neck,' adds Danny.

Danny has taken it too far. It's all a lie, of course – they have iPhones and laptops but this helps us detract attention from our good friends who don't have to get dragged into this Mintcake debacle.

Tim looks perplexed. 'Oh, well I can shoot that idea down again. Back to square one.'

'It was a good idea but I can vouch for this lot. They don't have the tech savvy and why would they have this exhibition on… as a sideline? This is loud, evocative, truthful in its message. It goes against Mintcake's clandestine approach.'

Danny smiles. The lady found her words. Tim nods.

'But given the Captain's interests, it's likely he might be in the room, right?'

'Maybe.' Danny is not subtle here. He turns to face a lino print of multiple vulvas. If you stand far enough back from it, it looks like rows of sea urchins.

'I'll go around and mingle. Maybe it will throw up some clues.'

I nod. 'Good plan.'

He leaves Danny, Stu and me watching him as he moves away slowly into the mass of people.

'You both didn't think to get me a drink?'

They both shrug.

'What do we do about Inspector Clouseau then?' asks Stu. 'Should I walk around with him?'

I shake my head. We've diverted attention from our friends. There are just too many people in here for Tim to question everyone. Steph suddenly appears again with her husband in tow.

'Mr Glendale, good to see you after all this time, sir,' mumbles Danny, his shoulders slouched, as he regresses into his moody teen years. I smirk a little.

'You can call me Bert, Daniel. I've not had you in my classroom for a while.'

He even has an old man name. He turns to me and extends his hand.

'You must be Daniel's wife.'

'That I am, lovely to meet you.'

'Glad he found a lass to rein him in. Did you pursue art in the end, Daniel? You were always so talented. Such an eye.'

'I dabble,' replies Danny. That he does. Maybe I have Mr Glendale to blame here. There's an awkward silence before Steph leans into us. 'So that young fella you were talking to, do you know him?'

'He works at the Wezzie, why?' I reply.

'It's just he were asking us some weird questions before about that online sex stuff. About Captain Mintcake...'

'You what?' I say smiling awkwardly.

'Haven't you heard? There's someone drawing erotic art and calls himself Captain Mintcake. My mum is a huge fan. It's brilliant, they're trying to work out who he is.'

Danny and I laugh at the same time in forced tones that don't harmonise well.

'Yeah, the Wezzie are trying to work it out. You got any tips?' I add.

'Well, it definitely ain't us. I reckon you're looking for a bloke but someone younger. From the way my mum puts it, he knows his way around,' murmurs Steph.

'Oi, stop you!' Bert chirps, playfully putting a hand on his wife's waist. I hold on to Danny's hand and squeeze it tightly. We're saved by a clink on a glass and the room going quiet. Ro is behind the mic on a small podium and has her hands together in a prayer position, thanking everyone. In the corner of the room, Jez wolf whistles and his lady companion laughs. I give them evils.

'People, friends... tonight is such an honour and a relief and I feel blessed. Truly. I have such amazing support from Ru and my family and the community of artists I know. Tonight's work is available for sale. Please speak to myself or The Brewery if you're interested or take a look on Instagram – we have all sorts of digital galleries online so we can create bespoke pieces. Anything really. There are some cards as you leave if you need details.'

I close my eyes, really slowly. Danny hasn't let go of my hand since Steph spoke and now I can feel the sweat of his palm transfer to mine. We just told Tim something very, very different. I can't see Tim. Where is Tim?

'Please continue to enjoy tonight's show and keep having discussions about what you see, how you feel. Involve me in this discourse and ask questions, and again, just thank you.'

'I have a question...' No, no, no, no. The room goes silent and I see hand pop up in a sea of heads.

'Yes, please... anything...'

'Love the exhibition but there're some things here today to suggest that you may be Captain Mintcake?' It's Tim's voice. I can't see him.

There is a snigger from Jez and his lady friend. Ro is calm and thoughtful.

'I am sorry. I have no idea who you're talking about.'

A few people in the room look perplexed but the interest that others are taking in the conversation confirms our suspicions that the Captain has indeed made his way around Kendal. Danny's nerves are not in a good way. Why did we lie to Tim? Idiots we are. Proper idiots. He'd have found their Insta accounts. We follow them for Pete's sake. And now she's gone and mentioned it on stage.

'There's a local erotic artist who *The Westmorland Gazette* are very interested in tracking down but we can't seem to find them?'

At this point, Tim turns to find me in the crowd, a look of pure disappointment on his face that I tried to waylay him. I feel all at once awful but incredibly nervous about what he might say now.

'Given some of the themes of your exhibition, we thought it might be you or your husband.'

Ro laughs, giving nothing away. 'I hate to disappoint but we're very honest about who we are and the art we produce. No hiding behind secret names. Exciting that he may be one of us though? Captain Mintcake, are you in the room?'

Ro looks over at us. Is she willing Danny to say something, to finally gain some ownership over this? I can see his nerves are torn to shreds. Stu looks lost for words or action. A hand pops up in the back of the room.

'Yep, that's me. I am Mintcake.' Fricking Jez. His lady friend thinks this hilarious and they fall about laughing in the silent room. 'Kendal through and through me, Mintcake's all me. You want a bit of raunch then you come to El Capitan.'

He salutes at this point. Tim ignores him but continues to look over at me for my reaction. Ro is not impressed and tries to maintain some sort of order.

'Well, there you are... he has revealed himself. Are there any more questions?'

It would seem Jez is not done. 'Yes, you mentioned custom-made pieces. I want a huge bespoke cock for my garden that doubles as a patio heater. I can model if you want...'

I see Ro's face on stage, hurt and embarrassed. You absolute twat. Not today.

'No need for that, Ro... just find a fun-sized Mars bar,' I boom from my corner of the room. I'm not sure why or how those words come out of my mouth but they do. It raises a few giggles and does enough to change the expression on my friend's face. Danny squeezes my hand so tight that I can feel his fingernails. Stu is mildly shocked that I can do gobby. However, there is fire in me. You don't piss over my friend's day nor poke fun at my husband's alter ego.

'Wouldn't you like to know, love.'

'Why are you here exactly?' I storm over, fighting Danny's feeble attempts to stop me.

'It was free. Your husband told me to—'

'To support our friend, I don't suppose he thought it might inject a bit of culture into your thick skull too.'

Ru takes to the stage to take over the microphone. 'Please, people. We'll end the questions here. Do keep looking at the pieces – and there are lots more nuts.' Both him and Ro skip off the stage to approach us.

'This ain't culture. This is up-your-own arse poncy art. It's as bad as that Mintcake shit going around town.'

'You were putting your name to it before.'

Lady friend suddenly has words. 'Bet my Jez could do much better. That Mintcake stuff gets passed around my work, it's rubbish.'

I see Danny's eyes lower to the ground. Stu's eyes look to both Jez and this woman not really knowing how to fight them. It's lucky I know. I'm a City lass, don't you know.

I smile and whisper into her ear, 'You know he's married, right? Your Jez? Two kids as well, one in the same class as my daughter.'

'He's separated.'

'Is that what he told you?'

Jez suddenly sobers up, the colour draining from his face.

'In fact, I'm surprised his dick ain't on exhibition here given most of Kendal have probably seen it.'

'JEZ!'

'She's just being a spiteful Southern bitch, love. Don't believe her…'

And this is when it all kicks off. You don't call a Morton a bitch in front of Danny or Stu. Both of them grab one of Jez's arms and escort him out of the building. His companion takes her heels off and storms off in the other direction. It takes mere seconds for everyone's attention to go back to the art.

'I'm sorry, Ru. I'm sorry that ruined Ro's moment.'

'Don't be sorry. It was that tosser, Jez. Can always rely on the Mortons to get rid of the riff-raff. I didn't realise the Mintcake thing was out there. How's Danny with it?'

I can still see Tim watching my every move from over Ru's shoulder.

'Not great. If my colleague from the Wezzie asks any more questions…'

'Then I'll tell him to go fish. We know nothing.' He winks in a strange exaggerated way that one does when they've consumed far too much alcohol. I go to hug him and hold him close. He whispers into my ear.

'Go check on our lad. Thank you for sticking up for my girl.'

'Any time.'

I run out of The Brewery in the only awkward way I can when wearing new footwear and a skirt. Where have the brothers gone? Are they putting his head down a toilet? My heart pounds a little as I open the front doors wondering how I can join in this fight. I could take off my shoes and give him a clobbering over his bald head or aim for his soft bits. However, I exit the doors worryingly out of breath to find the brothers Morton sat on some steps, laughing to each other.

'Where is he? Did you kill him?'

'Yes, and had him made into pies. Of course we didn't kill him,' replies Danny.

'Fun times putting the frighteners on him though. What a tool.'

I look around to check for blood splatter just in case. Danny is pensive. I can understand why so I go sit down next to him.

'Got us out of the exhibition at least.' I slap his arm at the comment. 'Tim's on to it then.'

I try and reassure him. 'We just got caught out. But this implies that we know who it is, not that it's one of us.'

As we say it, the doors of The Brewery open and Tim emerges. He sees us and gestures a wave but doesn't approach us given we all know there's been a strange moment where we lied to his face. You were my newfound friend, Meg Morton, I imagine him thinking. I've confided in you. You've seen me emerge from your kids' headteacher's bathroom in nothing but a towel. I can see there's one of Ro's business cards in his hands. He looks disappointed. I took him under my wing but now it looks like I just did it as some sort of professional ruse to dump him. Danny can sense that it crushes me a little to see Tim questioning my integrity, not just professionally but also as a person.

'I'm sorry,' he holds my hand. 'Is it really out there? This Mintcake stuff?'

'It would seem so. From soft play to The Brewery.'

We all sit here in silence. A small family are next to us, obviously tourists as they eat ice creams in November, all wearing very new matching outdoor jackets.

'Why Captain Mintcake, brother?' Stu asks.

'Just sounded right. Had a ring to it.'

'I'd have been Major Windermere. That's some classy shit, right there.'

'That sounds like porn with flatulence,' I tell him.

Both brothers who've never quite grown out of the little-boy fart joke, laugh.

'Lady Ravenglass,' I announce in tones posher than my own.

'Sounds like a *Game of Thrones* lass who shags her own cousins,' replies Danny.

Stu and I don't react to his jibe. There is a problem here – this is failing to be funny anymore. It's always been this secret that he's forced us to uphold for him. I'm awful at secrets; just ask my sisters how many

Christmases I ruined for them. I'm over why he does this, I'm liberal enough to appreciate it as art and a means of expression but we're lying to people we know. We're not well versed in having to do this either and after a while, we will trip. We almost tripped tonight. And when we do, people will feel we've been dishonest with them, people we care about.

'Your snatch sketches sold for £320 you know,' Stuart informs him.

Danny doesn't even flinch. I rub an eyebrow where a small migraine has started to form.

'Can I ask a question?'

The Morton brothers continue to stare into space. I ask the question anyway.

'You can draw as many minges as you like. Minge away. But if you don't want Captain Mintcake to be outed then take it all down off the internet. Draw all you want, I won't stop you, but it's stressful trying to keep this secret.'

'Minge Away. Sounds like a repellent of sorts. For when you want to frequent a nightclub full of drunk lasses,' says Danny.

This may raise a snigger from Stu, but I still don't get the joke. My eyes plead for a more serious response.

'I don't want to,' mutters Danny. I can't read the sentiment in his sentence. You don't want to because you're a stubborn arse or because you secretly like the attention?

'How many people know about him?' enquires Stu.

'Enough,' I say. 'It's just a case of someone digging around and they'll work it all out. I mean, I found out eventually. It feels like it's only a matter of time now.'

Stu inhales breath sharply. 'Just come out with it, man. It's good money that for drawing bits.'

'Stu, it were never meant to be…this. It was a hobby. It was me just doing something I liked. Ro told me to put it online as part of some artist's community thing and now it's this. I didn't ask for this.'

'So, make it a thing,' suggests Stu.

'But I can't? I'm not you, Stu,' Danny says. 'On my own, free to do my own thing. I've got a mortgage, got the girls. And folk down mill would love that, eh? Our boss left us up the swanny to become a glorified porn peddler.'

It silences Stu.

'You could do both?' I tell him. 'Why do they have to be mutually exclusive?'

'Because Morton's is a family-run business. You heard Mum the other day, I have a reputation to uphold. I can't leave that mill, I worked so hard to get it back on track. So I suddenly do this on the side and people's opinions change. It's sex, it's perverse. I lose accounts, people's trust and suddenly I've jeopardised that company because I wanted to be selfish and go off and do something else.'

Stu hears those words and I see instant guilt. While he was lording it up on several different continents, Danny went and did what was right by dad and the family. He sees things through a different lens. He hears hurt, and someone being held back trying to do what's right for them.

'So part of you wants to do this?'

'Well, not be some celeb and everyone know my business but… I don't know… I like drawing, I like painting. I'll admit, it's a boost to know other people like it too but…'

I take his hand and look him in the eye.

'But nothing… You can't stick with the mill out of sheer obligation. You'll get to sixty and wonder where your life went. You won't be fulfilled, happy.'

'I'll be fine. You're right. I can just downgrade this to a hobby and keep doing it but dump the Mintcake thing. I don't know. Was a stupid thing that just got out of hand. I'll be fine.'

'How will you be fine?'

'Because I'll have you…'

Stu takes a step back. I hold a hand out and Danny puts his in mine.

'You bloody idiot. So we make this work?'

'How?'

I hadn't really thought that far ahead but this is what he wants isn't it? A three-way marriage with the Captain. And why not? I've grown quite fond of the bugger.

'Leave that with me.'

Chapter Sixteen

I remember the first time I came down to Morton's Paper Mill. Both my parents had been teachers and I'd grown up in a comfortable suburb in London so had very little idea of what was rural or proper blue collar. Danny and I had not really known each other long but he wanted to show me his version of The Lakes. I've never told him but this was the trip where I fell in love with him.

I remember exactly what he was wearing on that drive up: a light blue shirt with the sleeves rolled up, jeans and old school shell toe Adidas trainers. We drove up on a Thursday; he was a brooding driver but every so often a hand would shift from the gearstick to find mine. He still does this. It still makes my heart glow. He was a fan of a car sweet but his taste in music left much to be desired. There was a lot of very hard rock: AC/DC in particular which wasn't the soundtrack I had in mind for a romantic weekend away.

By the time we came off the motorway at junction thirty-six, I couldn't feel my arse cheeks and my jaws hurt from having hit three packs of Starburst quite hard. It was the expression on Danny's face which made me fall for him I think. We hit these winding country roads, the sort where I still do a steady forty and panic every time I meet another car thinking I'll have to mount a hedgerow. He swept through them like they were etched into his memory, a swift fifty, reversing like some stunt driver every time we encountered a tractor. But he looked at home, a hazy look in his eyes that made the muscles in his body relax.

'Need to make a pit stop.'

I didn't query it. I thought he just needed a wee but we swept through a little town where I admired the quaint parades of shops selling menswear and woollen goods, painted signs of farms selling eggs by the dozen, scores of brick cottages. I didn't see the building to start off with but we stopped at a little security hut where a lad came out and grabbed his hand.

'Are you kidding me? Danny Morton, back on the manor.'

'Hobbsy! Now then…'

'Big fella expecting you?'

'Course not.'

'You up for long? Can grab an ale maybe?'

'Aye.'

I'd heard Danny do Northern with Stu but this was definitely a different vernacular. Hobbsy glanced over at me and raised his eyebrows like I wasn't even sitting there and looked back at Danny.

'C'mon, let us in yer bastard.'

That's when I saw the sign. *Morton's Paper Mill since 1923.*

'Where are we, Danny?' I asked.

'Family mill.'

This was not what I expected as a pit stop and there was not an actual Lake in sight but Danny clearly wasn't bothered. He parked up and came round to open my door. I'll admit it was a quaint building, well-landscaped with what looked like a factory at the back. I didn't want to feel stupid as I hadn't presumed paper to be something you milled. It was just shaved off trees, no? I kept my naivety to myself.

'Friend of yours, Hobbsy?' I asked.

Even now, I don't know his real name.

'Schoolmates. Mucked around back in the day.'

Danny knew everyone there that day: the ladies on reception, a couple of boys who were in the break room wearing blue overalls; I followed like a little lamb introducing myself as Danny's friend from the big smoke. We hadn't labelled our relationship yet. We were shagging and having fun. I had a toothbrush at his flat and a quarter of a drawer reserved for some face cream, a mascara and a few pairs of pants but that was it.

We didn't have to search for Bob Morton, he came looking for us. He emerged from his office while we were chatting to Sue on reception.

'Laddy, now this is a surprise!' There was a full-on embrace where he wrapped his arms around him and I smiled broadly. He spied me immediately.

'Are you the new one?'

'Does he bring a new one up every month then?'

He smiled. We've always had a good rapport, me and Bob. This is not how I'd imagined I'd ever meet him: I smelt like car sweets and my hair was bundled in a messy long car trip travel bun. He also had what looked like pastry crumbs in his beard but he bellowed with laughter at my response. And then he hugged me the same way he embraced his own son; the way you'd imagine a human would be cuddled by a big, cartoon bear.

'Lovely to have you here, Meg. Sue, be a dear and let's get kettle on.'

Sue made me a tea that was strong enough to bleach a toilet and followed me around with slices of fruit cake. I was given a tour of the mill. I got to wear a hard hat, I got to meet what felt like half of Kendal. Everyone was giving me the eye – I was Danny Morton's new thing. Danny didn't care. He welcomed everyone warmly. When there was a jam in one of the machines, Danny helped them to push some levers. In a hard hat, adopting a bit of a lunge and biceps bulging from both sleeves, I'll admit the image made an impression.

There was a wonderful feeling of camaraderie. Bob was warm and respectful and people showed that to him in return. It felt like if I had any knowledge of the paper production industry, this is where I'd want to work. Later when we left, I found out that Bob had hired Hobbsy as he'd been going off the rails after school (mounting farm animals was just the start). He created the job for him. They'd just relied on CCTV before that. Danny told me that story on the way to his family home and that's when I fell in love with him. He had no qualms in introducing me to his parents; he spoke of them with pride. He regaled stories of everyone who worked at the mill and it showed me that this was someone invested in people, someone with heart.

*

I drive up to the same security hut now where a new recruit called Martin sits with a cup of tea, wearing a hat that seems to be held up by his ears. He never quite knows what to do when he sees me. It's like the queen is here and no one told him to expect her. He scrambles with buttons and I think he may salute me as the barrier is raised. It's the end of a working day and people are getting into their cars and heading home. A smartly dressed Hobbsy, now head of operations, heads over to give me a hug.

'Madame Morton, always a pleasure…'

'How are you, love? How are the twins?'

'Grand.' He whips out his phone to show me a pic.

'Little beauties. Obviously take after Dee.'

He laughs. 'Don't you know it. I better be off or she'll have me guts.'

I wave him off and am accosted by Sue from reception who wraps her arms around me.

'How are you lovely? Last time I saw you was at Bob's seventy-fifth, getting mullered…'

Oh, Sue. You don't know the half of that story. 'We had a lot of celebrating to do. Is Danny still in?'

'Yes, him and Olive are just finishing an accounts thing. Make sure he doesn't stay here past six. I know what he's like.'

I salute her back and head into reception where Olive is packing away her lunchbox.

'You're looking well, Olive.'

'That'll be Slimming World, lost 10 lbs. Haven't got in this skirt since the nineties.'

It wasn't a comment on her weight but she glows all the same.

'Remind Danny to turn off the lights in the bathroom.'

'Will do. Say hello to George for me.'

I know everyone's names now too. It's what I did when Danny got this job. I felt it was almost an obligation, like marrying into royalty. Get involved in the annual fun day picnic, sign some Christmas cards, come in with the occasional cake. Times hadn't been easy here – a rival mill on the other side of town had merged with a Swedish manufacturer and a lot of Bob's health woes came about in the financial downturn. Gill was always adamant it was the guilt and stress which made him ill. When Danny came in, he turned things around. He convinced people to stay but take a lower wage. When things started looking up, he incremented their salaries slowly. Not one person queried it. I knock lightly on the door.

'Aye…'

I peek my head around the door.

'You're barred.'

'Whatever. Olive looks well.'

'Slimming World.' He's typing away on a computer and lets out an exasperated sigh.

'How do you spell "convenience"?'

'Con-ven-i-e-n-c-e.'

'I knew you were good for something.'

'Ta.'

Danny's office hardly changes despite my pleas to jazz it up with a rug or a sofa. What remains are the family photos on the desk: a strange selection of reportage shots and selfies including an awful photo of me on the beach looking like my hair has been styled by Mr Whippy. Danny stops typing and sits back from his chair.

'Done. Did you bring them?'

I bring out a roll of black bags from my handbag and wave it around. 'Let's do this then.'

It's been a strange week post Rowan's exhibition. We sat around outside The Brewery realising that Captain Mintcake was, locally at least, becoming something of a phenomenon. This was a chance for Danny to go either way: come out, wallow in the notoriety, make a bit of dosh – a fair bit if these London folk had anything to do with it. Or keep hiding, attempting to keep this under wraps: a hobby on a computer. Nothing was decided for sure but little things were discussed. We do a better job of covering our tracks, we protect the Captain until we find resolution and number one on that list was to tackle the filing cabinet full of sex paraphernalia. Of course, I could have just left this job to Danny but I'm here out of curiosity. How does one fill a whole cabinet full of the things? Are there those giant dildo things that you see in gay porn? I'm not naive. I know what exists out there.

Danny already has the key out and starts opening everything up. I peer over from the other side of the room. He glances over at me. 'What are you doing over there? I'm not throwing stuff over. You're a shit catch.'

I go over, curiously wondering if there's anything spring-loaded that may catch me by surprise.

'Has Olive actually left the building?'

'I think so. Anyway, would she know what any of this stuff is? We could tell her they're newfangled pencil sharpeners.'

Danny looks at me as he pulls out the first toy. It's a butt plug. We could easily say that was some sort of desk bookstand.

'Woah, did you try this one out?'

'Naturally. It has the suction cup. Just attached it to my chair, pulled down my underpants and had it in my arse while I checked my emails each morning.'

'I know you're lying. You have a fabric chair.'

He smiles. I peer over into the cabinet.

'Crikey, that's a lot of cock.'

The drawer seems to be made up of at least fifty per cent dildo. When Gill opened this up, she must have thought the very worst of me, like I was some sort of addict. There's quite an array of items in here, some opened and some in their original packaging. From anal beads to lube to harness-like contraptions. Danny doesn't seem too precious about anything so it mostly gets tossed in the bin bag. I have no idea where we're going to dispose of all of this but I'm thinking it'll be someone else's black bin on the way home.

Something suddenly starts vibrating in the cabinet like a wind-up toy one might find in a cracker. That'd be one way to spice up Christmas. What is this ring, Gill? It's a bit wide for my finger. I hold it up to my eye then realise Danny may have tried this on. I drop it quickly in the bag. I sift through the drawer like some very kinky lucky dip. This is when something is going to bite me, isn't it? I'm going to end up in A&E again in another sex-related incident. Instead, my hand happens across something strangely soft.

'What's this then? Is it a torch?'

I open it up. That is not a light.

'This is a vagina in a tube, Danny.'

'That it is. It's called a fleshlight.'

'I see what they're doing there. So you just lube up your cock and make love to the tube?'

Danny nods.

'Have you tried this one?'

'I may have.'

I fake indignancy. 'You cheated on me at the office with a fleshtube?'

'A fleshlight. It was only once and it didn't mean anything. It's you I want,' he utters completely deadpan.

I'm still intrigued by it. The vaginal lips are quite lifelike but I am pretty sure mine do not look like that anymore. I imagine mine are less pert, in the shape of a downturned mouth perhaps?

'To be honest at first it's a bit like putting your cock inside a Venus flytrap.'

'A penis flytrap, perhaps. May I?' I hover my fingers over the entrance of the fake vagina.

'I don't think she'll mind.'

I place the fingers inside carefully and marvel at the eye for design. It's really quite accurate.

Mentally, I'm doing a fair bit of maths here and working out that there is nigh on £500 worth of toys and accessories in this drawer. I'm winding my memory back to times when he must have been buying these items and hiding them here, times he must have been telling me we had to go easy on the food shopping as we were still paying off the service on the Volvo.

'So when did you draw these things? Here? Did you ever take them home?'

'All at home. You'd be surprised how much I got done when Polly was really little and you used to breastfeed upstairs with your box sets.'

'And then you'd sneak them in your work bag and back into the filing cabinet of filth.'

'The cabinet has a name now.'

'Yes, she's like some dominatrix's lair. The Captain's Cavern. We may have to burn it down after we've emptied it. Or clean it in holy water.'

It would have taken months of secrecy. My back being turned at the counter while I was pouring out bowls of cornflakes, he would have been transferring toys into the same rucksack in which he carried his tuna and sweetcorn roll and a packet of Hula Hoops. I am not sure if that's what still makes my heart ache, that he couldn't share this with me from the get-go. I reach into the drawer and pull out what looks like a lipstick; the cover is shiny and metallic. I tap it on the side of a drawer. Danny takes it out of my hands.

'It's a love bullet.'

'To kill the person you love?'

'I bought it but wasn't really sure if it worked or how it'd work.'

He unscrews the top to press a small button. It vibrates lightly in his hand. I suspect that would be something you wear in your knickers to spice up a dull commute. He then reaches in the cabinet and picks out a remote.

'That looks hi-tech.'

'Yep, it has apps and you can control it from other sources so you could be at work, writing your serious news stuff and I'd suddenly set this off.'

I laugh. 'You could try it out on me.'

He smiles. 'Is that an invitation?'

'Maybe…'

'Here?'

'Why not?'

He laughs. I don't know what I've just suggested here. We've never done it here, in his office. I feel the thrill, the same excitement when we were in the Volvo as he looks me in the eye and pulls me in with one arm. With his other hand, he unbuttons the top of my jeans. I'm not wearing the sexiest of pants – I think they may have cartoon llamas on them but he doesn't care. His fingers reach down, parting the lips of my pussy and locating my clit. His lips are next to my ear.

'You ready, Mrs Morton?'

I can barely handle this newfound intimacy between us. My breath quickens and I feel myself pulse at his touch. He pulls my jeans down past my hips and then brushes the bullet against my clit. Fuck. He alters the rhythm and lightness of the touch and my body jolts with pleasure.

'It works then.' I nod, my mouth agape. He slides a finger inside me, pressing towards my G-spot. I exhale deeply. Perched against his desk, he rolls my jeans down and unbuttons his trousers, pressing an erection against the inside of my thigh, still hovering the bullet over my clit that aches to feel the vibrations against it. He lifts my knees and penetrates me lightly, my hands steadied on the desk, his breath and lips light on the inside of my neck. He pushes harder, more rhythmically. The bin bag falls to the floor, sex toys everywhere, a huge rubber dildo bounces across the wooden floors with incredible momentum. A couple of toys start buzzing, one lights up. What the hell, Danny? But he does what he always does, he looks me in the eye and smiles broadly as I come, the sensation soaring up my spine, my arms giving way as I fall back on to his desk and a giant stack of paper is swept into the air and rains over us.

*

'What was that noise then?'

Of course, once Danny has finished then it's neither the time nor place for post-coital romance. He is even efficient enough to ask whether I had some baby wipes about my person so he could wipe himself down. Such is the sex we have as parents that we are now experts when it comes to the clean-up process so our kids know we weren't indulging in any sort of misbehaviour.

'That was the vibrator buzzing, no?'

'No, when you came... you kinda bayed like a cow.'

And this is Danny's version of pillow talk.

'Naff off. You can talk.'

'I don't make sex sounds.'

'No, just that weird spasmy orgasm thing when your nostrils flare like a bullock.'

Danny laughs. 'It was good though, eh?'

I find it hard to contain my smiles. 'Maybe.' It was better than good, frigging fantastic. We beam at each other like giggling teens as he adjusts his pants and pulls out a wedgie trying to not let it take away from five minutes ago, where I literally felt myself orgasm through my eyeballs. Office sex. Maybe it's something I should have instigated sooner. It feels naughty and I'm pretty sure that was part of the thrill.

'Do you ever think your dad had sex in here?'

'Stop talking now. Help me pick up this stuff. Make sure you check nothing's rolled under the desk too.'

The phone on his desk suddenly rings and Danny scrambles into action.

'Martin? The delivery was due tomorrow morning. But if they're here, they're here. Could you follow the van up to the main building and you can help me unload everything. Cheers lad.' He turns to me. 'Balls, they're delivering machine parts now. Look, handle this and I'll handle that…'

I look over to him and gesture that him doing up his flies may be handy. His cheeks are a bit flushed, that sort of bewildered look about his face whenever he's just come and it looks like he's run a 5K. He sorts himself out whilst I spy a gimp mask in the top of the filing cabinet and put it on. Danny looks up and trips over himself to see me. I do a little dance.

'You bloody clown. Take that off.'

'Can I wear this next time I'm modelling for you?'

'It'd keep you quiet at least.'

'Wouldn't be able to watch the telly though.'

He laughs and exits the room. I take off the mask, thinking it'd save me having to put on make-up. In the bin bag you go. I then sit by the edge of Danny's desk and survey the damage. It looks like there was an explosion of sex toys and administration here. I collect the toys and put them back in their black bags, heeding Danny's advice which was lucky as a vibrator had rolled under his desk. Marie on cleaning wouldn't have known what to do with herself. I count twenty-five dildos and wonder what one calls a collection of dildos? I have no control over the rules of the English language but I vote it should be a litter of dildos. Maybe a troop. I laugh to myself. I have an extended troop of dildos that I store next to my bevy of butt plugs.

I suddenly find the very dildo that started this whole affair; the one that arrived in the post that morning. Hello again, old friend. You are still abnormally huge and blue. I stare at it in my hands for longer than needs be. What if things had worked out differently that morning? What if Danny had met with the postie and done breakfast? Would this still be a secret? I am not sure if that still niggles. But it's progressed from that. I just have to rationalise that the whole Mintcake situation is a manifestation of being unhappy professionally, him wanting to spread his artistic wings. I have to stop thinking he wants more than me and the kids. I hear a door open to the main building downstairs and a straining noise which undeniably sounds like two men moving a box that's too heavy, meaning one of them will probably do his dodgy shoulder in. I hustle and grab the remaining sex harnesses and tubes of lube, squirreling them away into the black bag in my hands. Gin and tonic flavoured lube? They really like to cash in on current fads, don't they? Does it have alcohol content? That would make a blow job worthwhile if I could get caned at the same time. The office all clear, I tie the handles of the bag and move on to the piles of paper that are strewn across the floor. Oh, the joys of having a husband in paper. I shuffle a few pages together and glance over the words. Perhaps these are some new drawings? I may need to get nosy and have a gander.

I see a PO Box number at the top of the page. Do they still have PO Boxes? The letter is addressed to C Mintcake. Hey, I know him. Sat on the floor of the office, I start to read the letter addressed to him, every word making me heavy with emotion. Oh, Danny. I flick through the pages underneath me. This isn't just one letter. There's at least thirty of them. Some from agents, others from publishers – both big and independent. Letters from magazines, production companies, galleries. There are large numbers on every one, words of praise and hyperbole. They're talking about exhibitions and documentaries and merchandise, trying to lure him in with the promises of money and fame. And I start to tear up because a lesser man would have succumbed to such promises. He'd have run into the sunset, leaving me and his daughters behind and bought a mansion in the sun with his newfound sex empire earnings.

But he didn't. He stayed. There's even a letter here from the Wezzie, signed by Diana. We offered him money for an interview. The amount offered may be why we have to bring our own mugs to work. Tears start to blot the words as I look around this office and know why he didn't go anywhere. He stayed for this place, for his people, for his family. He stayed for me, the girls. He stayed because he's a decent sort of man. It's why I'm here too.

Chapter Seventeen

'Uncle Stu has peanut butter *and* marmite on his toast,' a little face grumbles to me beside the kitchen counter.

'That's why Uncle Stu is still single.'

Eve wrinkles her nose at me, taking her piece of toast begrudgingly, like I may have just smeared the dog's turds across the bread. 'Where is Uncle Stu anyway?'

I take that as a slur on my breakfast-making skills and return to my coffee. 'Uncle Stu lets us do that' is the common riposte that hums around the house at the minute. He gives us sweets, he doesn't wear socks, he lets us snorkel in the bath and ride the dog. He's slowly becoming the fun uncle who'll be remembered in years to come whilst I'll be the boring wench who cared more about health, safety and foot odour. The thing is we don't know where young Stu is; he left at nine last night and never came home. Do I worry about him? In the same way I worry about Magnum the cat when he's gone walkabout. He'll come back when he's hungry, though I hope he hasn't forgotten that we both have an important meeting this morning. As far as I hate to admit it, I need Stu today.

'He's on a sleepover with some friends,' I say.

'Do you think they watched films all night and fell asleep?' asks Eve.

'Exactly that.'

Tess sniggers. It's been a while since I had a morning like this with the girls. Having Stu made me lazy when it came to morning parenting and giving him the manic school runs felt like fitting punishment for recent sins. However, today makes me realise I've missed it and the guilt of having to balance work and home washes over me. So I sit here for a moment longer than I should. I've afforded myself a late start time so I can have a leisurely morning with my girls, walk them to school and do all those little things I used to do with them pre-Stu and really pre-Mintcake. I spy them lined up along the kitchen table, eating their breakfast, the morning still etched in their sleepy faces. Eve – you don't look like me at all, eh? That's all Danny. Tess is my clone from the dimples to the way she sucks yoghurt off her spoon. I marvel at little Polly's mop of platinum blonde hair. You get these moments sometimes when they're quiet and together. Where the hell did you little people come from? I can't even recall Tess being Polly's age, or even being pregnant three times. It's a mixture of pride and warmth but also sheer surprise.

We've kept the little ones at bay with all this Mintcake stuff being flung around the house. There were certain things around that were definitely not for the consumption of little eyes and ears but at the same time, amidst all the madness and confusion, the kids helped ground me. No matter what this Captain Mintcake fiasco meant, they were our girls, the epicentre of our family. For their sake, we owed it to them to work this out and see how it fit into our lives.

I sip at my coffee and stare at Mr T out of the kitchen window. He's now got so elderly that he can't even raise a leg to wee and I think of Danny who often sits down on the toilet, just so he can 'have a little rest'. On the table, I'm editing a couple of features that have been written by some of the office juniors: one where a prize-winning marrow has been described as 'elephantine' and a multi-storey car park as 'incongruous'. The office thesaurus wins again.

'Do you like writing?' asks Tess, watching my red pen scrawled across the print.

'I do. I think I'm good at it. I'm good at spelling. I'm not good at much else.'

Eve is surprised to hear this self-deprecating attitude. 'You're good at hair.' I laugh. Tess gives her a look knowing that my self-esteem is at stake here. They look a bit perplexed trying to come up with other things I'm good at. 'You also make good sandwiches?' she tries to redeem herself. Polly puts a handful of Weetos in her face and gurgles in what I hope is agreement.

'You are good at having babies,' suggests Tess.

Eve nods enthusiastically. 'Daddy said when they had to cut you a new minnie on your tummy that you were very brave.'

Tess and I pause for a moment. 'What was that, love?'

'Daddy said you had to squeeze me out the sunroof, not the boot.'

'They cut me open. I only have one minnie.'

'A person can't have two minnies, can they Mummy?' asks Tess.

I want to say no but I have no doubt that can exist in nature. I once saw a picture of a man with two johnsons. Maybe it's just best to clarify that I don't have a vag on my stomach. Geez, is that what she thought my belly button was, an extra vagina? How misshapen *is* my belly button now?

'I'm not sure how we started talking about minnies?'

'Daddy was telling us the other day that we have three holes: one for wee, one for babies and the other for poo. So are they all minnie holes?' asks Eve.

'No.' That much I know. Very like Danny to talk about things so plainly as a plumber would but a bit of elaboration is still needed. They stare at me inquisitively. Who was that person at their school who wanted to deny them sex education? This is what happens when we do. They piece things together and come up with absurdity. But I see innocence here, a simple need to understand the physical workings of the matter. Honesty feels like the best route.

'Well, Daddy has a poo hole and that is definitely not a minnie.' You see a little light appear in the irises of Eve's eyes for that realisation to dawn on her. At least we have that much sorted.

Tess interjects, 'But you can have a minnie and a willie. Rhys Griffin told me that. They have a special name.'

'You can call them intersex people, I think.' I make a note to consult Wikipedia later knowing my knowledge about the subject is pretty sparse. Eve's mind is blown. 'Biology works in different ways, sometimes,' I say, taking on an Attenborough style lilt in my voice.

'Rhys said a different word, he said… freak.' Tess mutters it quietly, letting me know it's the wrong thing to say.

'Well, Rhys is wrong; that's cruel and not very nice to say.'

'I told him that.' I smile, knowing that's typical Tess. 'And he said things like he-she and ladyboys and I told him there's nothing wrong with that at all.' Eve furrows her brow to take it in. 'As long as people are good and they are happy in their own skin then that's what's important.'

Hold the doors. There's a little someone right here who could give those sex education classes though I'm debating to what extent she knows how everything operates. 'Who taught you all of this?' I try to think when I last relayed such information to our eldest. There's a strong sense of empathy and understanding here that I for one have not imparted on her. I think.

'Aunty Lucy told me she once had a girlfriend. And Uncle Stu showed me pictures of Pride when he lived in Sydney, and he has friends who are very gay.'

I make it a point to call Lucy later. 'I don't think you can be very gay. It's not something you define on a scale.'

'Yes, you can. He had a friend called Marshall who painted himself silver and wore heels and feathers and once met Cher.'

I have no words. 'That's flamboyant, not very gay.'

'Like Elton John?' pipes in Eve.

'Yes but no. So what else has Uncle Stu said to you?' I hold my breath as there is plenty within this man's remit which he may have chosen to share.

'It was at the school gate the other week and there was a mum with a sign, George's mum in Year 4. It said: "Stop Sexualising Children's Innocence". He went up and had words.'

'Nice words?' I hold my breath, grimacing.

'Not really. She told him it was none of his business because he wasn't a parent. He told her to shove her sign up her bottom,' recalls Tess. I close my eyes very slowly.

'And then he called her a piggot,' adds Eve.

'You mean a bigot.'

Tess nods. 'And then he came home and sat us down and told us about stuff he's seen. He has lots of friends who are different and it's important we respect everyone and their choices in life. Except her because she's a…'

'Bigot.' I nod. 'And you're telling me this now? Why not last week when it happened?' I think of all the things they've chosen to tell me since, in depth conversations about what was eaten for lunch, who played with who and what colour their bowel movements have been.

'I dunno. We forgot,' replies Eve. I laugh. I hear the front door open and footsteps jog into the kitchen. A hooded figure appears.

'Well, speak of the devil. Stuart, good morning.'

The girls and I all smile at each other. Tess shakes her head. He clambers to the sink and finds a child's tumbler to pour himself a glass of water.

'I'm here. I made it for the school run. I didn't forget our meeting thing either.' He gurns and slaps at his cheeks. Polly giggles at the hollow sound of the slap. This goads him to do it again.

'Was it a nice sleepover that you had with your friends? Were there sweets?' asks Eve.

Stuart looks at me. Indulge the child.

'It were lovely, Steve.'

'My name is Eve.'

'Oops, I forgot again.'

She snarls at him. I look on as he steadies himself against the kitchen counter. When did I last do an all-nighter? I rewind my mind as far back as 2010: New Year's Eve in London. It wasn't even a big night out. There was wine, Scrabble and a cheese board. He empties his pockets on to the kitchen counter: receipts and coins, a johnny and a crumpled pack of cigarettes. Tess studies the contents and gives me a look of both judgement and concern.

'The girls were just filling me in on what happened last week with Kate, the mum.' It looks like it's painful for Stu to recall that far back.

'Is she the gym bunny with the Lycra?'

'No, she isn't.' I recoil to think about what else he's been up to. 'The one with the petition.'

'Oh her, on the solo crusade to protect the children. Yeah, told her to do one. Don't need that sort corrupting my nieces.'

'Nice work.' He studies my face for the sarcasm. This may indeed be a compliment that he has no idea how to handle. He nods back.

'Anything else I should know while we're all here gathered?'

Stu shrugs his shoulders.

'Uncle Stu wrote his telephone number in my reading record because he fancies Mrs Robinson?' announces Eve.

Seriously? Polly giggles then regurgitates all her Weetos on to the tray in her highchair.

'What the hell were you drinking last night, Stu?'

'Lord knows.'

I'm sat next to Stu in the artisan café next to my office. I should have made him shower and change before we came here as there is a strong scent of rum wafting off him but time was tight. I wonder if there's time for us to dash over to the chemist and douse him in body spray. Given what had been shared with me over breakfast, the school run was less eventful than I'd imagined. I got a wave from Mike McArthur from across the playground. I saw Ian Tipperton roll into the out-of-bounds staff car park to drop his boys off. No sign of petitions, and because he smelled and looked like a tramp, Stu really wasn't in a place to be on the pull. I learned a few things though. Stuart and Eve have a special handshake now. And Stu watches both girls as they walk away with a look that shows he might actually care and enjoy their company. We then made our way over to the cafe for our meeting, Polly in tow. At one point, we stopped as Stu thought he was going to throw up. He didn't. But he has made two visits to the bathroom since we got here.

In the corner of the café is Sarah, the last person who needs to be here but at least she's the other end of the room with another childminder and an array of kids who seem to have free reign of the place. She waved when she entered, fake smile plastered across her face, looking Stu up and down suspiciously. It wasn't hard to see why. I look over and wonder when he last washed his hair.

'Do I dare ask about last night?'

'Messy. All you need to know.' His face is pained. I push a glass of water in his direction.

'Do you still do drugs?'

'On occasion.'

'Keep that shit away from my girls, yeah?'

'Why yes, Baroness Mintcake,' he replies teasingly.

I look around in case anyone heard and gesture my disapproval for him to be saying it in public. I like the weight of that title though – we've not played around with the idea of nobility yet. I look over at Polly. Does that make her Princess Mintcake? Who knows? The fact is we sit here both slightly nervous at what we're about to do. Today is the day we launch a new plan, though when your fellow conspirator smells of booze and is having trouble keeping the contents of his stomach intact then you wonder about the success rate of said plan. Today hinges on us putting a lot of trust into one person and it has the potential to go very badly. Do we risk it? Or do we just sit on what we know? I spy the person we need entering the front doors and gesture him over.

'Is this going to work, Meggers?' whispers Stu.

'It's a start, try and stand upright.'

'Tim,' I say quietly as he approaches.

Stu nods and shakes his hand. I try to catch Tim's eye but nothing. He just takes his coat off and sits down, quietly. Not the best start. To be honest, Tim and I haven't really spoken since the exhibition furore two weeks ago. He made it clear I'd breached his trust and he distanced himself from me as a result. He stopped making me tea in the office. He stopped offering me biscuits. And it hurt. He had felt like a protégé up to that point. He'd confided personal information to me and I knew he was here, in the Lakes, totally alone. I was that person once. Today I want to greet him with clichés but he seems hesitant. A waitress with a fondness for gel nails and a magenta lip fills the awkwardness.

'What can I get you, dears?' she hollers at us.

'I'll have a green tea with ginseng and a slab of that hazelnut coffee cake,' I say.

'Like a pavement slab?' The waitress laughs. I nod.

'Macchiato, almond milk if you have it,' replies Tim.

She nods politely knowing that neither of us are from these parts. Stu rectifies that.

'Vat of tea, love. Full English, black pudding as extra and sub mushrooms for extra beans.'

'White or brown toast?'

'You joking me? White and some of them extra packets of butter.'

She laughs and wanders off. I allow Tim to get comfortable and greet the baby. Even if this meeting doesn't end well then we have the baby to distract us.

'One piece of cake between two. You're stingy,' Tim remarks.

'We can get seconds…'

'Good.' He jokes with antagonism in his tone. This could heal or be very painful.

'So…'

'So… how's Danny? The kids?'

'They're great. How are you?'

There is a long pause as he looks me in the eye. Why the grand gesture of cake? Why are we bothering to do niceties here?

'Good to see you, Stu.'

'Likewise, fella.'

Silence. I need to do this, don't I? Deep breath. 'So we asked you to meet us because we wanted to tell you something.'

'I think I know.'

Stu eyeballs me.

'So when is the big Captain Mintcake reveal?' Tim asks.

I was wrong. This will potentially play out like a poker match. What do I know? What does he think I know? What the hell do you know? I keep quiet.

'You've got the scoop, haven't you? Have you written the article yet? Told Diana?' he adds.

Stu looks at me. He can't quite read Tim's directness and tone. I'm confused too. Tim thinks I was hiding information from him for the scoop? Because I wanted the journalistic glory? I smile for a moment, hopefully in a way that doesn't look too smug.

'So you thought that I'd found out and lied to you because I didn't want to share the article?'

'Well, yeah… the way that you, Stu and Danny were trying to throw me off at the exhibition. It was kind of obvious. And yeah, kind of brutal… We'd been researching stuff together and suddenly, it felt like you didn't want me involved. I get it. It's the nature of our industry. It can get competitive. But I thought, I guess I thought wrongly that we were…'

'Friends.'

We take a moment for that to sink in. We are friends. I am extremely fond of him, which is why what I am going to do next is important because I trust him and I think he'll understand. I extract an orange folder from my handbag and lay it on the table.

'Green tea with ginseng, big tea and a macky-arrrr-toooe. And a slab of cake. Your brekkie is on its way, poppet.'

'Aye,' replies Stu, winking at her and making me slightly ill. I try to convince Tim to dive into the cake but he can't take his eyes off the folder. It's time.

'There is no article. The scoop is yours. Kind of…'

'I don't need your pity…'

'Not that at all. He's someone both Stu and I know and we don't want to be attached to it.'

For all his presumption, he suddenly goes very quiet. Stu is silent but nods in agreement. 'You know *him*?' He creases his eyes.

'And any journalist worth their salt will know you protect your sources and someone's right to privacy.'

I hand him a fork.

'Dig in. It's caramelised hazelnut. This cake got me through my third pregnancy.'

He's far too polite with the cake, I take a wedge with good cake/icing ratio. I push the orange folder over to him. Stu exhales loudly, though that could be wind.

'This is an interview with Captain Mintcake. It gives you the whys and the hows and all his opinions on this circus which has erupted around him but nothing about his identity. He doesn't want people to know.'

He stares at me for a moment then opens the folder and reads the first few lines.

'Wait, are you selling this to me?' he enquires.

Stu and I both laugh. 'Hell, no. It's yours. This has promise – it could be a big article for the Wezzie and good for you, too.'

'Good for me?'

'If nationals are after this then definitely. The Captain just wants to put this out there too, so people might stop digging.'

He runs his fingers across the first paragraphs. It's pretty easy to twig who it may be from the first few lines.

'Geez. Really?' There's a look of shock but also concern.

'Yup. Is that weird?'

'No.' He smiles at me. 'When you said it, I really thought it may have been your friend, Rowan.'

'Not surprised, given the tackle on display the other day.' Stu laughs.

He continues to read and then rather strangely reaches over to take my hand in his.

'You're Mrs Mintcake?'

I look around to see if anyone may have heard this, my eye on Sarah in particular only ten tables down.

Stu smiles. 'Mate, she's got rank. She's a Captain's wife. It's Lady Mintcake to you.'

I nod, I prefer that to Baroness.

'Are you collaborators? Contributors?'

Stu puts his hands up. 'We're allies, pal. It's all him.'

'Now I know why you want to keep this quiet.'

'We have daughters, he has a business. And now you know why I don't want this scoop at all,' I add.

He nods, letting me know he understands.

'Can I be frank?'

'Always…'

'You say all him. Is that his cock in the pics?'

'Some of them. That watercolour one you liked on my kitchen table, that's him.'

He grabs my hand a little harder. I blush.

'Well done, Mrs!'

Stu looks disgruntled as though it may be a competition.

'He just didn't look the sort…'

I laugh, a little too loudly to the confusion of a man opposite us enjoying a sausage bap.

'Like he didn't know what sex was?' I ask.

Tim blushes. 'I guess I thought you guys were a bit vanilla.' He most likely refers to when we saw him at the McArthurs and nothing could cover up Danny and me looking like our eyeballs were going to fall out. 'So these pics are you two?'

I shake my head and go slightly beetroot to think Tim would think some of those drawings were shenanigans that we got involved in. There's a lot of dildo and bendiness in those pics. 'Oh, trust me, there's a lot of artistic license.'

Tim scans the information in front of him. 'You know that time you almost choked on that biscuit in the office? I saw what was on your phone screen. I had an inkling something was up. I just thought it was marital problems. So this was all related to that?'

Stu looks confused. 'You almost choked on a biscuit?'

'Almost and yes. It was around the time I was piecing it all together. He'd been keeping it all from me. Turns out he'd been purchasing toys and such for research. Not bad stuff like hurty things but…'

I've used the word 'hurty' which I normally save for five-year-olds when they've jammed their finger in a door. Stu and Tim widen their eyes. I think this may have piqued Tim's interest but Stu looks a bit concerned about what I'm going to say next, as there are things a little brother doesn't need to know. The appearance of a full English breaks the tension.

'Legend,' Stu winks again at the waitress, shoving a piece of toast in his mouth.

'Aye. Enjoy, lovely. She's a bonny one? Aren't you petal?' She engages with the baby and we then wait until she's out of earshot, even though we say everything in front of Polly. Her first word better not be cock.

'How many toys?' asks Tim.

'This doesn't make the article, right? On the QT.'

Tim does a half-arsed Scout salute.

'Lots of toys that he used for research. It's been an education shall we say. I found out what a fleshlight was last week.'

Whilst Tim probably has no need for such contraptions, Stu bobs his head about to let us know he may have seen one in his lifetime. He shoves a whole sausage in his mouth. 'I've got a story about one of them. My mate, Wenters, he had one but forgot that you need to wash these things out every time you use them. Anyways, went back to use it and all the old lube had crystallised and sure enough, was like putting his cock in sandpaper. Ripped it to shreds.'

Tim breaks into laughter, enough for the nosy childminder across the way to glance over at us. How Stu can shovel that breakfast down him telling that story is beyond me.

'But an education in many other things too,' I say.

Stu ploughs through what looks like a trough of baked beans but Tim reads the double meaning in my words.

'As long as it's brought you and Danny together as opposed to it being a secret that's driven you apart. Does that make sense?'

Stu pauses for a moment. In one sentence, young Tim has dissected the situation beautifully. Because I guess I could have gone batshit crazy by the idea of a secret. With much indignation, I could have seen that secrecy as a betrayal. I could have raged even more with the content. But I didn't. Maybe there were just worse things he could have done. Maybe at the heart of it, I slowly realised this wasn't done to hurt me or because his feelings for me changed. When the fog cleared, I realised it was for him, I still loved the idiot and I'm here now protecting him and urging this to be a good thing for him.

'Perfect sense. It's just another part of him I guess. That's the joy of long-term relationships, you think you know someone and then they bring out something that totally surprises you. Like a year into our relationship, Danny found out that I'd never seen a *Star Wars* film, ever.'

Stu rolls his eyes back at this admission. Tim stops for a moment.

'How is that possible?'

'Just never appealed. And then it got worse… I watched it with him and Stu. The original one… and I didn't think it was very good.'

'Oh.'

Tim is silent. This may be something that affects his judgement of me.

'We nearly threw her out on street,' claims Stu.

'I thought it was too macho, not enough girls in it. There was Leia but I just didn't like it. I seriously thought I was going to get dumped over that. I nearly dumped him: he called me a moron.'

Tim laughs. 'So you didn't know he was doing this?'

I shake my head.

'Lois Lane didn't know Clark Kent was Superman and that was pretty obvious bar the glasses,' he replies.

I laugh. I love that, like myself, he uses the *Daily Planet* as a reference point to his career. And it's all very true but then Lois did find out in the seventies movies. I can't remember if that ended well for her. Or them. And maybe that's what still makes me feel a little cautious; this continued sense of secrecy, entrusting only a few more people with the info.

When Danny, Stu and I plotted this, we had no idea if this would work. Did we know Tim well enough to let him in on this? It was huge and it could totally backfire. But there was one thing which gave me hope: McArthur. Tim knew who he was in the community and he never uttered a word. He understood there was a line. I stood on that line and kept that secret with him. He was also a new journalist and needed to preserve integrity and professionalism if he was to ever move forward in his career. I take a giant gulp of my tea to steady myself and possibly burn off six layers of tongue.

'Shall I play this out like an interview or a feature piece?'

'Interview, definitely. Easier, more accessible.'

He makes notes on his phone.

'Remember, we don't want this to read like a promotional piece to increase sales or web traffic. It's got to read as sincere, capture the fact he's a normal person who's not out for fame or gain.' Tim nods. 'And when you've subbed to the Wezzie, I want a read and I'll then give you some names.'

'Names?'

'The idea is that we control how this is put to the public and I still have some contacts down South that you can use in some of the magazines.'

His eyes light up at the prospect of this being bigger, at least for him. I glance over at Stu to remind him why he's here. All our plans have been formulated over the kitchen table, late at night, and we realised now was the time to try and pick those over-educated brains of his.

'I've researched the legal aspect.' He leans over his breakfast clumsily to point out some disclaimers at the back of my research. 'Just some words for you to peruse to ensure we keep Danny's name out of this.' I expected a bit more lawyerly weight here – the thumbs-up doesn't help, neither do the slight grumbles of indigestion from his stomach. He gives Polly a piece of toast that's dipped in brown sauce.

'Wait, I saw those letters from the magazines and publicists. He doesn't want to capitalise on that?'

'His choice.'

Tim stops for a moment, remembering that just mere minutes ago we'd agreed we were still friends.

'How are you with this? This has so much potential for you, your family.'

'Seriously, it's his choice. His work. His call.'

He knows I'm not totally convinced by my own argument. 'You know this all happened, quite by accident. We have no idea what to do or how to work this out. This is a first step but after that we are clueless.' I try to laugh it off but this is the plan so far. We protect Danny's identity, we put out our version of events. People will then get bored and move on to different things like the outcomes of sporting events and *Love Island*. Tim's still taking notes.

'Again, this doesn't go in the article.'

He touches his nose and nods. 'Then I'm sorry that I assumed you were going all journo bitch on me and stealing headlines. I should have thought outside the box.'

'No big deal. I'm sorry I let this simmer and made you think that. We good?'

'Yeah. I might start making you tea again…'

'I can live with that. Stu is leaving soon. Come and hang out with us.'

Stu nods. 'And you? How's tricks?'

'You make me sound like a rent boy. There's a new fella but I don't think it's got legs. He doesn't use full stops.'

I knew I liked this kid. I smile but Tim can see beyond the chat. Unlike Stu who's downing his tea like water, Tim watches as I rub my brow, trying to process a million and one things at once. I remember a time when all I had to think about was whether I'd laundered the school cardigans or signed all the right school forms. Now, I worry about whether my husband will be exposed as an erotic artiste and my family made out to be pornmongers. Is that a word? It should be.

'Are you really OK?'

It's the first time anyone's asked me that since this started. Stu found everything hysterical, Emma thought it non-consequential, Rowan was her usual breezy self. When you have to hold on to secrets, it can cause anxiety, questions and I still have very few answers. I know it's ignited a spark with my husband. I know it's expanded my knowledge of all things sex. I know it makes me wonder how my husband's brain operates. Stu sits there quietly. She's fine, no?

'I'm getting there. I don't think he's a pervert which is a start. And I guess it's more exciting than if he was drawing trees or landscapes. But I'm OK too. Our love is more than a few well-conceived dick pics.'

He smiles. 'They are very good pictures though. The talent is surprising.'

'Right? He could have a flair for all number of things but my husband seems to be apt at sketching a johnson.'

'And muff,' Stu adds, laughing.

'So how did you find out? You saw him sketching a sex toy?'

'About the Captain? No, it was a dildo in the post.'

'That would be a great name for his first single. You could diversify here, the possibilities are endless.'

'Stu plays drums too.'

Stu's nostrils flare in horror. I smile to think of Danny in Spandex and leather. The chafing would kill him, the singing would hurt people. Tim studies me. I think he's waiting for the catch.

'You could have switched the scoop, still had this article for yourself. It would have been easy to divert it away from yourself.'

I smile. I could have. 'Maybe.' He still seems confused. 'Tell me, young Tim. What's your goal with journalism? Where do you want to go with this? Be honest with me.'

He hesitates for a moment like you would in an interview. I help him along. 'I was once you. I graduated from university, I got some small gigs in local papers and one of those inflight magazines writing filler articles. And then I worked for *InStyle* and *Red*, naturally.' I point down to my poor clothes selection for the day as proof. He smiles. 'And I did the big City thing, I met celebs and got to travel and attend events and it wasn't highbrow but it was fun and just part of a wider life experience.'

He starts to get where I'm going now.

'Do you miss it?'

I pause for a moment to think about that.

'We all miss and mourn our former selves but I traded up. I got Danny, the girls and I still get to write. I have an idea for an article in the pipeline anyway. About sex education in schools. One day, when Polly gets bigger and can wipe her own arse then maybe I'll go back to it proper…'

'And turn into Diana…'

'You are not that young that I can't give you a slap.'

He smiles. 'You're right. The Wezzie isn't my forever job.'

'I could have written an article about the Captain. I could have made this about myself and my career and used it as a step up from local stories about local people. But when it comes to what I want, it's not that.'

He seems surprised at the admission. Stu also studies my face, trying to read me.

'Nah, you need it more than I do. I like you, Tim, but you don't belong in Kendal. Use this. Meet people. Get into journalism that's worth your skill and talent. I've had the big City experience and you need that too. Come back here when you've discovered a love for fleece and mountain walks.'

'Or mint cake?'

I laugh. 'Exactly.'

Tim leaves when the cake runs out, the orange folder under his arm, whilst Stu and I hang around so we can finish this epic fried breakfast that could have easily fed a family of five. We all hug it out and in that moment, I'm comforted that we did the right thing. I'll have a glance over the piece so I can fact-check and correct his grammar but I have a feeling this is heading in the right direction, that he's on our side. We still don't know what will come of the

Captain but he's no longer lurking in the shadows. He's a proud alter ego with a story and a voice.

But still, I worry. I worry about Danny. I wonder how this story will end. Looking in the mirror opposite, I also am wondering what in the crap has happened to my hair. In the mornings, I think I'm fashioning a messy bun when in daylight it looks more like I've combed my barnet through with a hedgerow. Meg Morton, journalist at large… whatever happened to you?

A little hand reaches up and grabs at my cheek, smearing me with baked beans. Oh yeah, you happened. I hold Polly tight and smell the top of her head. She giggles. I'm sorry, little one. I seem to have palmed you off on your uncle of late. I'm sorry I dress you in hand-me-downs and we haven't really thought much about giving you a hairstyle with your platinum blonde locks. She smiles. I go to pick her up from her highchair. One of the few things I miss about my kids during the working day is the weight of their bodies on mine when I pick them up or hug them; little arms around my neck and wandering eyes that scan your face so they can imprint it into memory. Little Polly Lemon Drop. You and your sisters re-wrote the story. Bar a few days off here and there, I wouldn't give that up for anything. I go to find some baby wipes in her change bag. Instead I find three swimming nappies, half a pack of Doritos, a cuddly dinosaur and some Rizlas. Bloody Stu.

'You fancy some bacon? I think I'm done.'

I look down at Stu's plate, the scene of some sort of breakfast massacre. He rubs his belly. It is hard to think of an alternative life where this man is a high-flying legal expert but he's told us he's tied all the ends up for us and done what he can to protect his brother. I have to take his word for it, don't I? He has egg yolk down his top that he scoops up and licks off his fingers. A figure appears at our table. Sarah. I had a feeling that she would meander over to stick her oar in.

'Nice breakfast? Who was that before?'

I return her fake smile from earlier.

'A work colleague, Tim.' Tim who's gay and who I found in a threesome situation with our headteacher and his wife, and who'll be writing an article about my husband who is that Mintcake fella that all those people are talking about. Just smile, Meg…

'Is he single? New in town? Where's he living?'

I don't respond to any of the above but allow Stu to take over the conversation. 'Sarah Milner, always a pleasure,' says Stu, knocking back his tea but not looking too impressed. Both of them have sketchy knowledge on each other being locals but Stu also knows too much about this woman from the incident at the exhibition the other day.

'Stuart,' she replies, curtly. 'Just he's a new face. I'm curious.'

'You know what they say about curiosity, Sarah Milner,' says Stu, attempting to diffuse the situation with humour. She doesn't get the message.

'Anyway, I was hoping to bump into you as I heard from Natalie Walsh's brother that you and Danny were in the cop shop a couple of weeks ago?'

Stu smiles broadly. How the hell did that get out? I glare over at Stu. This was his doing and it's quite obvious that Natalie Walsh would have heard from her husband whose nose we broke. I look over at Stu to defend my honour. He smiles back. He glances over at Polly who grabs his fingers.

'Fender bender, innit? Danny had been at it behind the wheel.'

My glare intensifies.

'He was drunk?' replies a shocked Sarah.

'No. Have you not met my boring older brother? Just a bit of speeding and he clipped a cop car.'

My body relaxes. Sarah looks a little bored that the gossip wasn't worth hearing. Stu is finding it hard to contain his giggles. She looks over, wondering what's so funny.

'Just thought I'd check all was OK.' I like how she masquerades her nosiness for concern. 'And did you have fun last night? Have heard they had to close the whole pub and get a professional cleaner in.'

I turn to Stu. This information is not surprising and I'm just glad he wasn't doing the partying in my house. I won't give Sarah the satisfaction of telling Stu off like his own mother so I just smile through gritted teeth.

'I'm more than OK, Sarah. Good to see your husband down there as well. Saw him at that exhibition last week too?'

And that's all he needs to do.

'What exhibition was that then?' She registers an uncomfortable look, fakes another smile and leaves. Like a version of the Pied Piper except the kids under her remit are reluctant to follow and I think she may have forgotten one that sits under a table chowing down on a box of breadsticks.

Stu looks at me. 'Nothing much has changed from school, eh?'

'Was she always like that?'

'Yep. Gob like a black hole. That said, I also got busy with her cousin back in the day so she's never been keen on me.'

I close my eyes, slowly as he burps under his breath. Oh, Stuart. My phone bleeps. I look down at the texts waiting for me. It's always an assortment of school reminders and junk but there's one from Emma to tell me she's slept with the anaesthetist, another from my mother telling me that she thinks Emma is sleeping with someone.

There's also a message from Danny.

Is it done?

Done x

I let Stu wander off to settle the bill.

Did you know Stu had slept with Sarah Milner's cousin?

Quicker to work out who he hasn't slept with

I haven't slept with him

Good to know. Olive from work has brought in a pie that she won at a fair

Apple?

Like a giant pork pie. It's as big as Polly. She says her and Stan will never finish it so she's gifted it to us.

Dinner?

With chips?

That's the dirtiest thing you've ever said to me.

You love it

I do x

Chapter Eighteen

I'm not sure what has been the strangest part of this whole Mint-cake thing. For me, it might be how the story has veered from the ridiculous to the sublime. One moment I'm having sex in my husband's office, adopting positions I've not managed since the early noughties and feeling that sexual spark for my husband who in secret is some undercover erotic porn baron. The next I'm stood at a school Christmas Bazaar watching a donkey take a dump in the school playground. A gaggle of schoolchildren next to me roar with laughter and I giggle to myself. Polly hangs off my hip and smothers the last of a self-iced gingerbread man down my face. Thanks, Polly. I squeeze her tight and pick crumbs and sprinkles out of her hair. The donkey next to us is not done with leaving a huge steaming pile of dung here but now has revealed he also has a giant donkey dick. There are two boys next to me who are in hysterics. I look around for Danny. This is the stuff you should be drawing. The person in charge of the donkey approaches with a stack of newspapers to cover the offending pile and I recognise the top headline immediately.

I AM CAPTAIN MINTCAKE

I smile. The story went to print last week. Did it cause a sensation? It's left people guessing and, as predicted, for Tim it was a huge scoop that attracted the attention of a few nationals and magazines. People have found out that the Captain is a middle-class white man from Kendal who likes walks in the hills, a good cup of tea and is happily married. That's about fifty per cent of the population here. It was quite a dull article to be honest. I think people had hoped it was someone far more sensational: the vicar, the Tory MP, the little old lady who runs the post office.

I turn to read the headline of another article, written by some bird called Meg Morton. The juxtaposition next to the Captain Mintcake story was a bit dodgy but it's a sensitive opinion piece about sex education at schools. It was well-received by the masses, a few got the hump and wrote angry letters, but it also got a gold star from one Mike McArthur. Look at both us Mortons on the front of the Wezzie. It feels like an achievement were it not for this issue being used to hide some donkey crap.

The Ferney Green Primary School Christmas Bazaar is a very simple affair and having compared notes with Emma, there seems to be a stark difference in what her girls' private school offers. Down South, it's a hog roast, a paid actor as Santa, a raffle funded by Fortnum & Mason and a Christmas tree flown in from Norway. Here we have someone's granddad in a red suit that I hope has been fire-tested. There are burnt burgers and Styrofoam cups of mulled wine being served out of a slow cooker and the world's biggest tombola where I am destined to win back the bottle of Advocaat that I donated.

Eve comes running up to me with a bag of candy floss, a stuffed bear with a Christmas hat and a giant glitter tattoo of a horse on her forearm. 'This is amazing! Can I have another five pounds?'

'Errrrm, no. Where is Uncle Stu? He's supposed to be looking after you?'

'Jenna's mummy asked him to go on the coconut shy for a bit so he's doing that. Is that donkey doing a wee? Is that his willy?'

I look over and it's like a hose on the loose. A woman next to me has her phone out. Why would you want that video on your camera roll? Well, I can't judge really, can I?

'Piss,' says Polly. That'll be her uncle's influence there.

'Wowzers, look at the wang on him...' says a voice from behind me. Thank hell for that. An additional source of funds is here. He puts a hand to my back and delves into his pocket.

'Here's two pound for now,' says Danny. 'Where's Tess?'

Eve's not bothered, fleecing her father for the cash and running off.

'No doubt she's also pissing away more of our cash winning Christmas tat.'

Or maybe Polly's lexicon has been influenced more by her father. She holds her hands out for a cuddle and Danny being Danny grabs her tight and pretends to eat her cheeks. He spies the pile of donkey crap and the Mintcake headline.

'Is that...?'

'Yup.'

'I thought that smell were Polly.' I love how he thinks our daughter could produce a smell on that level and is unbothered by the newspaper in full view.

'How long do we have to stay?' he asks.

'Until they light up the tree and Tess has done her bit with the choir.'

'Kill me now.'

'Don't tempt me.'

'Why is it a bazaar and not a fair or fete?' Danny asks.

'I know the answer to this: it's because they asked all the farm shop people to come along and sell jams and things made out of hessian. Rufus is in the school cafeteria selling cheese and there are no rides either so that doesn't make it a fair.'

'You can ride the donkey…'

'Oi oi… I don't think he's for riding. You can pet the donkey.'

'He'd like that…'

We both giggle. We've always had our repartee. It's part of what made us work but I wonder now if we will spend an eternity talking in innuendo.

'Would you like to pet my donkey?' he replies jokingly.

I laugh but I'm aware that he's referred to his penis as a donkey and given the size of what's before us, he's a little short by about a foot.

'You got off lightly. You just need to stand around and buy stuff. Stu's on the coconut shy.'

We leave the pissing donkey to peer our heads into the hall. Stu loves the attention so is standing there like a ringmaster, buttering up a few of the mums who've partaken in a fair bit of the slow cooker wine. There's a lot of giggling and ruddy faces of people who should know better as their husbands are only outside manning the barbecue. Such is the draw of young Master Morton. One of the mums looks a bit familiar and I realise it's Jo McArthur.

Danny looks on slightly perturbed. 'Lad needs to tread careful there. If he goes after the headteacher's wife, I'll bloody kill him.'

Polly's face bounces between us trying to understand the conversation. One day she'll be verbal and recount all the gory details of the last six months: the giant blue dildo, the time she saw paintings of her dad's willy on the kitchen table. Joanne McArthur wears a posh Christmas jumper that you know is a cashmere mix, with well-fitting jeans and fancy boots. She's got a rubbish swing, so Stu does what he shouldn't and stands behind her, holding her arm to demonstrate. Bloody hell, Stu. He knows far too much and can't help but indulge in a bit of shit-stirring. We look on in the same way one would a car crash as she erupts into fits of giggles. Mike McArthur looks on as he sells raffle tickets. He's gone for a more casual Santa hat look with the rolled-up sleeve. Between him and Stu, they seem to have captured the imagination of the school mums in the main hall. Ladies, you have the option of a semi-tanned bit of rough or the swishy haired polished gent who likes a bit of three-way action. I don't know what to expect with Stu being so brazen but Mike watches and dare I say it, looks extremely calm, grinning. Is this getting him off? Is he turned on by Stu? Who effing knows?

I've seen Mike a few times since we visited his house. I've been very good. When I've seen him at assemblies and at the school gate, I've not given anything away. I've been the ultimate professional parent. Either way, you see him now squatting at a child's level and chatting to her, taking interest in her face painted like a penguin, and you realise what he gets up to behind closed doors is nothing to do with how he runs this school.

Stu, meanwhile, looks like he's presenting a game show. 'Terrible, Mrs McArthur. Right… who's up next? Roll up ladies – who's going to be the one who gives my nuts a good bashing?'

Danny and I have the good sense to walk away at this point. Who is that man? Never seen him before in our lives. We take off into a neighbouring classroom, home to the arts and crafts that the various classes have made.

Tess' teacher spies us. 'Mr and Mrs Morton, lovely to have you here!'

Mrs Randall is one of those overly pleasant ladies and you get that vibe that her throw cushions match and that she's had the same hairstyle for most of her adult life. One hopes she goes home, swigs at a bottle of vodka and swears like a sailor when she's not around the children.

'I have some things that Tess has made.'

Danny holds on to Polly so as to say that he can't access his wallet. She points over to decorations made with some sort of glittery clay, held together with gift ribbon and a crap load of PVA. Tess' face seems to be stuck on to the reverse. The second item is a reindeer made out of lollipop sticks.

'It's two pounds for both.'

'We might come back when we have change. The girls ran off with my wallet and—'

'I'll get these…'

It's going to be one of those evenings, isn't it? Briony Tipperton has shown up as Mrs Santa in a short woollen fur-cuffed dress. The lip is strong, the hair is big. I wonder how her earlobes are coping with the size of the baubles hanging off them.

'Tipperton, what the hell have you come as?'

I blush to hear Danny be so frank with her.

'You bastard, I'm spreading the Christmas joy about, aren't I?' She reaches over for the double air kiss and does the same with me. Since soft play, new battle lines have been drawn. I've seen that she cares and that changes everything.

Mrs Randall intervenes, 'I think you look radiant, especially with your news. Congratulations, Mrs Tipperton.'

Danny and I look at each other.

'Having another, innit? Another boy due May.'

'Fantastic, love…' Danny goes in to hug her, sandwiching Polly between them.

'It's in the air, eh? All this Captain Mintcake nonsense made us proper frisky.'

Danny and I freeze for a moment. She knows who he is too? That said, I believe you've sampled the Captain's goods before, Tipperton. Now he's inadvertently made you pregnant.

'You'll have to give me tips on what to do with three,' she gestures to me. I smile, holding up Tess' creations in my hands. 'Pay me back when you come in salon so we can sort that barnet of yours.'

Can I be insulted? Don't think you're allowed when the pregnant woman is the culprit and she's right, too – my hair has started to look like the manger where the sweet baby Jesus lay. She catches sight of someone behind me and her face suddenly drops. I glance back to see Sarah and her husband, Jez. It's an awkward family portrait of them walking together with the kids sandwiched between them. I know Danny is far from happy to be here but Jez looks murderous.

'She's told everyone this is our Band-Aid baby,' Briony says. 'That we're trying to save our marriage. Feel like telling her maybe that's what she needs.'

Mrs Randall, who is in earshot, pretends to look at the ceiling tiles.

'Poor girl,' says Danny, nonchalant. Briony and I look at him, curiously. 'Imagine what it's like to be in that marriage – torn between a shitty husband and your kids. It's like a call out for attention – try and throw shade at other people's relationships so yours doesn't look so bad.'

Mrs Randall, Briony and I are surprised by this clarity from Danny, of all people.

'Throw shade, what are you fifteen?' exclaims Briony. I giggle.

Jez suddenly catches Danny's eye. Balls. Not another confrontation here, in our kids' school and amongst the personalised handmade ornaments. Of course, Sarah is none the wiser about their altercation. Briony stares her up and down.

'Mrs Randall. Do you have ones for Maisy? Evening ladies.'

Sarah is not without her own brand of disapproving looks at Briony's outfit. That said, she's turned up in a jumper where Christmas puddings cover her boobs. Jez looks slightly pale making me wonder what Danny and Stu said to him outside The Brewery. Mrs Randall plasters a smile on knowing that what's about to unfold will at least be entertaining and worth her having to stay late.

'Where's Ian tonight, Briony?' Sarah asks.

And so it starts. Briony is wise to this game.

'Oh, he's visiting his granny in Storth. Taken her to a Christmas carol service.'

'Isn't that lovely? He should have brought her here. It's nice to bring your whole family to these things, isn't it?' She interlocks arms with Jez in the same way a constrictor may capture prey. Briony, who is here without allies, interlocks her arm in Danny's. I'm not entirely bothered but Sarah looks incredulous.

'Oh, I didn't realise you were all pals?' Sarah replies snidely, looking Briony up and down. 'How cosy.'

Jez giggles.

'What you trying to say?' Briony asks.

'Well, I guess you and Danny went out for a good while. It's lovely that he's back and you can reconnect.'

I cock my head to one side. Briony lets go of Danny who can sense something brewing here but doesn't know how to intervene.

'Reconnect as mates, get to know his lovely wife and family,' mentions Briony.

'I'm sure.'

Briony stares them both down. I can't breathe for the tension. And then Sarah looks down at Briony's stomach and then over at Danny. I laugh, quite hard. Danny shakes his head. But Briony? Well, this is where she loses her shit. I know what it's like to try and take the high road but I also know what it's like to be three months pregnant. The hormones are high, you really do not care who you insult or hurt and you become increasingly protective of your herd. And so like some angry Christmas cat, Briony literally goes in for the kill. I think about what she told me at soft play. *I'll have her.* Is this it? She hurls herself in Sarah's direction, Jez joins in, trying to drag her away. It's a blur of Christmas jumpers, manicured nails and teeth.

'Lying shit-stirring scumbags the two of you.'

There's a slap, someone grabs hair. I am secretly horrified and enthralled. Sarah puffs out her chest and uses her handbag as a weapon.

Briony loses her balance and her skirt flies up to reveal she's wearing a thong. A red sequinned thong. Danny hands me the baby and tries to calm everyone down. Good luck with that. Jez says words you really shouldn't be saying in a school. A random dad gets involved and calls Jez a plank. There's a spillage of glitter and pencil pots. People file into the room to watch. I hear a baby crying. I think there's a mum over there with popcorn. It's an actual bloody physical fight, the sort you wish most at the school gate would have to sort out all those petty issues over parking and lost cardigans. Mrs Randall glances over at me. There's a look that says this is not in her job description. I want to join in and cheer them on angry mob style. I don't. I look at Danny.

'Bird, you're pregnant. Calm down,' hollers Danny.

'Don't tell me to calm down. Tell her the gobshite!'

'What did you call my wife?'

'What do you care, you cheating bit of toerag! I've seen you coming out of the Winterburns' house!'

There are tears and fingers and accusations. Danny stands in the middle. He looks over at me and shrugs but also seems slightly bewildered that I am so calm in this melee. It's fine, Danny. I know that's not your baby. I know you're trying to do the right thing here like you always do. I know. I look down at Polly, laughing at the grown-ups in a pile on the floor, as she tries to eat some homemade decorations. She giggles. This is much better than that CBeebies rubbish you make me watch.

Twenty minutes later and Danny and I have found a school bench, freezing our arses off with a paper plate selection of cake sale items, cheap crisps, an incinerated barbecue mix and mulled wine which we're topping up with a few swigs of the cherry brandy we won in the tombola. We got sloshed pretty quickly to calm ourselves after that fracas, evident in the fact that I feel like I could strip and sprint home and it's easily only two degrees. Polly sleeps soundly next to us swathed in fleece and we've lost the other daughters to games involving skittles and twenty pence pieces.

Across the way, our good friend PC Gary Walsh is taking statements from people as he was called in to calm down the event. He's lost none of his sanctimony and waves his finger at a dad who trashed a fake Christmas tree. Naturally, we made ourselves scarce when Walshy entered the scene. We didn't see a thing guv'nor. But I make a mental note to tell Emma about this. I bet her highfalutin Christmas events down South don't come with fights where people use tinsel as lassos. I notice Danny glancing over as an interesting scene unfolds before us. Briony and Sarah share a picnic bench, one has a bleeding nose, the other a fat lip. Jez is nowhere to be seen. They share a tissue and then go in to hug each other. We must be drunk if those two are talking again.

'Can you wear thongs when you're pregnant, isn't that bad for your bits?'

I like that this is what Danny's got out of all of this.

'Well, she's a braver bird than me, that's for sure.'

We watch as Sarah cries on her shoulder and Briony continues to console her. Both of us are comforted by the fact that despite the comedy fighting, some good has possibly come of this.

'Were they ever mates?' I ask.

'Once. In school. Not sure what happened though.'

'I'd hazard a guess Jez happened. Do you think he ever hurt her?'

'Hurt comes in many forms,' mutters guru Danny, swaying slightly from the alcohol.

'I don't ever want it to be like that, you know? If you want to pork other women then just go for it. I don't want us to hate each other,' I tell Danny.

'Pork? That's feral, even for you.'

I feel Danny's hand in mine.

'So you're saying, there's an order to these things… If I get fed up of you then I need to just leave and then get porking?'

'Yes.'

'Can I have my daughters?'

'Well, no. I'll bloody wrestle you to the death for them. You could have the dog because he was your idea.'

We both stare at each other for a moment. Even talking hypothetically about splitting our family up feels weird. Even him taking the dog, of whom I've grown quite fond. But there's something inside me which reckons I could never really, truly hate him.

'If you cheated on me, it would break me,' mentions Danny.

'Like how? Man tears?'

'Like break my heart.'

'You must be drunk.'

'Don't ever do that, please.'

'I'll try… it's hard though. You know how I'm just hitting them away with a shitty stick most days,' I reply.

'Veritable buffet.'

'All-you-can-eat.'

'If you ever ate cock.' Oral sex, the sore point in any married couple's sex résumé.

I elbow him. 'Well, I can't even focus. Check the expiry date on that cherry brandy because you can have anything you want tonight.'

He doesn't quite believe me. 'Can I have a BJ tonight then, please?'

I applaud the good manners and forward planning.

'Well, I'm hammered. I'll eat kebabs from the van at the train station when I'm drunk so yeah, why not?'

He looks reasonably excited. 'Do you want anything special? I could dress up as something?'

'You know that sheepskin rug in the front room, could you wear it and pretend to be Ned Stark from *Game of Thrones*? Go all King in the North.'

'Honestly?'

'No.'

He smiles broadly. That smile that not many people get to see. He comes in to kiss me. I'd like to say it's tender but he's drunk and our tongues clash in the way moray eels might mate. I wipe a few multicoloured sprinkles from his stubble and he kisses my hands as it grazes over his chin. I love how we're achieving such levels of intimacy in a school playground.

A voice suddenly makes us part. 'There's always two that lower the tone.'

It's Stu. Of course, now complete with an elf hat that has mistletoe protruding from the front.

'Where you been lad?' asks Danny.

'Doing my bit for the children, naturally. I heard I missed a fight?'

'Indeed you did. You missed your brother trying to keep the peace,' I inform him.

Stu doesn't look impressed. 'Danny Morton I know would have got stuck in.'

'Danny Morton's a changed man now,' he replies, looking over at me.

Stu swipes Danny's Styrofoam cup and takes a swig. He chokes a little. 'Geez, this is where the party's at then. You could strip paint with that.' He takes the rucksack off his back and reveals a bottle of gin with a box of baby rusks. How we've changed this one.

'Let's crack this open too. Cin cin.' He pours himself a generous measure. 'So, I have news,' announces Stu.

Danny and I wait with bated breath.

'Just been on the phone with Craig Moon, remember him?'

'Moonsy? One with the big face?' replies Danny.

'Very one. Lad made money apparently reconditioning gypsy caravans for glamping. But guess where he's headed off season?'

Danny pauses and smiles. 'Chamonix, no doubt.' He laughs and shakes his head. 'When you off?'

'Tomorrow morning, my ride leaves at 5 a.m.'

He's going? There is a moment between the brothers. It's neither emotional nor angry; it's expected. Though I dare say there's a smidge of jealousy that Stu gets to drop everything, go off and have an adventure. The consolation being that Danny can release his brother back into the wild, to go beyond these hills and valleys, and live vicariously through Stu's Facebook posts and rude postcards. I throw my arms around Stu's neck in a feckless drunken manner.

'Will you miss me then?'

'Possibly. A tiny bit,' I admit.

'Mum and dad will cover the fort with littl'uns for a while. I need to go see them now and explain – stay the night there.'

'Mum will cry because you won't be here for Christmas,' Danny warns.

'Which is why I ordered her a set of festive placemats with my face on. And I left you guys a pressie too, it's on your bed. Hopefully, dog hasn't eaten it.' It will be shortbread knowing him – and knowing Mr T, he's gulped that down in one fell swoop.

Danny doesn't hug him. He does that thing the Morton brothers always do which is to punch each other in the arm.

'I've loved spending time with you lot by the way. Your daughters are my new favourite girls.'

I swoon. Danny is more sceptical. 'You won't be saying that in a week when you're knee deep in ski bunny.' I hit him across the head.

'True.'

'Look after your cock. Mind *les herpés*.'

'Your French is a bit good, eh? *Toujours*, big brother.'

And there's another look between them. I know that look. It's the one I give my sisters when we go our own ways. Stay in touch kid, tell us you're alive every so often. I love you but I'll never say that to your face.

'God, he's leaving us again? Couldn't have predicted that one.' Ru appears behind me, witnessing the brothers' parting gestures. He wears a baby and is carrying boxes of what I think are his homemade cheese. He is warm and sweet as ever and gives me a huge kiss on the cheek and hugs the Morton boys warmly.

'Who's up for free cheese?'

I put my hand up. Like I say, I'm drunk I'll eat anything.

'And how drunk are we all? I think everyone's got plastered waiting for this choir to come out. The school hall smells like a brewery.' He joins our party by swigging at a bottle of Babycham that he too obviously acquired from the tombola.

'You missed a proper fight too,' I tell him.

'I heard. I always miss the good stuff. Last year I missed the mum who fell off the sleigh.'

I know that mum and saw everything. She was drunk off her tits. Her name is Helen. She still gets called Jingle Hels.

'Stuart, I saw you getting up and personal with Jo McArthur too. You are incorrigible,' mentions Ru.

Danny and I stare at him intently. We didn't stay for all of that. Was he hoping for one last round before he left?

Stu smiles. 'Just playing it for laughs. Even with my questionable morals I don't think I'd go back there. She was very mean during sex too, she liked to bark out instructions like I were a Labrador.'

'Stay, lie down, good boy,' jokes Danny.

Ru laughs. 'Well, you'll never guess what I just heard on my stall. Couple of mums speculating that McArthur is your Mintcake man.'

Danny looks horrified. I forget that Ro and Ru know sometimes.

'Dirty bastard,' giggles Stu. 'What makes them think that?'

'That article in Wezzie said it were a local man, married, with three young kids. The ages tally up too.'

We all look up. Both the McArthurs are up on the stage, rearranging microphones, looking like they're about to announce their candidacy for the Presidency. Bollocks. Is it bad that we've diverted the attention to him? I don't know whether to feel guilt or relief. Is this what it will be like for the rest of time? He'll remain an urban legend, a myth of sorts. McArthur bends over and a few heads in the crowd turn.

Stu laments. 'Desperate housewives. My arse is much better than his.'

I don't have the heart to tell him otherwise. I think Danny's is the far superior of the lot in front of me.

'I tell thee though, the number of women who've been rubbing their tits in my face all night. No wonder Captain Mintcake is all they can talk about.'

It's a bold statement to make out in the open but luckily the only other people who surround us are sleeping children and the errant few Year 6 kids who've broken away from the bazaar to trash school property.

'Are you complaining?'

'Nah, but it's just sad. I don't understand that age when you suddenly buy a sensible motor, slap on some chinos, have a few kids and forget what sex is, or at least stop having fun with it,' says Stu.

'That's generalising it a little,' Ru argues. I can't help but look down at Ru's feet.

I intervene. 'They're just lonely, Stu. When you're a woman and the only people you ever meet are kids and other mums, then you go into some weird hyperdrive when you meet other men, especially ones who look like you.'

'Smeggsy, I do believe that is a compliment.'

I shake my head at him. I take back everything I said and thought. 'That or, like you say, it's just pure desperation…'

'Cow.'

'But seriously, if Captain Mintcake helps some people remember what it is to feel sexual, to feel desired and have a laugh then hell, he might be doing a good public service.'

Danny looks over at me and smiles. I love him for doing his bit for the community. But I also realise that maybe we fall under that category too. We forgot, didn't we? To have sex. To have fun. We flatlined and the Captain brought us back to life. I raise a cup in Danny's direction and he does the same.

'Finally…' mumbles Rufus.

Our attention is suddenly taken by the children filing out of the school building, including Tess who waves at us manically in a Santa hat that's two sizes too big and Rowan, who is ushering children and looking like she's going to break out a tambourine solo. Eve appears out of nowhere with something resembling an ylang ylang incense stick set and a bag full of marshmallows. Stu helps himself to her stockpile and we watch as a music teacher struggles to get to grips with the PA system.

'Errrm, hello. Hello? Hello! Ferney Green Primary School! Who's having fun tonight?' It's McArthur on the microphone. He laughs nervously, trying to regain a bit of calm amongst the drunk scrappy parents. I think he should sing. This is what this surreal evening needs, him and the wife banging out a Christmas duet. 'Firstly, can I say a huge thank you to our PTA tonight for their stellar work in bringing the joy of Christmas into our school…'

Both Morton brothers stand there swigging at alcoholic beverages and swaying slightly. Don't heckle the head teacher, lads. A hand falls into mine. Gorgeous little Eve, how are you daughter of mine?

'Mummy, who is Captain Mintcake?'

I stop hearing McArthur. Stu laughs. Ru looks mortified. It's a wonder the girls hadn't asked this before, given the time we've spent on the subject matter at home. Danny bends down to her level.

'Where'd you hear that from Buttons?'

'Uncle Stuart was talking about him. And someone was talking about it in the gym.' Danny tucks bits of errant fringe back into her hat, looking a little disturbed to see the words come out of her innocent mouth. 'Is he a bad person?'

'He can't be… he's a Captain,' says Danny. 'Like Captain America.'

'So he's saving the world?'

'One dong at a time,' whispers Stu out of the corner of his mouth. I have the urge to throw some wine at him. He bends down. 'He's a hero, a local legend, Steve.'

Eve punches him. 'My name is EVE! I still don't get it. Who is he? Is it Mr McArthur? Is it something you can dress up as? Maybe you could be Captain Mintcake? You like mint cake?'

'I do like mint cake. But I don't think I can be the Captain, Buttons. I'm not a hero,' replies Danny.

'Yes, you are.'

He smiles and my heart goes aflutter. He knows that to this little girl he'll always be a hero. I mean, half an hour ago he was breaking up actual fights.

'You told me something about mint cake once,' explains Eve.

'I did?' He can barely remember my name most days so I am sure it's not something he registered at the time.

'I was born in the North, in the Lakes. You told me I had mint cake and spring water in my veins like you.'

Stu chuckles. We all look down at the five-year-old in all her infinite wisdom.

'So, that means there is mint cake in all of us, except you. You Southern Jessie.' She points at me. Danny and Stu guffaw loudly. I'll have you know I've had a great deal of mint cake in me recently but even I'm not too drunk to say that out loud.

'So you are Captain Mintcake… we are all Captain Mintcake…'

The four adults stand over this child, who is high off squash and penny sweets, and pause for a moment.

Danny puts a hand to his chest. 'You are right. I AM CAPTAIN MINTCAKE!'

He picks up his daughter and swoops her around the playground. I hear a peal of laughter from her that will never grow old. Stu and Rufus inhale breath sharply. Naturally, he's a little drunk and he's said this within earshot to just a few, so it means nothing but in truth, it's probably the first time he's admitted it out loud and the words ring with some relief, some ownership.

The choir is lined up but no one can get the PA system to work. A few impatient parents who may also be drunk from the slow cooker wine start to cheer and chant. Everything starts to work again and we all wince from the feedback in the ancient speakers and wait for a bit of 'Hark! The Herald'. Ru waves at Sage in the front row. Stu cheers loudly for his niece. But wait. This music teacher has different ideas and the chords for 'Jingle Bell Rock' start beating out the speakers. You beauty. Danny, Rufus and Stu start moving their shoulders and dancing on the spot. Finest dad dancing I've ever seen. I go over and take Stu's hands and he spins me under his arms.

Eve intervenes. 'Why are you all doing that? Please stop…'

We don't. With a mixture of alcohol, joy and Christmas in our veins, we roll out our best exaggerated dance moves. I'd like to say we start a wave of dancing throughout the school. But no. I may be drunk but I think a donkey from across the way voices his approval too. The real donkey.

Oh, Stu. I can't believe he's leaving us. I look over at Danny. Wow. His eyes are fully closed. Like he's so drunk that he's passed out already but his body has not got the message. Those are some moves and ones I've not seen in public since when we first dated. Tess can see us from beyond the way and I throw a double thumbs up at her. Oh dear, she's not happy. I stumble a little. Fuck a bloody duck, something was in that slow cooker wine. It's a conspiracy. I put an arm around Stu to steady myself.

'You are such a lightweight, Smeggsy.'

'You are such a twat. I do love you though, you know that, right?'

He leans over. 'I know and I love you both too. That present. I sorted it. All those letters you gave me, I sorted it.'

I stop in my tracks. 'You did what?'

But before he can reply, he heads over to his brother and Rufus, and they start doing a strange jumping dance that has roots from an unfortunate teenage grounding in acid house. A swirling mix of drunken emotion swells in me. Is that emotion? What has Stu done? Because that isn't emotion either and I sprint to the nearest hedgerow and projectile the contents of my stomach all over it.

Chapter Nineteen

'I'm not getting that blow job, am I?' whispers Danny.

'Well, no.'

I think Danny might be crying. I'm not exactly sure if it's from the absence of fellatio this evening or the fact he may be in physical pain from carrying one medium-sized child home, along with the three bags of crap we acquired at the bazaar, whilst also having to hold my hair back so I could throw up all over the wheels of a Toyota Prius. Tess has gone into meltdown from having spent six pounds on the tombola and coming away with absolutely nothing whereas Eve was crafty and just spent all her money on sweets and some mysterious endeavour which means that she has acquired three giant cuddly toys. By the time we've pushed them through that door, they are banshees, wired on sugar and fatigue.

'BED! Just go upstairs, brush the candy floss out of your teeth and go to bed,' I say.

'But you said…'

Danny is having as much trouble as me putting sentences together and standing up straight.

'Bed. If you go to bed, I will give you actual money,' he pleads.

'Like the tooth fairy?'

'Yes, Dimples. Whatever.'

'But I'm thirsty.'

'And I'm Daddy. Bed.'

I stand at the bottom of the stairs watching the Captain usher the troops upstairs, trying his best to act sober and responsible, a tired limp baby on his shoulder. He's infinitely better at it than me because when they're out of sight, I collapse into a heap and put my cheek against the cold hard floor to remedy the woeful thumping in my head. I think of that hedge that housed some of the Christmas bunting created by Year 3, now speckled in maroon vomit. No one will ever know it came from me. We weren't there. We didn't get off our nut at a school Christmas bazaar.

Maybe I can sleep here. Mr T comes over and I heave slightly, thinking he may be licking the remnants of my spew off my face. Come lie with me furry creature and be my blanket. But the state of me obviously doesn't appeal as he doesn't budge. Stu's words echo in my head. He sorted it. Sorted what?

'Oi, wench.' Danny sits on the third step from the top. 'Get upstairs, I'm not carrying you. You know what happens when we try that.'

'Girls?'

'Getting in their onesies. Water all round. Tea for me.'

'But I'm dying.'

'Best to die in your own bed so we don't have to step over you in the morning.'

'Will you at least come to my funeral?'

'I'll sing at a fooking piano if you make me a cup of tea.'

For some reason, this makes me sit up. I hear a small child get whacked by a sibling in the bathroom and feel I may have got the better deal here. He returns to the bathroom to referee the action. I scrape myself off the floor and zombie walk to the kitchen, kicking off my boots halfway. Kettle. Tea. Crumbs, got to let the dog out to have a whizz too. I open up the back door and the cold hits me like a stab to the chest. I think about those slow cookers they used for the wine. Maybe they used them to cook meat. Raw meat. I may have salmonella. I rest my head against the doorframe. Mr T sidles up next to me to tell me he's done. Dog. I like you, dog. Have a biscuit and my affection. I'm supposed to make tea.

By the time I get upstairs, the girls are passed out and I find Danny in the bedroom sat on the edge of the bed in his pants and socks. He still looks pained and rubs his belly.

'I think those sausages were underdone.'

A loud fart resonates through our bedroom. Enough to make Magnum the cat who was sat in the hallway shriek a little and shoot down the stairs. For the love of monkeys, that's an ungodly smell.

'Danny, did you just soil yourself?'

I put the tray of drinks and mugs of tea on the bed. He hobbles to the bathroom and locks the door. I hear noises that no one should have to hear but when you've lived with a person for twelve odd years, they become part of the sketchy soundtrack of your marriage. The day you hear your partner through the bathroom door is the day when the love has crossed a threshold into forever and more.

'Are you OK?' I shout, trying to take off my dress, my eyes heavy.

I hear groans, flushing, taps running. The shower's going too which makes me fear the worst. He returns sopping wet, clutching his belly like a woman does when the first contractions kick in. Body hair clings to him like seaweed.

I chuck Danny a towel. He dries his undercarriage but then collapses into bed, naked and spread-eagled. It is a good arse but not today. He buries his head into the duvet.

'You're sopping wet, hun. Dry yourself, you're leaving an imprint on the bed.'

'I'll make you sopping wet.' He says, straining, trying to be sexual. 'Actually, I can't move,' he admits.

I take his towel and mop at the claggy hairs on his arms and legs. I try and turn him over and do the same. I then roll his body over and attempt to tuck him under the duvet.

'Why are you manhandling me? You're like a sex pest.'

'Drink your tea. Don't poo in my bed.'

I go to the bathroom to brush my teeth and spy my sorry state in the mirror. I grab some old T-shirt from behind the bathroom door and slip it on. When I return to the bedroom, Danny sits there sipping his tea in bed. He looks over.

'See, that is sexy.'

I shake my head and do some weird Beyoncé-style strut towards the bed.

'And that isn't. You look like a randy giraffe.'

I laugh, collapsing into bed. He puts his beloved tea down to rest his head on my lap.

'Where did they get those sausages from? Just went right through me. Who were on barbecue?'

I stroke his head. 'You're just getting old and can't handle your alcohol anymore.'

'You can talk.'

I laugh. I throw some of the clothes that litter the bed onto the floor and notice an A4-sized parcel in the middle of the bed. At first glance, it looks like some tombola shite we've picked up this evening but Danny sits up recognising the handwriting on the card.

'It's that present from Stu, innit? If it's biscuits, we may as well crack it open.'

I don't argue with him but think again about those words that Stu left me with. He sorted it. I sit and unwrap the parcel carefully. It's a huge pile of paper held together by coloured paperclips that I think belong to a ten-year-old's stationery set.

Danny has the attached card in his hands and reads aloud, '*After thirty years, I finally found a use for that wasted education of mine. Cheers Captain Mintcake. Have a good Christmas you fantastic fuckers xxx*'

Danny and I huddle around the papers and have a read. It's all on a solicitor's letterhead attached to an eighty-page document. Shit on an actual stick. Danny grabs his phone to try and ring Stu but it's going to voicemail.

'Oh my days, he did it. He actually did it.'

Danny looks at me, panicked. 'He did what? You had a hand in this?'

I browse through the literature, the hairs on the back of my neck standing up with guilt but dare I say it, some excitement.

'You had all those letters at the mill from agents and publicists and I may have made copies of them and shown Stu.' I can feel myself go a deeper shade of red. 'I just showed them to Stu though, when we were putting all that stuff together for Tim. I didn't tell him to act on them. I was just really proud of you…'

'They were addressed to me.'

'Yes… but… I never told him to do this. I didn't tell him to get out his law degree and make this happen. I swear.'

We sit there, half-naked, holding what looks like a few piles of contracts. Stu has carefully labelled and added Post-It notes along the way to explain it all to us.

Confidentiality Clause – publicist to act on your behalf.

Captain Mintcake LLC has been formed as a company to protect your anonymity.

Potential to get gagging orders to protect you as a 'trade secret'.

Danny and I are too far gone to be able to focus, let alone read. All I see is one contract has a hefty sum of money written across it. It's a contract for Danny to have an exhibition in a London gallery as part of a festival at the South Bank, two hardback books published and some of the copyright on the images sold. But Stu has done one better. He's allowed for Danny to do this without ever revealing his real identity.

'He's done everything he can to protect you, to make this happen for you. Geez, this is amazing.' My heart wells up because I know why he did it: he did it for his brother.

'This is what he were doing with Polly them mornings then. I thought he were at home eating our food and not cleaning our house.' He flicks through all of it. I can't quite read if this is the direction he wanted this to go, but it looks like Stu's done his homework; all the loopholes are covered and there's room for Danny to be as involved as he wants. 'And how I do explain this extra money… How would it appear to the people at the mill? I'll look like I'm bloody laundering it.'

'Lottery win, Australian uncle carked it? It's not like you're the sort who's going to buy a mansion and a Ferrari from the off.'

I haven't thought about these smaller details but I am relieved that someone shares this burden with me to help Danny feel fulfilled, happy. Danny has got to an added contract at the back of the pile – a letter is attached. He pauses for a moment. He smiles. He hands me the document. It's an employment contract. For the mill.

> *Time to think about yourself, brother. After I'm done in Chamonix, I'll come back for a year or two, try my hand at this paper business. I've let you do this for so long… time to do my bit, eh?*

Danny stops for a moment. This was probably the most telling action of all. Because for once, young Stu wasn't thinking about himself. He's taken a moment to think about this wider arc of family and is finally giving something back to them. It was something I couldn't do. I didn't have it in my power to help Danny like this but Stu did. It's gracious and endearing and dare I say it, a little grown up.

'Christ, we'll be buying him a pair of chinos next.'

I smile. But I still can't read Danny's reaction. Is this what he wants? Something tells me that he'd have preferred it if the parcel had been a box of value biscuits. He sighs quietly, exhaling air. He gets out of bed and starts pacing.

'I should be angry, you two hid this from me.'

'I didn't know what he was up to, seriously. He gave us advice with Tim and the paper but this was all him.'

'But you hid the fact you showed him the letters.'

'You hid Captain Mintcake from me for a whole year.' Touché.

'I'm still not sure I want it to be a thing. I don't know what I want…? I want a quiet life. My family.' He stares me out. 'I mean, what do you want?'

It's the first time he's asked me this since it all started. I've thought about this a lot recently. Pre-discovery of Mintcake I was actually doing OK. I was a bit tired and worn and my sexual self was somewhat lacklustre but Danny had given me a life up here in these Lakes that I had grown to love, and that had become everything. I think I was actually happy. So what I want more than anything is the same happiness for those I love, Danny in particular. I want for someone who's given me so much to own the person who he is, this person he's created, and turn it into something that will make his soul sing.

'You.' I whisper. His eyes glaze over and he comes back to lie next to me. 'All the versions of you. Captain Danny Mintcake Morton.'

'That's a mouthful.'

'It's just all innuendo with you now.'

He laughs. 'You think this could really be a thing?'

'It could. There could be merchandise.'

'Like T-shirts?'

'Condoms? Dildos? I could create you a logo. The only other Captain I know makes fish fingers though.'

'Oi oi, we could do a promotional tie-in.'

There's silence as we process this small step into the unknown.

'I can't process this, Meg. I'm a bit scared.'

We sit here in silence. He squeezes my hand tightly and our feet meet in the same place under the duvet where they've been meeting for years and years. It's rare to see Danny like this. He doesn't admit to fear. He craves security, our little bubble, that much I know and this element of risk is foreign to him. I cradle his head on my boobs, a classic hold of ours. He seeks comfort there when he needs reassurance in the same way a newborn listens to its mother's heartbeat. We'll be OK, Morton. Something rises in me which could still be drunken nausea, but it's excitement, for him: new chapters, new pages, the story going in a different direction.

'You'll stick around, right?' he asks.

'Well, I'm not going anywhere, it's just getting interesting.'

He sticks a tongue out at me. 'This could go tits up.'

'Quite literally.'

He guffaws a little unattractively then burps loudly. The scent of cherry and shop-bought mince pie lingers in the air.

'I feel ill.'

'That's the sausages talking.'

'Don't mention them sausages.'

He pauses. 'You know if this works out, I can get one of them big barbecues like at school but with the two tiers and the good tongs with the wooden handles.'

I marvel that after everything this could bring, this is his end goal. He sips his tea and I can see the cogs whirring, slowly but surely. The Captain is on standby, ready to launch. While I'm behind the curtain, fiddling with his cape so he can fly straight, keeping him in tea. Does that make Stu… Robin?

'It'll be grand,' I whisper.

'You're using Northern. I knew I'd break you eventually.'

'Fark off.'

He lies there taking it all in, paper scattered all over the bed, his body fizzing with a newfound energy.

'I won't sleep now.'

'I know.'

'A jump would have helped.'

'After what I've just heard in that bathroom? Jog on, not going near it.'

He laughs. I see his eyes scan my face for answers, about how this is going to work. I have nothing. But I am here. We'll do this together. Except the sex, mainly because I can't feel my face at this precise moment.

'Danny?'

'Meg?'

'I know you're excited but sleep now, those girls will be up at daybreak and I may need to barf again in a bit.'

He shows very little concern but the way he rubs his belly makes me think we'll be racing for the porcelain all evening.

'Instead of sex, we could finish off a box set?' I suggest.

'You're full of good ideas, eh?'

'It's why you married me.'

He doesn't disagree. There's a look between us. I call this look love because sometimes there are no other words to describe why two people end up together and why they stay that way. I grab my phone from the bedside table and he curls the duvet around his legs. He farts again but doesn't excuse himself. I'm far too tired to call him out on it.

'Did you put dog out?'

'Yep.'

'Well, whack something on Mrs. Nowt too romantic and none of that superhero shite.'

I smile.

'Aye aye, Captain.'

Epilogue

'He was the bestest dog in the world. He was warm and we used to watch the television together and when I gave him his toast, his willy used to come out because he was excited.'

Danny and I look at each other across this rather windy hilltop. Sometimes all that is really needed is a reminder from a dog that in life, we just need to relish the simple pleasures: walks, sunshine, the ends of someone's soggy toast. The girls giggle at each other. I wonder if Danny could ever get hard from toast. A decent cup of tea maybe.

It's a sombre day in the Lakes – there are glimmers of sunshine but today we are saying goodbye to the marvellous Mr T who finally succumbed to old age and poor health. It was a few days after Easter. It started with him not eating – we thought the girls had been feeding him mini eggs – but he was lethargic and had a look about him like he was resigned to the fact that his body was no longer working as it should. A visit to the vet confirmed this. The moment when we had to invite that vet into our home and give Mr T some medicine to put him to sleep was one of the saddest of my life. To see his spirit ebb away like that so slowly. But also to see him curled up in Danny's lap as Danny held him tight and whispered quiet words into his ear.

'Mummy, it's your turn.'

'Mr T, you were part of my family. I know you liked Danny more because he brought you up steeper hills and would give you offcuts from the roast but you were my first dog and you always remember your first of anything. I hope you are very happy in doggy heaven.'

'There's no such thing as heaven,' Eve informs me. 'He's just dust now and his dog ghost lives in the hills and will gallop around and sleep in the bushes scaring the squirrels.'

'Alright then,' says Danny. 'I am going to say, it were a pleasure to have you as our dog, Mr T, and thank you for all the walks and the licks and the laughs… We ready to do this then?'

This was not my idea. It was Tess'. She's not handled Mr T's passing very well. It's her first taste of loss and so we needed some ceremony for her to be able to grieve. We have Mr T's ashes in a Tupperware and the idea is for us to throw them here over Gummer's How, his favourite walking place, and say our official goodbyes. Danny keeps looking out over the clouds. He was forged in these Lakes so is very good at smelling out the slightest whiff of rain. Polly is strapped to his back and from what I can see has a very good view of old anorak and Danny's hairline. He is keen to get the show moving.

'Polly hasn't said anything yet?'

Danny and I look at each other, faking smiles. Polly's lexicon contains about twenty words, none of which she can string together as a sentence. We have to do this, don't we? Danny bends down and Tess walks up to her.

'Polly, do you have anything to say about Mr T?'

'Biscuit?'

'She knew Mr T liked biscuits,' says Eve.

'That's because she's a genius baby,' I add.

A group of people walk past.

'Ey Up,' greets Danny. They are obviously tourists as they have no way to respond and one of them is wearing bog standard Reebok Classics. I stand there clutching the Tupperware to my chest. We wait until they are out of earshot.

'OK then… Here's to Mr T. Farewell.'

I open the Tupperware and the plan is just to tip it out but the breeze picks up the ashes in the style of a frenzied hurricane and dusts my face gently. Danny sniggers. Christ, I have dead dog on my lips. I brush my face frantically. Tess takes the Tupperware from me and rolls her eyes.

'Maybe stand due East with your back to the wind?' she tells me.

'Alright then, Bear Grylls.'

She creases her eyes at me then tips the contents of the container over the rocks. The remnants skip over the air and chase those tourists down the hill. I put my hands to her shoulders and she sighs.

'Can we come back here every year and talk to him?'

'Whatever you want, Dimples,' says Danny. She smiles, grabbing her sister's hand to go explore the neighbouring bushes and pathways.

Danny turns to me. 'Tea? Should raise a cup to the pooch – I put some whisky in it.'

'Hell, why not.'

Polly's done with the ceremony for now and is having herself a nap, leaving a slug-like trail of saliva across Danny's back. Danny pours the tea out and we clink mugs. He brushes his thumb across my nose.

'Still got Mr T on yer.'

I shudder. 'Did you hear Eve on the way up? She asked why Captain Mintcake couldn't save Mr T,' I inform Danny.

'He's not that sort of hero.'

'Exactly what I said.'

He smiles. You couldn't escape that name recently. Captain Mintcake had caught on in The Lakes, naturally, but his first hardback book of pictures was also a bestseller in *The Sunday Times* and he had recently popped up on *Wired* magazine as being one of the most influential Instagrammers of the year. Beaten by the Obamas, a few YouTubers, and a girl on a raw diet who likes a bit of pastel tableware and a yoga trouser. Yet people were none the wiser. The Captain started conversations. He was a very rude Banksy. Was he a man? Was he a woman? Was he even real? Maybe he was a virtual invention created by a flagging publishing industry? Either way, he'd started some sort of storm in sex, in art, in social media.

In our house, the Captain had allowed us to purchase a new fridge freezer, that monster barbecue for the garden and paid for a holiday to Disney World which naturally Danny was less excited about as we made him pose with mouse ears. Like the sensible man he is, Danny set aside money for his girls to go to university and buy their first houses. He invested a lot of it in the mill, buying new machinery and setting up pension schemes for his staff. Like the romantic he was, he bought me a new car. It had cup holders, he told me, and heated seating. For all those times we want to go have sex in country lanes again and get caught by the coppers.

We perch ourselves on a rock nearby and take in the view, the breeze biting at my cheeks, and I'm all too conscious that I will need to have a wee with all this tea. It's something I'll never tire of here: these chocolate box vistas of swooping hills and valleys, infinite skies and bracing breezes. I think to a painting that Danny has just auctioned. It's similar to this but the hills are boobs, the wisps of clouds are trails of cum. It's very tastefully done all things considered and currently on exhibition at the Tate Modern. Has anything really changed? I don't know. There's the money that we could have used to take a helicopter up here and closed off the lanes to all tourists. Yet I am wearing old boots that I like because they're sturdy and reliable. I know Danny's biggest extravagance was an outdoor coat that cost three hundred pounds. We bought the cat a new bed. We don't sweat the small stuff.

The girls know nothing. They see their father more which is probably the best thing. Danny works three days a week at the Mill, Stu works the other two. He balances the routine of the nine to five with debauched long weekends in Europe with the lads from the factory. We still haven't told Danny's mum and dad either. Danny just said we'd finally got lucky on the Premium Bonds. They didn't query it but congratulated themselves on being the ones who bought them for us in the first place. My family simply commented that for once I seemed to have splurged on decent gift wrap and wine at Christmas. We've moved into fifteen pound a bottle territory.

'We getting a new dog then?' I ask.

'We might have to.'

'Only if we can call it Murdock.'

'Mad Dog Murdock Morton. The alliteration is winning.'

We hear the squeals of girls in the distance. Danny sways slightly to keep Polly asleep.

'Do you remember when we first dated? You brought me up here.'

'The least prepared mountaineer in history. You were wearing bootcut jeans and Adidas.'

'Well remembered.'

'I remember everything.'

'You don't even remember what we had for dinner last night.'

'When it comes to you, I remember everything. You were also wearing a vest with a rainbow on it and I could see your boobs through it.'

'Back when I didn't have to wear a bra.'

It'd been that first trip to the Lakes when I met his folks, saw the Mill; when I discovered a place that Danny loved so much, perhaps even more so than he loved me. He had described it as a light stroll. The most I'd ever walked uphill at that point was on the stairs at the Tube station when the escalators were out of order.

'It was just a small hill, you told me.'

'It is.'

'To the uninitiated, it's Everest. I got overtaken by grannies with walking poles and fleece headbands.'

'While I laughed.'

I shake my head at him. 'You're lucky the view was decent.'

'I'd say.'

We grin at each other knowing that much more happened when we got to the top of the meadow too. That was some decent sex, back in the day when sex was the priority. But the priorities change, I guess. Nowadays, I would worry about getting ticks on my unmentionables.

I stare over at my husband taking in the view and sipping tea noisily. He always pauses for a moment on any walk to drink it all in. He rustles in his bag and gets a packet out, opening the packaging awkwardly and offering me a bit. I raise my eyebrows at him. Mint Cake.

'You could have at least got the stuff covered in chocolate.'

'That's full luxury. I can't handle that sort of extravagance just yet.'

I put a piece in my mouth. Minty. I don't think it's given me much in the way of energy, but I'm suddenly ready for a full-on snog. I imagine it'd make a blowjob quite interesting too.

The one thing you forget about taking kids up mountains (small hills) is that for all that experience of green space and fresh air, eventually you will have to bring them down. Despite having three slabs of mint cake, we failed to remember to pack enough snacks and a fine drizzle is now scratching at our faces. It takes Eve much persuading to keep walking and by the time we return to the car, the sun is dipping behind the clouds and the twilight sits in the air. I haven't got anything in for dinner. We may have to swing by a supermarket. I also need to wee. Danny decided it was fine to park in a deserted car park in the middle of nowhere to escape the throngs of regular walkers and tourists but strangely enough, when we get back there, we are one of six parked up.

'Eve. Literally, just to the car. Like twenty more steps.'

'You lied! You said that twenty steps ago.'

'I have Haribo in the car.'

She progresses to a light canter.

'Where did all these cars come from?' Danny asks as he approaches our motor cautiously.

'Maybe you're not the only smart one in Kendal and people are following your lead.'

At this point, Polly is awake and alert and Danny straps her into the car. She's at a knife's edge of needing sustenance. Do we let her cry all the way home? I whip off my waterproofs and bend over in the back seat trying to locate muslins and the promised sweets.

'Mummy, your butt crack is showing,' says Tess and she clambers into the back seat.

Opposite a car flashes us.

'Someone else has obviously seen it too,' Danny laughs.

I look around at all the cars. People are sat in them. What are they waiting for? You see this sometimes when waiting for rain to pass or when people decide to eat their lunch in the car. I find a sippy cup for Polly but it spills over my fleece. Tits. I take off my fleece, shivering in just a T-shirt.

'I may need to have a wee before we go? I am busting.' I look around at the other cars realising I will need to go deep into the undergrowth to accomplish this.

'Will you wee yourself? asks Eve, giggling. 'Maybe you could just put some of Polly's nappies down.'

'Ladylike.' To entertain the girls, I do a little dance with my hands grasping my lady parts. I waft my top up and down to dry the wet patch of milk. Suddenly, I hear a car door open and a gentleman approach us. His footsteps are low.

I know you. Patrick. It's Postman Pat. I smile at recognising him, as do all of the occupants in our car.

'Daniel, girls. Fancy seeing you here, of all places.'

'Our poor dog died. We were having a walk to scatter his ashes,' I inform him.

'Oh, I'm so sorry. How terrible. Your dog were very lovely. What were his name, Tea Bag?'

The girls giggle. 'He was Mr T. Do you have a dog, Pat?' asks Tess.

'No, my wife's a cat lady. But funny you should mention dogs. This place here, people like to come here for that reason.'

'I've walked Mr T here plenty of times, it were his favourite,' pipes in Danny.

'That it is. People come here all the time for walking and with their dogs and other such endeavours.' His face looks slightly ashen at this point, his eyes darting towards the other cars. His eyes glance down to my top where the wet patch reveals a very pert and cold nipple underneath. 'And the other sense of the word… I just thought I would mention it as you have the girls and it's getting darker. I think someone just flashed his lights to warn you.'

Danny and I realise what he means exactly at the same time. 'OH!' we say at the same gobsmacked volume.

'Dogg… ing…' mumbles Danny. 'We should—'

'Leave, like definitely leave, like now,' I say, finishing his sentence.

The girls appear confused. I look around and shield my eyes. I should shield the children's eyes. His wife waves from the passenger seat.

'Give our regards to June,' I say.

'Will do.'

He salutes us and returns to his car. The girls have all the questions. 'People come here to look at dogs?' asks Eve. 'Where are the dogs?'

Danny's fists are clenched. I can hold this wee in, I think. Definitely. Polly can cry until kingdom come. I grab a jacket and cover myself up.

'Get. In. The. Car.' Danny mouths very deliberately.

I slink into the passenger seat. Our eyes dart in different directions trying to divert focus from any of the cars ahead. We'll be good if Danny doesn't drive us off a cliff face. He turns on the wipers, the engine roars to a start and he pulls away slowly.

'We could have stayed and seen the dogs,' says Eve, a little despondently.

I throw a bag of gummy bears at her. Danny and I are silent. I hear a baby burp in the back seat. We are both a little scarred.

'I tell you what was funny,' says Tess.

This was funny? The fact we strolled our children into an outdoor sex hotspot? We are terrible parents.

'That he thought our dog's name was Tea Bag.'

And with that Danny erupts into laughter. His roar echoes throughout the car, so much so a bit of snot cascades down his nose. The girls join in to see their Dad giggling with such force, tears running down his face. They don't understand it. But I do. That would complete our Mintcake family: Tea Bag the dog and Rimmer the Cat. That was our fifty-something postie. You couldn't make this up. I feel my shoulders surrender to join them, my face creasing, the sound of this laughter making my chest ache. I look out the window. The twilight has come for the hills, turning them into silhouettes. The twinkling lights of houses appear like stars. I smile, looking over at Danny. He changes gear, still giggling. He finds his girls in the rear-view mirror and studies their faces.

'Who fancies chips? There's a decent chippy down road.'

There's a chorus of approval from the back seat. He smiles. Chips and tea, it was all I ever wanted. He then moves his hand over from the gearstick to find mine, fingers interlocked, the sky glowing a thousand different colours.

A Letter from Kristen

Dear lovely reader,

You're bloody marvellous! Thank you from the bottom of my heart for reading my book. I hope it's provided plenty of escape and giggles along the way. I hope it wasn't too rude (I did my best to find as many synonyms for penis as I could…) and I hope, most of all, that you saw bits of your own relationship and family life in Meg and Danny Morton's story.

If you enjoyed this book, and want to keep up to date with all my latest releases, just sign up at the following link. Your email address will never be shared and you can unsubscribe at any time.

www.bookouture.com/kristen-bailey

Now, time for a disclaimer: my husband would like you to know that my sex life is absolutely fine. (He didn't really make me write that at all.) So what inspired this story? A few years ago, I thought (like many writers) that I'd have a go at writing erotica. It turns out, I couldn't. Instead I wrote about the sex that I knew: sex within a marriage. Because I think married sex is a lot of fun but pretty hilarious too. It's sex on a Friday night watching *Gogglebox*, right?

He's keeping his socks on, we're trying not to make too much noise so we don't wake the kids and halfway through someone gets cramp, and the other needs a wee break… Or is that just me? Please don't tell my husband that I told you that. Do tell him though that I tried to write an honest account of what it is to be married, of all the laughs, absurdity and intimacy that comes from sharing your life with someone. He'll like that.

I'd be thrilled to hear from any of my readers, whether it be with reviews, questions or just to say hello. If you like retweets of videos of dancing pandas then follow me on Twitter. Have a gander at Instagram, my Facebook author page and my website too for updates, ramblings, and to learn more about me. Like, share and follow away – it'd be much appreciated.

And if you enjoyed *Has Anyone Seen My Sex Life?* then I would be overjoyed if you could leave me a review on either Amazon or Goodreads to let people know. It's a brilliant way to reach out to new readers. And don't just stop there, tell everyone you know, send to all on your contacts list. Tell them there's a whole scene in this book involving a strap-on… that will go down well on the school WhatsApp group…

With much love and gratitude,
Kristen xx

kristenbaileywrites

kristenbaileywrites

@mrsbaileywrites

www.kristenbaileywrites.com

Acknowledgements

Thanks and praise to the wonderful Christina Demosthenous who is like some super editor from another dimension. She was the one who fought for me to join the Bookouture family and has supported and championed me ever since. I am truly indebted to you.

A special thank you to the Comedy Women in Print Prize. This story got on to your longlist for the unpublished prize in your inaugural year. It was after a year of writing ups and downs, so for you to reassure me that my work had potential was a motivational kick up the arse. You got me back on that writing horse and that was everything.

So time for some truth… I always knew what this story was going to be about but I was never very sure if I was going to be able to write anything really really filthy. I didn't know much about modern sex or dating either. So as I started writing, I had a chat with my mates in the know, Danny, Joe, Emma and Amy. I also joined Tinder (with my husband's full support and knowledge) to do some research. It was the best kind of research. I swiped, I heard your stories, I felt your dating scene pain, and some of you were just really lovely to talk to. You made me laugh, blush and once spit my tea out across my computer keyboard. I hope you all found the regular sex/hook-ups/threesomes/kink/potential girlfriends/wives/magic/NSF that you were looking for. And I meant it, height shouldn't be a thing. Prince was five foot nothing and he was fricking hot. I'm also one of those random people who could go on Tinder and make actual friends, so a special mention to Luke, Lewis, Leo, Leigh, Brendan, Chris and Peter. And most of all, Graham, who made me cry with laughter with a joke about Grace Jones (see Chapter Eleven). None of you ever tell my mother how we met please.

And last but not least, to my oft neglected husband. Without you, I wouldn't know what mint cake is. I owe you many cups of tea. Thank you for being my fiercest critic, letting me talk to those random men on Tinder, and for giving the occasional pep talk when I was being useless and wasting my time binge-watching Netflix. Thanks for all them babies too: my magnificent Bailey mandem. Love, always xx

Printed in Great Britain
by Amazon